JU
DRE

C000254496

DREAD DOMINION

Stephen Marley

Virgin

First published in 1994 by
Virgin Publishing
an imprint of Virgin Publishing Ltd
332 Ladbroke Grove
London W10 5AH

Reprinted 1995

Typeset by CentraCet Ltd, Cambridge
Printed and bound in Great Britain by
Cox & Wyman Ltd, Reading, Berkshire.

ISBN 0 352 32929 7

For Anita, for everything.

This book is also respectfully dedicated to the memory of Emperor Gaius Caesar Augustus Germanicus, otherwise known as Caligula, despite the fact that he was a homicidal megalomaniac.

ACKNOWLEDGEMENTS

I echo – and echo again – the full complement of acknowledgements to the creators and overseers of the Judge Dredd world listed in David Bishop's introduction to *The Savage Amusement*. The following are mentioned in recognition of stories, characterisations and ideas that apply specifically to *Dread Dominion* . . .

John Wagner, Archdemiurge of the Judge Dredd world, and writer of the 'lost' Dredd story, shrewdly censored from the first issue of *2000 AD* (and every succeeding issue), and which finally appears in this novel in a somewhat strange context; Alan Grant, for his major contributions over the years, especially the development of Cassandra Anderson, a central character in this book; Arthur Ranson, for his (to my mind) definitive depiction of Cassandra Anderson; John Gold, for the historical references. Thanks also to Peter Darvill-Evans, Rebecca Levene and Kerri Sharp at Virgin Publishing for the usual sterling effort, and Steve MacManus at Fleetway for the unqualified affirmative.

And special thanks to David Bishop for suggesting the crucial Rico tie-in that propelled my tale of dark deeds from its starting-blocks with maximum impetus.

PROLOGUE

Mega-City One: 2079

It was Judge Dredd versus Judge Dredd.

Clone-brother pitted against clone-brother: Joe versus Rico.

A slight squeeze on the trigger and the story would be Cain and Abel.

The two black-uniformed Judges confronted one another through helmet visors over the purple plasplex tables of the yellow-tiled Cafe Cesare.

Joe Dredd, gun arm extended, trained his Lawgiver pistol on Rico Dredd's heart. A shot – a single shot – and the bullet would drill a hole clean through the name-badge of Rico's Judge uniform.

The judicial warning had been given: the next move was up to Rico.

A burst of steam from the servo-kitchen's hatch hissed across the cafe, clouding the air.

Rico stubbornly retained a grip on his gun; a motion of just three or four centimetres would aim the muzzle straight at his brother's heart. 'Joe!' he appealed. 'Listen, we can make this look like an accident.'

Some accident. Rico crouched in a red sauce of blood that once belonged to Edward Gee, owner of the Cafe Cesare. Now it decorated the floor of his cafe, pooling out from under his prone corpse. A scorched hole in Edward Gee's back showed the exit wound of Rico's slug.

As his brother's Lawgiver lifted a centimetre, Joe Dredd

put a grim note of warning into his voice. 'No way, Rico. I'm taking you in.'

Rico's mouth wore a twisted smile, betraying the emotion that his visored helmet hid so effectively. 'Your own clone-twin? Come on, Joe, remember the Academy – who helped you on the firing-range? Me. Who was always there for you? Me. You can't turn me in. We're more than brothers – we're duplicates. One and the same.'

Joe Dredd bared his teeth. 'Not the same. A few months out of the Academy and you're running prostitution, protection, taking bribes. And now – ' He flicked a finger at the cafe owner's body. ' – Murder.'

Rico remained in a crouched stance, as if coiled to spring. 'A cafe owner refuses to pay his dues – he pays with his life. That's the way it goes. Wise up, Joe. A lot of Judges are making a tidy pile out of wearing a badge.'

'Save your breath. And drop the gun.' His tone lowered to a subterranean growl. 'Last warning.'

Rico expelled a sharp breath. 'You arrived a couple of seconds too early. Heard too much. Saw too much.'

'A couple of seconds too late for the guy on the floor,' Joe Dredd snapped back. He pressed the trigger a millimetre. 'I don't see your gun on the ground.'

Rico Dredd's Lawgiver stayed firmly put in his gauntleted hand. 'I don't think you'll shoot me, Joe. We're identical. It'd be like killing yourself.'

'Try me.'

'I always came first on the firing-range, remember? First in speed. First in accuracy. You were always second. Always.' His Lawgiver shifted another centimetre in Joe Dredd's direction. 'You wouldn't shoot me, *would you, Joe*?'

Joe Dredd was well aware that the man who intends to fire first has an overwhelming advantage: the opponent's reaction time – around one- to two-tenths of a second – means a hole in the heart or head before he gets off a single shot.

All his training demanded that he shoot first. *Two* warnings had already been delivered. If the perp had been anyone else but Rico he'd have been cold meat by now . . .

Rico's gun moved one more centimetre towards its target.

Joe Dredd's reaction time was a shade under a tenth of a second. Against his brother, it wouldn't be enough.

You wouldn't shoot me, would you, Joe?

Joe Dredd felt an itch in his trigger finger.

Shoot – *now*.

Rico's gun hand twitched.

SHOOT!

Joe could feel the pressure of the trigger as he squeezed it tight. Could see the bullet bore a hole in Rico's badge, leaving the marred inscription DRE*D where the letters had once spelt DREDD. Could hear the blast from his Lawgiver resounding from the yellow walls of the deserted Cafe Cesare.

The experience was so vivid that, for a stark moment, he thought he'd shot his clone-brother.

But Rico crouched as before, name-badge unmarked by a bullet, and Joe Dredd's gun was unfired.

Rico raised his gun.

And raised it higher. Above his head.

Then he let the weapon fall. It landed with a clatter on the yellow tiles.

'I couldn't shoot you, Joe. Be like killing myself.'

Joe Dredd released a low breath. 'Okay, Rico. Let's go.'

'You don't have to be here, lad,' Judge Morphy murmured, planting a big, friendly hand on Joe Dredd's shoulder.

'Yes, I do.'

Joe Dredd's mouth wore a scowl so tight that the blood had drained from the blanched lips. His visored gaze was

3

fixed on the spaceport ramp and the figure of his brother. Up in the night sky there was a big turnout of stars as if to witness the departure of the latest cargo of condemned souls into the indifferent heavens.

Bare-headed, bereft of weapons, pads and name-badge, Rico stood, wrists and ankles manacled, in a Judges-only section of Mega-City One's spaceport. He had two other comrades-in-woe on the ramp that arced up to the waiting space shuttle. The two convicted Judges, shoulders slumped, eyes downcast, waited to board the ship bound for the Titan penal colony. Rico, bolt upright, stared the guards right in the eye.

One of the guards stepped up to Rico. 'What you starin' at, creep?'

Rico gave him a slow, up-and-down glare. 'A piece of stomm on legs.'

The guard's fist slammed into Rico's stomach. The blow didn't even extract a wince from the crop-haired youth.

Joe Dredd started forward, but Judge Morphy caught his arm. 'Out of your hands, lad. Out of your hands now.'

Joe stayed put, a tremor at the corner of his mouth the only sign of the storm within.

The guard showed his teeth in a wide grin and leaned up close to Rico. 'Oh, we're *real* tough, ain't we, boy? Easy to be tough when you're eighteen and don't know no better. You know what Titan is, boy? Another name for hell. Twenty long years of hell. And we're gonna make you look like you belong in hell. Gonna rip you open – cram you full of pneumatic machinery. Seal up your face with circuit implants. You'll be a man-machine, slaving your mechanoid guts out on the airless surface of Titan. You're gonna look *real* ugly, boy. A monster in hell.'

He waited for a response, but Rico's craggy face remained impassive.

'Still not sunk in, huh, boy? I'll be one of your warders up there, and I'm gonna give you *special* treatment. I hate bent Judges, Rico, so I'm gonna bend you till you break.

4

And you will break, boy – oh, yeah. You won't live one year on Titan, let alone twenty.'

'I'll live,' Rico said tonelessly. 'Even in hell, I won't break – ' For the first time, he turned and looked straight at Joe. ' – I'm a Dredd.' He bent his lips into a hard smile, showing gritted teeth.

Then he wheeled round as the slide-ramp went into action and carried the convicts up to the ferry to hell, otherwise known as *Charon*, the Titan space shuttle.

Once Rico was out of sight Joe lowered his head. The deep scowl he'd worn since the Cafe Cesare seemed as permanent as an arced laser-razor cut: marked for life. As Joe's silence stretched to snapping point, Judge Morphy tapped him on the arm. 'Why not break the habit of a lifetime and share a little of the pain you're feeling?'

Joe Dredd straightened, squared his shoulders. 'A Judge keeps his feelings to himself. Better still, he treats feelings like wounds – he cauterizes them.'

Morphy took off his helmet, scratched his tousled hair. 'Well, perhaps I'm old-fashioned, or maybe it's the Irish in me, but I reckon there's a lot to be said for the old-style cop. Tough on the outside, but with a heart inside that's full of more than blood.'

The reply was flat. 'I've always respected you, Morphy, ever since I was your Rookie. But I'm a Judge, not a cop. I weakened back there, in the Cafe Cesare. I'll never weaken again.'

'Weakened?'

'Should've shot him dead after the first warning.'

'But he was your brother, your clone-twin . . .'

Joe stuck out his heavy jowl. 'Shouldn't count. I'm a Judge. Should've killed him. In fact. . .'

Morphy cocked an eyebrow at the sawn-off sentence. 'Yes?'

'Forget it.'

'No. Come on now, tell me.'

Joe Dredd's scowl became yet more pronounced. 'I – I

thought I *had* shot him. Clean through the badge, straight through the heart. Some kind of hallucination. It's all in my report.'

'Severe stress reaction,' Morphy shrugged. 'Nothing unusual.'

'I keep dreaming about it,' Joe said, staring at the empty ramp.

'You've been using the sleep machines since the Cafe Cesare,' Morphy remarked. 'It's rare to recall dreams from micro-sleep.'

'I remember *this* dream well enough. I'm in the Cafe Cesare, gun trained on Rico's badge. I fire a slug into the name-badge, leaving a bullet hole where the second D in DREDD used to be. The badge runs red. He yells out as he drops. Then he's dead. End of dream.'

'And for a little while after you've woken up, you're convinced the dream's real,' Morphy shrewdly observed. 'You believe you shot your brother.'

Joe Dredd swung round on the older Judge. 'How did you know that?'

'Sure, it didn't take much guessing,' Morphy smiled. 'You're a fine young Judge, but you've a lot to learn about human nature.' The smile faded. 'I'm glad you didn't shoot Rico in cold blood – for your sake. Would have been like firing a bullet into your own heart. Oh, you'd have lived, sure enough, but the killing would have marked you for life.'

'Marked me as a true Judge,' Joe dourly responded.

'Oh, you're a true Judge, right enough. But you're also a man. Remember the old story of Cain and Abel? You know as well as I that Titan will destroy him, in spirit if not body. He'll soon be a dead man.'

The young Judge gave a dismissive lift of his wide shoulders and swung away, heading for his Lawmaster motorbike. 'Rico's as good as dead to me now. There's only one Judge Dredd left in this city, and that leaves me the work of two men.'

Judge Morphy pursed his lips as he watched Judge Dredd vault on to the Lawmaster and ignite the armoured motorbike into thunderous action, swerving onto the sleek curve of a megway.

Yes, Morphy reflected bleakly, *Judge Dredd* – not Joe. Judge Dredd: one man doing the work of two.

As Dredd's mighty Lawmaster rapidly shrank to a small dot in the distance, the rumble of the *Charon* ferry to Titan shook the skies as it lifted off to a distant hell in the heavens.

Morphy ruefully shook his head. 'Double trouble.'

Breaking into the Cafe Cesare was easy. The munceburger joint had been closed down for six weeks since some bent Judge plugged Edward Gee. No security staff. No surveillance. Easy pickings.

Easy pickings were Manny Porlock's speciality. Scraps. Leftovers. Low-risk looting. You didn't take chances when you were past seventy and your cardiovascular system was shot to hell.

Porlock kept his torch to low light as he picked his way around the cafe, searching for light movables, spare change, a little food.

All he found after twenty minutes' scouring was a button and a chunk of mouldy munceburger. The joint had been cleared out by earlier looters.

Apart from the tables and chairs, Cafe Cesare contained nothing but dust and crowded shadows. The shadows, tall and askew, leaned in too close for comfort.

'Drokk it,' he muttered, sitting glumly on the yellow-tiled floor. 'Drokk it drokk it drokk it.'

Mrs Porlock would chew his ears off if he came home empty-handed.

He scratched his white-stubbled chin. 'Drokk it.'

Planted his hand on the floor. 'Drokk – '

He felt metal under his palm. Flat, cold metal, almost the size of his hand. He lifted it up, puzzled that he'd

7

missed it in his exhaustive search: he was certain he'd scanned every floor tile in the place.

Angling the torch, he studied his find. A gap-toothed grin split his lined features.

A Justice badge, stained rust-brown with old blood. That would fetch a fair price on the black market.

Pity there was a bullet hole in it – cut the value by half. Still . . .

He tried to read the name on the badge, but the hole had obliterated the fourth letter: DRE*D.

Porlock was still studying the name when the badge vanished. The looter's eyes bulged at his empty palm.

It *had* been in his hand. Solid and real. But now it had gone to Grud knows where.

He cast a nervy glance at the enfolding shadows: they seemed to shrivel the dithery beam of torchlight.

Spooky.

Objects shouldn't disappear. Not like that.

'Spooks,' he muttered hoarsely.

Something chill tingled the nape of his neck. An icy breath. He could feel the condensation on his skin.

Porlock's dicky heart banged out of tempo. He wanted to turn round, and simultaneously knew that was the last thing he intended to do.

The cold breath sighed like the wind and the rain. And whispered its wind-rain words:

> *'Like one that on a lonesome road*
> *Doth walk in fear and dread.*
> *And having once turned round walks on,*
> *And turns no more his head . . .'*

Porlock's better judgement was screaming at him not to look over his shoulder. But a mixture of know-thine-enemy and face-the-devil forced him round.

8

What he saw shocked his dicky heart to a thud of finality; a thumping full stop.

He was dead seconds before he hit the floor.

Porlock's death failed to merit even a nine-minute wonder. When his week-old corpse was discovered it was unceremoniously dumped into a meat wagon for Resyk. Dead bodies littering streets and derelict interiors were part and parcel of the little annoyances that comprised everyday existence in the Big Meg. The estate agent didn't think to mention the incident to the new proprietor of the Cafe Cesare.

After a month of dwindling custom and rising debt, the owner shut up shop and left. The customers had complained of – an atmosphere. He hadn't been too successful in allaying their fears; he shared them. There was something wrong about the Cafe Cesare. One uneasy patron murmured that a bad soul had soaked into the plasteen tiles and plascrete walls. That about summed it up for the proprietor. He had sunk all his savings into the munceburger joint. But enough was enough.

The cafe stayed empty for three months.

Its next proprietor lasted less than a week. He was carted off to the local psycho-cubes where he lived out his mortal span, his eyes forever jiggling like glass beads, his mouth pouring forth an incessant flood of jabberwocky.

For two years the Cafe Cesare lay boarded up and tenantless, dark and dust gathering under the weight of its sinister reputation.

Then it found a new proprietor who stoutly rejected all superstitions concerning ghosts and goblins and ghoulies.

Three days later he was found in the kitchen, drowned in a vat of munce soup. His eyes were missing. An autopsy uncovered them in his stomach: he had swallowed them whole before plunging to his soupy end.

After that, there were no more takers. The Cafe Cesare was left to rest in peace in its shadows and silence. Even the rats refused to disturb its thick carpet of dust, its grimy walls.

Conflict and perils shook the outside world: the Civil War, Judge Cal's despotic reign, the Apocalypse War, Necropolis, Judgement Day. But the Cafe Cesare, enclosed in its own quiet dark, was untouched. The great events that swamped the world stirred not a wave in those shut-away rooms where time hung in suspension, breathless.

And with the lapse of decades, shadows congealed in the locked chambers.

Darkness coagulated into what might be called a shape.

The shape of darkness reached out . . .

And one fine morning in the spring of 2116 the door of Cafe Cesare was finally opened.

It was opened from the inside.

Part One

In Fear and Dread

'Like one that on a lonesome road
Doth walk in fear and dread.
And having once turned round walks on,
And turns no more his head;
Because he knows, a frightful fiend
Doth close behind him tread.'

Samuel Taylor Coleridge,
The Rime of the Ancient Mariner

ONE

A jump-start of the heart jolted Edgar Allen back from the dead.

Moments flickered as he phased between the dark and a dream.

Then the dream blazed in full glory.

A dream of good times in motion, the city flying by . . .

. . . Jenny's eyes flashed warm as her smile at the sight of Mega-City One's bulbous citi-blocks gliding by on all sides. Her red hair flared in the dance of sunlight.

She had an arm round each of the twins, hugging them tight. The two six-year-old girls grinned at the embrace: Sally and Caroline had their mother back again, the way she used to be before the illness. And Edgar had his wife back, recovered from the trauma reaction that had stolen a year of her life. There were new lines on her face, but he hardly noticed them. Jenny was her old self, and they were a family again.

And they rode as a family on Sky-Bullet 3, the favourite vacuum tube train for sightseers. The luxury train, whose transparent materials, including the seats, gave you the illusion that you were sitting on thin air, hurtled at 700 kph a full five kilometres above ground level. It was an exhilarating experience, and one that he'd inwardly promised Jenny all through those long months of psychiatric purgatory in the white-tiled clinic.

Now they were flying through the air with the greatest of ease as though between trapeze and trapeze, with no safety net in sight. There were times you needed to stamp the train's translucent floor to convince yourself it was really there.

The Sky-Bullet executed a roller-coaster dive, and Jenny and the twins let loose delighted squeals.

'Way to go!' she chuckled, winking at her peas-in-a-pod daughters. She glanced at Edgar, and mouthed a silent 'thanks'.

'Way to go!' Sally and Caroline chorused.

Edgar expelled a contented sigh. Life in the Big Meg was usually one long duck-and-dodge flirtation with trouble and danger. But sometimes life worked out.

He leaned across to plant a quick kiss on his wife's lips. 'Way to go, Jenny.'

His vision of Jenny and the kids abruptly tilted.

A sudden lurch of the train threw him off his seat. The air *whooshed* from his lungs as he landed on his back. He heard the nervous laughter of the twins, the uncertainty in Jenny's voice.

He couldn't respond. His throat had gone dry.

Something wrong.

He sensed it through the muscles of his back, responsive to the magneto-accelerators' low thrumming. The Sky-Bullet's vibrations were all wrong.

A deep shudder ran through the sky train.

Then the air seemed to congeal into a rockcrete wall. And Edgar crashed straight through it . . .

The dark returned to Edgar's brain, dallied a while, then retreated.

He felt a low vibration beneath his back, a sense of steady motion.

Edgar's eyelids struggled to open: damn things felt as if someone had glued them shut.

Am I dead? he wondered. Dead in a sky train crash?

No. Cancel that thought. There hadn't been a crash. The Sky-Bullet's emergency brakes had cut in, the deceleration sending him spinning to the end of the carriage.

A bump on the head – that's all he'd received. No harm

14

done. And Jenny and the kids were all right. Sure, he'd be a little groggy the rest of the day. Dizzy spells. And sleepy. Very sleepy.

He must be lying in bed. If Jenny wasn't at his side, she'd be close by.

But what was this vibration thrumming in his back muscles, this continuous sensation of gradual motion?

He managed to force his eyelids open. A grey blur swiftly focused into what he identified as a ceiling. It should have been the ceiling of his bedroom.

It wasn't his bedroom ceiling.

It was more of a vaulted roof than a ceiling. The longer he looked, the surer he became. A vaulted roof, at least a hundred metres above his head.

Unable to move his head, eye muscles straining, Edgar forced his gaze to the right. Three tiers of plasteel galleries came into view. A sparse scatter of people, mostly in tiny clumps, were dotted along the galleries. Behind them, every fifty metres or so, was a giant sign:

RESYK

At sight of the sign, and what it signified, Edgar Allen tasted something on his tongue: the flavour of pure dread.

Resyk . . . Recycling.

Mega-City One didn't bury or cremate its dead. They were recycled: flesh sliced, juices sucked from glands, bones ground to powder. Recycled into fuel to oil the cogs of the city.

He tried to scream, but his numb mouth refused to open. Struggled to lift his arm, but the limb was cold and unresponsive. Attempted to twitch a finger – nothing. No sensation.

Thanatonic narcolepsy

The clinical term was like a frosty breath from the morgue. Death-like sleep. Suspended animation. Twenty-second-century pathology abounded in victims of thanatonic narcolepsy. Some of them ended up as food for Resyk.

15

For Grud's sake – let me move, let me speak!

A flip of the heart triggered a small spasm in the neck and shoulder muscles, and his head flopped to the left. For the first time, he had a view of his silent companions.

Naked corpses; men, woman, children, lay like broken dolls on a wide, moving surface of grey rubbereen. The dead of Resyk left this world as bare-skinned as they entered. Many had limbs missing. Some were mashed into bizarre flesh sculptures. One was bereft of a head. Others had flesh unfolded, displaying the purple viscera. The dead were strewn all around him, evidence that Death was a democrat: billionaires and vagrants, saints and sinners, peach-young and prune-old – all reduced to the democracy of pale, cool meat.

Beside Edgar was a man in two neat halves, bisected from groin to crown. Some Resyk technician had made a botched job of matching the two halves. The right side was a half-head lower than the left, revealing the grey brain matter of the left lobe. Edgar regarded the man's lopsided state as blessed; he was as dead as you can get. He couldn't see what Edgar saw, a hundred metres down the rubbereen belt.

The dead couldn't see the Mouth.

Edgar had witnessed the macabre workings of Resyk once before, at his father's death. Only once. Never again.

The cadavers were loaded on to a fifty-metre-wide rubbereen belt that conveyed its passengers at a steady four kilometres per hour along the three-hundred-metre length of Resyk hall. A slow, final journey to the waiting Mouth.

The Mouth was a fifty-metre-wide rectangle in the wall that separated the Hall of Passage from Resyk proper. A rectangular mouth of whirling blades and buzzing saws in place of teeth, ready and eager to chew up the dead. The entire process was computer controlled, robotically performed. The Mouth crunched you up, then gulped you down into the mechanical Stomach, where organs were

16

plucked out by robotic arms, valuable secretions teased from glands by suction tubes.

Edgar was lying at a forty-five-degree angle to the direction of the conveyor belt. The blade-toothed Mouth was clearly in his line of sight.

It was a mere fifty to sixty metres away. Not much more than a minute left before the spinning blades made mince-meat of him.

Why is this happening to me? he screamed inwardly.

Resyk's Hall of Passage was supposed to be crammed with a range of sensors aimed at detecting a living body. The audio-sensors should have picked up his heartbeat, the thermal sensors should have registered his body heat. He should have been identified as a Waker the instant he recovered from narcolepsy, and the belt automatically halted. But the sensory net had failed to catch this far-from-dead fish. It was letting Edgar slip.

Mesmerised, he stared at the approaching Mouth.

Eaten alive.

No! He wouldn't let it happen. He swerved his eyes up to the lowest gallery, seeking out the figures of mourners, who were few and far between.

Look at my eyes! he pleaded. *I'm alive! Look at my eyes!*

Then he saw her. Red-haired Jenny. His wife, slumped in grief, leaning on the railing.

Jenny! I'm alive!

She wasn't looking. He hadn't looked either, two years ago, when his father's stripped carcass was carried towards the Mouth.

If only he could speak – move his hand . . .

The Mouth was less than forty metres away.

Jenny!

A prickling sensation suddenly broke out over his entire body, mounting swiftly in intensity. In seconds he was suffering an attack of pins and needles that was exquisite agony.

17

The pain evoked a silent shout of joy. Circulation was being restored to his numb muscles. His nerve endings were coming alive.

Thirty metres to the Mouth.

A faint hiss was all that escaped his lips as he fought to cry out to Jenny.

A finger twitched.

A foot spasmed.

Look at me! I'm alive! I'M ALIVE!

Jenny hadn't seen. She covered her eyes, sobbing, then turned and trudged along the gallery.

No, Jenny, don't go! Look at me! Pleeease . . .

Edgar's hand balled into a fist.

STOP THE DAMN BELT!

Just twenty metres to the Mouth. He could feel the wind of its whistling blades on his skin.

Inadvertently, he glanced at the half-and-half man beside him. The corpse was a dour symbol of Edgar's impending fate. The sight drove him to a final effort.

He battled to gain control of his legs, kick his heels into the rubbereen and shove back against the flow of the belt.

His limbs refused to respond.

Ten metres to the mouth of spinning blades.

'Help me!' he heard himself croak. 'I'm alive!'

The sound of his voice, feeble though it was, impelled him to lash out with both arms and legs.

He rolled over with the violent thrash of his restored limbs. A hurtling blade missed his feet by centimetres.

Sheer panic forced him to his legs, pumping with adrenalin.

He staggered back up the belt, drawing away from the Mouth.

'*Jenny!*' he yelled triumphantly, waving heavy arms.

She spun round, gaped for a moment.

'*I'm alive!*'

She burst into a wordless shout of delight and wonder, hands reaching out to him.

He tumbled to his knees as the belt came to a sudden stop. At last, one of Resyk's Tek-Judges had spotted him, pressed the HALT button.

Head whirling with joy, his eyesight blurred.

His sense of direction deserted him.

Reaction to trauma. Shock setting in. He had literally been delivered from the jaws of death.

The world spun around him. Flickered.

Receded.

Then came back with a low, humming murmur.

Groggily, he regained his footing. For a moment he was puzzled by a sensation of motion. Then he realised that the belt was rolling again.

He ran several metres, putting a healthy distance between himself and the Mouth, then turned round, back-pedalling.

Edgar glanced around Resyk, and speech froze on his tongue.

There were no more corpses on the belt. The dead had been replaced by the living.

Naked as the dead, a host of wretches whimpered and wriggled on the smooth surface, jerking up only to flop back, like stranded fish. From youngster to eldster, their eyes were raw with terror as they were carried to a Mouth shaped to look like a mouth: the rectangle was replaced by a gaping oval of stretched, plasteen lips, with a mouth-ful of flashing blades and spikes.

Edgar looked up, bewildered. Resyk's architecture had changed. Uniformly dark grey, it soared in a series of Gothic arches, its walls ornamented with baroque imagery that gave the surface the appearance of tormented metal.

The galleries, which seemed to have acquired two extra tiers, were crammed with Judges. Jenny was nowhere to be seen.

Peals of laughter rang from the vaulted roof. Derisory laughter. Edgar was thunderstruck. The Judges were treating the plight of the victims on the belt as a spectacle. An amusement. They thought it was *funny*.

A Judge floated down from a lower gallery, the shimmer from a hidden anti-grav device rippling the air under his boots. He alighted on the upper lip of the Mouth, arms folded, booted feet planted wide. Under the visor of the helmet, his teeth were bared in a grin. He raised a gauntleted hand and pointed at Edgar. His voice was bad news, like the first rumble of distant thunder.

'Another fresh one.'

'Judge Dredd,' Edgar whispered. The physique – the voice – were unmistakable. Only the savage smile belied the man's identity. He'd heard that Judge Dredd never smiled. Obviously he'd heard wrong.

'Make him run!' a Judge shouted from above.

Judge Dredd shook his head. 'We'll wind this one up now.' Again he pointed his finger at Edgar. A crackle of blue electricity zigzagged from Dredd's finger to impact with Edgar's heart, stunning his nervous system. He dropped, poleaxed.

'Speed up the meat grinder,' he heard Judge Dredd command.

The belt doubled its speed.

Edgard shared his companions' helplessness, his drained limbs unable to accomplish more than a slow slither as he sped towards the meat-grinding Mouth. The whimpers of the condemned rose to wails. Edgar's voice was part of the chorus of dread.

Twenty metres to the Mouth's curtain of hot red rain.

Ten metres.

Edgar's last sight of a human shape was Dredd's bulky outline above the Mouth. Dredd's lips were curved in a lethal smile.

For a fleeting instant, Edgar registered the name on the Judge's badge, and a thought whisked through his head:

The name's wrong.

Then the Mouth swallowed him. A rotary blade greeted his arrival with the sharpest of welcomes.

'Jenny,' he whispered as the blade severed his legs at a single stroke.

A chainsaw cracked open his breast-bone.

'Jenny . . .'

'Jenn – '

Judge Corman stood amidst the corpses sprawled on Resyk's stationary belt and watched as a distraught Mrs Jennifer Allen, wife of Edgar Allen, was led out of the Hall of Passage.

'I've heard of this kind of hallucination before,' Judge Murray drawled, scratching the stubble on his sagging jowls. 'Grieving wives imagine things – ya know? Hell, she didn't wanna see her husband chewed up in the meat grinder, so she – ya know – sees things. Gets it into her head that he vanished before the slicers got to him.'

Corman subjected Murray to a withering stare. 'This is all down to you and Spooner. You should have been keeping an eye on the monitors, and Spooner should have picked up the glitch in the sensors.'

'Aw, come on, Chief, it was just bad luck we got a Waker when the system went on the blink. Chance in a million.'

'You're on report, both of you,' Corman snapped. 'And Mrs Allen didn't hallucinate. Edgar Allen vanished into thin air. I saw it with my own eyes.'

Murray gave an aw-shucks grin. 'Stress of the job, Chief. You did your best – stopped the belt. You've been here too long, is all. It's getting to ya. People don't vanish.'

'Then where is he?' Corman waved a hand over the spread of corpses on Resyk's still, silent surface. 'Go on, Murray, find him if he's still around.'

Murray shrugged. 'I know he ain't around. You pulled

21

the plug on the belt too late. The meat grinder got him. You just didn't see it happen.'

Corman lifted the hand-held playback screen. 'Let's see what story the vid tells.'

The vid, linked to Resyk's computer, replayed Edgar Allen's desperate struggle to drag himself from the Mouth. Recorded his triumphant escape – the arms flung up as if to embrace his wife, twenty metres overhead – the exultant shout of '*I'm alive!*'

Then the sudden disappearance. Exit Edgar Allen – swallowed by the air.

'See that, Murray? Or were you looking the other way again?'

Murray gave a non-committal grunt.

'Like I said, you're on report,' Corman said, and stormed off the belt, muttering, 'Grud, I hate this job.'

On the paternoster elevator up to the Observation Deck, the Resyk Chief shut his eyes. He tried to black out what he'd seen, not on the vid, but with his own eyes as he stepped on to the lower gallery and witnessed Edgar Allen's frantic struggle. The luckless man's predicament was bad enough, but Corman had thought his dive for the emergency halt switch had saved Allen's life. What Corman saw next made his senses reel.

For a long moment, he stood in *two* Resyks, one superimposed on the other. One Resyk was this Gruddam recycling plant he'd worked in for the last four years, the other was –

Hard to find a comparison – a Gothic cathedral, maybe, deprived of its windows and stripped of religious images, and crossed with an abattoir? He shook his head. The cathedrals he'd viewed on historical holo-vids and in virtual worlds didn't come near to the grotesque architecture of that other Resyk. And the alternative Resyk was crammed with Judges.

The only Judge he recognised was Dredd.

Logic insisted that the second Resyk was a hallucination.

'It couldn't have been real,' Corman murmured. 'But I know it was.'

TWO

Judge Ferenzi's fingers played the Devil's tattoo on the black, reflective surface of the desk in Room 102 of Psi Division headquarters. Two lesser Psi Judges flanked him on each side, their attention fixed on the Street Judge sitting bolt upright in front of the desk.

The room was crammed with wall-to-wall silence.

Ferenzi's fingers finally finished their tap dance. 'Please feel free to open up to us emotionally, Judge Dredd.'

Judge Dredd sat impassive, arms folded, mouth tight shut in a scowl.

Silence.

Ferenzi's fingers recommenced tapping, then stopped. 'Perhaps you'd care to remove your helmet,' he invited.

'No.'

'Uh-huh.' The psychiatrist nodded significantly.

More silence.

Ferenzi glanced at Kraft and Ebbing, his fellow psychiatric specialists, and the three lifted six eyebrows in unison.

'Joe – ' Psi Judge Kraft began, an understanding smile decorating his young, round face. ' – may I call you Joe? Are you familiar with the term "helmet fixation"?'

Silence.

Ebbing thrust forward her thin, pinched face, the severity of her features accentuated by the back-combed hair, pulled tight to the scalp and gathered into a compact bun. 'Do you think it's possible that you *hide* behind your helmet for a – *reason*? Perhaps you habitually wear the helmet because it represents the womb.'

Dredd's lip curled a centimetre. 'That's the last place I'd stick my head.'

'We're straying from the point,' Ferenzi muttered, stroking the balding dome of his skull. 'The Chief Judge had good cause to order this psych-analysis. Talking during micro-sleep in the somno-machines is unusual behaviour, to say the least. Would you care to hear what you said in your sleep?' Without waiting for an answer, he pressed a button, and Dredd's recorded voice filled the room:

'*I shot Dredd – shot him right through the badge – slam in the heart . . .*' A brief pause, then Dredd's grim monotone changed markedly to a hoarse cry. '*Mother of God – is this the end of Rico?*'

The recording clicked off. Ferenzi leaned back in his plush chair, lean lips pursed, fingers steepled. 'On the last twenty-nine occasions you've used the somno-machines the same words are repeated. The symptom of a traumatic event which you've repressed, hum? Well now, let's look at the facts.' He glanced at a monitor readout. 'You arrested your clone-twin Rico in 2079. He returned from Titan twenty years later – '

'Returned as a monster, an unbreathing cyborg better suited to Titan than Earth,' Kraft interrupted, with a touch of relish. 'In a sense, a dead man.'

'As I was saying,' Ferenzi continued, 'on Rico's return he forced you to shoot him, and he died shortly afterwards. But he was dressed in civvies when you put a bullet in him. He was an ex-Judge: no uniform, no badge to shoot through.'

'In other words,' Kraft broke in, 'you dream of killing your brother in 2079 when he was still a Judge, not in 2099. Is it possible that your arrest of Rico, with the inevitable consequence of his spending twenty years on

Titan, appears to you as a symbolic murder of your brother?'

'Yes,' Ebbing concurred. 'The Cain syndrome. Fratricide is one of the most traumatic – '

'Quite so,' Ferenzi said curtly. 'You dream of killing Rico way back in 2079 because that's when you destroyed him as a human being.' He swerved a look from Ebbing to Kraft. 'That's pretty straightforward, don't you think?'

'Absolutely,' said Ebbing.

'Not a doubt of it,' said Kraft.

'*But* . . .' Ferenzi thrust up a finger in a dramatic gesture. 'Why do you say, "I shot *Dredd*"? Why not "I shot *Rico*"? Any ideas on the subject – er, Joe?'

A brief silence.

'No.'

Ebbing leaned forwards. 'Don't you think that, in an existential-phenomenological meaning-nexus, you killed yourself when you destroyed your clone-twin? Thus, Dredd shot Dredd.'

Dredd's compressed lips were a long curve of silence.

A deep frown creased Ferenzi's forehead. 'I must warn you, Judge Dre – er, Joe – I must warn you that Chief Judge McGruder has suspected your mental stability ever since you demanded her resignation on the quite preposterous presumption that *she's* the one suffering from mental problems. Why, the Chief Judge – ' He glanced furtively at the Eye camera on the wall, an electronic spy that transmitted every word and gesture to Justice Central's data banks. ' – the Chief Judge is a model of sanity for us all. Isn't it possible you projected your own psychological disorders on to our eminently stable leader?'

Dredd glared straight at the Eye. 'McGruder knows exactly what I think of her.'

Kraft dropped all pretence of amiability. 'I don't think you realise the seriousness of your position, Dredd. Seven months ago you brought in Mandra, the notorious Anti-Judge and friend of the Judge-killer, Mister Cairo. You

26

wished Mandra "good luck". She escaped just two minutes later, and has eluded capture to this day.' He studied his fingernails. 'Some people say she had help, from someone who wished her – luck.'

'And she recited a code while in your custody,' Ebbing cut in. 'A code couched in a refrain from a nursery rhyme, but she clammed her lips tight before pronouncing the final word. Why was that? What cryptic message did she pass on to you?'

Dredd snorted contemptuously. 'If it was a code, it wasn't intended for me.' He returned his stare to the Eye. 'I wished Mandra luck because she helped save Mega-City One. And she escaped *after* I left, when she was in the hands of McGruder and the SJS.'

'You turning into a rogue Judge, Dredd?' demanded Kraft. 'Think you're above the Chief Judge?'

The corner of Dredd's mouth twisted. 'Now we're getting to the real reason why I'm here.'

Ferenzi raised his hands, showing conciliatory palms. 'Not at all, not at all – Joe. We're concerned with the sleep-talk in the somno-machines. The rest is merely – detail. Now – ' He threw a look at the readout. ' – This expression: "Mother of God – is this the end of Rico?" Why should you voice such a curious line in your sleep? The use of the title "Mother of God" implies an atavistic Christian impulse, inimical to mental hygiene.'

'Do you have problems with the Judges' code of celibacy?' Kraft broke in. 'Many Judges find – difficulties coping with their celibate status.'

'*Is* the problem sexual?' inquired Ebbing, narrowing her eyes to slits. 'Clones from males sometimes seek association with a mother figure. Do you wish you'd had a mother? If so, do you have sexual fantasies about her?'

Kraft nodded sagely. 'That's where the helmet comes in.'

Dredd stood up. 'And this is where I get out. I'm not listening to any more stomm from a bunch of mother-

27

drokking psych-shrinks.' He swerved round and marched across the polished floor.

'You can't leave until psych-analysis is completed!' shrilled Ebbing, approaching falsetto.

'You've got to stay!' thundered Ferenzi. 'I have a psych-probe warrant from the Chief Judge!'

'Stick it in your helmet,' Dredd growled, slamming the door behind him.

McGruder's bony fist thumped the plasteen desktop. 'He said *what*?'

Ferenzi's holo-image, hovering above the black transmit disc in the middle of the Chief Judge's desk, seemed to shiver at her vehement reaction. 'He – he said, "Stick it in – "'

'We heard you the first time!' McGruder snapped, cutting off holo-transmission with a jab of the finger. Ferenzi fizzled into thin air.

The Chief Judge leaned back in her swivel chair, fingers scratching the stubbly beard on her jutting chin, the bristles as steely grey as her back-combed hair. Even the beard reminded her of Dredd's intransigence. Dredd had persistently made pointed remarks concerning her beard, the most visible side-effect of a rapid testosterone increase from long-ago exposure to the Cursed Earth's radioactive wastelands beyond the city walls. More than once she'd accepted Dredd's advice to take a shave: he didn't even approve of facial hair on *male* Judges, let alone a female Chief Judge.

She darted wary glances around the oval of her austere office, whose walls were an identical steel-grey to the colour of her hair.

'Well, we're gonna grow this beard good and long, Joe Dredd,' she muttered. 'And it's gonna stay that way.'

Who's Chief Judge around here, anyway?

'We are,' she snapped. 'Damn right.'

The Justice system wasn't pulling as a team any more.

Didn't accord McGruder the respect her status commanded. The rot had set in with Judge Cassandra Anderson, luminary of Psi Division and closet rebel. And close colleague of Judge Dredd. Anderson had finally shown her true colours and thrown in her badge. Good riddance. Then Judge Hershey had taken it on herself to pry into the secret workings of the SJS, the Special Judicial Squad of elite Judges that judged the Judges – and anyone else it saw fit to investigate or punish. McGruder didn't take kindly to Hershey's interference: the Chief Judge had once been head of the SJS before assuming the supreme seat of power. Hershey, member of the on-off Council of Five – and potential trouble-maker. And close colleague of Judge Dredd.

Joe Dredd, the same Senior Judge who'd had the *nerve* to demand McGruder's resignation.

McGruder fingered her death's-head earrings, mementoes of her SJS days, and pursed her thin lips in vexation.

'Who's Chief Judge around here?'

We are. Damn right.

And *she* decided who was mad and who wasn't.

'You played right into our hands, Joe Dredd,' she murmured. 'Shouldn't talk in your sleep.'

She pressed a stud that activated a vid-link with SJS headquarters on the underground levels of the Halls of Justice, hundreds of metres below her feet. Judge Eliphas's angular, Luciferian features, accentuated by a goatee beard, appeared on a central screen amidst a wall of monitors. 'Chief Judge,' he nodded. 'I'm alone, but – '

'You can talk freely,' she said. 'This channel's secure.'

A smile bent his lips but did nothing for his face. 'How did the psych-analysis go?'

'Dredd walked out.'

'Doesn't surprise me. Want an update?'

McGruder tugged impatiently at a death's-head earring. 'Why else would we call?'

'Well – ' His eyes lowered. 'I've intercepted two Dredd-

29

related anomaly reports in the last hour. One from Sector 39, the other from Sector 38. The incidents are increasing in frequency. The full total stands at – ' He checked some sources offscreen. ' – ninety-seven, all from the same general area.'

The Chief Judge stroked her stubble. 'And all during Dredd's periods of micro-sleep.'

'Or just after,' he observed. 'The latest – sightings – occurred ten to twenty minutes after Dredd awoke. Of course, that's no reason to discount a connection between the micro-sleep and the sightings.'

'Tell me about the latest incidents.'

'Well, one of my own officers saw Dredd walk into a rockcrete wall over in Sector 39. Disappeared into the wall as if he were a ghost. And he was smiling.'

'Dredd hasn't smiled in almost forty years,' McGruder snorted. 'Did anything show up on a spy camera?'

'There were three Eyes covering the location, recording everything. They showed a faint blur moving to the wall, then vanishing into it. Nothing as detailed as the officer witnessed. We've run the recordings through enhancement, and come up with *nada*. The blur could be anything or nothing.'

'Okay,' she sighed. 'Next sighting.'

'Resyk,' he responded.

'Resyk again,' she pondered. 'That makes – how many? Eleven Resyk incidents?'

'Twelve. This report came from Judge Corman. In most respects it's identical to the rest. A Waker, name of Edgar Allen, came to on the belt. Then vanished into thin air. But this one didn't shout out Dredd's name, like the rest of them.'

'So what makes it Dredd-related?'

'Judge Corman reported seeing Dredd in some weird version of Resyk. The glimpse was momentary. Corman claims it was an illusion, but I don't trust him. You demoted him to Resyk for suspected liberal sympathies, remember? Permission to bring him in for interrogation and torture?'

'Permission granted. Anything show up on Resyk's monitors?'

'Yes, but not much. Something like a blanket shadow, duration four nanoseconds, coinciding with the Waker's disappearance. Enhancement can't do anything with it. Normally it'd be dismissed as a technical glitch. By the way, Tek Division discovered the reason for the high number of Wakers in the last four months. Seems there's a drug, Thanatonia, that induces the symptoms of thanatonic narcolepsy. A handy way of disposing of someone you don't like. Doesn't apply to Edgar Allen, though. Tek was already on to the drug before he was fed to the belt. He tested Thanatonia negative.'

'I don't give a drokk about Thanatonia. I want to know why people are seeing Dredd's image all over the place. What have we got here? Apparitions of the living? Bilocation? If Dredd's gone off the rails, he'll need a long rest. Intensive psych-probing. And the word will get around that he's the crazy one, not me.'

Eliphas shrugged. 'There's his dream-talking in the sleep machines – evidence of mental disorder.'

'Not sufficient. Not nearly sufficient. We have to establish a link between Dredd's micro-sleep and the unexplained sightings. Something that makes him look – out of control. Dangerous. Once that's done, it'll be fairly straightforward to implicate Hershey. She's after our job, you know.'

For the first time, the SJS Judge adopted a tentative air. 'Those two were marked down for extra-judicial killing some six months ago. Why not put an EJK squad on them? We could use a plain-clothes team, untraceable. Nice and simple.'

'Nice and simple!' McGruder burst out, spit flying. 'What happened last time, huh? Dredd and Hershey wiped out an entire squad of SJS trained killers! And what if a

31

new team succeeded, and the truth got out? We'd have a Judge riot on our hands.'

Eliphas gave another shrug. 'Whatever you say, Chief Judge.'

'Damn right! Now find a connection between Dredd's dream and the sightings, and you'll be next in line for our chair. Fail us, and we'll post you to a rad-pit. Got it?'

'Got it,' he replied in a subdued tone.

'Then get to it,' she ordered, terminating the vid-link.

As Eliphas blinked out of sight, McGruder shut her eyes and leaned back in the capacious chair.

'Things ain't what they used to be,' she whispered.

Times had changed.

Not so long ago she'd have trusted Dredd – and Hershey – with her life. Gruddam it, she'd even trusted Anderson once. Now she knew better. She should have remembered the central axiom of her SJS training: *No one can be trusted*.

It wasn't just Dredd, Hershey and Anderson. Half the Justice force was against her. Oh, they hid it well, behind a show of obedience, a smiling mask. But secretly, they hated her.

The enemy within.

They're scheming against me right now, she thought. In corners. Behind locked doors. They think I'm mad.

All against me – plotting my downfall.

'Treachery with a smile,' she hissed.

Then, in a faint voice:

'What game are you playing, Dredd?'

THREE

'Chick-a-chick-a-chick-a-chick . . .' chuckled a voice in the night.

Eleanor froze at the dire laughter in the shadows. Oh hell. Oh *hell*. They'd found her again. After two hours hiding in a corner of the Stews' labyrinthine alleyways, they'd ferreted her out.

The momentary paralysis was dispelled in an adrenalin rush as she darted down a short tunnel in a desperate attempt to escape her pursuers. The soft pad of numerous feet followed in her tracks. So did the unremitting chorus of giggles.

'Chick-a-chick-a-chick-a-chick . . .'

They were back. After two hours of hiding in the Stews, hope growing with each passing minute that the threat had passed by, moved on, they were back. She'd almost begun to believe that she might see her sixteenth birthday after all.

'Chick-a-chick-a-chick-a-chick . . .'

Some hope.

All she had was her athleticism and will to live.

Eleanor sprinted uphill with grim determination, zigzagging through the maze of alleys that made up the Stews, a hotchpotch slum clinging like a barnacle to the sloping flanks of a three-kilometre-tall citi-block.

Panic sped her feet, and the mindless laughter receded. She was outdistancing them. But she had no illusions.

They'd already killed two Judges a couple of hours past. Didn't say much for her chances.

If only Dredd had stayed. He wouldn't have failed like his two replacements.

She spotted a ragged hole in a wall, skidded to a halt, hesitated a moment, then crawled inside. Her small frame barely fitted the recess.

If the hunters missed her – fine. If they saw her, she was trapped.

Eleanor shut her eyes tight, bit her lip, balled her fists.

Don't let them see me. Please don't let them see me.

Why had Judge Dredd been called away? He'd been so close to nailing the giggling maniacs when she heard him snap into his helmet-com, reacting angrily to some message from Control. 'What the drokk do you mean, report to Psych-analysis right now? I'm in the middle of doing my job – fighting crime. And there's a girl here – ' The roar of Lawmaster motorbikes made him glance up as two Street Judges streaked into sight.

Dredd's lip twisted. 'Yeah, I see 'em,' he growled into the communications mike. 'Just hope they've got what it takes. Make sure they know what they're up against.' He glanced at Eleanor. 'Better hide yourself until the show's over.'

With that, he was on his Lawmaster and away.

The replacement lawmen lasted three minutes before the Tittering tore them to shreds.

Dredd's doubts had been confirmed. The newcomers didn't have what it took, and hadn't a clue what they were up against.

The Tittering wasn't so much a gang as an epidemic. A form of psychopathic reaction to the frenzy of modern living, characterised by an inane tittering in those it afflicted. Once it struck, it spread like wildfire, almost exclusively among disaffected youths. The giggling juves merged into a mindless mob bent on a rampage of rape and murder. Individual identity dissolved into the pack mentality. The many became One. They became the Tittering.

And the Tittering had picked on Eleanor as prey.

'Chick-a-chick-a-chick-a-chick . . .'

Her heart flipped over. The Tittering was coming close, scenting out its quarry. She tried to squeeze tighter into the hole, curling into a foetal position.

The Tittering increased in volume.

'Chick-a-chick-a-chick-a-chick . . .'

Eleanor prayed that they – it – would go away. Leave her alone. Then the prayer turned into a protest, the protest of every Mega-City victim: *Why pick on me? What have I ever done to you? WHY ME?*

But if she stayed still, very still, and breathed quietly, very quietly, the Tittering might pass over her like the Angel of Death, and travel on into the night.

A hand grabbed her ankle and yanked her out of the hiding place before she had time to scream. Her black dress tore as she was dragged along the gritty ground, speeding past the host of vacant faces that composed the Tittering.

'CHICK-A-CHICK-A-CHICK-A-CHICK . . .'

The hand let go of her ankle and she slid to a halt, banging her head on a plascrete wall. The Tittering surrounded her in a wide crescent, an arc composed of dozens of youths, each wearing the same empty expression, giggling in concert.

The Tittering was like a creature with dozens of hands, each wielding a weapon, ranging from a knife to a photon gun.

Eleanor stared death in its composite face.

'CHICK-A-CHICK-A-CHICK-A-CHICK . . .'

This was it. No hiding-place. No escape. At times in her life she'd wondered, idly, where she would die, and when.

Now she knew.

First would come the multiple rape. Then the slow carving.

She lifted her eyes to the black sky.

'SOMEBODY HELP ME!'

And somebody up there answered.

A black, metallic beast roared down from above, trailing fire.

A voice boomed, echoing down the Stews' maze of alleyways:

'Judge Dredd! Surrender – *now!*'

The metal beast was a Lawmaster. Dredd's Lawmaster, descending in wrath.

The Tittering raised its dozens of faces.

'CHICK-A-CHICK-A-CHICK-A-CHICK . . .'

The turbo-boosted bike crash-landed in front of Eleanor. The dark figure of Dredd reared up from the seat, his back to Eleanor as he confronted the Tittering, his Lawgiver pistol extended from a straight arm.

'Okay, chickens,' he growled. 'Welcome to the chopping block.'

Then he startled Eleanor by pointing the Lawgiver over his shoulder without turning his head. To her stunned wits, the muzzle seemed to be aimed straight at her.

'Armour-piercing,' he said.

A slug spat from the barrel and slammed through a door a metre from where she sprawled. The bullet left a scorching hole where the sturdy lock had been.

'Inside, young lady,' he ordered, his back still to her. 'Fast.'

Eleanor didn't need any prompting. She was on her feet and inside the house in a single leap. She kicked the door shut too hard. The recoil swung it wide open.

She reached for the door, then dived flat as red hell erupted in the dark of the Stews.

'CHICK-A . . . AARRGGHH!'

The Tittering was cut short in a series of thunderclaps punctuated by Dredd's bellow of 'Hi-ex!' as he pumped high explosive slugs into the threshing mess of subhumanity. From her prone position, she glanced up and gaped at the flame and the fury. Moist clumps of flesh soared like lava from a volcanic inferno and fell in a sloppy mess amidst a hot red rain.

A severed head flew through the doorway and nutted her on the brow.

'Drokk!' she swore, tumbling backwards while the head rolled to rest against a table leg. She gave it a kick that sent it spinning to the far wall.

'Titter now, titterhead.'

By the time she shook the circling black stars from inside her skull, the noise of battle had abated.

Then there was silence.

Eleanor counted twenty breaths, then eased round the door-frame.

The entire alley was decorated with the Tittering's remains.

Dredd, wearing more of the Tittering's shattered flesh and spattered blood than his own tattered black uniform, sat astride his Lawmaster, barking instructions to Justice Central.

'One Med-Wagon. Two meat-wagons. And tell Med to make it quick.' A pause. 'No, it's for a girl who's probably in shock. I'm okay – just a broken arm and a few broken ribs. Judges Washer and Lolland are dead.' His tone lowered to a canine growl. 'And pass this message up the line: next time any jerk wants to call me off a job for a shrink session, don't bother to call. I won't be coming.'

Eleanor had heard all about Judge Dredd. Arrest you as soon as look at you. But no better man to have at your side in a tight corner. She fully expected him to haul her in for some transgression or other, but that didn't matter. He'd come back, just in time. Saved her life.

'Thanks,' she said, confronting his visored gaze.

'None needed. Just doing my job.'

'Thanks all the same. Now what are you going to book me for? Wearing a skimpy dress in public? Venturing into the Stews at night? My father would have said I was asking for it.'

'Where is your father?'

'Dead. Like my whole family. Wiped out in a Floor War in Jane Austen Block. Left me homeless. The Stews was the only place left to look for a home.'

His lips tightened. 'Aiming to pay the rent through prostitution?'

She shrugged. 'I've got to eat.'

'Name?' he demanded.

'Eleanor Quinlan.'

Eleanor knew, for certain, that Dredd was about to arrest her. That's what the man did. No exceptions.

'Control,' he addressed the helmet-com.

Here it comes, she thought in resignation. Fair enough. A few months in the cubes is a small price to pay for your life.

'Citizen name of Eleanor Quinlan in need of food and accommodation,' he said. 'Find her a place in a women's refuge house.'

Her mouth fell open. 'You mean a *real* women's refuge, not some lock-up?'

Dredd stuck out his jaw, blistered and bloody from battle. 'You heard me, lady. If you'd sooner walk the streets, that's your business.'

She laughed, happy for the first time in weeks. 'No. A women's refuge would be just fine.' She glanced at her scuffed shoes, looked up. 'Would – would you mind if I kissed you?'

Dredd rubbed scarred knuckles across his stubbled chin. 'Yeah – I'd mind.'

Eleanor waved goodbye as the Med-Wagon drew away in the wake of a meat-wagon. Dredd, half covered in magnetic med-patches, didn't respond.

To one side, the remaining meat-wagon was operating its mechanical scoop and shovelling the bits and pieces of the Tittering into the refrigerated interior of the morgue vehicle.

Dredd's right arm, encrusted with med-aids, hung limp at his side. The bones were already knitting, grace of Med technology, but the severed nerves would take a few hours to reknit. By then he'd be asleep in his conapt in Rowdy Yates Block. Apart from the wasted hour in psych-session, he'd been tearing into crime on the streets for a full thirty-eight hours, and a rest was overdue. His bed for tonight was his own, not the sleep machines of Justice Central. Once a fortnight each Judge was obliged to spend a short time in his conapt. Dredd's term of home leave was due.

As the meat-wagon scooped up the last kilo of bone and tissue and departed the scene, Dredd approached his Lawmaster, swung a leg over the monster motorbike, and prepared to leave.

The rumble of a nearing Lawmaster stayed his hand. A Justice bike swerved round the corner and screeched to a halt at his side. The rider made a sign that told him to break radio communications.

He switched off his mike, and nodded. 'Hershey.'

Hershey doffed her helmet, barely disturbing the black bob of shoulder-length hair. Unlike Anderson, who was of similar age, Hershey's stern face bore all the faint lines and general wear and tear of a woman in her early thirties. Tonight there were more lines than usual in her frowning brow.

'Trouble,' she announced, her muscled, curvy figure swinging off the bike with military precision. 'Right here in Mega-City One.'

'Tell me something new,' he said, wheezing slightly from a cracked ribcage.

'Your ghost has been up and about again. And McGruder's got you in her sights. She's flipped, Joe. She's finally flipped.'

'Like I said, tell me something new.'

'Okay. Corman got through to me just before the SJS came for him. He saw your image in Resyk. Included it in a report to Justice Central. And probably signed his death warrant.'

Dredd expelled a low breath. 'Good Judge, Corman. Deserved better than Resyk.'

'Resyk's paradise compared to the SJS dungeons. He's done for. No way I can help him. McGruder doesn't listen to me any more. It's yourself you've got to watch out for. This doppelganger of yours is giving the SJS the ammunition it needs to bury you.'

'You're hardly the flavour of the month with the death's-head brigade, either,' he remarked.

'Sure, but I'm not talking in my sleep about my dead brother and bilocating all over the megalopolis.'

'Whatever's happening, I'm not Gruddam well appearing in different places at the same time. It's either some kind of psi creation or a – '

'A ghost?' she queried, arching an eyebrow.

His downturned mouth betrayed nothing. 'Maybe.'

'Ghost as in an apparition of the living?' she asked. 'Your ghost?'

'Ghosts belong to the dead.'

A half-smile brushed her mouth. 'You keeping a secret to yourself?'

'No. Just working on my own case.'

'Uh-huh. Well, I've got no more updates. Go get some rest. And remember – watch your back.' She gave a wry look as she studied the rags of his uniform. 'As a matter of fact, most of your back's on show – and a lot more besides. I can almost see the skin beneath the scars.'

He gunned the Lawmaster into action. The thunder of its engine reverberated around the labyrinthine alleys of the Stews. 'Best go our own ways now, Hershey. Might look like we're plotting to one of the Night Eyes. What with McGruder and the SJS turning on their own troops we could be heading for another Judge Cal scenario, with our necks first for the chop.'

She snorted disbelievingly. 'Judge Cal! That was almost

two decades ago. We've learned from the experience. And McGruder at her worst wouldn't end up parading around as a reincarnation of Emperor Caligula and ordering the extermination of the entire city. Cal was a one-off. Can you imagine McGruder appointing a goldfish as Deputy Chief Judge?'

'If she goes right over the edge, it won't be in the same way as Judge Cal, but the consequences mightn't be much better. Demented tyrants come in all shapes and sizes, each with their own speciality.'

Hershey looked askance. 'You seriously think McGruder's that dangerous?'

He shook his head. 'No. I think there's something much worse heading our way.'

Her full lips formed a pensive twist. 'By the pricking of my thumbs, something wicked this way comes,' she quoted. 'One hell of a play, *Macbeth*. You should see it some time.'

'Something wicked this way comes,' he murmured. 'Yes. I think so.'

Deep lines in Hershey's forehead betrayed her concern. 'Joe – what's got into you? You don't seem yourself. What's wrong?'

'So long, Hershey,' he said, releasing the Lawmaster's brake. 'And do me a favour.'

'What's that?' she called out as he rode away.

'Don't prick your thumbs.'

The door to the Cafe Cesare was open.

Dredd sat on his Lawmaster, its motor quietly purring, and stared at the dilapidated cafe from the opposite side of the street.

The sign above the door had faded with the passing of decades, its letters barely legible.

The black rectangle of the doorway looked like an open invitation:

Walk right in. Come into my parlour.

41

The derelict cafe's silence cast its spell over the street. Silence and emptiness stretched up and down the length of Robinson Street. A watchful silence.

He hadn't visited the Cafe Cesare's precincts since his brother's arrest. Not once in thirty-seven years.

But all the recent sightings of Dredd's 'ghost' were located within a twenty-kilometre radius of this cafe, here in Sector 38. McGruder had gone to some pains to keep Dredd in the dark about the sightings of his apparition. But he had his means of finding out.

He kept his gaze fixed on the open door for long minutes.

Then he eased the bike down the road, gradually gathering speed. Not once did he look back. As he put distance between himself and the cafe, he mouthed an extract from a poem that Rico had been fond of quoting:

> *'Like one that on a lonesome road*
> *Doth walk in fear and dread.*
> *And having once turned round walks on,*
> *And turns no more his head;*
> *Because he knows, a frightful fiend*
> *Doth close behind him tread . . .'*

The Firerock tyres devoured the kilometres to the lawman's conapt, the bulging, cloud-piercing tower blocks blurring by. Throughout the journey he kept his eyes fixed straight ahead.

He spoke only once, somewhere below a breath:

'Something wicked this way comes.'

FOUR

'Do it by the book.'

Hershey spoke in a whisper so low that even Justice Central's hypersensitive audio sensors wouldn't pick it up.

No matter how crazy McGruder or how insidious the Special Judicial Squad, you don't stir up a revolt. Storming the palace gates wasn't Hershey's way.

Do it by the book.

When the time was ripe, she would persuade/cajole/threaten the disbanded Council of Five into deposing McGruder – legally. The apparatus for deposition was in place. It was simply a matter of using it effectively and speedily before the SJS blew your head off.

She strode down a green corridor off a middle tier of the Grand Hall of Justice, heading for the holo-firing-range. A Judge had to keep in practice, no matter how much of a sharpshooter she fancied herself. Besides, she needed to keep her mind off the trouble brewing in Justice Central. And she had a greater need to forget the eerie sightings of Dredd, just for a little while.

Something wicked this way comes . . .

Yeah, well, let it come. She'd face it, whatever it was. Even if it killed her.

The arched door to the firing-range *whished* open and she found, to her pleasure, that one of the fifty chambers was free. Fifteen minutes' holo-shooting should get some of the spooks out of her nervous system, spooks that Dredd's uncharacteristic behaviour had evoked.

Marching into a thirty-metre-square chamber, walled,

43

floored and ceilinged with dull grey image-conductive plasteen, she drew the Lawgiver from her boot holster, converted it to holo-fire.

'Activate,' she ordered.

The grey chamber was instantly converted into a riotous amalgamation of a number of Mega-City One's deadlier locales.

Populated with the deadliest of enemies.

A holographic Mean Machine, dial implanted in his head, a lethal mechanical arm sprouting from one shoulder, sprang out of a sadomaso parlour door, metallic arm stretched to snap off her head.

She put two bullets in each of Mean Machine's eyes before he got halfway to his quarry. Holo-blood spurted and splattered the black leathereen of her uniform.

A figure darted in from the right.

She swung and stopped a millisecond from firing. A Judge. Serious infraction if you shot a holo-Judge.

Faint footsteps behind her.

Hershey whirled and drilled a hole each in two members of the Angel gang.

A flash of an airborne knife to the left. She dived sideways, evading the blade by centimetres while pumping a bullet into Orlok, the East-Meg assassin, partially visible inside a round window. He dropped.

Nice one.

The street cleared.

Senses on red alert, she prowled down the narrow street, eyes darting to and fro.

The enemy hid its face. Held back.

Test of nerve time.

Reaching the crossroads, she launched into a forward roll, peripheral vision taking in figures to right and left.

Her boot knife was out and hurtling at the left-hand perp, simultaneous with the volley she let loose on the shambling shape to the right, its hand pulling out a glittering object from an inside jacket pocket.

She threw herself back into a doorway and darted a glance to the left. Yes, she'd assessed the situation correctly. A thug lay dead, her knife in his throat, a Gotterdammerung combined assault rifle and missile-launcher loose in his uncurling hand. To the right –

Hershey stalked up to the mutant behemoth with a bullet hole in the centre of his forehead, her intent grey eyes still on the lookout for any sudden appearance of friend or foe.

She saw what the lumpy-headed mutant had drawn from his jacket. Not a weapon – a plastiplex card with an embossed message:

MY NAME IS JOHN MERRECAR. I AM OF GRADE ZERO-TWO INTELLECT AND CAN ONLY UNDERSTAND VERY SIMPLE INSTRUCTIONS. PLEASE DO NOT FIRE IF I FAIL TO RESPOND TO JUSTICE OFFICERS' COMMANDS.

Hershey's skin chilled. Guilt welled up on her tongue, and tasted sour.

She had fatally shot a similar low-intellect citizen a year ago. For real. She'd thought he was drawing a gun when he reached for his low intellect exemption card.

It was a killing that still haunted her dreams.

A flicker of light to one side –

She spun, squeezing the trigger. And halted, a hair's breadth from firing a slug.

Chief Judge McGruder stood three metres away, arms folded.

Drokk! She'd almost shot a holo of the Chief Judge. That would have looked bad on the firing-range vid-record. In the present state of affairs, potentially treacherous.

'Good judgement,' complimented the holo-McGruder, giving the thumbs-up.

Enough was enough.

'Deactivate,' she ordered.

The light-and-shadow-play dissolved into the dull grey chamber.

She expelled a sharp breath, cancelled the Lawgiver's holo-function, and walked to the exit with slow, deliberate paces.

Bad idea, using the holo-range. Didn't exorcise a single spook. Just resurrected a ghost she'd begun to hope would lie still. She should have known she'd never be rid of that guilt. The dead can't forgive.

Back in the green-tiled corridor, she straightened her back, squared her shoulders. Okay, she'd once killed a harmless man because she was too damn quick on the damn trigger. Just live with it. Life's a bitch.

She got her mind back on track. There were people to meet, plans to be formulated. Step by step, the Chief Judge had to be ousted. Legally.

By the book.

Hershey emerged on the middle balcony of the Grand Hall of Justice, turned left for the grav-chute to the Hall floor. And halted abruptly.

She spun on her heel and headed right, stepped into the grav-chute for the upper balcony, and stared unblinkingly ahead as the magneto-powered anti-gravity elevator whisked her upwards.

Emerging from the chute, she strode purposefully through a series of branching corridors.

Two more turns and she'd reach McGruder's office.

McGruder was likely to be alone at this hour.

Hershey could walk right in.

And shoot that man-bitch McGruder in her foul brain.

The office door came into sight.

Hershey pulled the gun from its boot holster.

One bullet in the right head and Hershey would rule the roost.

He wouldn't object. *He'd* understand.

You've got five seconds, McGruder . . .

She raised the Lawgiver, readied herself to kick the door open . . .

Kill the old crow . . .

Hershey froze.

Shuddered.

Shook her head.

Her puzzled gaze alighted on the pistol at the end of her extended arm.

Her confusion increased when she realised where she was standing.

How in the name of Jovus Drokk did she get up here, in front of the Chief Judge's office? And what the hell was she doing with her gun out and levelled at the door?

A quick glance disclosed that there was no one around. A swift sigh of relief. She returned the gun to its holster, and beat a hasty exit, her wits whirling.

What the *drokk* had happened? The last she remembered she was on the middle balcony, heading for the grav-chute to the ground floor.

After that – what?

A blank.

As she made her way down to the floor of the Grand Hall, Hershey struggled to recall what had occurred in those lost minutes.

Couldn't recollect a Gruddam thing.

But she'd finished up pointing a gun at McGruder's door.

Had some suppressed homicidal impulse possessed her, driven her like an automaton to drill a hole in the Chief Judge?

She believed herself incapable of such deliberate murder. But then, who could tell about the inner dark?

'What's happening to me?' she whispered hoarsely.

Something wicked . . .

FIVE

A toneless voice buzzed in Dredd's spartan conapt.

'They seal up your mouth and nose, adapt your body to work in vacuum without a clumsy spacesuit. And every day I looked at the little pinprick of light in the sky that was the planet Earth . . . And I swore I'd get even with you, Joe.'

Dredd, free of his helmet but still clad in the rags of his uniform and the crimson mess of the Tittering, sat in front of his compact vid-screen and watched a conapt-eye recording of an event that occurred in this same conapt, seventeen years ago. The flicker of the vid-screen was reflected in the Judge's eyes:

Rico pulled back his hood, revealing a freak-show face. The plasteen-based features had the botched-job look of work laid on with a slapdash trowel, mish-mashed with a patchwork of circuit implants. The mouth was permi-sealed. The buzzing voice vibrated from his throat-mike:

'Swore I'd get revenge for what you did to me! Look at me, Joe old buddy! LOOK AT ME!'

Rico had been adapted on the Titan penal colony to survive without external sources of air. On returning to earth, he'd lain in wait inside Dredd's apartment, sealing it tight, draining it of air and warmth. A miniature Titan. That ruse had taken Dredd unawares; it almost stole his breath away for good in the moments it took to pull the helmet respirator into place. Rico stood waiting, with the patience of twenty years, as Dredd made an appeal to the monster who'd once been his brother:

'Rico . . . Stop . . . While there's time.'

'No,' buzzed Rico's throat-mike. 'But I'll do you one last favour. I'll shoot you quick. Your gun's back in your boot holster. Draw!'

'No, Rico. Don't make me kill you.'

'Because you know I'm faster, huh? You're yellow, Joe! Draw!'

Rico's hand moved to his shoulder-holster. Dredd still held back.

'DRAW, I SAID!' Rico ordered, quivering with rage.

'Okay, Rico. If that's the way you want it . . .'

The two men stood motionless as freeze-frames, hands dangling over their guns.

Dredd drew in a blur of speed, drilling Rico's heart while his brother's gun was halfway out of its holster.

Rico spun and dropped. Dredd rushed to his side, propped him up.

The faint buzz from Rico's throat voiced its disbelief that Joe could be faster than Rico.

Dredd's breathing was laboured, the respirator's air running out. 'Twenty years on Titan . . . slowed you down a split-second . . . But you were the best, Rico . . . The best . . .'

Dredd stared at the vid-screen for a brief space, listening grim-mouthed to his clone-twin's final words – those fateful last words – then fast-forwarded the recording to the arrival of Chief Judge Goodman and a Tek team, who restored air and warmth to the apartment.

Chief Judge Goodman glanced up at Dredd, who leaned against a wall, temporarily disabled from oxygen deprivation and exposure to sub-sub-zero temperature.

'He's just died,' Goodman quietly informed him.

'No,' Dredd husked. 'Rico died a long time ago . . .'

'Terminate,' Dredd ordered the computer. The vid-screen instantly went blank.

Dredd leaned back in his chair, shut his eyes.

Yes, Rico died a long time ago. In the Cafe Cesare. The arrest was as effective as a bullet to the heart. There was only one punishment for bent Judges: Titan. And the convicts on Titan were dead men in all but name.

Rico died thirty-seven years ago. What came back from Titan was part robot, part wretched beast. And Dredd put him out of his misery with a well-aimed slug. Vengeance wasn't the motive force that drove Rico to confront Dredd in a shoot-out. Rico desired the oblivion of true death, and he wanted it from the hand of his brother.

For a few seconds, Dredd reflected on those last words – those very last words – of his one-time brother.

'Mother of God – is this the end of Rico?'

'Drokk it.' He stood up and walked into the bathroom, kicked off his boots, unhooked the Justice name-badge and placed it on a small table. After turning on the taps of the antique pedestal bath of white enamel, he stripped off the one-piece leathereen uniform and disposed of it in a chute that led to UnderBlock recycling.

He lowered his jigsaw-scarred body, decorated with med-pads from the Stews mayhem, into the near-boiling water, watched the organic muck of the Stews flow, dissolve, merge with the steaming liquid. The skin on his injured arm was starting to prickle; the severed nerves were realigning.

Ten minutes later he emerged from the bathroom, dressed in strictly functional sleep-vest and shorts, the name-badge in his hand. He left it by the vid-screen.

He approached the narrow bed that was one of the few items of furniture in his dour conapt. As he was on the brink of climbing under the rough sheets, the voice of Control issued from the audio-com.

'Judge Dredd. You're required to attend psych-analysis tomorrow at eighteen hundred hours in Room 102, Psi Division. Said analysis may be extended over an indeterminate number of days. Please confirm.'

Dredd paused for a moment, then: 'No.'

'No?'

'I won't be coming.'

'Er – attendance is compulsory. Orders from the Chief Judge's office. Please confirm.'

'I confirm that I'm not coming. Now sign off and let me get some sleep.'

'May I point out that the Chief Judge is most concerned about your psychological welfare. You *must* attend psych-analysis. Please confirm.'

'Drokk off!'

'Er – ' said Control, then fell silent.

Dredd glanced at the vid-screen, pondered a few seconds, then resumed his seat in front of the screen. A swift selection brought a replay on to the screen.

The Cafe Cesare, 2079.

Unknown to the cafe-owner, and Rico, an Eye had been planted in the cafe in response to rumours of drug sales, later proved unfounded.

Dredd watched his younger self face out Rico over the body of Edward Gee. Watched his clone-twin drop his Lawgiver in surrender.

Replay concluded, he slumped back in the chair, gaze remaining on the glowing white of the screen.

'All "ghost" sightings located within twenty kays of Cafe Cesare,' he muttered. 'They started when the dream came back, after all these years. Why?'

A minute passed. He reached to turn off the computer.

His hand halted in mid-reach.

Bold black words had appeared on the screen: SOME-THING WICKED THIS WAY COMES.

The sinister message remained for several seconds, then vanished.

The Cafe Cesare replay took its place. An eighteen-year-old Joe Dredd aimed his Lawgiver at Rico. The events unfolded as before, right up to the final lines:

'I don't think you'll shoot me, Joe. We're identical. It'd be like killing yourself.'

'Try me.'

'I always came first on the firing-range, remember? First

51

in speed. First in accuracy. You were always second. Always.' Rico's gun moved a centimetre. 'You wouldn't shoot me, would you, Joe?'

The confrontation lengthened to breaking point.

Rico's gun-hand twitched.

And Joe Dredd fired.

The slug bored a hole in Rico's name-badge. He spasmed, crumpled to the floor.

He sprawled, glazed eyes wandering aimlessly.

'Mother of God,' he croaked, 'is this the end of Rico?'

Joe rushed to his side, cradled him in his arms. The body went limp. He let it fall.

'You weren't the best, after all, Rico,' he said.

Then he picked up Rico's DREDD name-badge, whose bullet-holed metal showed DRE*D.

He gripped it tight.

Two Judges rushed into the cafe. 'Saw it on the Eye, Joe. Drokk – who'd have thought Rico would have turned out as one of the heavies?' Judge Gunning said, staring at the corpse. 'Grud – that's tough, having to kill your own brother.'

Joe Dredd gazed down on Rico. 'He – he ain't my brother – he's a heavy.'

Gunning and the other Judge left him alone with the corpse while they waited for the meat-wagon's arrival.

Joe glanced at the bullet-drilled badge in his hand, then returned his gaze to Rico.

'I owe you, twin brother. You've taught me a lesson I won't forget.'

The screen image wavered; the pixels danced, jostled. The picture degenerated into a variegated swirl.

Then the vid-screen resumed its familiar bland white.

Dredd stared for a time, then released a long breath. 'What the drokk was that?' he growled. 'The ghost in the machine?'

He eased back in the seat, gaze settling on his name-badge. His shoulders sank.

Dredd barely heard his own voice: 'Rico's ghost?'

52

Part Two

Rico's Ghost?

'Thou canst not say I did it: never shake
Thy gory locks at me [. . .]
The times have been,
That when the brains were out, the man would die,
And there an end; but now they rise again,
With twenty mortal murders on their crowns [. . .]
Hence, horrible shadow!
Unreal mockery, hence!'

William Shakespeare
Macbeth: Act 3, Scene 4

SIX

The Muttering was one of the last districts in Mega-City One in which you'd wish to be alone at night.

She was alone.

It was night.

She was in it.

Jessie Merrow hurried along in the shadows of bulbous citi-blocks two kilometres tall, and wished she was up there somewhere, in the tangle of skedways, megways, zoomways and slipways, crammed with speeding vehicles, five hundred metres overhead. Or higher, in the cobweb of interlaced pedestrian glideways and slideways, around a kilometre above the grimy ground level in which she found herself.

Toxic rain began to fall.

'Oh *great*,' she muttered, then realised she'd already fallen into the morose muttering that typified the denizens of this low-city area, and gave it its name.

There was something about the Muttering's crooked streets, the overbearing citi-blocks that bulged overhead, that cowed any dweller or visitor into subdued speech. Permanent occupants never spoke above a low mutter. The Muttering district might not be as violent as the Mumbles or as depressing as the Grumbles, but it had an intimidating air, an oppressive sense of *weight*.

'Drokk,' she muttered, slipping on one of the lumps of stomm fouling the zigzag length of Degradability Avenue, one of the Muttering's meaner streets. 'Damn and drokk.'

The evening had started out so well. A call from Bazza,

proposing a date at the Schlockfest fly-in cinema. She'd fancied Bazza since she was sixteen. Four years was a long time to wait for the first date, but she'd kept up her hopes. And tonight her patience was rewarded.

So she thought.

The motherdrokker hadn't turned up. She should have guessed it was a hoax when he suggested meeting *inside* the anti-gravity cinema. Dead giveaway, now she thought about it.

But Jessie, like a mug, had flown her hov-pod to the Schlockfest and parked her vehicle in the anti-grav spaces of the auditorium, midway between roof and floor.

As the minutes passed, it gradually dawned that Bazza had stood her up. Stommhead.

She'd hated the horror double bill: *Maniac Judge VII* and *Maniac Judge VIII* in HyperHolovision and Feel-around. Tacky. Seriously tacky. A decomposing Judge charging about with an axe and chopping up teenage couples every time they started screwing or decided to put on blast music.

What really unsettled her was the Schlockfest's Feel-around system. Every physical sensation experienced by the movie characters was passed on to the audience in muted form. If one of the actors barked his shins, you experienced a dull, fleeting pain in your own shins. Feelaround was fine a lot of the time (especially the sex scenes), but when the Maniac Judge sliced his axe into a victim's throat . . . Ouch and yuck.

Jessie had left in the middle of the second feature and flown at max power, intent on getting home and burying her face in a pillow.

She shouldn't have pushed her seventh-hand hov-pod so hard. Damn thing conked out over the Muttering. She was lucky to glide the old banger down to a mild thump of a landing. Her luck didn't extend to the communication system: drokking thing was dead as a night out in Antarctic City.

She'd been looking for a hov-taxi for the past twenty minutes. They were never around when you wanted one.

The toxic downpour increased in intensity. Thank Grud wide-brimmed hats were all the vogue. Combined with her Omni-Repellent overcoat, her metre-wide hat provided ample protection from the chemical crud in solution that battered down from the acidic sky.

Of course, she had more than the weather to worry about. The Mega-City was a cauldron of violent crime. And the Muttering's crime statistics were higher than most.

That's why Jessie kept up a brisk pace. The street ahead was deserted, but someone was walking behind her. Had been for the last ten minutes. She'd looked over her shoulder at first sound of the footsteps, discerned merely a shambling blur in the darkness.

It was probably quite innocent; just someone heading the same way as her.

All the same, the sooner she found a hov-taxi, the better.

She squinted ahead through the rain. Where was this avenue leading? The jagged thoroughfare seemed to be bending back on itself.

Spying an opening to her left, she decided to make for it. At least the side street was fairly straight, more likely to lead to a somewhere out of this nowhere. The name was barely legible through the teeming rain: Robinson Street.

The first anomaly that struck her was the silence in Robinson Street. Despite the thrash of rain, a profound silence permeated the walls of the empty street, which seemed to be lined with derelict cafes and clubs.

Covering the first fifty metres, she tried to fight off a growing unease.

'Spooky,' she muttered.

A couple of lines from English Lit sprang out of her schooldays and haunted the present:

Like one that on a lonesome road
Doth walk in fear and dread . . .

She shuddered. Erase that memory for now. Another time, another place.

The soft pad of footsteps echoed at her back. An icicle scraped down her spine.

The man in the rain had followed her into Robinson Street. Could be coincidence. More likely she was being stalked.

Keep walking, and don't turn round.

She spurred her paces to greater speed.

The following footfalls more than matched her accelerated pace. The pursuer's steps were louder.

Nearer.

Sweat popped in beads on her brow. *If I run, he'll start running, then I'll know he's after me. And I don't want to know.*

Her frightened glance darted left and right, seeking out a lighted window, a sign of human company. But the whole Gruddam street, which must have swung in its heyday, was an abandoned project, lightless, lifeless. She peered into the burnt-out husk of a streetcar, praying to see someone inside, sheltering from the rain. No such luck.

Twenty strides on, she neared a cafe whose dereliction approached the outright ruinous. Years of neglect had almost corroded the lettering on the old sign: CAFE CESARE.

The cafe door was open, and clogged with shadow.

A dark figure stepped out of the shadow of the door.

He took a couple of paces and entered the dithery aura of a street lamp.

Jessie heaved a sigh of relief. It was a Judge.

She shot a look over her shoulder. The pursuer had vanished. Must have ducked into a hiding place when the lawman appeared.

'Thank Grud,' she sighed, approaching the motionless figure of the Judge.

Then the memory of the Schlockfest's Maniac Judge surfaced, with its creepy Feelaround effects.

What if it's the Maniac Judge?

Stupid thought.

Reassurance came when she halted within five paces of the law officer. That physique, that inimitable jaw-line, were unmistakable. They were famous all over the Mega-City. No two men could be so alike. The name-badge was partially obscured in shadow, but with this man a badge was unnecessary for recognition.

'Judge Dredd,' she said.

He didn't move. Didn't speak.

Then, slowly, his lips parted and curved into a smile, displaying clenched teeth.

Her eyed widened with a touch of surprise. Word had it that Dredd never smiled. Evidently the word had it wrong.

Anyway, it could hardly be called a *friendly* smile.

'Judge Dredd?' she repeated.

'*The one and only*,' he said.

The resonance of his voice stunned her: although strong and clear as Dredd's distinctive tones, it seemed to come from a distant place, like the boom of a giant on the far edge of the world.

Unnerved, she took a step back.

'*Stay*,' he commanded, raising an arm.

A power radiated from the arm, immobilising her limbs. Her scalp prickled as she sensed a merciless consciousness probing her brain.

'*I see what you are*,' the Judge said. '*You're all heart. You must be shown up for what you are.*'

He pointed a finger.

A blinding light blazed from the fingertip.

A jagged bolt of blue-white light crackled an erratic course through the air.

59

And slammed into her heart, hurling her backwards to a bone-jarring impact with the sidewalk.

The Judge's voice rang out, remote and clear:

'*I've fed your heart a hunger. Your heart will feed on your body. And your heart will grow. And grow . . .*'

Jessie tried to scream, but her lungs felt suddenly constricted.

And there was a lump in her throat. A lump forcing upwards.

A swelling bulged out the centre of her chest, like a third breast.

A lump inside her – growing – her heart –

The pain was excruciating.

She felt her arms and legs shrivelling, retracting into a torso that pulsed and pulsed with the heart's mighty expansion and contraction.

'*Yes,*' she heard, distant and distinct. '*You'll soon be all heart.*'

He stood over her, fully illuminated by the street light, the golden badge glistening in its flickering radiance. The name stood out on the badge, gold letters on black:

DREAD

It was the last thing Jessie saw.

He saw it all, through the shattered window of a burnt-out car.

When the Judge first appeared, Grubber had dived for cover. The car was within diving distance.

Grubber didn't like Judges. That's because Judges didn't like mutants, and Grubber was a mutant from his lumpy head to his seven-toed feet. All Grubber wanted to do was forage in the garbage that littered the Muttering, but the Helmets were always hassling him. Always insisting that he give his name, often irate when he hand-signed that he was a mute, born without a tongue.

No, Grubber didn't like Judges. But he liked people. Well, *nice* people. The young lady had looked like a nice person, and he was worried on her behalf, travelling alone through this plascrete jungle. He'd followed her all the way, keeping one of his three eyes on her, making sure that no one tried anything. With him following, not a soul would have dared touch her. Grubber was a little man, but he had a big, big gun.

Anybody tried to hurt the nice lady, they'd get a big, big bullet.

Shame the lady didn't realise he was protecting her. He couldn't call out a reassurance, and she probably wouldn't have believed him anyway. She'd walked faster and faster to get away from him, and he had to force his thick, wobbly legs to their utmost to keep up.

When the Judge stepped into the street, Grubber was glad for the young lady. Then he noticed which door the lawman had stepped out of.

Bad. Oh, bad.

Bad place.

He'd put on his magni-specs and viewed the encounter with mounting consternation.

Judge Dredd. Yuch. Loud-mouth Judge. Pain in the neck.

Then came the forked lightning from the Judge's hand. It hurt Grubber's eyes.

When his vision swam back into focus, the young lady was lying on her back. And –

He adjusted the magnification on the specs.

Oh no! The poor lady was getting very fat. Very fat and very red. And what was happening to her arms and legs? They were getting smaller and smaller.

He increased the magnification to maximum.

Funny. Judge Dredd was smiling. No – not possible. Dredd was a sourpuss.

That's not Dredd, Grubber thought.

He concentrated on the badge. On the name inscribed in capitals:

DREAD

Dread, he mouthed. Judge Dread.

Grubber returned his attention to the lady.

Lady? What lady?

All he saw was a – lump, resting on top of a spread of torn clothing. The lump got bigger and smaller, bigger and smaller. It reminded him of –

Fiddles and ferkins! It *was*. It was a heart. And it had a hat on.

Judge Dread had vanished, Grud knew where.

Grubber waited, not daring to move for a while. At length, he stole out of the car, crept towards the heart with a hat that sheltered it from the rain.

It was the size of a boulder, at least half a metre in span. And it kept on beating. Steam rose from its pumping chambers and flexing tubes, curling under the wide hat brim.

Fiddles and ferkins!

Judge Dread had done something bad to the nice lady.

Judge Dread was a very bad man.

But who was he?

Grubber looked at the open door of the Cafe Cesare, and tried to think. The effort hurt his head, but a memory stirred in his brain.

Dredd had had a brother, a long time ago, when Grubber was a little sprog. What was his name? Rico. There'd been big trouble between Dredd and Rico in that cafe. After that, the cafe had gone – bad.

Nobody had ever wanted to use the word 'haunted'. Or 'ghost'.

Bad luck, using words like that.

I'm slow in my head, Grubber admitted. But I know who you are, Judge Dread.

The knowledge spooked him.

Slowly, he backed away from the open door, then turned and hurried down Robinson Street, oblivious to the pelting rain.

Rico's ghost, he muttered inwardly.

* * *

The Judge switched off the hi-magnification mode of his visor, and slipped round the corner of Robinson Street into Degradability Avenue.

All the signs had pointed to this spot. He'd been observing it for the best part of two days. The long wait had been worth it. His patience was rewarded.

He'd finally seen the dark Judge of the night. Observed his name through visor-magnification.

Judge Dread.

'I might have known,' he murmured.

He located his hidden Lawmaster, voice-activated its systems. The glare of headlamps illuminated his lean figure, picked out the name on his Justice name-badge:

MAXIMIN

He eased into the motorbike's seat, gripped the handlebars.

'Judge Dread. I might have known.'

SEVEN

'You're all mine.'

Chief Judge McGruder surveyed the bulbous tower blocks, the spidery network of suspended highways and walkways – in short, the soaring monumentalism of Mega-City One – through the curved panel of a plastiplex window. Mega-City One, the summits of its citi-blocks resembling domed mountain peaks, gleaming in the morning sun above the clouds, while perennial shadow cloaked the sloping lower flanks of the gargantuan buildings, home to four hundred million souls (damned or otherwise).

'All ours.'

Damn right.

'Huh!' she snorted. 'Chief Judge thinks he's Grud Almighty. We'll show him, won't we, darling?'

'Ma'am?' came Judge Vogel's puzzled query.

She spun round. 'What? Ah yes, manning levels.'

McGruder stomped across the twenty metres of floor to her desk, sat down and faced Vogel. 'Right,' she snapped. 'Why are we below target on Academy recruitment? There must be plenty of parents who wouldn't say no to handing over their infants.'

The harassed Vogel ran stubby fingers through his grey, thinning hair. 'Nuclear families were never a prime source of cadet material. Basically, it boils down to the orphanages, which we've cleared out of all semi-suitable candidates. To be frank, we're scraping the barrel there. That leaves the genetic banks . . .'

She jabbed a bony finger over the desk. 'Don't give me

any more of that stomm about drokking clones. Clones already make up a third of the force. If we push the genetics department any harder we'll end up with two-headed freaks.'

He threw up his hands. 'Then what do you suggest, Chief Judge?'

Her eyes glazed. The eyelids slid shut. Snapped open.

Vogel gulped. McGruder's eyes were never mellow at the best of times, but those eyes were now hard and sharp as flints.

'Chief Judge? What are you talking about, Dekker?' she growled.

Vogel blinked in astonishment. How could she confuse him with Dekker? Firstly, Judge Dekker was a woman. Secondly, she'd been dead for years.

'Now listen,' she continued. 'We've got to kill that upstart Hershey. Then we can really go to town on that bitch Anderson and her rebel army.'

His mouth fell open. 'Huh?'

'Hershey and Anderson – pah! He fancies them both, you know.'

'Huh?'

'Dread does, drokkhead. He wants to screw them both.'
'!'

'And Dread's getting far too pally with Judge Caligula for my liking. I mean – we've got the drokking Roman Empire back again, haven't we darling? Do you call that sane, eh? Well, *do you*?'

'!??!'

Her eyelids flickered. The flinty glare vanished.

'We'd suggest you scour every orphanage in the city,' she said. 'You must have overlooked some candidates. We can't overstretch genetics – too dangerous. All right?'

His mouth fished for speech. 'Er . . . Ah . . .'

'What's wrong with you, man?'

'Oh – you – you realise I'm a man.'

'Realise . . . You crazy or something?'

65

Vogel's cheeks purpled. 'You – you thought I was Dekker. And you thought Caligula – Judge Cal – was alive. And – and you said Dredd wanted to screw Hershey and Anderson.'

McGruder's eyes bugged as her eyebrows vaulted. 'We don't believe what we're hearing.'

'That's what you said,' he insisted, shifting nervously. 'Honest.'

'You're barking mad!' she roared, banging the table with her fist.

'Then check the Eye replay,' he pleaded. 'I swear I'm right. If I'm not, you can execute me. That's how sure I am. *Please* – just replay the last two minutes.'

She lofted her fist, then lowered it slowly. 'Okay, it's your Resyk.'

Vogel heaved a sigh of relief as McGruder punched in the codes for replay.

The two watched the vid-screen in silence as it relayed McGruder's bizarre behaviour.

The silence persisted a full minute after the recording concluded.

'Ahem,' she coughed. 'Well – er – what can I say?'

'Don't know,' he shrugged, expertly hiding an exquisite feeling of smugness.

She stroked her beard. 'Vogel – do you think I'm going senile?'

'I – I'm not qualified in that department, Chief Judge. That's Psi Division's territory.'

She waved him away. 'Very well, you can go. I must give this matter some serious consideration.'

He stood up and headed for the door. 'Good morning, Chief Judge.'

'Oh – one last thing,' she called out.

Vogel, halfway through the door, looked over his shoulder. 'Yes?'

'You've got a real cute butt, Dekker,' she winked.

'When you get tired of rolling in the sheets with Dread, look me up, okay?' The flinty gaze was back.

'Oh – okay.'

He shut the door quietly behind him.

And walked numbly down the corridor.

Jovus Drokk on a Titzy-bike, he swore inwardly. *Come back, Caligula – all is forgiven.*

'That's the way it happened. I swear.'

'Okay,' Hershey nodded, lips pressed tight. 'You were right to come to me. Don't repeat this to anyone else. Understand?'

'Of course,' Vogel agreed. 'What are we going to do? I mean – McGruder's crazy. Crazy as a loon.'

'Keep your voice down,' she hissed, glancing at the milling crowds surrounding them in the glaring sunlight of Pagliacci Plaza, every last one of them juggling coloured balls – all the rage this spring. 'I've already spotted three SJS plain-clothes spies.'

'Sorry,' he apologised. 'What are we going to do?'

'What's this "we"? You're out of this, and be glad of it. You'd best go now.'

He lifted his weary shoulders as he moved away. 'Oh well, can't say I'm too sad about that.'

Hershey watched Vogel's dumpy figure until it was lost in the crowds.

Vogel's information convinced her that action was imperative, but whom to trust?

Not for the first time, she wished that Cassandra Anderson was around, instead of roaming in deep space. Anderson was brilliant crystal, Dredd was impenetrable granite. Together, they were formidable.

Well, one out of two was better than none.

She and Dredd had established an ultra-secure channel that circumvented Justice Central surveillance, in case of another emergency on the lines of Judge Cal's reign of terror.

Jumping on her Lawmaster, she nosed the motorbike to a nearby drop-square, parked it in the middle of the four-metre-wide slab, and issued the DROP command via her bike computer.

The slab dropped beneath her at five metres a second. Ten seconds later it slowed to a halt in a straight tunnel illuminated by Hi-Glo. The instant she rode off the drop-square it ascended back to the surface, leaving a clear view to front and back.

She accelerated close to 500 kph along the Justice Express, as the Judges-only network of underground thoroughfares were nicknamed. They afforded swift access to all areas of the megalopolis whenever speedy response was urgent.

More to the point, in the present situation, the Justice Express merited a mere token surveillance. Anything said in the tunnels was unlikely to be picked up by Justice Central.

'Situation Caligula,' she instructed the computer, the code-words initiating a bypass that cut out Control and connected her with Dredd, person to person. A panel flashed blue-green-blue, acknowledging the bypass.

'Right,' she breathed.

A hand tapped her on the shoulder.

Shocked, she twisted round.

A Judge was riding pillion on Hershey's bike.

The Judge sitting behind Hershey was – Hershey.

Hershey gaped at the double of herself, too stunned to wonder where the drokk this doppelganger had come from.

'*You!*' snarled the doppelganger in an exact reproduction of Hershey's own voice.

The Hershey-double flung one arm around Hershey's throat as the other removed the Lawgiver from her holster. 'There's no room for the two of us in this world, *Barbara* . . .'

The encircling arm tightened, squeezing Hershey's windpipe. She fought to keep the bike from crashing.

'Come on over to *my* place, *Barbara*,' Hershey's double hissed.

Hershey's vision shimmered.

Suddenly she wasn't in the tunnel anymore. Cyclopean grey walls, sprouting huge gargoyles, rose on all sides as she sped on her Lawmaster, her other self at her back, throttling the life out of her.

'Bye-bye, *Barbara* . . .'

EIGHT

McGruder slumped back in her chair, eyes fixed on Judge Maximin's vid-screen image.

'It's got to be a mistake,' she snorted.

The head of crime statistics was unmoved. Maximin was one of the few officers in Control that refused to be intimidated by McGruder. His youthful, elegant features, framed with a blond mop of hair, regarded her with a hint of disdain.

'We don't make mistakes,' he asserted calmly, his grey eyes impassive. 'A crime-free zone seems to have been established on the border of Sectors 38 and 39. Nothing to do with our policing, needless to say. I've designated the area Zone Pacifica.'

'Crime-free zone,' she grunted, scratching her eagle's-beak of a nose. 'That'll be the day.'

An Eye-in-the-sky view of Zone Pacifica appeared on another screen.

'The crime rate, originally way above average, began to dip a month ago,' Maximin continued, unfazed. 'After two weeks it was half the Mega-City average. Over the last three days not a single crime has been reported. Zone Pacifica, as you can see, is roughly circular, blurring into low-level crime at its edge.'

The Chief Judge snapped her fingers. 'That's the same area where Dredd's phantom has been sighted.'

'You noticed,' Maximin said, lifting a languid eyebrow. 'And may I point out the time-scale? The first report of a

70

phantasmal Dredd coincides with the initial dip in crime levels.'

'Got to be a connection,' she mused.

'Indeed. The question is *what* connection. Hard to believe Dredd's ghost has scared all perps into law-abiding citizens. May I suggest you put Dredd on the case? Set the man whose ghost it is to hunt the ghost. And how about Hershey as his partner? They make a good team.'

'We make the decisions around here, Maximin,' she snapped. 'But you wish someone else was in our chair, don't you?'

'Of course,' he shrugged, cool as an ice floe. 'I've always said so. Dredd, Hershey . . . either would be infinitely preferable to you. That goes for a thousand others.'

She opened her mouth to vent a stream of invective, then clamped it shut. When she spoke, her tone was thoughtful. 'You've always been straight with us, Maximin. We'll give you that. Tell us – ' A pause. 'Do you think we're insane? Be frank. Speak your mind.'

'Insane? No. Mentally unbalanced. Prone to paranoia. Unsuitable for office, from day one. And downright uncouth, to boot. But not insane. However . . .' He let the silence hang in the air. 'Lately, your paranoia and incipient megalomania have worsened. I mean, turning against *Dredd*? That's tantamount to treason in my book. That man saved this city a dozen times while you were still in the Special Judicial Squad, torturing any *real* Judges that stood up to you.'

'That's your candid opinion?' she said, softly, dangerously.

'You wanted my opinion. You got it.'

She nodded. 'All right. Fair enough.'

'Incidentally,' he said. 'The recent downturn in your psychological state started about a month ago. Just like Zone Pacifica's crime rate. And the sightings of Dredd's phantom. Food for thought.'

McGruder shook her head and sighed. 'We don't – we don't know any more . . .'

Maximin pursed his lips, as if engaged in an internal debate. He came to a quick decision. 'If Anderson was around, you might find some answers.' He raised his hand to prevent her outburst. 'Yes, yes, I know. Anderson's a renegade and you wouldn't touch her with a ten-metre day-stick. But there are others in Psi Division, not so adept, but still – '

'What are you getting at?'

'If you extended your confidence to officers outside the SJS you might pick up on a little trouble, right here in Justice Central. The SJS are so busy suspecting everyone of everything that they never identify genuine dangers right under their noses. That's always been your chief drawback: you've never forgotten your SJS allegiance. If I were you, I'd contact an empath and precog from Psi.'

Her eyes narrowed. 'We thought your sideline was time vectors, not psi. You know something we don't? What have you got up your sleeve?'

'Nothing up my sleeve. It's in my head. Unlike most Judges, I'm educated. That's the trouble with Judges – they're *trained*, not educated. Worse, they can't tell the difference between the two. It'll be the death of them one day.'

'Don't make a meal of it, Maximin,' she warned. 'Okay, I'll contact Psi.'

'And don't rely on any of those yes-Judges from Psi. Get advice from one of the mavericks, someone that isn't afraid to hit you on the jaw with the truth.'

'*That's enough!*' she exploded. 'Get back to crime-stats, and don't waste any more Justice time on that time-vector hobby of yours!'

He signed off with a wave of the hand. '*Sayonara.*'

Eliphas turned to Mathers, his SJS subordinate.

'Always disliked that stuck-up Maximin. He's trouble. Step up surveillance on the motherdrokker.'

Mathers kept his attention on McGruder's office on the vid-screen. Eliphas had planted a vid-bug in the Chief Judge's sanctum, and the monitor in Room 101 of SJS underground headquarters was the sole receiver of the bug's transmissions. The SJS judged all Judges, including the Chief Judge. That was a necessity she'd have understood in the old days. Not now. They spied on McGruder in secret.

'Maximin needs taking out,' Mathers stated.

Eliphas shook his head. 'Too risky now he's blabbed to McGruder. Might rouse her suspicions. Not that I wouldn't like to get him on a pain-induction slab. Gruddam creep made out we're a bunch of imbeciles.'

'Yeah,' snarled Mathers. He glanced at his superior. 'What's an imbecile?'

'Shut up. I'm thinking.'

After a prolonged period of stroking his pointed beard, a hint of light dawned in Eliphas's eyes. 'Dredd's behind all this weird stuff. Got to be. Could be he's stirring up some kind of psychic brew, without knowing it. And the effects are driving McGruder over the edge. Bad news, Mathers.'

'Yeah, bad news . . . Why?'

'McGruder goes ga-ga, she gets replaced. And who's odds-on favourite to take her place?'

'Er – head of SJS?'

'*Hershey*, you – ' He controlled his exasperation. 'Hershey'll be Chief Judge. Can you imagine what she'd do to the Specials if she were in power? She hates us, Mathers. We might even be disbanded.'

'Jovus Drokk!' Mathers exclaimed, horrified at the prospect.

'We've got to keep McGruder in the Chief's seat,' Eliphas said firmly. 'With Hershey out the way, that'll be easier. It's time she was taken out for good.'

'But her and Dredd, they're real close. If she dies, he'll snoop and snoop until he traces the killing to us.'

'Obviously. So we waste both of them. These "ghost Dredd" sightings have given us the best chance in years to kill Dredd and get away with it. Whatever she said to Maximin, McGruder's afraid of Dredd. Now he's mixed up with spook stuff she won't be sorry to see him on a slab. With Hershey and Dredd out the picture, we're in the clear and back in charge.'

'Yeah. Back in charge.'

Eliphas stood up, adjusted his double-breasted jacket. 'Let's see if Corman's ready to talk.'

'You kidding, chief? Sure you are. He didn't know nothing. I killed him off with a magni-blast of pain induction. Boy, how he screamed!'

'He's dead.'

'Yeah – right.'

'You killed him.'

'Sure did, chief. Killed him *hard*.'

'We had a Judge who saw the phantom Dredd in Resyk – and you killed him.'

'Uh – yeah. You told me to kill all detainees. Kill 'em slow and *hard*. Hey, you got a real laugh out of that, chief!'

Eliphas grabbed Mathers by the throat. 'Don't take the stomm out of me, drokkhead.'

'Check – check the record,' Mathers croaked. 'Here – let me . . .' He reached for Interrogation vid-scan, pressed for replay, time 08-46.

One of four large vid-screens came to life.

Eliphas let go of the man's throat as he witnessed himself, in full tri-D, march into the Interrogation section and order all prisoners tortured to death, beginning with Corman.

'See, chief?' husked Mather, massaging his throat muscles.

In response, Eliphas pressed for Internal Records vid-scan, time 08-46. Eliphas appeared on another screen, running through files on a computer terminal.

74

Mathers gawped at one screen, then the other. 'That's you, chief, and – and *that's* you, ch-chief.'

'I was in Records for ninety minutes.'

'Then, how come you were in Interrogation at the same time?'

'That's not me, you – imbecile!'

'But I was there. I know you. Couldn't have been fooled by an imposter. Besides, the sensors would have spotted a phony. They recognised you.'

Eliphas's face drained of blood. 'Voice-recognition. Cornea-recognition. Even DNA matching. Are the sensors functioning properly?'

'Sure.'

'And this – double, he told you to kill Corman first?'

'Yeah. Like I told you.'

'A double. Remind you of anything? Oh, don't strain your brain. Dredd's ghost, get the idea? That's sure as hell what it reminds me of.'

'But you – he – wasn't no ghost.'

Eliphas glared at the scenes in the interrogation cells. 'And maybe Dredd's ghost isn't a ghost either.'

'Tchaikovsky's Piano Concerto,' Maximin requested, sprawling across his burgundy-upholstered hover-chair, a small, black signature-box in one hand, a Lawgiver in the other.

'Which concerto?' asked the curved, Wedgwood-blue walls of Maximin's private office.

'The first, you buffoon. What else?'

He released a deep sigh at the first crash of piano notes. 'Yeees . . . Flamboyance – that's the ticket.'

A fitting finale.

His grip tightened on the gun and the black signature-box.

The right lobe of his brain attuned itself to the concerto, drifted through Russian forests and wheatfields. The left lobe considered Hershey.

Hershey, marching up to McGruder's office, her Lawgiver drawn.

Hershey, blinking her eyes as if waking from a dream, studying the Chief Judge's door with puzzlement.

What am I doing? How did I get here? It was all written on her face.

The SJS, morons that they were, had no idea that he'd hacked into their surveillance system. He liked to keep an eye on things. Knowledge was survival. Hershey was lucky that the Specials hadn't observed her strange fit. Too busy torturing suspects, most likely.

Even before that incident, the phenomenon of Zone Pacifica had directed his attention to Robinson Street, epicentre of the crime-free zone. Alone, he had kept the street under intermittent observation. On the second night he'd witnessed the emergence of Judge Dread, and the grisly end of the lost young woman.

'Double trouble,' he'd said.

After that, Maximin kept an eye on all high-ranking Judges, studying their behaviour, alert to the tell-tale glazing of the eyes, however momentary, and the minutiae of body language, with a vocabulary all its own. Hershey's aberration had been the first of many, discounting McGruder's mad fits.

Five hours' viewing convinced him that some unknown force was influencing the minds of at least half the officers in Justice Central.

As for Psi Division, that was a revelation: the empaths and precogs walked with uneasy steps, looked with uncertain eyes. As the hours passed, an air of confusion reigned. Psi Judge Wu-li, an empath, had confided to Warner, a fellow empath, that she kept receiving messages – from *herself*. Warner admitted that he was undergoing the same experience. It soon became evident that the experience was widespread.

Should they tell the Chief Judge? Tell her what? That

they were talking to themselves? Best pool their minds and discover the nature of the mystery.

It was Anna Rotheram, a combined empath and precog, and one of the most rebellious of the young Judges, who had made Maximin really sit up and pay attention to the vid-screen.

She had clutched her temples, swayed, shouted out loud:

'The Mimics the Mimics the Mimics! No – no – these are *real*.' Her mouth gaped wide. 'THEY'RE COMING! THEY'RE *HERE*!'

'Yes,' whispered Maximin. 'I think they are.'

He glanced at the black signature-box, marked FOR DREDD ONLY.

The concerto reached its triumphant conclusion. A fitting finale.

THEY'RE COMING . . .

'But they're not coming for me,' he said, thrusting the Lawgiver's muzzle into his mouth.

A pull on the trigger made a red mush of his head.

The signature-box glided across the anti-grav chamber.

NINE

Something wicked this way comes . . .

Dredd, seated on the hard surface of the single chair in his conapt, pressed for replay of the Cafe Cesare confrontation.

The vid-screen replayed the incident, from Dredd's entrance to Rico's surrender. Just as it had happened.

He pressed again.

The scene was repeated – until the point where Dredd fired into Rico's heart through the badge on his chest. The young Joe Dredd picked up the holed badge, gripped it tight . . .

Another replay.

Joe Dredd arrested his brother. No bloodshed.

Replay.

Joe Dredd killed his brother.

He jabbed a button, and the screen went blank.

'Dredd killed Dredd,' he rumbled, leaning back, eyes hooded.

BOOOOM . . .

A thunderous knock shook the plasteel door on its reinforced hinges.

He sprang up, grabbing his Lawgiver.

BOOOOM . . .

Still dressed in sleep-vest and shorts, he padded across the floor, gun levelled.

BOOOOM . . .

The door trembled in its frame.

'Who's there?' he demanded. 'Declare yourself or take the consequences!'

BOOOOM . . .

The ultra-security door shuddered as though a giant were hammering it with a boulder-sized fist.

He pressed a stud to activate the doorspy-vid.

BOOOOM . . .

A small door-screen sprang to life.

A helmeted Judge was revealed on the screen. Nose, jaw, mouth – they were grimly familiar, even though the mouth bared its clenched teeth in a smile.

BOOOOM . . .

The image of Dredd stood outside his door, knocking for admittance with the force of a battering ram.

Dredd slammed back the security bolts.

BOOOOM . . .

Swung open the door and leaped out, Lawgiver trained on –

Nothing.

No one in sight on stair or corridor.

'Bye-bye, *Barbara*.'

Hershey struggled against the Hershey double's throttling grip as the motorbike sped along the bottom of a granite canyon of bizarre architecture.

She could take in only the barest impressions as the towering walls streaked by. Thousands of grotesque faces sculpted from the granite, interspersed with artificial caves carved as mouths.

Hershey wrenched her neck this way – that way. She couldn't budge the doppelganger's neckhold.

The double's strength was astounding. Hershey had met herself, and been outmatched.

Wheezing for breath, she threshed violently in an upsurge of rage.

This is my world. I belong here. You don't. DROKK OFF!

The granite world shimmered. Shuddered.

The neck-grip became a phantasmal caress.

A Justice Express tunnel flickered into view. And solidified.

She was riding halfway up one of its curved walls. Easing back on the throttle, she guided the bike back to the floor. Darted a look over her shoulder.

No passenger.

Hershey's double had vanished.

Illusion? It damn well hadn't felt like an illusion. The sensation of strangulation was still with her, good and strong.

She touched her throat. It was swollen and throbbing.

Some illusion.

The bike console was flashing its green panel for access to Dredd.

'Connect – ' She gasped at the ring of fire round her neck. 'Connect – Hershey to – Dredd.'

The panel changed from green to strobing red. The call was through. She slowed the Lawmaster to a halt.

Waiting for the Judge to respond, she gulped precious swigs of air. The sense of asphyxiation receded. Thank Grud.

Dredd's rugged features came on screen. 'Hershey, I was . . . What's wrong with your throat? It's black and blue.'

'Well,' she croaked, 'I had this – passenger – who tried to – strangle me. She – was me.'

Hershey didn't expect Dredd to grasp the situation so readily.

'You saw your double? Another Hershey? Did she appear out of nowhere?'

'Ah – yeah. She was me. But – stronger. You don't – think I'm – crazy?'

He shook his head. 'I just saw myself, outside the door. A doppelganger. It vanished.'

'You too? What's – going on?'

Dredd folded his scar-mazed arms. 'Remember the

80

Mimics, a few years back? We were attacked by our own images. You, Anderson, me – we all had our counterparts from what we thought was another dimension.'

'But Anderson – said – '

'I know, let me talk for a while. Save your breath. The Mimics looked like us, but there wasn't much going on in their heads. They were just one step up from reflections in a mirror. They didn't come from a real world. And they weren't alternative versions of ourselves. Let's face it, a quick gun battle, and we finished them off. Anderson called them – '

'Epiphenomenal geeks,' Hershey smiled. 'See – I said that in – one go.'

'But it's different this time,' he remarked dourly.

She rubbed her throat. 'Tell me about it. Listen – I called you – because of McGruder. She's gone – crazy. Remember what you – said in the Stews? About Caligula? You thought she was – going the same way.'

'And I said there was something worse coming. McGruder's always been a little screwy, but something's driving her over the edge now.'

'Something – or someone?'

'Someone.'

'Another McGruder? From another world?'

His features betrayed nothing. 'Could be.'

'I think I – tried to kill her. Or did – another Hershey – take control?'

'Could be.'

'Joe, you know something – and you're not telling.'

'I will, in front of McGruder. I've got your location. Wait there, and I'll be with you in twenty minutes. We'll walk into the Chief's office together.'

'Okay,' she nodded. 'We'll play it – your way.'

McGruder twitched and scratched.

Psi Judges always made her uncomfortable. Too clever by half.

81

And they looked deep into you. McGruder didn't like that.

'We didn't get where we are today by looking deep into ourselves,' she mumbled, eyeing Psi Judges Warner and Rotheram with distaste.

'Thank you,' Warner smiled.

'Take a seat,' McGruder invited a microsecond later, then bit her lip. Gruddam Psis, always knew what you were going to say before you said it. 'Wait till we speak before you answer, right? Grud – *Psis* . . . You're only here at Maximin's suggestion, and then *he* went and blew his brains out.'

Her eyes focused on a signature-box close to her hand: FOR DREDD ONLY. Then she returned her attention to her visitors.

Tall, rangy Warner, grey-haired at forty from the occupational hazard of psychic stress, sat with a good grace. Not so Rotheram, a supple, curvy blonde of twenty-two with a pair of cloudy blue eyes that some men would die for. She dropped into a chair and glared at the Chief Judge with more than a trace of contempt.

McGruder banged the desk and thrust her face at Rotheram.

'You think you're something special, young lady?'

'Yes.' The girl's tone was remarkably low and penetrating.

McGruder's voice rose in pitch. 'Oh yeah? Good enough to be Chief Judge, huh?'

'I wouldn't aim that low.'

McGruder jabbed a knobbled finger. '*Now listen, you* – '

'Now, now,' soothed Warner, raising placatory palms. 'We're here for a purpose. Let's not allow personal conflicts to muddy the issue.'

The Chief Judge seethed. 'All right, girlie – talk.'

'Certainly, old woman.' Disregarding McGruder's trembling fist, Rotheram eased back in the chair, closed her eyes. 'There's a world,' she said. 'Another Mega-City One. It's very close. Next door. Bad neighbours. I can't see them, but they can see us. The next-door neighbours want to move in. And you can't stop them. Compared to them, we're all gnats.'

'Oh yeah?' snarled McGruder. 'Well maybe you haven't learned this city's history, girlie. Anyone tries to move on to our patch, they get clobbered.'

'Why do you talk like a Neanderthal?' Rotheram asked, briefly opening her eyes.

'Because we're Chief Judge, and we talk how we like! Damn right!'

'Hmm,' Rotheram responded, lifting an eyebrow, then closed her eyes again. 'I can sense them. They are the brothers and sisters of the Law. They're coming, drawn by the Eagle. They're near.' She lapsed into silence, muscles limp.

'You sure they're not another bunch of Mimics?' McGruder asked, darting a glance at Warner.

'We're not sure of much, except that they can affect our minds but we can't touch theirs,' he replied. 'As for Mimics – no. These aren't epiphenomenal geeks, as Anderson would have put it. They're all too real.'

'Epiphenomenal geeks!' she growled. 'Anderson fancy-talk. What the hell's it mean, anyhow?'

'Well, in this case an epiphenomenon is a sensory by-product, a reflection of consciousness. If you imagine your image in a mirror – '

'We know what an epiphenomenon is!' she snapped. 'Of course we do. We're Chief Judge, Gruddammit! What we want to know is – ah, drokk it.'

The distinctive report of a Lawgiver sounded in the distance.

'Now what?' McGruder groaned.

Rotheram's eyes sprang open, revealing a distant blue. 'They're coming.'

Another shot rang out.

And another.

Rotheram's body was a-shudder from head to toe as she rose, swaying, from the chair. *'They're coming!'*

A volley of shots resounded from deep within Justice Central.

McGruder and Warner sprang to their feet as a muffled explosion shook the floor.

Rotheram's hands flew to her head, fingers digging into the temples:

'THEY'RE COMING!'

'What the drokk?' Dredd exclaimed as a bullet zinged past his helmet and ricocheted from the plasteen wall of the Grand Hall of Justice.

The Hall boiled with Judges, most with Lawgivers drawn, swinging the muzzles to and fro, wondering what the hell to do. It was hard to tell who was firing at another Judge out of sheer craziness and who was firing at a Judge because *that* Judge had gone crazy and –

'Hell on Firerock wheels,' Hershey groaned. 'It's a Gruddam shambles.'

A burst of hi-ex sent several bodies flying, ruptured intestines blossoming like red flowers.

Hershey opened her mouth to bellow an order. Dredd beat her to the bellow:

'Drop flat – all of you!' His booming tone travelled the entire length of the Hall, drowning out the gunfire.

'Hundreds of men and women dropped flat on the spot.

A score of Judges, widely scattered, remained upright, Lawgivers spraying lead in all directions.

'Shoot to immobilise all those standing!' Dredd bellowed, simultaneously downing two of the upright officers with bullets that left wounds just one artery away from fatality.

By the time he'd taken out a third, the rest of the rebellious crew had toppled, two of them with a bullet each from Hershey.

'Winstanley!' Dredd barked to a nearby Senior Judge. 'Take charge. Patch those renegades up fast. Then grill them.'

'Good job you weren't taken literally,' Hershey wryly observed, rising from her prone position. 'You stayed on your feet after telling them to shoot all those standing.'

He turned on his heel. 'Big joke.'

Hershey matched him, pace for pace, as they traversed the floor and entered a grav-chute to the top balcony.

'We're being followed,' she remarked as they sped upwards. 'Those two down there; they'll be into the chute the moment we're out of sight.'

He nodded. 'I know. They're Eliphas's men. Shouldn't have riled them up so much when you investigated the SJS.'

'You can talk,' she grunted.

The debacle below had emptied the upper corridors. Their footsteps echoed as they headed for the Chief Judge's office.

'Still not going to fill me in?' Hershey inquired, eyebrow raised.

'Not till we're in front of McGruder. We're gonna have this out in the open.'

'When your enemies work in the dark, that may not be too clever,' she murmured.

A door opened to one side. A young man stepped out that Hershey recognised as Judge Toby, fresh from the Cadets. He flashed an amiable smile at her, turned to walk past, then halted in his tracks. His eyes hardened.

Then a Lawgiver was in his hand.

Dredd and Hershey nose-dived as one, escaping the bullet by centimetres.

Judge Toby immediately clasped a hand over the horrified oval of his mouth. 'Oh Grud – I didn't recognise you. Oh Grud . . . I'm sorry, Chief Judge.'

'I'm not the Chief Judge, you stommhead!' Dredd bellowed, rising to one knee.

'Oh,' Toby said, 'that's all right then.' And fired another shot.

It went astray as he spun from the impact of a slug from Dredd's gun, fired a microsecond earlier than Toby's.

'Call Med,' Dredd said into his helmet-com. 'Judge Toby. Corridor E-79. Patch up and grill.'

'Everyone's going loco,' Hershey muttered.

'Only a few, so far.'

'There'll be more.'

'Yeah,' he nodded. 'And when soldiers in the same uniform start shooting at each other, you've got chaos on a grand scale.'

'Then we'd better get to McGruder before someone else bushwhacks us, huh?' She started down the passage with determined strides.

Dredd soon drew abreast, and they arrived at the Chief Judge's door side by side. He knocked and walked in without invitation.

'Warner,' Hershey nodded. 'Rotheram . . .' The young Psi Judge was sprawled on the floor, fingers gripping her head as she moaned softly.

Hershey glanced at McGruder. 'What's wrong with her?'

'Aw, she spouted something about someone coming. From some kind of alternative Mega-City One. If you ask us, she's got a screw loose.'

Hershey slanted a look at Dredd. 'Another Mega-City One. Maybe with our counterparts in it. It fits.'

'And a different Chief Judge.' Dredd added. 'Remember Judge Toby?'

'Yeah – he thought *you* were Chief Judge. Do you think you *are* Chief Judge in this alternative Mega-City?'

'Could be. Me, or someone who looks like me.'

McGruder's eyes contracted to slits. 'What're you two saying? We've got better things to do than listen to you when Justice Central's coming apart. And who asked you in here anyway?'

86

Hershey matched McGruder, glare for glare. 'Sooner have your SJS friends here? A couple of them should be down the corridor. Why not give a whistle?'

'We're here for a good reason, McGruder,' Dredd said, forestalling further escalation. 'And you'd better listen.'

'Still want us to resign?' she asked, lip curled.

'Not till this is over. Unless you've been seeing things. Like yourself.'

'What?'

'Have you seen your doppelganger?'

'A double, Dredd. Talk Mega-City. A double.'

'Well, have you?'

She shook her head. 'No. But it seems we've had – hallucinations. Thinking Dekker was alive. And Judge Cal, except we called him Caligula.'

'Uh-huh. And what about the city? Anything strange been reported from the border of Sectors 38 and 39?'

She frowned. 'How did you guess?'

Dredd angled his jutting chin. 'Better fill me in on the reports; then I'll give you my guesses.'

She threw up her hands. 'Okay. But your guesses had better be good.'

While Rotheram recovered from her trance, McGruder launched into a terse account of the phantom Dredd sightings, the Resyk disappearances, the tie-in with Dredd's sleep periods, Maximin's information and Rotheram's warnings.

Account concluded, she leaned back, tapped her fingers on an armrest. 'Now let's hear the guesses.'

'Not yet.' He flicked a finger at the signature-box. 'Who signed that to me – Maximin? Yeah? Then hand it over.'

'Guy who found the box tried to open it,' she said, sliding it across the desk towards him. 'Must have forgotten all he was taught about signature-boxes and DNA recognition. His interference triggered the defence mechanisms. It took an hour to scoop all the bits of him together. You gonna open it now?'

'In a moment. What about the Resyk disappearances? They turn up anywhere else as apports?'

'No record of it.'

Hershey stroked her lip. 'What d'you think, Joe? They disappeared into this other world?'

'Seems likely. But why Resyk?' He shrugged. 'I'll figure it out.' He turned back to McGruder. 'About the Muttering district – anything unusual, apart from the zero crime?'

She chuckled. 'Funny you should say that. An Eye spotted something real weird an hour ago. A huge heart, with a hat on.'

'Show me the exact location,' Dredd demanded.

'It's on the Zone Pacifica map,' she said grudgingly, punching up an aerial view on one of the screens. 'There, marked with a red dot.'

Only Hershey heard his whisper:

'Robinson Street.'

'Something wicked this way comes,' she said, meeting his visored stare.

He inclined his head a fraction, then faced McGruder. 'Don't you notice anything particular about the heart's location?'

'Dead centre of the Zone Pacifica,' she responded. 'Sure. What are we supposed to make of that?'

'Up to you, Chief Judge.'

She slammed a fist on the desk. 'You haven't told me a drokking thing yet!'

His mouth twisted a centimetre. 'All right. I'd say Rotheram was on the right lines. There's another Mega-City One, another world, and it's *close*. A next-door neighbour. And yeah, I'd say the next-door neighbours make us look pretty feeble. Maximin must have got some idea what they were like. The thought of it drove him to suicide – and Maximin was no coward. Should give you an idea what we're up against. They're moving in, and we can't stop them from this end.'

'Are you suggesting we hop into another dimension?' McGruder asked.

'Not so much a dimension. A time-line. One that diverged from ours thirty-seven years ago.'

Hershey caught on quick. 'Rico.'

The Chief Judge wore a dubious expression. 'I don't see how Rico's arrest created a parallel time-line.'

'Maximin's sideline was time-vector theory, right?' He placed a palm on the lid of the signature-box, allowing it to read his DNA. A soft click signalled that the defence mechanisms were disarmed.

Doubts suspended, the Chief Judge leaned forwards eagerly. 'Open the box, Joe.'

He flipped the lid, studied the contents, then slammed the box shut.

'I've got to go,' he said. 'I may be quite a while.'

He spun on his heel and marched to the door.

Hershey made to follow him. Rotheram's spaced-out voice stopped her in her tracks.

'Where he goes, only he can go.'

'What the drokk's that supposed to mean?' McGruder grimaced. 'Grud save us from the Voice of Fate!'

Hershey thumped her chest. 'Where Dredd goes, I go.'

'Rotheram's right,' Dredd said, his back to them as he strode out of the door. 'I'm going alone. Don't wait up for me.'

The door slammed shut.

'Thanks a lot, Joe,' Hershey scowled.

TEN

The door of the Cafe Cesare was still open.

The grey quiet of dusk rested on the deserted length of Robinson Street.

Dredd sat on his Lawmaster on the opposite side of the street, visored stare fixed on the decay of the facade, the congealed dark of the door.

He took out a small, black box, extracted an antique parchment, and read the lines written on the sheet in an elegant calligraphy that belonged to another age. Maximin always had been something of a cultural throwback.

From a dead man to a man who stubbornly refuses to die, salutations. I don't envy you. Where you must go, you must go alone. And no one must know where you've gone.

You've been much in my thoughts of late, Dredd. So many outlandish signs point to you. I could wax lyrical about post-Pfliger time-vector theory, composing an ode to the node and the nexus, but what would be the point? You'd only skip to the end. So here, my dour friend, is the end . . .

The epicentre of the Zone Pacifica, with its ghostly Dredd, is the Cafe Cesare, where you arrested your clone-twin. Yet, in your dreams, you kill him in that same cafe. Yes, you arrested Rico. And you simultaneously shot him through the badge. Confused? Try this on for size: at any given moment each of us can make a number of different decisions. The truth is (take it on trust) that we make all the decisions simultaneously. The Joe Dredd who is reading this decided to arrest Rico. But the Joe Dredd who pulled the trigger is somewhere else entirely, in another time-line. Time branched one way for you, a different way for your other self. Have you already guessed that? Whatever. The Dredd who killed Rico must have developed in a very different way from you. The time-line he occupies would have diverged radically from the one you inhabit. I have reason to believe your other self became Chief Judge. And I also have reason to believe he is the embodiment of evil. But remember, he is you. You. The you that did pull the trigger, long ago. And he must have corrupted the Mega-City One he lives in beyond all recognition. Let's call it hell. And now he's bringing hell to our world. You've got to stop him. The gateway is the point where the time-lines originally forked: the Cafe Cesare. You must go there and relive the past. With luck, you'll be drawn back in time. When your other self shoots Rico, you then shoot your other self. That will cut off the other time-line at source. Now – if you haven't understood a single word of the above, let's just leave it to your instincts: they were always your strong point. Just go into the Cafe Cesare and play it by ear, okay? You'll work something out. I hope.

Regards, Maximin

Dredd reread the letter, then torched it to a crisp. The box he kept; he had a use for it in mind.

He swung off the motorbike. Glared at the decrepit cafe.

'I'll play it by ear.'

Crossing the road, he eyed the massive, pumping heart a few strides from the open door. A heart with a hat on.

The hesitation was momentary. Four long paces took him to the pulsing organ. He kicked off the hat.

Sure enough, it was a human heart, but what power had bloated it to boulder size and kept it beating was anybody's guess.

And he hadn't the time to investigate. Higher priorities.

He planted a magnetic palm-sized disc inside his helmet. It was the latest in compact computers from Tek Division, fresh from the laboratories. The last word in UltraTek. It was known as CORA: Conversation Or Rigorous Assessment.

He didn't think he'd need it, but no point in taking chances.

'Good evening, sir,' CORA greeted.

'Stow it,' Dredd growled. 'I'll call you if I want you.'

'No need to take that tone, sir. It costs nothing to be polite.'

'Drokk,' he grunted. 'A computer encoded with an artificial personality. That's really made my evening.'

'Do you wish me to switch to hold mode, sir?'

'Just shut it!'

'Ah – "shut it". What your speech patterns lack in elegance they almost compensate for in a certain primitive cogency. Signing off for the nonce. *A bientôt.*'

Dredd expelled a sharp breath. Clenched his right fist.

Then he pulled out a microcorder from his green utility belt, lifted it to his mouth.

'Hershey, if you hear this, consider me dead. A while back I wondered if I'd have to take on Rico's ghost. I was wrong. The man I'm going after is – myself. My alter ego. He's the me that shot Rico back in '79. I'm the me that didn't. Yeah, I know, I sound like an UltraTek seminar. What it comes down to is that I've got to move back in time, back to '79, and kill the Joe Dredd that shot Rico. That'll stop the growth of this alternative Mega-City One that's drokking up everyone's minds. Maximin confirmed that I became Chief Judge in this parallel time-line. Seems I turned out pretty bad. It's up to me to set things right. If I don't make it, I know you'll put up a hell of a fight.

You've got my posthumous vote for Chief Judge, if you want it. See you on the streets, Hershey.'

Placing the microcorder in the signature-box, he activated the box's defences, then coded it to respond exclusively to Hershey's touch. Her name appeared on the lid when the process was completed.

Box in hand, he turned and walked to the door. The silence closed in, muffling his footfalls.

The dark within the door-frame had a density, a presence, that defied any intruder to breach its black membrane:

Enter if you *dare*.

Dredd strode straight through, his visor automatically switching to night-sight.

Despite the visor's night-sight, and his own enhanced vision, the interior was a dull grey monochrome, all details indistinct. Congregations of shadows leaned up close, crowding the air.

Hard to breathe.

Dredd drew his Lawgiver and traced a path through the dusty tables, festooned with cobwebs. Under one table he deposited the signature-box. Hershey would soon work out where he'd headed for. Smartest Judge on the force. She'd find it.

Eyes still roving the murky interior, he moved stealthily to the far end of the cafe. The shadows moved with him.

Thirty-seven years was a long time, but he could recall the exact spot where he'd stood, confronting Rico.

He halted five paces from the servo-hatch. *Here*. This was the space he'd occupied, back in 2079. His gaze moved to a spot one metre from a grimy wall. *There*. That was where Rico had knelt, over the corpse of Edward Gee.

Dredd assumed the position of long ago, legs widely planted, Lawgiver trained half a metre from the floor.

With luck, a lot of luck, he'd be swept back to 2079, shoot his other self the moment his alter ego fired at Rico.

Sever the alternative time-line at root, then hope to Grud he was propelled back to 2116.

It would require some leap of the imagination, mentally resurrecting the Cafe Cesare of nearly four decades past. But the cafe's haunted air evoked the phantoms of the past, all on its own.

A blink of light in the dark.

Yellow light.

The cafe burst into a flood of illumination.

Gleaming yellow tiles on walls and floor. Glossy purple tables.

And a semi-opaque Rico, crouched over the smudged outline of Edward Gee. Phantasmal blood spreading over the yellow floor.

Back to the beginning.

Rico's mouth moved. The voice was faint, like a cry from a distant place:

'I don't think you'll shoot me, Joe. We're identical. It'd be like killing yourself.'

'Try me,' Dredd heard himself reply.

Rico's voice was clearer now. Closer. 'I always came first in the firing-range, remember? First in speed. First in accuracy. You were always second. Always.' His pistol shifted a centimetre in Joe Dredd's direction. 'You wouldn't shoot me, *would you, Joe*?'

Dredd suddenly sensed a third man close by. Very close. Just this side of his own breath, occupying the same space as himself. The third man was as familiar as Dredd's face in a mirror.

Rico's gun moved another centimetre.

Dredd felt an itch in his trigger finger.

Shoot – *now*.

Rico's gun hand twitched.

SHOOT!

He held back from that final pull of the trigger.

Then his mind split in two.

He fired – and didn't fire.

94

Rico's name-badge was drilled – the name-badge was unmarked.

Dredd's senses tilted as he saw the cafe speed away from him in an impossible up-down-sideways bolt of speed.

A yellow smear of light, streaked with purple.

Then the impossible direction converted into a sideways race against the velocity of light. Dredd's being was accelerated to one side, his atoms trailing in a sparkling dance like a comet's tail.

Blackness gulped up the shimmering comet.

The dark lasted a nanosecond or a kalpa.

A rainbow shattered into splinters. Rained all the colours of the spectrum.

He fell with the rain, his essence a multi-coloured host of droplets.

The droplets rushed together, organised themselves into a combination of cells.

His body solidified as he continued to fall.

Colours swirled into semi-recognisable patterns as his fall slowed. He felt the weight of his body, felt the nerve endings screaming their protest at an experience above or beyond pain.

Black flooded his brain the moment he hit the ground. Hovering on the edge of consciousness, he gradually became aware of the rough surface under his prone body.

Grunting, he focused his blurred vision on his surroundings. They swam slowly into clarity.

Yellow tiles. Purple tables.

The Cafe Cesare. He was in the Cafe Cesare.

But this wasn't the cafe of 2079.

Nor was it the cafe of 2116.

At least, not the 2116 of his world.

Head spinning with vertigo, he rose groggily to his feet.

The yellow floor tiles were cracked and grimed with age. The walls had shed most of their tiles where the surfaces bulged inward. The tileless ceiling sagged in the middle, drooping midway to the floor.

He glanced at the door. Robinson Street was nowhere in sight. A tunnel of rock sloped steeply upwards from the buckled doorway.

His fist tightened. 'CORA?'

'Nice to hear from you again,' the microcomputer responded inside his helmet. 'What do you wish? Conversation or rigorous assessment? Or both?'

'Assessment. Where are we? No, *when* are we?'

'In May of 2116, sir. Surely your chronometer would have supplied the requisite information? Did you really need to pose such a simple question to an UltraTek miracle the likes of myself?'

'Chronometers are unreliable in time travel.'

'Oh, you haven't travelled in time, sir. Not at all. You've side-slipped into another time-line, a parallel Mega-City One.'

'Jovus Drokk! Is there any way back to 2079?'

'No sir, there never was. If you'd seen fit to seek my opinion before launching on this venture, I would have advised you against it.'

'Better watch your mouth,' Dredd snapped. 'How do I get back to my own time-line?'

'You can't, I'm afraid. You've undertaken a one-way journey, sir. You're stuck here for the duration.'

Dredd compressed his lips into a hard, tight line as he digested the news.

'Okay, I'm stuck here. Better look round.'

'I suggest you *turn* round, sir. My sensors detect a plaque that is not without some measure of interest.'

Dredd swivelled round, and confronted a man-high plaque in the shape of a Justice badge, mounted on the far wall. The corner of his mouth twitched at the inscription on the plaque:

DREAD

'Judge Dread,' he said. 'I've got a strong feeling that's me.'

'I lack the requisite data to arrive at an informed conclusion on the subject,' CORA remarked.

Dredd grimaced. The voice in his helmet irritated him like a fly buzzing in his ear. 'Then extend your sensor range and access some data on this world. Locate Judge Dread. Fill me in on this time-line.'

'My sensors are purely local. Besides, any contact with this world's data banks may well alert them to the presence of an intruder – to wit, yourself.'

'Then sign off!' Dredd snapped. 'I'll work this out on my own.'

'Whatever you say, sir. The best of luck. I suspect you'll need it.'

CORA fell silent.

Dredd took a firm grip on his Lawgiver, and headed for the door. He found himself in a rounded tunnel that snaked up through rock that resembled granite. He gave the smooth surface a hard push. The apparent granite gave a little under the pressure. More like tough rubbereen than stone.

He followed the winding, upward path for several minutes.

The night-sight function of his visor phased from high to low as he neared an arch of grey dusk.

If his own guesses – along with Maximin's calculations and McGruder's fugue rantings – were correct, what waited out there in the dusk was a world full of familiar strangers.

A world in which Cassandra Anderson led a rebel army. In which Dekker had never died. Where Judge Cal was alive and well.

And in which Judge Dread ruled as Chief Judge.

His very own self. The man he might have been.

The man Maximin believed was the embodiment of evil.

Approaching the end of the tunnel, Dredd slowed his

paces. He was entering Dread's domain, and he had to be ready for anything.

He listened for footsteps, voices, any sign of activity. Heard nothing.

Taking a deep breath, he sprang out into the fading light . . .

Slam into a bolt of lightning that whacked him to the ground.

He fought to rear upright, but his muscles had gone to sleep. Every drokking one of them. He couldn't twitch a finger.

Helmeted heads appeared over him, teeth bared in grins.

'Welcome to Dreadcity,' one of the grinning mouths said. 'That's D-R-E-*A*-D.'

'Come to visit the next-door neighbours, Judge D-R-E-*D*-D?' mocked another Judge. 'Chief Judge Dread's been expecting you. You should be honoured – it's not often you get to meet your better self.'

The Judges' attire was almost identical to that of the law officers of Mega-City One. The differences were manifested in the belts and boots. Instead of pouches, the green belts sprouted peculiar hooks and studs. And bulky guns, twice the size of the Lawgiver, jutted from the holsters of both boots.

As for what Dredd could see of Dreadcity, it bore scant resemblance to Mega-City One. He lay in what seemed to be the bottom of a man-made canyon. The towering architecture was uniformly dark grey, composed of the same synthetic granite as the tunnel from the Cafe Cesare.

The buildings were a bewildering hotch-potch of severe lines and baroque extravagance. A confusing meld of order and chaos.

The clumped towers reminded him of stalagmites. Huge, contorted stalagmites that pierced the dull grey canopy of cloud.

Dreadcity's overall effect was overwhelmingly *grim*. Grim – and deranged.

A sprinkling of frost, too light to mute the omnipresent granite grey, covered every surface.

The overhead vista was blocked out as a Judge bent over Dredd, his breath steaming in the icy air. 'Like what you see? The Chief Judge oversaw the rebuilding of the entire city. His concept. His creation.'

If Dredd's facial muscles hadn't been struck into immobility, he'd have registered some reaction to the name on the Judge's badge.

MAXIMIN

Yes, the same jaw-line. The same voice.

But there was an unfamiliar stamp of cruelty on the lips, a callous tone to the voice.

It was Maximin. But a Maximin that would have chilled his Mega-City counterpart to the bone.

'You know what you're in for when we take you to Chief Judge Dread?' Maximin whispered softly. 'A real *treat*.' The lips pulled back, exposing the teeth in a grin. 'Judge Dread will make you a part of him.'

Maximin's head bent closer. The bared teeth all but filled Dredd's field of vision. 'He'll have your brain served up on a plate. And then he'll eat it – every last morsel. What greater honour could you hope for? You should be glad.'

The toothy grin widened.

'Come on now, Dredd. *Smile*.'

Part Three

Dreadhead

He doth bestride the narrow world
Like a Colossus; and we petty men
Walk under his huge legs, and peep about
To find ourselves dishonourable graves.'

William Shakespeare
Julius Caesar: Act 1, Scene 2

ELEVEN

Emperor Caligula, Caesar of Nova Roma, swirled his diaphanous, scarlet cloak over a short, purple tunic as he strutted across the stage of the Palatine Palace, watched by an audience of millions under the hot blue skies that perennially covered the white, classical architecture of the Second Roman Empire.

'Friends, Romans, countrymen, lend me your ears,' he declaimed in a shrill voice, striking a melodramatic pose, finger thrust upwards. 'I come to bury Caesar, not to praise him.'

A long, dramatic pause.

Then, inexplicably, he stuck a finger up his nose and broke into a slow, archaic dance.

Caligula's short, slender figure – rejuvenated to a man in his mid-twenties – weaved to and fro, supple as a dancing maiden. As he trod the measure of the dance, his free hand stroked his spiky shock of auburn hair; at times his goofy teeth flashed a dreamy smile in concert with a flicker of the pale blue, bugging eyes.

The dance stopped as abruptly as it began. Finger was removed from nostril and pointed once more at the sky. 'In the pot, nine days old, and don't spare the warthogs,' he muttered under his breath. Then, in a high-pitched screech:

'The evil that men do lives after them;
The good is oft interred with their bones . . .'

The performance of *Julius Caesar* continued without further ado. He completed Mark Antony's speech to the plebs, then played a servant talking to Mark Antony, then Mark Antony talking to the servant, jumping madly from one side to the other as he changed roles.

Scene concluded, he charged off-stage. A split second later he charged on-stage again and performed the roles of Cinna the poet and four plebs, hip-hopping frenetically from place to place.

Caligula frequently performed the great plays solo, on the grounds that no one could come near his mastery of the Thespian's art. Earlier in the play, as Cassius and Brutus, he had plotted against himself as Caesar, then assassinated himself with a clutch of holo-knives as he virtually tied himself in a knot playing both Caesar and assassins.

But that bizarre accomplishment paled beside the *tour de force* at the conclusion of the final act: Caligula's enactment of the Battle of Philippi, in which he single-handedly embodied two armies locked in battle.

Whirling like a dervish as he leapt like a frog, he spun himself into a frenzy, spit flying, holo-swords slashing up-down-sideways.

Battle concluded, he lay winded for a full minute, flushed cheeks puffing furiously.

Breath finally regained, he staggered to his feet and managed to wheeze his way to Mark Antony's and Octavian's finishing speeches.

'So call the field to rest, and let's away to part the glories of this happy day,' he concluded, rounding off his performance with a bow and a flourish of the hand.

Panting, he looked up expectantly. The multitudes burst into uproarious applause.

Not quite uproarious enough for Caligula's liking. By the breasts of Artemis, had these unworthy mortals not witnessed the consummate performance of an incarnate god?

He scowled at the plebeian hosts of the Second Roman

Empire. 'I wish you had one neck so I could hack it off,' he snarled, departing the stage.

Inside the shaded interior of the Palatine Palace, his rage cooled as he skirted the atrium and entered the chamber of the Anti-Gravitorium pool. Naked nymphs disported themselves in the pool, splashing up holo-spray to the echo of laughter. The sight quenched the last embers of anger.

No, of course he didn't want the Roman populace to have one neck, let alone hack it off. That sort of wish belonged to his wild, carefree years of youth. He was a reformed character these days. Why, he hadn't even killed a slave – not for *hours*.

Doffing his garb, he splished and sploshed a while in the tactile illusion of water, pinching nymphs' bottoms. Then he jumped on to the pool-side, spread out his arms for the semi-sentient Imperial robes to descend and autoclad his nakedness.

'Drusilla!' he called out as a wreath of golden laurel leaves crowned his head. 'Agrippinilla! Lesbia!'

Three young women, dressed in flimsy gowns, rushed into the Anti-Gravitorium and bowed in unison.

Caligula smiled fondly at the women. They were so beautiful. And so they should be. They were female versions of himself, each cloned from his own divine body. Drusilla, Agrippinilla and Lesbia were his sister-clones. And his wives.

Let's face it, nobody else was good enough for him.

He was, after all, the reincarnation of Gaius Caesar Augustus Germanicus, affectionately known as Caligula – Little Boots. More than two thousand years ago – ah, he remembered it like yesterday – he'd ruled ancient Rome as Emperor and Supreme Pontiff in his original incarnation. At first he'd resisted the truth that he was a god: natural humility. But facts must be faced. Not only was he a god, he was the lord of gods. Zeus-Jupiter himself. Indeed, he was greater than Zeus-Jupiter; Caligula was *all* the gods. At least, he *could* be all the gods, if he felt like it. Just couldn't be bothered, that's all.

He held his arms wide. 'Beloved sisters, is the statue ready yet?'

Three eager nods. 'Yes, O God above Gods, Aphrodite awaits you in yon Temple of Love,' Drusilla announced.

'Oh great!' he beamed. 'Let's have a gander.'

He whistled for a hover-litter and reclined in its sumptuous embrace as it carried him through the labyrinthine interior of the Palatine Palace, twenty times the size of the ancient palace of the Caesars. For that matter, the Palatine Hill was twenty times larger than the hill he'd inherited, many years ago. The expansion of the hill had been his second decision as Nova Roman Emperor. The first had been to chuck out all the Italians, on the patently obvious grounds that those incompetents couldn't possibly be the descendants of the ancient Romans. Seven years later, his grand scheme was completed: Nova Roma was built on the ruins of Euro-City and Brit-Cit, the two linked by the kilometre-wide Janus bridge over the Channel. He'd overseen the entire building project, faithfully reproducing the Rome of twentieth-century Hollywood epics.

'All right,' he said, as the litter whispered to the gates of the Temple of Love. 'Nova Roma is thousands of times bigger than ancient Rome. But I'm a god, and gods have to think big.'

The litter came to rest in the Temple of Love, flanked with various towering images of Aphrodite, each morphed from flexiplast by psionic sculpting – a couple of hours work, tops. Ignoring the older statues – Aphrodite-Sharon Stone, Aphrodite-Rosanna Arquette, Aphrodite-Nastassja Kinski – he walked up to the new Aphrodite, his new love. *This* time it was the real thing.

Goggle-eyed, Caligula gazed up at the twenty-metre image.

'Helena Bonham-Carter,' he sighed.

106

Oh yes, there she stood, larger than life, straight out of the old 2-D movies.

He reached out his hand, activated the psionic implants in the fingers, and initiated the giant effigy's programmed speech centres.

Shyly, he fingered the collar of his robe. 'Hi, Helena. How – how do you feel about me?'

'Oh, *Caligula*,' she moaned soulfully. 'You're the *best*. I really *fancy* you.'

He tilted his head, smiled winsomely. 'You're – you're not just saying that?'

'Of *course* not. You're so – so tall – and handsome – and good – and noble – and sexy – and – '

'CALIGULA!' The booming tone dinned out Aphrodite-Helena's string of praises.

Caligula stamped his foot. 'Hecate's teeth! It's *him*. Damn damn damn damn damn. Big, crude bully. Well I'm chatting up Helena Bonham-Carter, so I'm not coming. So there.' A hand flew to his mouth. 'Er, you didn't hear that, did you, Ruler of the Seven Suns?'

'*CALIGULA* . . .'

Crestfallen, he climbed on to the litter, cast a longing backward look at Aphrodite-Helena. 'I'll be back soon, darling. I – I love you. Heaps.'

Sighing, he waved the litter forwards. 'Hall of Visitation.'

The litter wound its way through the palace and glided into a vast, dark hall, its spartan austerity out of keeping with the rest of the palace.

He alighted from the litter and knelt, facing the centre of the hall.

A shape of darkness welled up from the middle of the floor. It soared up into a figure fifty metres tall, the helmeted head almost reaching the ceiling.

Caligula prostrated himself before his lord and master. It was hard to believe this intimidating apparition was a

107

holo-transmission. The image radiated a terrifying presence.

'All hail, Judge Dread.'

'Still playing the little emperor, Little Boots?' The sneer was magnified to a rumble of thunder. 'Play your games, but don't take them too seriously. There's only one emperor of this world. Remember that – and you'll live.'

'Yes, Emperor of the Seven Suns. You're the supreme power. The Lord of Might. You're the tops.'

'Are you prepared for the invasion?'

Caligula knew better than to lie. Judge Dread was testing him. 'Oh, you don't need little old me to invade the next-door continuum. I'd only muck it up. Besides, my legions are rubbish compared to your armies. Trained by Italians, you know. Never got over it.'

'The state of the legions is your own handiwork, slug. After all, who ordered them to spend the last three years attacking the Channel?'

Forgetting himself, Caligula sprang to his feet. 'My troops must do battle with the sea god Neptune! He's never forgiven me for riding across the Black Atlantic on the bridge of boats, you know. Without my legions' heroic struggle, Neptune would flood his oceans over entire continents! Every day my soldiers beat him back. But he's strong – every day he returns . . .'

'A novel way of regarding the ebb and advance of the tides.' Judge Dread's withering contempt beat down on him. Caligula lowered his head.

'But I don't give a drokk about your ridiculous legions,' the booming voice declared. 'Your sole purpose in life is to amuse me. My jester, all the more amusing because you don't realise what a fool you are. I want my jester at court. Come to DreadCourt immediately.'

Caligula's voice was tiny. 'What for?'

'To witness the invasion, fool. And also – a little taster before the main course. My little brother is on the menu.'

'Rico? But he died years ago.'

108

'My double. My lesser self from the world next door. He's just been captured. You're invited to the torture-entertainment before I dine on his brain.'

'Well, I'm rather busy here,' Caligula prevaricated. 'Things to do, people to see. You know how it is . . .'

'Come now, slug, or you'll be added to the menu.'

Caligula forced a smile on his lips. He hated Dreadcity. He loathed DreadCourt.

'On my way, Chief Judge Dread.'

A knife and red rose between her teeth, grime on her sweating face and Undercity slime on her weathered, black battle-jacket, Cassandra Anderson wriggled out of the hole and dropped into the underground room.

Flicking her sweat-slicked yellow hair from her eyes, she glanced at the muck on her left sleeve. A quick brush of her hand dislodged the dirt, revealing a bleeding-heart badge sewn into the sleeve. The heart was pierced with a dagger and underlined with the motto LOVE HURTS.

A Judge nosedived out of the hole she'd emerged from, propelled by an ankle-booted foot. He thumped to the tiled floor, blood swilling his broken teeth.

The Judge's uniform was split open down the middle. So was the flesh underneath. The viscera bulged forth, free at last. He gave a final spasm, then subsided into death.

Anderson, a finely tuned empath, unfolded her empathy to the man in his death throes. Her sensitive psyche was flooded with his red pain, his raw terror. Shared his horror at the black pit of oblivion that sucked in his withering soul.

She was with him in spirit to the end; tasted the flavour of his suffering on her tongue.

Bowing her head, Anderson gave vent to a low sigh.

'Groovy,' she smiled.

She knelt down, groped under the corpse's ribcage, and ripped out the heart. Chucking the heart over her shoulder without a second thought, she plucked the red rose from her teeth and thrust it into the heart cavity.

'Regards from the Bleeding Hearts,' the young woman sneered, rising back to her feet.

She glanced at her comrades who slipped through the melt-hole in the crumpled wall. Giant, a dark-skinned renegade Judge who lived up to his nickname, landed at Anderson's side and stretched to his full two-metre-plus height as Corey, a young woman who served as Anderson's second-in-command, slithered down to the tile-strewn floor.

One by one, five other members of Anderson's rebel army emerged from the rounded gap in the wall.

Corey, dressed in the Bleeding Hearts' uniform of black, heart-badged battle-jacket and black trousers tucked into black ankle-boots, took three long strides to the corpse. Then kicked it hard. She swept her light brown hair from her pretty, fine-boned features and threw a quizzical look at Anderson. 'If we'd taken more time over him, we might have found out more about Dreadhead.'

Anderson shook her head, stirring her shoulder-length mop of hair. Her mesmerising eyes – their colour a grey that might be blue, a blue that might be grey – roved about the scattered yellow tiles of the ruinous cafe. Her face, hauntingly beautiful despite the coating of underground slime, radiated a powerful intelligence, assessing action and consequence, sifting a hundred possibilities. 'We haven't the time. We've got a captive to set free.'

'Why bother?' rumbled Giant's basso profundo tones. He planted meaty fists on his hips, muscles almost bursting the battle-jacket's seams. 'He's one of the Goons. Got to be.'

'Maybe yes. Maybe no.' Anderson lifted her hands, splayed the fingers. 'Let's find out.'

Giant and the three non-psychics moved well clear as Corey and two other comrades copied her actions.

The four Psis shut their eyes, held their breath.

A shape of blue light extruded from Anderson's finger-tips. It mingled with the radiance spilling from her companions' fingers.

The streams of light coalesced into a shining sphere.

And exploded in a blast of blue-white lightning.

Judge Maximin kicked Dredd on the jaw.

'You ain't smiling, Dredd.'

'No big surprise,' another remarked, booting the captive in the stomach. 'Takes muscle response to smile, don't it, *Dredd*?' He raised his gauntleted hand, spread the fingers. 'Psionic finger implants, enhanced by the gauntlets. Packs a real punch. Knocks the drokk out of the central nervous system. Face it, Mega-City man, your technology's a joke. We're light years ahead.'

'Fist coming,' someone announced, peering up at the frosty swirl of cloud enveloping the summits of the twisted stalagmite buildings. 'ETA one minute.'

Dredd kept up the mental fight. *Move* . . . Twitch a finger. Bat an eyelid. *Move* . . .

Zilch. Might as well be a hunk of meat on a butcher's floor.

The flood of warmth came without warning. Gushed from head to feet, restoring sensation and mobility.

So did the screams of the Judges.

Dredd launched himself to his feet, Lawgiver drawn.

He counted eighteen Judges, finger already squeezing the trigger as he counted.

The bullets had no effect. They ignited before impact.

'Force shield,' he muttered. The ultimate body armour.

But if his slugs weren't getting through, something else was. A force as invisible as the body-shields. It tore cries of anguish from its targets.

The Judges were wrenching off helmets as if the metal was red-hot. Once they were helmetless, the reason for their tormented wails was apparent. Each head was throbbing, expanding. Swelling up like a threatened toad.

111

In seconds, the men's heads resembled huge, purple boils with protruding tongue and eyes.

Some inner pressure shot the reddened eyes from the sockets in jets of steaming blood.

The sightless boil-heads bulged, and bulged.

And burst in a hot, crimson mess.

'Groovy,' said a voice at his back.

He whirled round, Lawgiver levelled.

And found he was aiming it at a familiar face.

'Anderson!'

Cassandra Anderson flicked her fingers, and a flicker of light stabbed into the gun.

The Lawgiver wilted in his hand. The barrel drooped. As he stared, it liquefied in his grasp and spilled on to the ground.

'Primitive weapon,' Anderson sniffed contemptuously.

Two black-clad figures behind her caught his attention. 'Giant!' he greeted. 'And – Corey. You're both dead in my world.' They reacted with a glare.

'And you'll be dead in this world if we don't get back to the Cafe Cesare – fast,' Anderson said, ducking into the round mouth of the tunnel. 'There's a Fist on the way down. So move.'

He glanced up at the snow-heavy clouds above the gloomy pinnacles. The cloudy canopy was churning at the centre, as if whipped to a frenzy. 'What's a Fist?' he demanded, watching the mounting agitation of the clouds.

'Stay and find out if you want to die,' Anderson snapped back as she disappeared into the tunnel's darkness.

He hesitated for a long moment, then followed Anderson's band into the murky passage.

'Where we going?' he demanded, thumping down the twisting incline. 'Cafe's enclosed in this granite-like stuff.'

'Graniteen,' he heard Anderson call back. 'And there's a way out now. You're about to discover what it's like to crawl down one of our melt-holes.'

'Where does it lead?'

'Do me a favour . . .' Her voice echoed back.

'What favour?'

'Shut your big, stupid mouth.'

'We're gonna have to *talk*, Anderson,' he growled.

'You're going to have to *listen*,' she replied.

A gauntleted hand curled round a bare throat, forcing a choked cry from the woman at the foot of the DreadThrone.

A menacing voice rumbled around the hall of vaulted pillars, clustered shadows:

'What – did – you – say?'

'The Conglomeration has reported that Joe Dredd has been rescued,' informed Judge Omar, head of Psi Division. He lay prostrate on the floor, eyes lowered.

The gauntleted hand let go of the woman's throat, tightened into a fist, slammed the armrest of the Dread-Throne. 'Rescued by whom? Anderson? Was it *Anderson*?'

'At a guess – yes, Lord.'

'*Find her.*'

'But the invasion preparation . . . Can we spare the extra psi-power? The Conglomeration is set to absorb Mega-City One within a couple of days. If it's distracted, there may be a delay.'

'*Find her.*'

'Yes, Lord.'

'And don't let the news of Joe Dredd's rescue spread, or I'll feed you into the Conglomeration.'

'Rely on my discretion, Lord.'

'And on no account must Caligula hear this news. My clown must not be allowed a secret laugh at my expense.'

'But you ordered him here. It'll be difficult to keep the truth from him once he arrives.'

'I'm aware of that. I'll deal with the situation. Leave.'

'Yes, Lord,' Judge Omar acknowledged, bowing as he backed away. 'You are the Law.'

'I am the Law.'

A helmeted head watched Omar's departure, then waved a beak-nosed, bearded woman from the shadow of an arch. McGruder, Judge Governor of EastDread, approached with swift but respectful steps.

'You are the Law, Chief Judge,' she greeted him.

'Well, McGruder,' he said, slanting his gaze from EastDread's governor to the skimpily clad woman at the throne's foot, wrists bound to ankles. 'It seems you were right to suspect this female of disloyalty. Being governor of SinoDread has gone to her head, perhaps.'

His hand encircled her throat once more, squeezed tight, forcing a pained gasp from the constricted larynx.

He smiled at her helplessness, her – dread.

'What shall we do with the SinoDread Governor, do you think, McGruder?'

McGruder gloated over her hated rival's plight. 'Strip her. Then let me kill the bitch *my* way.'

His smile broadened as he inhaled the scent of fear from his captive. 'Tell me, how would you like to die, Hershey?'

TWELVE

She was being strangled.

Hershey rubbed her throat but the illusion of strangulation persisted.

She lost track of the debate in the Grand Chamber of the temporarily reconvened Council of Five. Couldn't breathe. Couldn't speak.

Through hazy eyesight, she saw Chief Judge McGruder stare in her direction.

'What's wrong, Hershey?'

'I – ' As quick as it was stolen, her voice was restored. The strangling sensation rapidly receded. She flashed a feeble smile at the concerned faces of Shenker, Kelleher and Coker, divisional heads and members of the Council of Five. 'I'm all right.'

McGruder, sitting at the centre of the crescent table, studied Hershey for a brief space. Then she lifted her eyes to the golden holo-eagle that hovered under a crimson dome, and gave a peremptory wave of the hand to Kelleher, head of the Street Judges. 'Go on.'

'Well,' the youthful Kelleher commenced, 'I'm inclined to believe the trouble stems from an experiment that's gone haywire.'

'That's right,' Coker snorted. 'Go on. Blame it on Tek Division. We always get it in the neck.'

Kelleher swerved his glance towards the icy blue eyes of the bald-headed Shenker, head of Psi Division.

'I don't look *anything* like Donald Pleasence,' Shenker was muttering to himself.

'I was thinking of a Psi experiment that's got out of hand,' Kelleher said. 'Judges attacking Judges. And shooting citizens without any cause. Sounds like a mental attack, a form of psychic virus.'

'Yeah,' Coker weighed in. 'Psi Division's the worst hit. Your empaths and telepaths and precogs have been climbing the walls, Shenker. What's freaked them out? Some weird experiment in mind control that's gone off the rails?'

'I don't look *anything* like Donald Pleasence . . .'

McGruder banged the desk. 'Shenker! Come out of Xanadu and start talking.'

He looked up. 'What?'

'You been drokkin' around with any unauthorised experiments?'

He shook his head. 'No.'

'Then why's Psi Division turned into one big psycho ward?'

Shenker steepled his fingers. Gazed into an abstract distance. 'Only 23 per cent of operatives are affected. Of those, the vast majority are empaths. They're receiving signals from an unidentified source. And may I point out that the *whole* of Justice Central is comparably affected. Judges are shooting Judges at an increasing rate.'

'An average of twenty-two shootings an hour,' Coker nodded. 'Projections suggest the rate will be two hundred an hour this time tomorrow.'

Hershey expelled an exasperated breath. 'You're missing the point. Look at the *location*. Justice Central. The Sector Houses are largely unaffected. And the rest of Mega-City One is carrying on as normally as can be expected, considering the mayhem at the heart of the Justice force. And don't forget the Zone Pacifica. Still not a single crime reported from the Muttering district. We've got two anomalies: Justice Central and the Zone Pacifica. Reports show that every member of the Muttering's population is living in a state of ill-defined dread, too *terrified* to break the law. My opinion is that whatever's

116

cowed the Zone Pacifica is also driving Justice Central crazy. Besides, it's not just the shootings. A lot of Judges are starting to admit that they don't feel – real.'

McGruder raised a supercilious eyebrow. 'Don't feel *real*? What kind of wimp Judges have you been talking to?'

Hershey restrained her anger. 'Unreal. Drained of reality. Like something's sucking us dry.' Hershey looked to Shenker for support. 'You know what I'm talking about, don't you?'

Shenker's mouth gave the merest hint of a wince. 'Psis *always* feel unreal. But I must admit – '

'We're wandering from the point,' McGruder cut in. 'An unidentified source is drokking up Justice Central. And – yeah – okay, it may be tied in with the Zone Pacifica somehow.'

Kelleher stroked his lip. 'That may be so, but the source remains unidentified. A superbeing from another dimension, perhaps?'

'Not *another* one,' groaned Coker.

'Brain-scrambling rays from deep space?' suggested McGruder, looking round for reactions.

There were none.

'Maybe Judge Death's up to his tricks from inside his prison,' Coker said, keeping a straight face.

'You think so?' McGruder frowned.

'I don't believe this!' Hershey burst out, staring McGruder square in the face. 'You *know* what's going on! We're being psychically invaded by a parallel continuum, almost certainly one in which Dredd became Chief Judge. We're the targets of our doppelgangers. Dredd and I talked about it right in front of you. Have you forgotten Maximin and Rotheram? Jeez!'

McGruder's eyes acquired a flinty hardness. She rose up, pointed a finger at Hershey.

'Strip her!' she shrieked. 'Then let me kill the bitch *my* way!'

'Huh?' gasped Kelleher and Coker in unison. Even Shenker saw fit to raise an eyebrow.

Hershey's hand flew to her throat. The strangling sensation was back, but not so fiercely as the first time. Her Lawgiver was out of its boot holster in a blur of speed.

McGruder dived for cover an instant before slugs from Hershey's gun thwacked into the Chief Judge's vacated chair.

Then McGruder was up and firing, and *everyone* dived for cover to the sound of banshee alarms.

'SinoDread bitch!' McGruder spat, loosing another round as Hershey popped up her head.

'EastDread sex-freak!' Hershey snarled, missing McGruder by a centimetre as the Chief Judge dropped under the desk.

Both women stayed under cover for several seconds. Hershey felt the throat pressure ease . . .

She and McGruder holstered their guns and stood up. Then sat down, staring curiously at the crouching men.

Warily, the divisional heads resumed their seats.

The eagle-emblazoned door swung open and a troop of guards rushed in. They skidded to a halt, uncertain whether or where to point their Lawgivers. Behind the bemused guards came Eliphas and Mathers.

'What's going on?' Eliphas demanded.

McGruder shrugged, looked at the Council members.

'Search me,' said Hershey.

Coker's pensive gaze alternated between McGruder and Hershey, weighing pros and cons, profit and loss. 'Hershey went insane,' he concluded. 'Tried to assassinate the Chief Judge.'

Kelleher hesitated, then made up his mind. 'Hershey fired first. I'd say the Chief Judge fired back out of self-defence.'

McGruder glanced at the head of Psi. 'Shenker?'

He gave an almost imperceptible lift of the shoulders. 'Hershey fired first.'

Eliphas looked to the Chief Judge. 'Assassination attempt. SJS business. We judge the Judges.'

McGruder stared at Hershey for the best part of a minute. She didn't blink once. Finally, she gave the nod.

'Judge Hershey, surrender your weapons. You're under arrest. Eliphas, take her down to Interrogation. She's yours. Do whatever you see fit to make her talk.'

Expressionless, Hershey stood up, handed over her weapons. Mathers cuffed her wrists behind her back.

Eliphas walked up close. Breathed right in her face. 'Let's go.'

Kelleher and Coker averted their gaze as she was frogmarched out of the Grand Chamber.

McGruder tracked her exit with a steely stare.

Three sets of footsteps echoed in the dark passages of Level 7, the deepest of Interrogation's subterranean quarters.

Eliphas had ordered the guards to return to their duties after they'd passed Level 6. Eliphas and Mathers had Hershey all to themselves.

'I've been waiting for this a *long* time,' Eliphas grinned. 'You're gonna pay for treading on SJS toes. Snooping. Telling tales. You think McGruder wanted to pat you on the back for snooping into SJS affairs a year ago? Grud, you're dumb, Hershey. McGruder started out as one of us. Once SJS, always SJS.'

She stared ahead, down past the rows of ultra-security cell doors, her expression unreadable.

'McGruder didn't even question why a whole floor of suspects got wasted this morning,' Mathers tittered. 'Bought our cover story without blinking. McGruder knows the score. *We're* the Law.'

'And now you're all ours,' observed Eliphas, studying the curves of her figure. 'You won't die quickly, Hershey. Gonna take our time.'

She hardly caught the threat. It was getting hard to keep

hold on reality. Form and substance were slip-sliding away.

We're being drained. *Drained of essence by another world.*

Push the thought to the back of your head. Hold on.

She told herself the corridor was solid, the plastisteel doors all too real.

This is really happening.

Sure, so it was.

Just didn't *feel* like it. The hazy memory of the Council of Five, punctuated by a blank gap, concluding in the wailing alarms and the guards storming in – unreal.

Like a dream.

As if reality was an old coat that was wearing thin. Showing holes. Holes that let another, harder reality in.

Walking down the passage, Hershey felt . . . She fished about for the word . . .

Displaced.

Another world was muscling in.

They're coming . . .

She began to understand Rotheram's distress.

They're coming, right enough. And they're wearing our faces. They're welcome to them. We soon won't need them any more.

And when they come, we go.

Into the nearest nowhere.

Drokk, she swore, pushing her attention back to the dismal actuality of Interrogation's Level 7. Nearly lost it there. Got to hold on.

'Here we are,' announced Eliphas, halting in front of the double doors of Interrogation Chamber 7. 'You're about to become familiar with a pain-induction slab, and many other novelties of ours. Say goodbye to the world, Hershey.'

Now or never, she thought. Her wrists were cuffed at her back. But her legs were free. Free to kick.

Trouble was, Mathers had a Lawgiver trained on her

head. The chances were a thousand to one that she'd manage to kick the gun out of his hand before a bullet took her head off.

A remote chance, but better than none. Once she was inside the interrogation chamber, the chances were zero.

Planting her left leg firmly on the floor, she shifted her centre of balance fractionally to one side, tensed her right leg –

'Grud!' Eliphas exclaimed, gaping past her.

She looked down the corridor for the source of Eliphas's amazement. Her eyes widened.

Eliphas was standing twenty paces down the corridor, arm raised, fingers extended.

And Eliphas was also rooted to the spot beside her. The SJS official was in two places at the same time.

'H-He's back, Chief,' Mathers stuttered. 'See – the vid-screens didn't lie. It's *you*. I mean – '

Hershey's mind was in hyperdrive. Eliphas's double was equally hostile to his counterpart.

'I'm from your world!' Hershey shouted to the doppelganger. 'Get me out of this!'

At her cry, Mathers pressed the Lawgiver's muzzle to her forehead. Squeezed the trigger.

A flash of lightning . . .

That flash told Hershey she was dead. A Lawgiver slug had blasted her brain.

Then she wondered why she was still standing. She glanced down. Mathers lay senseless on the ground, a liquefying Lawgiver in his hand, puddling into a mercuric mess.

A blur of motion to one side. Eliphas had drawn his gun.

An instant later he was flung back by a blue-white bolt of forked lightning. He sailed several metres and landed with a satisfying thump, the Lawgiver rolling from his nerveless hand. Blank eyes fixed upwards, he didn't twitch a muscle.

The doppelganger Eliphas covered the ground with long, swift strides. His brow knitted. 'Governor Hershey? Who gave you permission to act as a probe?'

'The Chief Judge,' she replied, adopting what she hoped was a convincingly casual air. 'Who else?'

He glared hard into her eyes. 'And what's the Chief Judge's name?'

That was an answer she didn't have to guess at. 'Judge Dredd, of course.'

Governor . . . He called me Governor. Take a risk. . .

'Listen, Eliphas, I outrank you. Don't dare question me. Undo these cuffs.' She turned her back to him, held out the cuffed hands. 'That's an order!'

She blinked at the burst of light, then felt the plasteel cuffs literally *flowing* off her wrists.

Spinning round, she gave a curt nod. 'That's better. You can go now. I'm on a special reconnaissance of Level 7 for Chief Judge Dredd. You take the upper Interrogation levels. Go on, hurry!'

He was dubious, but equally, he didn't want to get on the wrong side of Governor Hershey. 'Can't understand why you didn't melt your own cuffs,' he murmered, moving slowly away. 'For that matter, why didn't you immobilise these feeble creatures yourself? Their technology is as pitiful as their intellects.'

Hershey had already noted that the doppelganger bore no weapon in his hand. When she'd first glimpsed him, he'd had his arm raised, fingers stretched. Was the gauntlet a weapon? Better be, or he'd see clean through her sham.

She lifted her hands, wiggled the fingers. 'Systems failure. Hardly ever happens. Just my luck they packed up on me now.'

He studied her fingers with renewed suspicion. 'Psionic failure? Almost unheard of.'

She squared up to him. 'In *our* world, yeah, but did it

occur to you that our psionics are less reliable in this continuum?'

'First I've heard of it.' He pondered a brief space. 'I'd better go back and check. Shouldn't take long.'

She folded her arms. 'Sure, go ahead. But make sure you check *properly*. You should have been informed of my mission in the first place. Someone's getting sloppy, Eliphas.'

'Real sloppy,' he agreed, still eyeing her with caution. 'Last I heard, the Chief Judge was down on you for misgovernment of SinoDread.'

'You shouldn't take any notice of rumours, Eliphas.'

'We'll see,' he responded, closing his eyes. He placed his hands together, fingertips joined. A look of intense concentration filled his face.

Then he departed in a bewildering up-down-sideways direction to the accompaniment of a fierce explosion of light.

'*Whooo* . . .' she breathed as the sparks stopped jiggling before her eyes. 'Close one.'

Hershey had no idea how soon the doppelganger Eliphas would return. She had no intention of hanging around to find out.

Eliphas hadn't moved a centimetre since he'd been hit by the strange lightning, but when she leaned over him she realized he was still alive.

Too bad.

She grabbed her Lawgiver from him, rose to make a run for it, then halted as an appealing thought struck.

If there was time, she could haul the SJS creep on to his own SJS pain-induction slab. Turn on the power. Listen to the screams.

No time. The doppelganger might be back in seconds. Eliphas would be spared the torments of the black slab. Shame.

Breaking into a run, she hurtled down the passage.

Thirty breaths later she skidded to a halt by the grav-chute. And almost made the mistake of stepping in.

Uh-uh – no way: her arrest would be in Records, and the chute sensors would recognise her as an escapee and act accordingly, probably with a faceful of stun gas.

She made for the stairs and took them three at a time.

No guards in sight on Level 6. First piece of luck.

Racing up the steps to Level 5, she emerged into an empty corridor. Second piece of luck.

Level 4. More luck.

Same for Level 3.

'Might make it,' she panted, pounding up the stairs to Level 2. There was a welcome silence up there. 'Might make it.'

The silence shattered.

Alarms rang hell's bells from every side. An urgent voice sounded from the audios:

'Judge Hershey has escaped SJS custody! Shoot on sight! Repeat – shoot on sight!'

Drokk! The Specials would shoot, sure enough. Shoot to kill. They hated her guts.

Well, it was kill or be killed. The odds were stacked against her, but that was nothing new.

She had to escape Justice Central. She was the only one in the Mega-City who had a clue about the cataclysm about to overwhelm it. Whatever it took, she had to get clear.

A leap took her on to Level 2, her Lawgiver spouting Hi-Ex to left and right. A series of thunderclaps from the explosive bullets. A momentary impression of arms, legs and heads going their own sweet, separate ways . . .

Then she was on the stairs up to Level 1.

Rushing up to meet a downrush of SJS guards.

Instinctively adopting a duck-and-weave ascent, her wits raced on fast-forward as she identified the optimum targets, the appropriate sequence of killing.

She took a hit in the shoulder-blade. And downed three Judges for that hit. A slug bit into her thigh.

She wasted four guards for that single slug.

Five men remaining. They ran upstairs for cover. The SJS weren't renowned for heroism. And they were up against a Street Judge. A *real* Judge.

Fast as they fled, Hershey outpaced them. If they were expecting a bullet in the back, they didn't get one. She needed them for cover.

She was right at their back when she emerged on Level 1, shielded by their bodies for a precious moment as she swerved on to the final flight of stairs.

Firing hi-ex over her shoulder, she barely noticed the thunderous explosions and agonised screams. Her gaze was fixed on the arch up ahead. The entrance to the Grand Hall.

A bullet slammed into her lower back. She bit her lip and carried on.

A last leap took her into the Grand Hall.

The alarms were ringing just as loudly up here, echoing from the vaulted roof. And the voice persisted in its command:

'SHOOT HERSHEY ON SIGHT!'

Her boots skidded on the smooth floor as she ran smack into a crescent of Street Judges. At least thirty of them.

They greeted her with a hail of bullets.

THIRTEEN

Caligula's Head flew silently over the polluted wastes of the Black Atlantic.

The marbleen head, wreathed in synthetic laurels, was two hundred metres in span, its configuration an idealised version of the Emperor of Nova Roma. Gone was the spiky shock of hair, replaced by a mass of curls that swept decoratively over the noble forehead. Absent was the goofiness of the long, protruding upper teeth. The gnashers of the *Head Imperial* were small and even.

The *Head Imperial*, Caligula's personal airship, powered by some sort of magneto-anti-gravitational-polarity-alternation-something-or-other that he didn't have a clue about and cared about even less, had been moulded into the emperor's image of himself. 'A perfect likeness!' he had acclaimed at the unveiling ceremony. 'It's absolutely *me*.'

Flying the cursed thing was another matter. Seated at the console behind the blue glasseen of the giant Head's right eye, Caligula swore by the private parts of a score of gods as he struggled with the controls. 'This is all too fiddly-faddly for a visionary genius like me,' he snorted.

Despite the blue skies of holo-day that the emperor had switched on to illuminate a radius of fifty kilometres, he might just as well be flying through the encircling dark of the night for all the control he managed to exercise. Gods! Flying this thing was blue murder.

Quintus Bulbus, chief Head pilot, seated in an assistant pilot's chair, leaned towards the miffed ruler. 'You're just

126

out of practice, Caesar. You haven't flown in – what – two years?'

'You trying to be funny?'

Beads of sweat popped on the pilot's brow. 'Why – no . . .'

'The Head's been impounded for two years by Judge Dread. Is that my fault? *Is it?*'

'Of – of course not, mighty Caesar . . .'

Drusilla, sensing a major imperial fit on the way, stroked her imperial husband's hair. 'But you *did* blow up that planet, darling.'

'Huh!' he grunted. '*He* blows up planets all the time. And for no reason at all. *I* had just cause.' The pale blue eyes almost bugged out of their sockets. Foam flecked his pouting lips. 'There I was, flying through space, minding my own business, not so much as harming an asteroid, and then suddenly there's this planet right in front of me. Slam in the middle of my flight path, with all of space to choose from! Of course, I realised instantly this was no coincidence. The planet had *deliberately* guided its orbital path to obstruct my right of way. Damn cheek! So I blew it up. Can't have stroppy planets thumbing their noses at me. Bad example.' His lower lip pushed forwards into a pronounced sulk. 'How was I supposed to know it was the home of the most advanced civilisation in the galaxy? Nobody told me. Not my fault.'

'They'd just discovered the secret of corporeal immortality, and were about to pass it on to us,' Quintus Bulbus muttered.

'I don't *care* about their gift of immortality!' Caligula shrieked. 'I'm a god and I've already got it! How dare you defy your emperor!'

'Oh, sire, I didn't mean – '

Caligula glanced down at the turgid black waves. 'Ah, *yes*. We're flying over Neptune's realm. The old fish god has been whispering treachery in your ear. You've sided with Neptune. Plotted with him. That sea god's always had it in for me.'

'But – '

Foam flew from Caligula's mouth. 'Side with Neptune – then to Neptune you go!'

'But – '

The emperor jabbed an EJECT button.

A coiled spring shot up and propelled the pilot's chair to the domed roof. He disappeared through an open-shut slide panel, leaving the vacated chair boinging up and down on the high-tensile spring.

Caligula watched a vid-screen that showed a tiny, wriggling figure arc down to splosh into the sea.

'Whoops! We shall now observe two seconds' silence for Quintus Bulbus.'

A console panel flashed an urgent signal. 'Oh, now what?' he groaned, pressing for call acceptance.

A head and shoulders appeared on the main screen. Caligula's manner sobered. 'Patchwork,' he said.

Patchwork nodded his head. The emperor considered the mysterious man well named. Rightly so. It was the emperor who'd given him the nickname. The features that looked out of the screen were, to put it mildly, a bit of a mess. Patchwork was a veritable patchwork of tissue: bits and bobs of flesh crudely slotted together into a skewwhiff jigsaw. The clothes he wore were also patchwork: a hundred different coloured rags sewn together without rhyme or reason. And the clownish clothes hid an equally patchwork body.

'You left without telling me,' Patchwork reproached in a harsh, grating voice, his mashed lips barely moving.

'Why do you let him talk to you so disrespectfully?' Lesbia frowned.

'Because he's come back from the dead. *Twice*,' Caligula hissed out the corner of his mouth. 'You don't fool around with a man like that.' He bent an apologetic smile

128

at Patchwork. 'I had to leave in a bit of a hurry. About five minutes ago, in fact. His Dreadness insisted.'

'I hear,' husked Patchwork, 'that the Chief Judge's double has just arrived from another continuum.'

'Yes. Captured the moment he arrived. His brain's on the menu for Dread's delectation. Part of the pre-invasion celebrations. Your humble emperor is obliged to witness the barbaric spectacle.'

Patchwork was silent a moment. Then he resumed in a still harsher tone: 'If you wish to be Emperor of the Seven Suns, you must do everything to save Judge Dread's double. *Everything*. If you need me, call.'

Transmission concluded, the screen went blank.

Caligula shot a barbed look at Drusilla. 'We'd best keep quiet about this, Mrs Caligula.' He turned to his other clone-sister wives. 'The same goes for all the Mrs Caligulas. Play your cards right, and you'll end up as wives of the Supreme Ruler.'

Agrippinilla's mouth angled into a crooked slant. 'If you're Supreme God, how come Dread's got you under his thumb?'

Caligula tilted his head. Pouted. 'He cheats.'

'How?'

'He's got magic socks.'

'Oh!' Drusilla exclaimed. 'He's starting to flip again!' She yelled out loud: 'Autopilot!' and heaved a sigh of relief when the autopilot kicked in.

Caligula's bulging eyes glazed. 'Yes, your Dreadness,' he growled. 'I know about you and your magic socks. Don't think I don't. A gift from Neptune, I'll be bound. Those terrible socks – spun of seaweed. Giving me – giving. . .'

He clutched his temples. 'Oh God!' he cried, features stretched in pain. 'Yes?' he answered, face momentarily clearing. Then the anguish returned. 'When he treads the ground in those magic socks, the earth rejects me. And his helmet – I'll wager Mercury gave him that, he always was a slippery sod of a god – his helmet . . . Gets in – my head . . .'

'He's getting one of his headaches!' Lesbia screamed. 'Ooo, we're in for it now!'

'My *heeeeead*!' he screeched, swaying to and fro in a crouched stance.

'Easy, god-husband. Kissie-kissie,' Drusilla soothed, simultaneously fighting off her own panic. 'The socks and helmet can't hurt you while Drusy and Aggy and Lesby are here. We'll keep the nasty socks and helmet away, won't we, girls?'

He straightened, glowered at her. 'Socks? Helmet? What are you talking about, you stupid woman? Neptune doesn't wear socks and a helmet.'

She threw up her arms. 'Oh, you can't win. Why bother?'

Cupping his forehead in both hands, eyes shut tight, he groaned soulfully. 'I've got horses pounding in my head. Sea horses. Ah, the *pain* . . .'

Suddenly, grim determination hardened the line of his mouth. Rage forced his eyes open. The abstracted gaze roved the vid-screens showing the tumbling Atlantic wastes.

'*There!*' He pointed. 'There he rises, crowned with seaweed, wielding his trident!'

Instinctively, the sister-clones looked. Nothing there, of course.

Caligula lurched for the weapons console. 'I'll teach you to stick sea horses in my head!' he yelled. Jabbing manically at a series of missile launch buttons, he screamed triumphantly: 'Take that! And that! And that!'

Sleek missiles streaked down and gave the Atlantic one hell of a time. A series of explosions rocked the *Head Imperial*.

The ocean rose to meet the sky.

'Ha ha ha ha ha ha ha . . .' exulted Caligula. 'That's it, go and hide! Scaredy-cat! Scaredy-cat!'

'CALIGULA,' a voiced boomed about the flight-deck.

'*Dread*,' the women chorused, instantly recognising the hard, implacable tones reverberating from the audio.

Arms folded, Caligula strutted up and down, several kilometres out of his head. 'Too late for apologies, Neptune. Sink in silence to your bed of shells.'

'CALIGULA, RETURN TO ROME . . . *NOW*.'

'Don't you tell me what to do, fishmonger! You've lost and I've won, so there!'

The order from Chief Judge Dread was not repeated.

The clone-sisters exchanged nervous glances.

'Do you think the Chief Judge heard?' Lesbia whispered.

Drusilla shook her head. 'He was transmitting, not receiving.'

'Hah!' exclaimed Caligula, fist lofted to the ocean. 'That shut you up. Now who's God around here?'

'You've got to tell him the voice was Dread's,' Agrippinilla urged Drusilla.

'In the mood he's in? You tell him.'

'Lesbia, you tell him,' pleaded Agrippinilla.

'Get lost. *You* tell him.'

'No. You tell him.'

'Oh, forget it,' sighed Drusilla. 'Lord Dread will probably kill him for disobedience, and that'll be that.'

'You think so?' the others chorused, horrified at the prospect.

Drusilla grimaced. 'And then we'll belong to Dread.'

A short dread-struck silence.

'Maybe Patchwork could help,' whispered Agrippinilla.

Caligula spun round. 'What are you lot whispering about?'

Drusilla smiled sweetly. 'Nothing, darling. Just – women's talk.'

FOURTEEN

Chief Judge Dread stretched out his hand, an engram ring the size of a wristband resting on the palm.

A larger version of the engram ring encircled Hershey's neck, tight to the flesh. She stood five paces from Dread's throne in the hall of DreadCourt, eyes glued to the ring in his hand.

'Are you familiar with asphyxion rings?' he asked in a voice as dark as the soaring spaces of DreadCourt. 'I have one in my hand. You have another around your neck. They expand and contract in concert. A small demonstration . . .'

He squeezed the asphyxion ring. It contracted a millimetre, still preserving its perfectly circular shape. Hershey's metallic collar dug into her neck, creasing the skin, suffusing it with blood. She winced, bit her lip.

'As your collar is twice the span of the ring in my grasp, the effect for you is doubled,' he smiled, baring his teeth. 'If I should press tighter, the collar would slice through your skin. And if I should compress the ring to a tiny, compact mass, the neck-collar would likewise contract – and cut off your head.'

He released the pressure. Hershey gulped in a strained breath as the collar relaxed its deadly grip.

'Point taken, Judge Governor Hershey?'

She nodded. 'Point taken, Chief Judge Dread, Lord of the Seven Suns.'

'Good girl. Good little girl.' He leaned back. 'I think you look better dressed – if that's the word – in those little

132

strips of leathereen.' His visored gaze descended to her calf-hugging black boots. 'I'd estimate that there's twenty times more leathereen in your boots than covering the rest of your body. Feeling cold?'

The question was superfluous. Goose-flesh was much in evidence over Hershey's skin. 'We can't all endure the cold as you can, Chief Judge,' she said, breath frosting the air.

'You'll learn, Hershey, you'll learn. Warmth makes us comfortable and sluggish. A cold body is a sharp mind.'

'Whatever you say, Lord Dread.'

'You'll be interested to know that I'm giving you a chance to live. If you live, you'll be reinstated as Sino-Dread Governor, and *this* time I'll expect you to stamp hard on the population. No more lapses into the merciful behaviour which McGruder quite rightly reported.'

She glanced up, her grey eyes an unsettled meld of doubt and hope. 'It's – not a trick?'

'No trick. I've decided on trial by combat. You against McGruder, with pain-induction body-pads. A gladiatorial contest, viewed by a select audience.'

Seeing the glad glint in her gaze, he quenched it with a few words. 'Of course, I've thought up a serious handicap for you. In a fair fight, you'd defeat McGruder in seconds. Can't have that. Your disadvantage will be severe. If you win, you'll be reinstated and McGruder will have to live with it, if she survives. If you lose, but still have breath in your lungs . . .' He allowed the pause to hang over her like the impending wrath of God. 'You'll become a permanent member of the Orchestra.'

Blood drained from her face. 'If I lose, I'd better die.'

Judge Dread loomed up from the throne, descended the steps. 'Speaking of the Orchestra,' he said, lifting a hand. 'Music! Animation!'

The high walls, whose buckled, protruding expanses gave the appearance of tortured metal, began to heave

133

and writhe in tempo with the symphony that burst from every crevice of the animated surfaces.

It was a symphony of lost souls. Otherwise known as the Orchestra.

The members of the Orchestra, picked randomly from Dreadcity's slave population, were entombed in the walls, their bodies enclosed in graniteen and riddled with oxygenation and preservation tubes. Filaments from the Conglomeration, an organic computer two kilometres beneath Dread's throne, threaded the brains of the 'musicians'. The filaments conducted ultraterror. And ultraterror modulated the precise level of pain and fear to every entombed slave, producing a particular pitch and tone of agony from each throat.

From bass groan to soprano scream, the Conglomeration conducted the five-thousand-strong Orchestra in a symphony of torment.

'Music to my ears,' Judge Dread smiled. 'The Third Anguish Symphony in Black Minor. One of my favourites.'

He stepped up to Hershey. And booted her hard in the stomach.

Air whooshing from her lungs, she crumpled.

'That's for taking it on yourself to leap the continua just to put a scare into your Mega-City double,' he said. 'Now what does a good girl say when she's been chastised by her master?'

'Th-thank you,' she gasped.

He kicked her on the jaw, snapping her head back. *'What do you say?'* he repeated.

'Thank – thank you, *sir.*'

'Better, but let's continue the lesson, shall we?' He stamped on her hand, cracking finger bones.

Face creased in pain, she forced a 'Thank you, sir' between gritted teeth.

He turned on his heel and strode back to the throne. 'Good girl. You're getting the idea. Now go back to your quarters and ready yourself for the combat. And crawl all the way.'

Hershey crawled.

'I am my own name,' Dread said.

Slouched on the throne, Judge Dread drank in the last, tortured strains of the Third Anguish Symphony as he thought ahead to the Grand Audience, here in DreadCourt.

Caligula, he'd learned, had ignored his order. The self-styled Roman Emperor was already nearing the Atlantic Wall in the *Head Imperial*. Well, Caligula would be taught not to do that again. After that, he'd be too terrified to spread gossip about Joe Dredd's rescue, Anderson's continuing defence.

Nothing must detract from Judge Dread's omnipotence. Anderson's seizure of Dredd from a squad of Judgement troops reflected on the Chief Judge's authority. He could trust his Elite of Five, the Hammerfist, to keep silence. But Caligula – he'd need the lesson drummed into him.

Enough. These were trivialities.

Within two days, he would control another continuum, thanks to the steaming, stinking mess known as the Conglomeration: the greatest miracle in the interplanetary dominion of Dread.

A voice murmured in his helmet. 'Eliphas here, Lord Dread. Speech request.'

'What is it?' Dread growled.

'Could you confirm that Hershey's been with you in DreadCourt for the last hour?'

'Yes. Why ask?'

'I met a Hershey in the other continuum. She claimed to be the Hershey of our world. I consulted Memory and it informed me that the ex-Governor was here. I just wanted confirmation because – '

'Now you've got it,' Judge Dread interjected. 'Don't bother me with trifles. If you're concerned that this alternative Hershey poses a threat, you're a fool. The Judges of the parallel world are feeble. We could drain their brains with a single glance.'

The multiple voice of the Conglomeration streamed into Dread's helmet and drowned out Eliphas's farewell response.

«Lord Dread,» it bubbled, like a hundred mouths awash with saliva. «The history of Joe Dredd's time-line has been partially reconstructed. Do you wish to hear?»

'Just the gist, for the moment.'

«Yes, sire. After Joe Dredd arrested Rico in 2079, there was no radical divergence in events until the civil wars of 2083 to '86. Joe Dredd acted purely as a Street Judge during the wars, eschewing any political ambitions. The civil war between the three Mega-Cities ended in stalemate and the declaration of each city's independence. Mega-City Three was renamed Texas City. Luna 1 moonbase was founded in 2088, but its government was divided between the three cities.»

'Did Dredd play any political part in any of these developments?' Judge Dread asked. 'Mutual independence of the three Mega-Cities after the civil wars, a shared moonbase: quite a contrast with our own history.'

«No strictly political input by Joe Dredd. From what I can gather, he saw his role simply as fighting crime. Bringing Law to the streets.»

'The man's a moron,' Dread sneered. 'Continue.'

«Next event of interest is in 2101. Judge Cal, Head of the SJS, murdered Chief Judge Goodman and assumed the role of Chief Judge. After a hundred days, Joe Dredd led a popular revolt against the new Chief Judge. Judge Cal was overthrown and killed, and Judge Griffin took his place. The position was offered to Joe Dredd, but he refused.»

'My alter ego is obviously afraid of the big issues. Compared to me, he's a small, small man. What happened to Rico?'

«He returned from Titan in 2099, and Joe Dredd was forced to kill him.»

'Twenty years late,' Judge Dread sniffed contemptuously. 'Continue history.'

«The Apocalypse War started in 2104, initiated by Supreme Judge Bulgarin of East-Meg One. He delivered a full nuclear strike on Mega-City One. East-Meg was finally defeated, but Mega-City One was devastated. Chief Judge Griffin died in the conflict, and was replaced by McGruder.»

'And Joe Dredd agreed to McGruder's appointment?'

«Yes, sire.»

'He really is a moron. Continue.'

«From the Apocalypse War on, the two continua diverge radically. Joe Dredd's world suffered an attack by one Judge Death during what was known as Necropolis. Some years later the necromancer Sabbat invaded the continuum. Under Sabbat's influence, half the world's population became zombies, and the Judges ordered a global nuclear strike. Their world is still suffering the consequences.»

'Sabbat!' the Chief Judge snorted. 'We drove that tedious clown out of our world in a matter of minutes. He wasn't even a joke. Grud, Joe Dredd's world is beneath contempt.'

«As for Judge Death,» the Conglomeration resumed, «there is evidence that he came to the borders of our continuum, but decided not to enter.»

'Very wise of him.'

«Of course, where Judge Death failed to enter, Judge Joe Dredd stepped right in,» the Conglomeration observed. «It seems he is unaware that you provided the clues for him to follow. My assessment is that he hasn't grasped that you wanted to destroy him in our own continuum before launching the invasion.»

Dread's fist clenched. 'He'll know by now. Anderson will have told him. It's apparent that Anderson breached our security. She knew when and where to intercept when he arrived.'

«Sire, are you quite sure Joe Dredd is worth the trouble? All indicators point to Anderson as a greater irritant to the power of Judgement.»

'I don't like the idea of another me in the same world, no matter how inferior,' Dread murmured. 'Easier to dispose of my inferior double here, in my domain, than in Joe Dredd's home world.'

«Permission to offer an opinion, Lord Dread?»

'Just one.'

«Joe Dredd is no threat to you, in any world. And Anderson has only survived because you wish to take her alive and make her one of your concubines. You could destroy both with a word, should you choose to give it. You have made yourself into the most powerful being in history. Why not swat Anderson and Dredd for the flies they are?»

Dread's fist thumped the throne's arm rest. 'I want Anderson alive and under my thumb. As for Joe Dredd – I'm intrigued to met this lesser version of myself. See for myself what I might have become if I'd taken the wrong turning. Now leave me. I sense Caligula's arrival.'

The symphony of tortured souls had concluded. The walls ceased their writhing. Chief Judge Dread waved his hand, and curtains of coagulated shadows parted.

It was time for the pre-invasion games to begin. First on the list was the combat between Hershey and McGruder. Next would come the chastisement of Caligula. After that, the entertainment would move into full swing as the audience enjoyed the latest novelties of ultraterror.

Ultraterror.

And dread.

He rested his helmeted head on the back of the black throne.

'I am my own name.'

FIFTEEN

Cassandra Anderson plucked the knife from her teeth. 'Any more lip from you, Joe Dredd, and I'll make grungemeat out of you.'

Scowling, he reared up, casting a long shadow in the underground chamber hollowed out of solid plascrete. 'That's enough of *your* lip, Anderson. The Anderson I knew back in the Mega-City could be pretty wayward at times, but she always showed me some respect. You're a rebel leader. I'm the Law. Don't you forget it. The *Law*.'

'Don't say the L-word around here without spitting,' she rejoined, grey-blue eyes flashing. 'The Law's what's wrong with this world.' She flicked a glance at the rapidly sealing melt-hold in the plascrete. 'Who freed you from the Judges? Who got you out of the Cafe Cesare through a melt-hole tunnel? The rebels, *Judge*. The rebels against the Law.'

Giant rose to his intimidating height, dwarfing even Dredd. 'Get this straight, man. You're nothing in this world. A primitive. And a *lawman* to boot. You ought to thank Anderson for what she's done for you. If it were left to the rest of us, you'd be dead meat.'

Dredd glared up at the familiar face with its unfamiliar hostility. 'We were friends for years, Giant. You were my Rookie once. Different continuum, but you can't be that different from the man I knew back in the Big Meg.'

'Big Meg,' mused Corey, leaning against a wall. 'There's a name from the past. Haven't heard it spoken in decades.'

Anderson was still glaring at Dredd. 'You're with us. Or with the Judges. That's the choice.'

He glared back. 'What about the straight Judges who care about justice? Let's get them together, go against the Chief Judge. Like I did against Judge Cal.'

A gale of grim laughter greeted his proposal. Anderson laughed the loudest. Her dour mirth subsiding, she stowed the knife in one of the pockets of her black combat gear.

'Judges who care about justice?' she mocked, eyebrow arched. 'There aren't any. The few who once did left the Justice force when you – your alter ego – took over. Judges uphold the Law. *We* fight for justice. Chief Judge Dread called us the Bleeding Hearts. We got to like the name.'

Dredd glanced around. 'You were all Judges?'

Anderson nodded. 'Most of us. I was the first to leave. One year of watching the gradual enslavement of citizens was plenty for me. I hid out in the Undercity. Corey joined me a couple of weeks later. A few years later there were hundreds of us. A small army of Bleeding Hearts.'

'Bleeding Hearts,' Joe Dredd growled, lip curled.

Anderson's hypnotic stare intensified. 'That's just the way *he* said it. Same tone, same sneer. Yeah, you're Judge Dread's double all right.'

'I say kill him,' Giant rumbled. 'Same mentality as the Judge goons. He's on their side.'

'Don't think so.' Anderson shook her head. 'I've looked into his mind. Learned a lot about his world into the bargain.'

Corey looked surprised. 'You did? I tried. Couldn't read him at all.'

'He has a remarkably low level of self-reflection, Corey. You were looking for subtleties of character, profound depths. There are none. I caught some doubts about the job he does, but he deals with them by wearing boots a size too small.'

140

'What?' Corey exclaimed. 'That's the dumbest thing I've ever heard.'

A smile played over Anderson's full lips. 'Yeah. I'm getting a name . . . Judge Morphy. He advised you to wear tight boots to keep your mind from reflecting on the rights and wrongs of upholding a police state. If your boots pinch, you don't think too much. That's the idea, isn't it? Don't think about right and wrong. Get on with the job. Haul in the perps.'

'A job that needs doing,' Dredd growled. 'Without the Judges, the city would drown in crime.'

Anderson expelled a sharp breath. 'If you'd bothered to use the brain Grud gave you, you'd have realised a lot of the crime feeds on hatred of the Judges. Besides, in a police state, the Judges *are* the criminals. They rob the people of their most precious right: freedom.'

'*Freedom*,' Dredd snapped. 'Freedom to kill, torture, maim . . .'

'Strictly the preserve of Judges, right?' Her smile was hard. 'Your system stinks, Joe Dredd.' Her expression softened slightly. 'But this world stinks ten times worse. Thanks to you – the other you.'

He stuck out his jaw. 'I don't give a drokk about your world. I came to stop it invading ours, that's my only interest.'

'Then you'll have to take on Chief Judge Dread and the entire Judgement force. They're the ones about to swamp your continuum. If you want to save your Mega-City, you'll have to take on the Law, *Judge* Dredd.'

He folded his brawny arms. 'I'll string along with you for a while. See how it turns out.'

Giant waved a chunky hand in the air. 'Not good enough.'

'It'll do,' Anderson countered. 'He could be useful. The Chief Judge is afraid of him.'

'No way,' Giant glowered. 'The Chief Judge isn't even

afraid of *you*, Anderson. How come he's nervous of this creep?'

She kept her gaze fixed on the Mega-City Judge. 'Because Chief Judge Dread regards himself as a man set apart. The one and only. The thought of a doppelganger makes him uneasy. He's afraid of himself.'

'Okay,' Giant conceded. 'You're the boss. The creep goes with us.'

Dredd's scowl was fierce as a scimitar. 'I'm stringing along for my own reasons, *creep*. I've got a job to do. It's gonna be done.'

'The old routine about getting the job done,' Anderson remarked. 'His mind's fixed on one track. Tunnel vision. It's a weakness that might prove a strength against Judge Dread. Tunnel vision is an effective block to psi attack.'

'What are we going to call him?' asked Corey, flicking a finger at the Judge. 'Dredd and Dread sound the same. Downright confusing.'

Anderson was on her feet, checking that the melt-hole was fully sealed. 'Oh, we'd better call him Joe.'

His lip twisted. 'I might take that from you and a few other familiar faces,' he growled. 'But no other Gruddam rebel strangers are gonna call me Joe.'

'What about Big Mouth?' Giant suggested.

Anderson heaved a sigh. 'We'll make it Joe Dredd. Everyone satisfied?'

'No,' Dredd retorted.

'Tough.' She turned to the far corner of the chamber from the sealed melt-hole. 'Okay, *Joe* Dredd, we're going to get out of here.' She raised her hand, pointed a finger at a blank expanse of plascrete. Her companions imitated her actions.

Several streaks of zigzag lightning shot from the pointing fingers and conjoined on the plascrete face, searing into its hard substance. In seconds, a metre-wide hole was burned out of the plascrete. It bored swiftly into the synthetic stone for several metres, then revealed the blackness of an open space beyond.

The blue-white lightning sped back into the fingers. Anderson threw a glance at Dredd. 'Our tunnels and chambers have plugs that we can unseal and seal by psionics. Once in the next tunnel, it's an unimpeded path to the Undercity. That's where we'll muster the rebel forces.'

Dredd followed the others towards the melt-hole. 'How long to muster the forces?'

'A few hours,' Anderson answered. 'We haven't much time. Judge Dread's about to invade your continuum in a day or so. From our point of view, a welcome diversion. While he's concentrating on your home world, his attention will be diverted from us. It's the one chance we'll ever have to attack Dreadhead and destroy the Conglomeration. Wiping out the Conglomeration will serve both our purposes.'

'Dreadhead and the Conglomeration?' he echoed, ducking into the melt-hole. 'What are they?'

She glanced back with a half-smile. 'You'll know Dreadhead when you see it. As for the Conglomeration, you'll smell it before you see it, and it's not a pretty sight.'

'Anderson!' he called out to her rounded rear as she wriggled along the tunnel. 'You've got to fill me in on this continuum's history. I need to get a line on this world.'

'Ask that gizmo in your helmet,' she said. 'I've fed it info on a sub-psionic mode.'

'How the drokk did you – ' He clammed his lips shut. Then, the corner of his mouth twitching, he growled, 'CORA.'

'Ah – greetings, sir,' welcomed the microcomputer. 'I'd like to say that it's pleasant to hear your growl again, but it isn't, so I won't. Would you care to learn your present location?'

'That'll do for a start.'

'Well, we're crawling through one of thousands of

143

tunnels that honeycomb the plascrete lid that covers old New York, the Undercity of our own continuum. You'll find that this Undercity is virtually identical to the one beneath Mega-City One. Home from home, sir. Anyway, these tunnels are unknown to Chief Judge Dread. He has always assumed the rebel headquarters to be located in the streets of the Undercity. Apparently he has refrained from destroying the Undercity because he wishes to capture Anderson alive. Taken a bit of a shine to the lady, if I may make so bold. Have you ever had any inclination – '

'Get on with Dreadcity's history, creep!'

'"Creep" – hmm . . . Must do something about that vocabulary, sir. Some people might assume you possessed a limited intellect.'

'*Get on with it!*'

'No need to shout. Potted history about to be delivered. It's quite a history, sir, in which you're the central protagonist. Oh yes, I have quite a tale to tell . . .'

The ennobled features of Caligula glimmered in the moon-lit clouds as the marbleen *Head Imperial* descended through the ice-crystal-seeded vapour that canopied Dreadcity in a perpetual shroud.

Caligula peered through the Head's blue glasseen eye, and called out in a ringing tone:

'Dreadhead dead ahead.'

'Oh, shades of Hades,' groaned Drusilla as she and her clone-sisters clustered round to view the daunting sight.

Judge Dread's head, resting on the summit of Judgement Central, loomed into the clouds, three kilometres high from the neck-base to the crown of the helmet. An exact likeness of Judge Dread's helmeted head, it was the largest airship/spaceship in the five continents. It dwarfed Caligula's *Head Imperial* as the Earth dwarfed the moon.

It was Dreadhead, the biosteel head of a Titan, and it glowered down on the City of Dread.

'The biggest head in the world,' murmured Caligula. Then covered his mouth with his hand. 'Oops. Hope he didn't hear that.'

'Just try not to bang the *Head Imperial* on Dreadhead's nose,' Lesbia said urgently, indicating the airship's erratic course.

Caligula fiddled about with the controls. 'I know what I'm doing.' After several lurches, he directed his craft towards the gaping oval of Dreadhead's mouth.

He breathed a sigh of relief as his Head flew into Judge Dread's mouth.

'Home and dry,' announced the Nova Roman emperor, releasing the controls as Dreadhead's systems auto-guided his ship through a dark conduit leading up to DreadCourt in the dome of the helmeted head.

Swiftly though the ship flew, several minutes passed before the exterior darkness lifted and the *Head Imperial* sank to rest.

'DreadCourt,' Caligula muttered. He turned to his wives and did a twirl. 'How do I look?'

Above the waist, he resembled a Roman soldier with imperial pretensions: a golden plasteen breastplate glittered over a simple white tunic, bordered in red. Below the waist, he was decidedly un-Roman: tight black leathereen trousers were tucked into tight crimson leathereen boots.

'You look like Apollo on a good day, my adored Little Boots,' acclaimed Drusilla, nudging her sisters into agreement.

'Right, let's go,' he beamed. He shouted an order to the Head's computer. 'Open mouth!'

A low whirr sounded as the Head airship opened its mouth.

'Come, sisters,' he summoned. 'The Lord of the Seven Suns awaits.'

Caligula leading, they progressed down to the ship's open mouth and on to the ribbed floor of DreadCourt.

Way in the distance, the throne area was dimly visible through curtains of shifting shadows.

'I'm not scared,' Caligula whispered to his wives. 'I always tremble like mad in Dreadcity. It's so accursedly *cold* here. I'm not scared. Honest.'

Drusilla gave an anxious glance. 'You're – you're not getting another of your headaches, are you, dear?'

'Never felt fitter.' He stumbled. 'Hecate's teeth! I wish his Dreadness wasn't so keen on these bumpy floors. Look like giant's bones stuck together. What's wrong with smooth floors, I ask you!'

'Shhh,' the three sisters silenced as one.

'Don't you "shhhh" me,' he pouted.

'Lord Dread,' Agrippinilla warned, eyes darting to the distant smudge of the DreadThrone.

'Oh – right.'

They progressed in silence over the ridges of the floor.

Minutes later, they reached the comparatively smooth Circle of Dread around the throne-mount.

The sisters prostrated themselves. 'All hail, Lord Dread.'

Caligula sank to his knees in front of the throne. 'You called, Judge Dread. I came.'

The black figure on the obsidian throne sat still and silent. The DreadThrone, mounted on a miniature hill, was a stylised replica of the man who sat on it.

The black throne was shaped in the image of a seated Judge Dread, in the manner of the effigies of Pharaoh Rameses II at Abu Simbel. The obsidian head looked down from a height of five metres. Stone fists rested on the thighs of tight-pressed stone legs.

Judge Dread sat in his own stony lap, elbow leaning on an obsidian fist that served as an armrest.

As the silence lengthened, Caligula peered apprehensively about the court. Some one hundred dignitaries were strung around the Circle of Dread, each in standard Judge regalia. The living shadows that haunted DreadCourt reared tall at their backs.

His gaze returned to the man on the throne.

Unbidden, words issued from Caligula's mouth:

'Weave a circle round him thrice,
And close your eyes with holy dread . . .'

Dread's lifted hand struck him dumb. 'How dare you enter my presence?'

'Uh! You summoned me . . .'

Judge Dread waved him away. 'And ordered you back. Take your sister-wives and retreat to the edge of the Circle. I'll deal with you later.'

Caligula, heart thumping, bustled his sisters to the Circle's edge.

Dread spread his arms. 'Music! Animation!'

The gloomy walls began to writhe, a flexing graniteen skin with five thousand opening pores. And the five thousand human instruments entombed in their folds screamed their symphonic agony through the mouth-wide pores.

'The Second Torture Symphony in Blood Major,' Dread rumbled, his voluminous voice encompassing the hideous music. 'Most excellent.'

Even Caligula winced at the torment of the Orchestra, resonant with ultraterror.

'McGruder – Hershey,' Judge Dread summoned.

McGruder, clad in her glistening black Judge Governor uniform, strode into the Circle. Small metallic pads glowed red on her feet, knees, elbows and fists.

Pain-induction pads, Caligula observed. And tuned up to red: maximum pain delivery.

Hershey shuffled behind McGruder, wearing black boots, a metal neckband, and very little else. Like McGruder, she was kitted up with pain-pads. But Hershey's pain-pads shone a weak yellow: low-level pain delivery. That more than evened the odds against the aged and less skilled McGruder.

'Healed up from those kicks of chastisement?' Dread asked Hershey.

She nodded. 'Pretty much. Fingers still haven't mended, though.' Her eyes lowered to the yellow glowing pain-pads. 'So this is the handicap you mentioned.'

Dread shook his head, lips peeled back in a savage smile. 'No, Hershey.' He opened his left hand, revealing an engram ring in his palm. 'I'll be squeezing this from time to time. I think you'll find your engram collar a serious handicap. In fact, the chances are high that you'll soon be dead or – ' He indicated the chorus of condemned souls in the animated walls. ' – you'll be the latest addition to the Orchestra.'

Hershey blanched, then curled her lip and glared at McGruder. 'I won't make this easy, you old crow.'

McGruder grinned, brandishing the bright red pain-pads. 'I'm gonna make it *slow* for you, Hershey. Real slow.'

The two women began to circle round each other, crouched low.

The Orchestra rose to a crescendo of torment.

'Begin combat!' Dread bellowed.

The women sprang like tigers.

SIXTEEN

The tunnel descended in a gradual spiral through the thick plascrete lid to the ruins of Old New York, better known as the Undercity.

Crawling down the gradual incline, Joe Dredd listened to the voice in his helmet, the voice that told him the history of Dreadcity, which was at the same time the history of the planet once called Earth, now renamed Dread in honour of its ruler.

'It started thirty-seven years ago,' hummed CORA in Joe Dredd's helmet. 'The Judge Dredd of this continuum shot Rico, and kept Rico's name-badge for several months. Then he inserted an A in place of the bullet hole. He took the badge as his own, and assumed the name DREAD. In the following years, Judge Dredd became progressively more brutal in his policing, adopting a shoot-first policy. Increasingly irritated by what he regarded as Chief Judge Goodman's "bleeding-heart liberalism", he fixed his sights on becoming Chief Judge and showing the bleeding hearts how the job should *really* be done. He read omnivorously, aspiring to an intellectual excellence that would outshine all his peers. *Very* different from you, Joe – may I call you Joe?'

'Make it "Sir", and keep talking, creep,' Dredd snarled.

'Succinctly put, if I may say so, sir. During the civil wars of the early '80s, Judge Dread was instrumental in subjugating Mega-City Three, against Goodman's better judgement. By 2099 Dread achieved the position of Deputy Chief Judge and initiated a war against Mega-City Two.

149

He was victorious, and MC2's total defeat made him a hero among the hawks and jingoists. Mega-City One was now in total control of the North American area. Two years later, he made his move . . .'

'Forget the dramatic pause,' Joe Dredd snapped. 'Keep spouting.'

'Yes, sir. In 2101 Dread prepared the way for Judge Cal to assassinate Judge Goodman and take his place as Chief Judge. Chief Judge Cal performed as Dread expected. Cal started to believe that he was a reincarnation of the Emperor Gaius Caligula, and acted accordingly. The ancient Roman emperor is said to have made his horse Incitatus a Consul – Judge Cal proclaimed a goldfish to be Deputy Chief Judge. He copied his role model in other respects, too numerous to mention. Eventually he announced himself as the reborn Emperor Caligula. The Judge Cal of our own continuum did not go that far, according to the records, although he must have secretly had thoughts in that direction. One might speculate that – '

'Keep to the point, CORA! I want Dreadcity's history, not Mega-City One's.'

'I hear and obey. Dread kept himself hidden through Chief Judge Caligula's hundred-day reign of terror; then, when Caligula ordered the extermination of the entire population, he emerged as a saviour at the head of an army of Judges and defeated Caligula with ease. On the tide of jubilation, Dread was instated as Chief Judge and invested with absolute power by popular acclaim. To crown his triumph, he arranged for a Caligula look-alike to be kicked off the top of the Statue of Judgement by an overgrown halfwit named Fergie. The look-alike, however, didn't share Caligula's high-pitched tones. He roared "Fascist bastard!" in a strong baritone at Dread as he toppled, realising he'd been duped. Dread then kicked the halfwit in the look-alike's wake, just in case his dull brain registered the markedly un-Caligulan pitch of the stand-

150

in's final cry. The genuine Judge Caligula was kept locked away from sight and sound of all but a few of Dread's most trusted guards. Time for you to interrupt in a gruff manner, sir.'

'What?'

'You keep interrupting in a gruff manner. You've refrained for several sentences now. I thought you might like to interrupt gruffly.'

'*I'll* decide when to interrupt! Get on with it!'

'Post-haste, sir. Ensconced as Chief Judge of three Mega-Cities, Dread reformed the Council of Five into the Hammerfist, whose work was to carry out Dread's orders without question, as well as overseeing a spy network to ensure all Judges were kept in line. Several hundred Judges went underground at this point, swelling Anderson's rebel band. In 2103, Mega-City One was renamed Dreadcity. The following year, Judge Dread organised Caligula's escape and engineered his flight to East-Meg One with a bagful of bogus information on Dreadcity's defences. Caligula, incidentally, was under the misapprehension that he'd escaped to the East of his own volition. He had no knowledge of Dread's hand in the affair. Through the work of Judge Dread's secret agents in the Eastern Bloc, Caligula appeared beside Supreme Judge Bulgarin in a global vid-transmission from East-Meg One. Caligula exhorted the populace of Dreadcity to rise in revolt against their tyrant, promising, "I shall return!". Needless to say, everyone turned to Chief Judge Dread at the prospect of Caligula's return, many demanding the nuclear annihilation of the Eastern Bloc. Dread unleashed a first strike, on the pretext that the East-Megs had fired first. To make the claim credible, he delivered limited nuclear strikes on Dreadcities 2 and 3, as well as blasting a few sectors of Dreadcity well away from Judgement Central, which was renamed from Justice Central years before. Caligula was spirited away and hidden once more.'

'Stop,' commanded Joe Dredd. 'There's some kind of log-jam ahead.'

All that was visible in front was a pair of ankle-boots. Their owner was evidently stuck. A muffled voice came down the narrow tunnel. 'Slope-chute up ahead. Always causes a delay. When I drop out of sight, wait a few seconds. Then get ready for a fast slide down to the old World Trade Center.'

'I was in that building seven months ago,' Dredd muttered. 'Twin Tower Two. Seems there's a lot of parallels between the continua.'

'Shall I continue, sir, or do you wish to indulge in muttered ramblings?' inquired CORA.

Dredd snarled. 'I was just gonna tell you to talk. So talk.'

'Hmm . . . Well, off we go. The Eastern Bloc cities were rebuilt under the names of EastDread One and Two, and placed under the governorship of McGruder. Other Mega-Cities quickly fell to Judge Dread, leaving only Oz, Euro-City and Brit-Cit. Oz resistance was so determined that Dread decided on total destruction, resulting in the entire continent becoming one, vast, radioactive wasteland, seething with mutagens. The devastated continent was renamed Woz.'

Dredd inched forwards into the tunnel's tight squeeze, watching the boots in front for the moment they vanished down the slide.

'Are you listening, sir?'

'Yeah. Get on with it, for Grud's sake.'

'Getting on with it, as ordered. After the example that made a Woz of Oz, Euro-City and Brit-Cit capitulated. At this point, Chief Judge Dread, his grip on power unbreakable, showed his contempt for all and sundry by producing Caligula and nominating him Judge Governor of the unified Euro-City and Brit-Cit, with full freedom to do what he would with his new domain. The reasons are open to debate, but the most likely explanation is that

Judge Dread gradually acquired a taste for dark humour, and regarded Caligula as a master exponent of the art. Once instated as Judge Governor, Caligula promptly proclaimed himself Jupiter, Zeus, Mercury, Venus and King of the Jews, and dubbed his domain Nova Roma. He later encountered a mysterious figure whom he called Patchwork. The extent of Patchwork's influence on Caligula is unknown. In all matters, however, the self-styled Nova Roman emperor defers to Dread. One suspects, however, that he dreams of supreme power. As for Chief Judge Dread, he gave Earth a new name – his own – and extended his sway over seven solar systems – the Lord of the Seven Suns – bringing his particular brand of Law to each. With a series of rejuvenations stretching to the crack of doom, he looks forward to becoming Emperor of the Universe. Recently, however, yet another option has presented itself: ruler of a range of space-time continua, the nearest of which is our own, accessed by the fistula created in the Cafe Cesare.'

'Run that last line past me again.'

'A fistula is an abnormal opening between one hollow organ and another. Imagine the two continua as branching veins. The fistula has occurred at the branching point of the veins. Your shift from one vein to the other is so singular that it must have been effected by Judge Dread. The anomaly of your continuum shift aside, all motion is from Dread's world to our own. No one else comes in after you. And Judge Dread's power is blocking your return. I trust that's sufficient working knowledge for you, sir.'

The boots ahead slid out of sight. Joe Dredd inched forwards.

'Tell me about Dreadcity's citizens. How many can be recruited in an uprising?'

'Virtually none out of a population of eight hundred million. There are no citizens, only slaves, known as the Nameless. Their subjugation is near absolute, being cowed into submission by psionic ultraterror waves transmitted by the Conglomeration.'

'Ultraterror? The Conglomeration?'

'Much too complicated to explicate for the nonce, sir. Another time, another place.'

Dredd bit back a retort as he launched forwards. The floor fell away and he hurtled headlong down the steepest of slopes.

'Keep talking, CORA,' he hissed. 'Tell me about the Tek level around here. Fill me in on psionics.'

'Fill you in on psionics? That would take months. Sorry, this world's far too advanced to explain to the likes of you. Too much even for Judge Coker to take in.'

Dredd sped down the slide-chute with increasing speed. 'Give me some idea, you drokking junk disc!'

'Hmmm . . . Well, the power of psi is the strongest force in the universe. Our own Psi Division back home has been kept under the thumb, and thus far failed to realise its potential. Has it ever occurred to you that a Psi operative should beat any Street Judge in so small an affair as a fist-fight? They always know when and where you intend to kick or punch even before you're aware of it. They should defeat you every time. But they hold back. In Dread's world, far from holding back, psi is unleashed in full flood, enhanced and modulated by bioplast psionic implants. Thought is transformed into directed energy. Energy is transformed into matter. And vice versa. That's the best I can do. Now don't pretend you can understand it, because you can't. By the way, you're about to plunge into the seventy-second floor of the World Trade Center, Twin Tower One. The ceiling presses against the Under-city's plascrete lid. The building used to be thirty stories taller before – '

'Shut it, CORA!'

'Shutting it, sir. Over and out. And don't forget to give Jerry a wizard prang.'

'Gruddam screwball computer,' Dredd muttered, glimpsing light at the end of the sloping tunnel.

He emerged from the chute and dropped several metres to a tumbling halt on a dusty floor. He was back on his feet in a single second and facing Anderson.

'I want a psionic implant!' he barked.

'And I want universal love and peace,' she riposted. 'Neither of us are going to get it.' She spun on her heel. 'Come on, Mega-City One man, let's head down the stairs. The Bleeding Hearts are gathering in the plaza.'

Fists clenched, he followed Anderson's curvy, athletic figure down the stairs.

Corey leaned close. 'You couldn't handle psionic implants, Joe Dredd,' she explained. 'Your psi potential's near zero. Besides, it takes months for them to grow into the fingers, and years before you can utilise them without blowing yourself to atoms.'

His mouth formed a resolute line. 'I can handle it.'

'You sound just like Chief Judge Dread,' Anderson retorted over her shoulder. 'Always on top of everything. Always knows best. Always in the right. Pain in the drokking butt.'

He took three bounds down the steps, drew level with the lemon-haired woman in black. 'Pity you can't meet your counterpart in my continuum,' he hissed, low and lethal. 'You could learn something from her. You could do with a few lessons, lady. As the real Anderson's not around to give them, I might oblige.'

She slanted a withering look. 'I *am* the real Anderson, drokkhead. So's the one in your time-line.' Her expression switched to thoughtful. 'What's she like, your Anderson? Know her well?'

His anger subsided. 'Known her since she was fresh out of the Academy. She took on Judge Death three times. Helluva Judge, Anderson.'

'She's still a Judge? Hell, I'm ashamed of my other self.'

155

'Her Judge days are over. She's had doubts for five years or more. Threw in her badge a year ago.'

Anderson looked askance. 'She was a Judge for – what – about seventeen years?'

'About that.'

'Took her long enough to wake up. I rammed my badge in Judge Dread's mouth before my nineteenth birthday.' She threw a glance at what was visible of Dredd's features. 'You look a lot rougher than the Chief Judge. Rejuve must be pretty basic in your world, huh? Doesn't cover a load of hard living. You've had a tougher time than Judge Dread. And you've lost your eyes – bionic replacements.'

'You got X-ray vision or something?' he snapped, turning his visored gaze on her.

She shrugged. 'No. But I can tell. I can see right into you. You can't hide your guilty secrets from me.'

He stiffened. 'That's what Judge Anderson said when we first met. I'll tell you what I told her: I *have* no guilty secrets.'

'Oh yeah – that's what you think. You have stuff you keep hidden. And a lot of it you damn well *ought* to feel guilty about.'

'Keep your mind out of my head,' he warned.

The warning passed right by her. 'I've seen all I want to see. Learned what I needed to know. I don't think you'll side with the Judge goons. You're chock-a-block with Mega-City Law. Dreadcity Judges don't fit your mental set. You'll come in useful.'

'I'm nobody's pawn, girl!'

'Get this straight, *Joe* – this *girl* has lived in the underworld for seventeen years. In rotting cellars. In sewers. Fed on garbage, when I could get it. Never slept in a bed. Fought tooth and nail every black hour of every stinking day. I earned the rebel leadership, twenty times over. I make the decisions. Accept it, or drokk off!'

He stuck out his jaw. 'When I decide, you'll be the first to hear about it.'

She tilted her head, cast a warning look. 'You're not indispensable, although you act it. Better make up your mind fast, Joe Dredd. Time's running out fast.'

'Oh yeah? Then you'd better try and keep up with me, Anderson.'

Dredd speeded his paces, taking the stairs four steps at a time. After thirty flights, Anderson was still at his side.

As a growing crowd noise from below rose to meet them, she flashed a glance at the grim Judge. Her lips widened in a thin smile.

'Pace not too fast for you, Joe?'

He grunted something.

'Cassandra! Cassandra!'

Eight hundred fists, human and mutant, shot upwards, as if defying the plascrete sky of the Undercity, dimly visible by the bonfires that lit up every street in the ruins of Manhattan.

'Cassandra! Cassandra!' The acclaim resonated from hundreds of throats, echoing from tilted skyscrapers as Cassandra Anderson emerged from Twin Tower One.

Then silence spread like a dose of bad news. Gathered in the plaza at the foot of the World Trade Center, Anderson's rebel army, from the two-hundred-strong hard core of black-uniformed Bleeding Hearts to a rag-tag assembly of malcontents, observed Dredd's appearance with fear and loathing.

'Judge Dread,' someone whispered. The whisper travelled the way bad news will. It expanded to a momentous rumble, reverberating down West Street and up the winding length of Broadway.

'JUDGE DREAD . . . JUDGE DREAD . . .'

Anderson jumped on to a makeshift stage, threw up her hands, closed her eyes. Features flickering in the streaming torchlight, her brow knitted in intense concentration . . .

Each member of the mustered host heard her voice in their head. A quiet, calming reassurance:

Be still. Be silent. This man is not Judge Dread. To look alike does not mean to think alike. He is Joe Dredd, come from another world. Joe Dredd is what Judge Dread most fears. And what Judge Dread fears is welcome in our ranks.

Her words of calm restored a measure of silence to the crowds. The silence gave way to a renewed roar.

'CASSANDRA! CASSANDRA!'

Telepathic effort expended, Anderson reeled, fought to regain her balance as she sucked in breaths of foetid Undercity air.

Corey sprang on to the stage, gripped her friend's arm. 'You shouldn't have transmitted to so many minds at a time.'

Anderson steadied herself. 'I'll survive. I always do.'

Drawing a deep, slow breath, Anderson straightened her back, planted her feet wide. Thrust a fist upwards . . .

'Do you want *war*?'

The response bounced back and forth from the crumbling skyscrapers of Old New York, buried in eternal night under a concrete sky:

'YES!'

'Do you want to dine on Judges' hearts?'

'YES!'

'Do you want to tear down *everything*, even if *nothing* is built in its place?'

'YES!'

She brandished her fist. 'Then it's *war*! Blood red WAR!'

'YES! YES! YES!'

Fist lowering, her shining eyes moved to the implacable figure of Joe Dredd. A ghost of humour tweaked her lips. 'Want to arrest them for riotous assembly?'

He replied in a bass monotone. 'If I wanted to, I would.'

She tilted an eyebrow. 'I'm beginning to wonder about your sanity.'

Corey, who had stood with head cocked, as though

straining to listen to a distant call, darted a glance at Anderson. 'Weller's started, Cassandra.'

Anderson nodded. 'Good. The war's begun in earnest.'

His eyes of brown more sad than warlike, Weller raised his lumpy hands, bristling with bio-psionic implants from wrist to fingertip. The fingers throbbed rhythmically.

'I've got rhythm,' he smiled wanly. 'How about you?'

The thickset, middle-aged man surveyed his squad of ten Bleeding Hearts. They were a suicide squad. They were ready. They were not all willing. But they were ready.

The bared hands of the squad throbbed with as many psionic implants as Weller, their mentor and leader.

'Joshua,' Weller announced. 'Let's go.'

A swarthy, dark-haired man nodded, and placed his hands on a wall of the tunnel. The rest took up their positions, palms pressed on the walls of one of the numerous tunnels riddling the thick plascrete lid on the Undercity.

The elite squad had prepared a long time for this night. Now the moment had come, tension crackled the air.

Even for these veterans, the narrow tunnel was claustrophobic after hours of waiting for Anderson's telepathic signal to commence.

It would be a long battle against claustrophobia in the ensuing hours as the band traversed tunnel after tunnel.

But they were devoted to Cassandra Anderson. They'd make it, for her sake. They had to.

Weller thrust his own palms on the smooth plascrete.

'We've got rhythm,' he murmured. 'Let's make music.'

SEVENTEEN

The animated walls of graniteen vibrated to the Second Torture Symphony in Blood Major in the ever-shifting shadows of DreadCourt.

Chief Judge Dread leaned forwards in his Pharaonic Judge Dread effigy throne as the circle of DreadCourt dignitaries raised a cheer at the declaration of combat.

Teeth bared in snarls, Hershey and McGruder flew at each other feet first.

Sole to sole, their boots met with a thump in mid-air. McGruder's bright red pain-pad flashed a scarlet signal of pain into Hershey's feet.

Hershey gasped as the two women tumbled to the floor, her feeble yellow pain-pad no match for McGruder's high-tuned agony transmitter.

Rolling away to gain seconds while the pain decreased, Hershey sprang upright, wincing a little at the remaining discomfort in her feet.

McGruder thrust forward her bearded jut of a chin. 'Gonna make you *crawl*, girlie. Gonna make you *beg*. Gonna make – '

Hershey leaped like a streak of light. Her boot banged McGruder on her beaky nose, crunching cartilage as it darted a yellow stab from the pain-pad. She had twisted in the air before McGruder could retaliate, and vaulted clear of the red pad on the older woman's gauntlet as it swiped at nothing.

'Nice one, Hershey!' Caligula acknowledged, clapping his appreciation.

A visored glare from Judge Dread silenced the Nova Roman emperor. You could never see his eyes, but you could *feel* his stare right to your marrow. Caligula lifted an apologetic hand. 'Sorry, Chief.'

Blood streaming from her broken nose, McGruder rushed Hershey, shrieking fit to burst. 'I'll rip you, girlie! Crack every drokking bone!'

Hershey somersaulted over the charging Judge and landed lightly on her feet.

Skidding to a halt, McGruder spun round. 'Hopping out of trouble, eh? Can't keep dodging, *Barbara*. Gotta come in close sometime. Get a dose of the shiny red pain-pads.'

Hershey kept her distance as her adversary advanced. The contest was heavily weighted in favour of McGruder, and both fighters knew it. Once within kicking or punching range, the younger Judge was at a severe disadvantage from the glowing red pads. If accurately delivered, the pads could administer a killing punch, the heart shocked into eternal silence by a bolt of ultrapain.

McGruder advanced, crouching low. Hershey backed away, her heel straying close to the edge of the Circle of Dread. One step over that boundary meant instant execution.

'Watch out, Hershey!' Caligula warned.

Heeding the warning, she darted to one side. But McGruder was already on her.

A punch to Hershey's bare stomach. A stab of red lightning. She gasped and staggered back.

Another punch. Red lightning.

Hershey stumbled backwards, arms flailing, mouth open in a scream that almost outdid the tormented din of the Orchestra. Her stomach muscles were visibly contorted, as animated as the living graniteen walls.

Teeth gritted, she managed to evade the following kicks and punches, recouping strength as the torture of the pain-pads subsided to the comparatively minor hurt of bruised muscles and tendons.

161

McGruder dashed at her opponent, fists lashing.

Hershey dropped like a stone before the first blow struck. The fists flew overhead, punching empty air.

A kick from Hershey caught McGruder slam in the midriff. A rapid sequence of double kicks was unleashed from the prone woman, targeted on McGruder's stomach.

Crumpling from the assault, the older Judge managed to let loose a kick at the figure on the ground.

Her booted foot landed on the floor, centimetres from the swiftly rolling, twisting Hershey.

Hershey was on her feet and behind McGruder with a speed that evoked muffled applause from the onlookers. And rammed her yellow-padded elbow into McGruder's back. Again and again and again, a blur of speed.

Howling, McGruder spun round.

Her gutsy adversary had anticipated the move and jumped out of harm's way.

Pained and enraged, McGruder threw a wild punch, missed, went off balance.

Hershey stormed in with a growl and slammed a double kick into McGruder's solar plexus. A fraction of a second later she delivered a thrust-kick whose recoil propelled her backwards while simultaneously sending her opponent flying.

Sliding to a stop, McGruder groaned and threshed, contorted with the damage to spine and stomach.

A burst of applause rose to mingle with the Torture Symphony in Blood Major.

Covering the intervening floor in two bounds, Hershey sprang at her distracted enemy, boot raised to land a decisive kick to the midriff.

At that instant, Judge Dread's right hand tightened on the engram ring.

Hershey's kick faltered, grazed McGruder's stomach. She tumbled across the floor, wrenching off her gauntlets and scrabbling helplessly at the contracting collar. Cheeks puffing, she wheezed as she fought for air.

The neck-ring dug deeper, disappearing into folds of flesh. She thrashed on the ground, a thin rattle issuing from her gaping mouth.

A ring of blood trickled down from the neck, as red as the face was blue.

McGruder crawled towards her adversary, a toothy grin spreading on her bony face. 'Curtains, girlie,' she cackled. 'Curtains for you, bitch.'

She leaned over the choking figure, reached down a gauntleted hand, its knuckle pad blazing red. Then she hesitated.

Pointed two fingers at Hershey's eyes.

'Never did like the way you looked at me,' McGruder chuckled. 'You won't be looking any more.'

The two fingers descended.

And Hershey wrenched her head back and caught the fingers in her mouth, teeth crushing to the bone.

McGruder yelped and jerked back. And left the gauntlet between Hershey's teeth.

Mouth working in breathless spasms, near-blinded by oxygen deprivation from the tightening collar, Hershey thrust her hand into McGruder's gauntlet.

Bellowing, McGruder leaped on to her with a furious roar.

Her face impacted with her own gauntlet in a punch from Hershey's fist.

McGruder's features were mashed by the blow as red lightning seared from the pain-pad on the gauntlet's knuckle.

Screeching, her hands covered the exquisite agony that was her face. Then she slumped back and thudded to the floor, out for the count.

The applause was uproarious. Even McGruder's supporters felt obliged to give a grudging hand.

Judge Dread's head inclined in a slow nod. He relinquished his grip on the engram ring. It expanded to its former size.

Hershey's collar released its stranglehold. Croaking hoarsely, her neck a mass of sticky red, she sucked in air in small, strained gulps.

Gradually a flush of pink suffused her features. The blue of asphyxiation receded from the cheeks.

She staggered to her feet, stumbled over to the dazed McGruder. Still swaying, she stood over her prone enemy.

Hershey lifted her booted foot over McGruder's throat. The older woman's eyes flickered open; regarded her adversary with growing horror.

Glancing up at the enthroned Dread, Hershey raised a quizzical eyebrow.

Judge Dread waved a dismissive hand.

'What you do now is up to you,' he declared.

She looked down and met McGruder's wild glare.

Then pressed the boot into McGruder's throat, transmitting cumulative waves of suffering from the yellow pain-pad.

McGruder's eyes bugged as her neck gurgled.

A smile curved Hershey's lips. She ground her heel harder into the pulsing throat and forced out grim words of farewell from her own pained larynx:

'Choke, you drokking bull-dyke.'

EIGHTEEN

A crescent of Judges fired at Hershey, their Lawgivers spitting flame. The Grand Hall of Justice resounded to the thunder of the continuous salvos.

Her heart changed to lead and sank. She'd blazed a path all the way up from the subterranean levels of the SJS to run into an arc of firepower from her own people. She was the target of dozens of Street Judges.

Street Judges were firing at her.

And missing.

Hundreds of slugs must have blasted from the barrels. And thunked harmlessly into the hall's plasteen walls.

Deliberate misses.

She suddenly grasped the situation. Even in normal times, Street Judges would be reluctant to kill Hershey on the say-so of the hated SJS. Now that Justice Central was going crazy, Street Judges would be inclined to ignore a highly dubious SJS order to shoot a high-ranking colleague on sight.

Judge Mellor, an old friend, darted a look at a nearby emergency chute and mouthed, '*Run!*'

The crescent of Judges was giving her *cover*. Blocking the view of any hostiles in the Grand Hall.

But that wouldn't hide her from the SJS guards charging up the stairs at her back.

She took the advice and ran, leaping feet first into the emergency chute.

She slid down a couple of metres to a horizontal tunnel where the chute's magnetic field swept her along at a dizzying speed. Emergency chutes were designed for rapid-response situations when a Judge needed to reach a Lawmaster in seconds. Just what she needed for a quick getaway.

After a couple of breaths she was deposited in a Lawmaster parking area. She was on one of the motorbikes and donning the helmet left on its seat before any of the attendants grasped what was happening. By the time they realised who she was, Hershey had gunned the bike into action and was hurtling up the exit ramp.

No shots followed. A thin smile brushed her lips. The attendants were Street Judges, and these were strange times.

She laughed aloud as she raced onto a slipway that swerved up to merge with a megway. In moments she was racing down the megway, accelerating to 550 kph, a full 150 kph faster than the average traffic speed.

From Level 7 of Interrogation to the open megway. Pretty good going.

The exhilaration soon faded. She was one woman on a motorbike in the most heavily policed city in history, scanned by numerous surveillance Eyes. Her body throbbed from bullet wounds to her back and legs. And she was under sentence of death.

There was no way she could outrun the long arm of Justice Central, with its fleets of hover-wagons and Gunbirds. And a Lawmaster-mounted Judge at every corner, a lot of whom would obey the shoot-on-sight order without question. Come to think of it, McGruder would have confirmed the order by now. They would *all* be gunning for her.

Gruddam it, how the drokk did you get the Helmets off your back? Now she knew how a hunted perp felt. Not too good.

Hard to lie low in Mega-City One, but she had to try.

A glance in the rear-view mirror. Three Judges, matching her pace on their Lawmasters, guns drawn and aimed in her direction. For the first time in her life, the Justice motorbikes looked ominous. Black, menacing monsters.

'No wonder the perps call them the Beasts of the Streets,' she muttered. Spying a slipway, she swerved the bike into it, shaving a Wolfhound express coach and damn near launching herself off the megway with the torque of the sharp turn. A heart-stopping instant as she grazed the barrier, then her bike was clear and zooming down the slipway.

Grud on wheels! If she'd smashed through the barrier it was a kilometre-plus drop to Ground Level. Plenty of time to scream before you hit rock bottom.

One of the pursuing Judges had crashed the barrier in the tight turn. Bike and rider went spinning, down and down. She couldn't hear if he was screaming.

But two lawmen were still on her tail, although they were losing ground to her suicidal speed on the bends.

Luck was with her so far. No sign of Justice vehicles in the air. Wouldn't stay that way for long.

Tyres screeching, she veered on to an old slipway, heading down. About thirty seconds to Ground Level if she maintained her breakneck speed.

She heard the zing of a bullet as it winged her helmet, snapping her head to one side.

All right – if that's the way they wanted it.

Hershey slowed the bike, switched to auto, and swivelled round in the seat, Lawgiver in her hand.

The gun spat bullets at the tracking riders. One caught a slug and did a backward somersault, leaving the bike to career into a small car. Bike and car went over the edge in a shriek of tortured metal.

She aimed at the remaining Judge.

Her aim went astray as a sudden lurch of her bike nearly threw her from the saddle. Darting a glance over her shoulder, her skin went cold. She was on a hairpin bend, and the bike's auto-sensors had been lax in picking up a dark green chemical truck that lay on its side, blocking the road from barrier to barrier.

At 550 kph they'd be scraping her off the truck for hours. And no time to brake.

'*Hell!*' She swung round, ignoring the bullet that clipped her arm, and cut to manual, simultaneously pressing for turbo-boost.

The bike's side-mounted micro-rockets blasted into action, launching bike and rider into the air.

She held on to the handlebars for dear life as the chemical truck seemed to hurtle at her.

She wasn't going to clear it. Insufficient elevation. A split second earlier on the boost and she'd have made it.

All she could do was pull on the handlebars and heave her body back in a desperate attempt to tilt the bike a fraction – gain a few centimetres . . .

Her muscles tensed for the imminent crash.

So long, Mega-City One. It's been – real.

Her muscles were still tensed as the tyres skimmed the edge of the truck by the skin of their rubbereen.

'Yes!'

She looked over her shoulder.

The following Lawmaster was copying her example, its side-rockets firing on turbo-boost.

An instant later she'd dipped over the truck, and focused all her wits on landing the bike without skidding sideways or performing a series of lethal somersaults.

The Firerock tyres hit, skidded, then steadied.

A Grud-almighty crash sounded at her back.

The pursuing Judge hadn't made it. He'd slammed straight into the chemical truck.

The explosion hurled a white-yellow inferno at the sky and rocked the ground with a minor earthquake.

A searing heat-wave hit her back, accelerating the bike to a speed clean off the counter. Teeth clenched, she fought for control as the wheels threatened to take her off the slipway.

The Lawmaster scraped the right-hand barrier, veered left and skimmed along the opposite barrier.

Then she was back in control.

She whistled between her teeth. They didn't come any closer.

Racing around a couple more turns, she glimpsed Ground Level some hundred metres below.

She'd made it to the dark and slime of the city's lowest level, known to its denizens as the Pits. It was the most lawless level in Mega-City One.

Right now, that suited her fine.

Helmet visor automatically adjusting to the permanent murk of the Pits, overborne by the bulbous bellies of kilometres-high citi-blocks, she nosed the bike down one of the crooked streets of the Ground Level shanty towns. This was the lowest you could get in the Mega-City. You *could* go deeper – into the Undercity – but that meant using a Justice access tunnel through the thick plascrete lid that covered the ruins of Old New York in eternal night. She'd gone down there with Dredd seven months ago. The thought of a return visit didn't appeal.

If she boxed clever, the Pits would provide an adequate hideout. She could lose herself in the shadows.

The bullet wounds from the Lawgivers beat a steady pulse of pain in her body. The blood was still draining from her veins, spinning her head, sparkling her eyesight.

She had to locate an underworld doctor pretty soon, otherwise she'd end up on the ground with all her blood on the outside.

First she had to get rid of the Lawmaster: it was as good as a huge, hi-glo arrow pointing at her back.

She spotted an alco-vagrant slumped in a muddy puddle in a corner between two lean-tos. Hershey halted the motorbike and approached the woman. At first sight she looked dead to the world. On closer inspection she was just plain dead.

The dead woman's ragged black overcoat and torn

trousers stank. The brown calf-boots didn't smell much better. That didn't bother Hershey; the clothes were the right size. And the flat-brimmed hat would help shadow her features in the scattered pools of light where the unreliable street lamps were still working.

Five minutes later Hershey was dressed as the vagrant and the vagrant was dressed as Judge Hershey: helmet, badge – the whole works.

Another couple of minutes and Hershey had succeeded in positioning the corpse on the Lawmaster, her seated stance a passable imitation of a rider, thanks to skilful application of the latest in adhesives.

Hershey voice-activated the bike to auto, and instructed it to exit on a slipway a few blocks away, then head up to Megway 3265.

'Optimum speed up the slipway,' Hershey commanded. 'Max speed on megway, heading due west to the Wall. Stop for nothing. Go!'

The Lawmaster rode off with a roar, bearing its dead rider into the night. That should lead Justice Central a merry dance.

The echoes of the engine soon died away, and Hershey was left alone with the dark and dangers of the Pits. She was ready for anything that came her way. Her Lawgiver was still in her possession, tucked into an inside pocket of the overcoat.

Pulling the hat brim low over her face, she stepped into a lane cluttered with old, worn-out techno detritus. Something was crawling inside her borrowed clothes, and it wasn't her. Bugs. Well, what did she expect? Live with them like they lived with her. She had to keep on the move, flitting from shadow to shadow. Biding her time, staying alive, while Dredd finished doing whatever it was he was doing. *Wherever* he was doing it.

'Another world?' she questioned somewhere under a breath.

Keep moving. Stay alive.

Padding softly, she ran down a zigzag alley, occasionally tripping over discarded metal junk. The helmet had to go with the vagrant on the Lawmaster, and it wasn't easy travelling through near-darkness without the visor's night-sight.

Ah, a flicker of ruddy light ahead, beyond the next corner. She quickened her pace.

Emerging from the alley, she blinked in the sudden illumination of a circle of strobing lamp standards, left-overs from the twentieth century. The thrum and sizzle of an antiquated electric generator filled the enclosed space of what she discerned as a courtyard walled with rusting steel buildings, clumped shoulder to shoulder.

A loud clang made her whirl round. A metal gate had swung shut on the alleyway, pushed by a gangling man who wore nothing but three-quarter-length leathereen trousers and head-to-toe tattoos. The tattoos were variations on a single theme – eyes: heads sprouting dozens of eyes, an eye on a tongue poking from a gaping mouth, an eye in the middle of each of a clutch of hooked hands, eyes gouged from sockets. She didn't have time to take it all in before a soft, sucking *schlup* trickled from every side.

Vision adjusting to the light level, she picked out a dozen or so tattooed goons gliding out of recesses in the walls, each sporting the eye motif in all its grisly glory. They weren't mutants. Just depraved humans – which was a hell of a sight worse.

The freaks closed in like a tightening noose.

'Briiight eyeees,' sounded the rattlesnake hiss of one. The gap-toothed mouth performed a sucking action. *Schlup.*

'Niiice eyeees – suckie-suckie,' came the sibilant whisper from another. 'One eeeach. One for Sleeth's belly. One for Slith's belly. Suck 'em out. Suck 'em down, niiice and smoooth . . .'

schlup

She was locked into a small space that was big on trouble.

Well, Hershey could be big trouble too.

She whisked out the Lawgiver. 'Back off, creeps, or you'll be swallowing what's left of your heads.'

'Briiight eyeees . . .'

schlup

'Niiice eyeees . . .'

schlup-schlup

'You asked for it.' She squeezed off a round that made a red mush of a goon's head. He continued for two faltering paces, then crashed to the ground.

The rest kept on coming, regardless.

schlup-schlup-schlup

Hershey aimed again, pressed the trigger . . . Then released the pressure.

The gun swung loose, fell from her hand.

Some wrongness was fooling with the inside of her skull. She was – almost naked . . . A blurred impression of a vast court of living shadows . . .

For a skimmed moment, she was dimly aware of tattooed figures approaching as she dropped to her knees, weaponless.

schlup

Then all she could see was –

McGruder.

McGruder, her black uniform studded with bright red pain-pads.

Her enemy. Her adversary in mortal combat.

When wet lips touched her eyes, she thought it was McGruder's foul kiss.

schlup

Judge Kelleher's mouth fell open. 'Chief Judge!'

Judges Shenker and Coker joined in Kelleher's surprise.

In the middle of issuing a string of emergency measures from her red and gold chair in the Grand Chamber of the

172

Council of Five, Chief Judge McGruder had been struck dumb, eyes glazing.

She'd sat immobile, unresponsive, for several seconds.

Then leaped clean over the crescent table, mouth extended in a rabid howl.

Her booted foot barely brushed the floor before she sprang and kicked at empty air, then spun and crouched low.

'Chief Judge!' Kelleher repeated, glancing at his colleagues for support.

McGruder stuck out her bearded chin, mad eyes glaring at an invisible enemy. 'Gonna make you *crawl*, girlie. Gonna make you *beg*. Gonna make – '

The watching Judges gasped as McGruder's beak of a nose imploded in a crack of cartilage and she flew backwards, sticky red spurting from her flared nostrils.

Coker cast a dazed look at Kelleher. 'Invisible attacker. Got to be – she couldn't do that to herself.'

Shenker, observing McGruder's frenzied battle against nothing, a singularly deadly nothing, shook his head. 'There's no other presence in this room. I'd know. She's reacting. It's a form of possession – McGruder could never move that fast of her own will.'

Kelleher gazed numbly as McGruder whirled like a dervish, growling. 'We should have backed Hershey,' he mumbled. 'She must have known something we don't when she went for McGruder.'

'Hershey was as – possessed – as McGruder,' Shenker said, tilting a thin eyebrow as the Chief Judge executed a quickfire somersault that would have done credit to an acrobat on hyperadrenalin. 'We should have turned them both in, but not to the SJS. This is a mental attack. They should both be locked in Psi's psycho-cells.'

'Who's going to make the decision to lock up McGruder?' asked Kelleher.

Shenker interlaced his long fingers. 'Not me.'

Further dialogue was ended by McGruder's increasing

frenzy. Intermittently muttering incomprehensible words, she ducked, dived, punched, kicked, her face a mask of unparalleled ferocity.

Finally she went on one knee, stared at an invisible something on the floor, and pointed two rigid fingers at the unseen opponent. 'Never did like the way you looked at me,' she chuckled insanely. 'You won't be looking any more.'

McGruder's expression was hard-core evil. Concentration camp evil. Hardened veterans though they were, the three men were chilled to the heart. Frost in the blood.

'That's not McGruder,' whispered Coker.

'As a matter of fact,' murmured Shenker, 'it is.'

'But that's – '

Coker was cut short by McGruder's abrupt yell as she staggered back, rallied, and launched once again into the fray.

Her face slammed into an invisible wall. The features crumpled as she hurtled on to her back.

Kelleher slammed a fist on the desk. 'That's it! I'm taking over as acting Chief Judge!' He threw an interrogative glance at his fellow Council members. 'You'll back me on this?' Their shrugs showed that he was welcome to the responsibility.

He yelled into the public address. 'Judge Kelleher speaking! The Chief Judge is indisposed. I will be acting Chief Judge until further notice. Cease pursuit of Judge Hershey immediately, repeat – *immediately*. Hershey has been cleared of all charges. Wait on stand-by for emergency orders.'

The decision made, Kelleher was all efficiency. He nodded at Shenker. 'Take her to a psycho-cell and call Med in to patch up her face. And make all the moves discreet – Justice Central's torn apart enough as it is without word of a psychotic Chief Judge getting around.'

'Better call Med in first,' Shenker said, pointing at McGruder.

A harsh croak rattled from her throat. And the throat was compressing, as if a boot was grinding its heel into the flesh.

'Whatever's doing that, I wouldn't like to meet it,' muttered Coker. Then he frowned. 'How come we're not affected?'

Shenker's Arctic blue eyes gazed beyond the walls, beyond the city. 'I sense we don't exist in that other world. McGruder and Hershey do.'

'So we're immune?'

'No one's immune. When that other world comes, it'll come for all of us.'

schlup

CRACK!

Another tattooed head split open.

Hershey unleashed a flurry of punches and kicks as she somersaulted in the strobing illumination of the locked courtyard.

McGruder. She had to kill McGruder.

But McGruder had so many faces, so many reaching hands . . .

Her fist lashed out.

CRACK!

A ribcage imploded, the infolding bones beating a skeletal percussion as they jostled one another.

She punched a face. The face finished up somewhere inside the head. There were so many McGruders . . .

She sprang on a prone but still breathing figure, planted her boot heel on the throbbing throat.

A wide smile spread her lips as she ground the heel deeper, deeper.

A harsh croak rattled from the throat.

'*Choke, you drokking bull-dyke.*'

The sharp snap of neck-bones brought her back to reality.

Hershey shook her befuddled head and took in her surroundings. A courtyard with flickering lamp standards.

The tattooed goons.

A red alert zinged down her nerves. She ducked into a spinning crouch.

And slowed to a halt.

There were only two goons left standing. The rest provided a messy flooring for the courtyard. There were something in the region of twelve bodies on the ground. Hard to tell the precise number: the corpses were in a hundred pieces.

Did I do that? With my bare hands? Impossible.

Having spotted the butt of her Lawgiver sticking out from a mess of brains that had somehow ended up inside a shattered ribcage, she grabbed it, brushed off the red slop from the barrel and aimed the muzzle at the two survivors. 'Out of my way, or join the mess on the floor.'

Vacant-eyed, they kept advancing.

schlup

'Briiight eyeees . . .'

schlup

'Niiice eyeees . . .'

Schl-

A mouthful of bullet stopped the slurp in mid-suck.

'Niiice ey – '

Hershey spared two slugs for the final goon. One for each eye.

He'd hardly splashed into the slushy meat of his companions when Hershey unlocked the gate and swung it wide. A quick glance at her once black overcoat disclosed that not all the blood was on the ground. She'd changed from the woman in black to the woman in red.

'What happened?' she murmured as she ran down the crooked alleyway. 'What possessed me?'

Pointless question. The whole episode was a blood-red blank. Keeping her head low, she sprinted through the dark of the Pits.

The bullet wounds were bleeding afresh; she could sense the bugs in the vagrant's clothes lapping up the blood. She must have put one hell of a strain on her physique back there in the strobing yard.

If she didn't get to a doctor soon, it was over for her.

It was going to be a long night, and she had a lot of surviving to do.

The *Watcher*, one of the Special Judicial Squad's sleek hover-ships, thrummed gently as it hung half a metre from the shell-battered megway.

Scores of smashed vehicles were scattered over a radius of half a kilometre, the wreckage from two Ragnarok missiles launched from the *Watcher*'s side-ports. SJS Judge Eliphas was interested in only one of the wrecks.

'You sure it's not Hershey?' he asked, rage muffling his tone.

The Tek operative glanced up from the scorching, twisted metal of the Lawmaster and the burnt-out corpse that had heat-melded with the rags of a Justice uniform. The badge had partially melted, displaying HERSH on its wrinkled surface.

'Can't be Hershey, sir. The dentition doesn't fit.'

'And no sign of her Lawgiver?'

'No sir.'

'That woman's got a charmed life,' Eliphas snarled, swinging round to Mathers. 'Come on. Let's keep looking.'

Eliphas stumbled and winced as he climbed into the hover-ship.

'You okay?' Mathers inquired, as they seated themselves ready for the ship's swift ascent. 'Feel pretty rough myself after that freaky double of yours zapped me.'

'I don't give a drokk about my double,' Eliphas seethed. 'I want Hershey screaming on the black slab. And we'll get no better chance to put her there.'

A vid-screen flashed into life. A fresh-faced Control

operative appeared on the screen. 'Pursuit of Judge Hershey has been called off,' he announced. 'Hershey has been cleared of all charges.'

Eliphas, tight-lipped, glared at the screen, then peered through a window at the city below.

'You hear that?' he finally said, through clenched teeth.

'Uh – yeah,' Mathers answered.

Eliphas stared his subordinate full in the face. 'I said, *you hear that*?'

Catching on, Mathers tapped the side of his broken-veined nose. 'No, boss – didn't hear a thing.'

Turning to the thirty-strong elite squad of SJS executioners (technically listed as a Special Attack Squad), Eliphas studied his black-visored troops, each armed with the high-powered assault weapon known as the Widow-maker. 'Any of you hear anything about calling off the Hershey hunt?'

They shook their heads in unison. The SJS hated Hershey, every last one of them.

One of the executioners hefted a Widow-maker. 'Vid-screen's right out, sir. No messages coming through. Hershey hunt up and running.'

Eliphas gave a curt nod. Nothing less would be expected of the Specials. They had iron loyalty to their own division. All those outside – Chief Judge and Council of Five included – were potential enemies.

'How we gonna track her down?' Mathers asked.

A glint came to Eliphas's cold eye. 'Around the last place she was seen, heading down to Ground Level. She won't have ridden far before leaving her bike. She must have switched clothes. Without her Lawmaster communications she won't know the pursuit's been called off. She'll be on the run or lying low, just like any perp. And you know what happens to perps when we go after them. Hershey won't see morning.'

'What if Control gets on to us?' Mathers frowned. 'They

might send out a fleet of bikes to stop us – maybe even h-wagons.'

'Justice Central's got its hands full just keeping itself from blowing sky-high. The field's wide open.' His gaze moved back to the window, studied the glittering lights of the massive citi-blocks, with roads and pedways suspended between them like the glistening threads of a cobweb. 'Look down there,' he ruminated. 'Tens of thousands of people in every block, each block a little city in itself. Totally insulated in their protected environments. Indulging in every sport in and out of the book, fed full on every entertainment, legal or otherwise. Sealed in their secure little worlds. Safe and secure.' He heaved a deep breath. 'They don't appreciate what we do for them, Mathers.'

'Ah – um – I guess not, boss.'

'We're the people's friend. Judges like Hershey are their enemy,' Eliphas continued, lost in reverie. 'You know why, Mathers?'

'Uh – no idea. Did you say the people's *friend*?'

'I did. The people want walls. High walls. Thick walls. They want security. High security. We give them walls, high and thick. Metre by metre, we're making a prison of Mega-City One. When the prison's complete, the people will be content, protected by impenetrable walls, and watched by us, their guards – and masters.' His fist tightened. 'Judges like Hershey never understood that. She thinks our job should be dealing with crime, imprisoning the criminals. Hershey thinks we're the people's servants. When she sees fit, she takes their side against *us*. That breeds uncertainty, and uncertainty gives rise to discontent. If all Judges were like Hershey, the walls would one day come tumbling down.'

Mathers scratched his head. 'But Hershey's no Anderson, boss. Sure, I hate the bitch, but she'd never bring down the system.'

'Anderson's in deep space. Out of the picture. Hershey's right here.'

He flicked a finger at the night city. 'Down *there*. And the way she acts, she undermines the system, whether she intends to or not.'

'So – uh – we're helping the people by wasting Hershey, right, boss?'

Ignoring Mathers, Eliphas stared down at the Mega-City. 'She's down there, where she belongs. Without Justice backup, virtually weaponless. A sitting duck.' A smile curved his lips. 'The shooting party's on its way, Hershey.'

NINETEEN

'Choke, you drokking bull-dyke.'

'STOP!'

The voice of Dread reverberated around the soaring arches of DreadCourt, underscoring the Torture Symphony in Blood Major.

There was a power in that booming voice: it struck Hershey like a body-blow, lifting her off McGruder and flinging her several metres to land with a bone-jarring thump. Rolling twice, she was back on her feet, crouching like a panther coiled to spring.

'You said what I do is up to me!' she accused, glaring at Judge Dread, seated in the Dread-effigy throne. 'I want that bull-dyke dead.'

Judge Dread rose from the DreadThrone like the dawn of a black sun. All but a few quaked in the vast, shadowy hall.

'And what I do is up to me!' he thundered. 'And I want my Judge Governor of EastDread alive! The combat's over, Hershey. Take my advice – withdraw, and live.'

Her hesitation was fleeting. She nodded acquiescence and departed the Circle of Dread. You didn't gainsay the Ruler of the Seven Suns, not unless you wished to be fed to the Conglomeration.

Dread brandished the engram ring. 'The device is deactivated, Hershey,' he called out. 'You can snap the neck-collar with those strong fingers of yours. And you're reinstated as SinoDread Governor. See how well you're treated when you do as you're told.'

She knew what was expected. Turning, she gave a deep bow. 'Thank you, Lord Dread. I'm your slave in all things.'

Still rearing above the throne-mount, Dread pointed at the floor beneath Hershey's feet. 'As a last gesture of compliance, leave our presence on your knees. Crawl.'

Dread's laughter counterpointed the agonised strains of the Torture Symphony as Hershey, reinstated Judge Governor of SinoDread, sank to her knees and crawled from the Court.

The laughter faded. He jabbed a finger at the semi-conscious McGruder. 'Take her away and patch her up.'

One of the amorphous, living shadows whispered down on the EastDread Governor, gathered her in its murky folds and bore her out of the Court.

With slow, deliberate steps, Judge Dread descended the rumpled plasrock of the throne-mount, arms outstretched, fingers hooked.

Caligula shook in his leathereen boots: *Now I'm in for it. How was I supposed to know he'd ordered me back to Roma? Nobody told me.*

Drusilla gave him a faint nudge, leaned her mouth close to his ear. 'Beg forgiveness,' she whispered. 'Grovel. He likes that sort of thing. It's the only chance you've got.'

'Right.'

Caligula flung himself prostrate. 'I am but a worm, unworthy to be trodden under your foot, O Judge of the Seven Suns! Forgive me, O my Lord and Master! I never heard your command, else I would have obeyed it with aplomb, nay, sheer joy, for my sole delight is in pleasing my Emperor. Blame me not for my importunate actions, O Awe and Splendour of the World, for it is the visiting madness that is to blame for the occasional folly of my deeds.' Propping himself up on his elbows, he turned and glanced questioningly at Drusilla. 'Was that all right? Not too over the top?'

She thumped her brow and groaned. 'That's torn it.'

182

Judge Dread ignored them both. He raised his arms higher. 'The Testing!' he commanded.

The command voice-activated Dread's Chief Judge uniform to dissolve above the waist, vanishing in two blinks of an eye.

A muscle-roped torso was revealed, wrapped in bioplast skin – visually indistinguishable from living flesh – which was nine times stronger than the toughest plasteen. Beneath that impenetrable skin was a skeleton of adamantinium, the strongest biometal in the known universe. All this, added to a musculature enhanced by magnihormones, made Judge Dread the most invulnerable and indomitable human in history. The Chief Judge had reconstructed his anatomy over the last decade, beginning with the adamantinium skeletal replacement, bone by bone.

As for the face behind the helmet, no one could say. He hadn't removed the helmet for fifteen years, not even in bed, not for a single second. For all the officials of DreadCourt knew, the head and helmet had fused into a biometallic unity.

The mighty Chief Judge Dread was truly a figure of awe, but he was not a man immune to pain. Far from it; his pain centres had been artificially boosted. Dread didn't flinch from pain: he revelled in it. He was hooked on suffering, both the giving and receiving of it. Whatever UltraTek had made of his physiology, Judge Dread still lived for the thrill of challenge.

The command which had left him half-naked also summoned a dozen hardened veterans of the Judgement force into the Circle. Each was clad in the spiked, plasteen-reinforced uniform of full combat, replete with a small armoury, the king of which was the Exterminans psionic rifle, dispenser of ultraterror waves that killed with raw fear. The men's expressions were blanked out by the black visors, but the watching dignitaries had no doubt of what the helmets hid: sheer terror.

The terror of men about to die.

These were Dread's opponents in combat, and only one outcome was possible when anyone opposed Judge Dread. For the Chief Judge, the combat of the Testing was merely an exercise, a test of his skill and endurance. He indulged in a Testing at least once a day.

For his twelve reluctant adversaries, it was anything but a test: it was simple mass murder.

'Shield,' ordered Dread, flexing his muscles for battle.

A vague shimmer was all that showed of the energy shield which sprang up and enclosed the Circle of Dread, protecting the audience from the fearful weaponry.

Inside the Circle, Caligula sprang to his feet in alarm. 'Hey!' he shouted, banging a fist on the invisible wall. 'I'm on the wrong side of the shield! Let me out! *Help!*'

Dread showed his teeth in a harsh smile. 'You're on the right side. Inside. If you survive the havoc of the Testing, you're free and forgiven. I don't expect you to fight – just run for cover.'

Panicked, Caligula's eyes darted hither and thither. 'There's only the throne-mount . . .'

'Feel free to hide behind it, but I hope you remember the fate of anyone who touches the Throne.'

'I know, I know,' grumped Caligula. 'One touch and the Throne will turn my body inside out. But, your Dreadness, listen – '

'Begin!' Dread bellowed at his opponents.

Twelve Exterminans rifles spouted red waves of ultra-terror at the Chief Judge. A split-second ultraterror burst from a single rifle would have stopped any normal man's heart with fear-shock overload.

Dread simply drank it all in, wave on wave.

'Yeeesss,' he sighed. 'Yeeesss . . .'

'Oh, no,' moaned Caligula, sprinting around the Circle's perimeter, gaze desperately searching out a way to the cover of the throne-mount without crossing one of those deadly red beams. 'Nothing's going to harm me,' he told himself in a shrill squeal. 'I'm a god. You can't hurt a god. Oh hell! Help!'

Dread's opponents gave up on the Exterminans rifles.

You can't destroy Dread with Terror.

Caligula made a bolt for the mount, dived behind its rumpled slopes. 'Leave me alone!' he shrieked. 'Don't shoot at me – I'm on *everybody's* side. Stay away! Clear off!'

Blue-white lightning crazed the shadowy air as the twelve fighters projected psionic rays from extended fingers.

The lightning played about Judge Dread's awesome figure: a god wreathed in fire.

Dread smiled a thin smile at the exquisite pain. 'What puny opposition. Not worth my time. I should give you to the Conglomeration.'

'No!' one of the men screeched. 'Kill us, Lord Dread – I beg you!'

'Cowards!' Caligula called out from the shelter of the throne-mount, then put a muffling hand over his mouth.

Still wreathed in lightning, the Chief Judge raised his fist. 'I AM THE LAW!'

Then he swept through the air like a thunderstorm and descended in wrath on his adversaries.

His fists and feet of adamantinium and bioplast tore into the luckless men, punching holes clean through chests and helmets.

Within ten seconds of his attack, Dread had made mashed meat and cracked bone of eleven men.

The survivor had fled the instant Dread leapt. He stood, quivering, by the throne-mount.

Dread snarled in contempt. 'If there's one thing I can't stand, it's a yellow Judge.' He pointed a finger at the hapless Judge. 'Join the Orchestra.'

'NOOOO!'

A lazy streak of light meandered from Dread's pointing finger and enveloped the victim in a glowing blue haze.

The man's helmet melted on his head, spilled down in droplets. The uniform dissolved.

In moments, he was naked and screaming.

'You'll soon scream a different tune,' Dread chuckled, moving his finger to aim at the animated wall.

The haze swept the Judge to the fleshy wall with its five thousand pores, each bleeding in sympathy with the Torture Symphony in Blood Major.

The flexing graniteen skin sucked the man in. For an instant his head was visible, howling its horror. Then it was ingested, leaving a pouting pore in its place.

The Orchestra had one more instrument.

Dread twisted his lip in distaste. 'Nothing but weaklings. No one's worthy to be my enemy.'

'Certainly not me, Chief!' said Caligula, popping out from behind the mount. 'Splendid show you put on. Er – mind if I toddle off now? Got to get back to Nova Roma, like you said.'

'Now you're here, you stay. You can take part in the invasion.'

Caligula's face fell. Then he adopted a cheerful mask. 'Oh, good. That'll be – great.' He crept towards his sisters as the energy shield was lifted.

Judge Dread marched back to his throne. 'Leave me, all of you!' he roared. 'You're scum. You don't deserve to be in my presence.'

He sat on the DreadThrone, chin on fist, and glared at the departing figures.

Scum.

Not one worthy enemy.

The line of his mouth tightened.

There had been a worthy enemy once.

Rico.

The Torture Symphony concluded its final movement.

The walls smoothed out into still, flat surfaces as silence filled the court.

'Fifth Despair Symphony in Grey Minor,' he commanded.

The graniteen walls swelled and subsided in slow, solemn waves in concert with a doleful chorus of misery.

'Rico,' he murmured.

Rico had been a worthy enemy. If the draw had been simultaneous, back in the Cafe Cesare, Rico would have beaten him.

That thought still rankled, after all these years.

So did the memory of watching Rico's body on the Resyk belt, gliding towards the meat-grinder Mouth.

It started there . . .

«Lord Dread?»

The multi-tongued voice of the Conglomeration sounded in his helmet, a slurping echo.

'What is it?'

«I sense an uprising in the Undercity. I sense Anderson at its head. There's a man close to her. Your brother . . .»

'My brother's dead!' Dread snapped, gripping the arm-rest shaped as his own fist.

«Your inferior brother from the other world. Your other self. I feel that he's joined forces with Anderson. The uprising must not take place. This is a very delicate time. Nothing must distract from the invasion. The uprising must be crushed now.»

Dread rubbed his chin. 'I want Anderson alive. And Joe Dredd.'

«The invasion is paramount, sire. Once it's completed, you will find an alternative Anderson in the neighbouring continuum.»

'And Joe Dredd?'

«He's nothing, Lord Dread. While you grew and flourished over thirty-seven years, he stayed the same.»

'Not a worthy enemy,' Dread muttered.

«Not even worthy to bear the name of an enemy. May I suggest that you quash the rebellion at source?»

Dread considered the suggestion. 'Very well,' he

decided. 'I've tolerated the Undercity dissidents long enough for the sake of hauling in Anderson alive. As for Joe Dredd – well, you said it – he's nothing. I wasted my time luring him into my world. Not a worthy enemy.'

«By what means do you wish to wipe out the rebels?»

A slow smile curved Dread's mouth. 'The Secretion. Steep them in hell.'

«The Secretion will not kill the rebels, sire.»

'I know.' The smile widened. 'Why be merciful?'

TWENTY

Manhattan was silent. Broadway was dark.

Muster completed, the Undercity rebels crept stealthily to their positions, infra-red lenses serving in place of the quenched bonfires.

Crouched on a makeshift stage in front of the World Trade Center, Cassandra Anderson clenched and unclenched her right fist. 'Twelve hundred and thirty,' she sighed. 'Twelve hundred and thirty against ten million.'

'Ten million?' Joe Dredd echoed, standing over her, fists planted on his hips. 'Ten million *Judges*?'

She nodded. 'Ten million Judges.'

'How does the civilian population support that much manpower?'

Cassandra heaved weary shoulders. 'There is no civilian population. The people don't even have names, only numbers. That's how come they're called the Nameless. Dreadcity's a prison, each citi-block's a prison block. Everyone's a convict from birth. First principle of Dread's Law: everyone is guilty. A life sentence from the moment of birth. Hard labour from the age of five. Then there's the alien civilisations Judge Dread's conquered. A plentiful source of wealth and power generation.'

'Where are the Judges drawn from, clone banks?'

'The clone banks were closed down long ago. Chief Judge Dread has systematically eliminated clones since his rise to power. Only a few clone Judges remain. Soon Dread will be the only clone left. I've a feeling the Chief Judge is afraid of clones.'

'Afraid of clones,' Dredd murmured. 'Why should a clone be afraid of clones?'

'Can't tell. There's a permanent dark around his psyche. I can't pierce it.'

'Okay, so how are the Judges recruited?'

'The majority are recruited from the Nameless, every Carnal Carnival.'

'What the drokk's a Carnal Carnival?'

She stood up and moved away. 'Ask CORA. I've fed all the information you need into it. I can't waste any more time chewing the fat with you.'

Dredd glowered at Anderson's departing figure, then lifted his shoulders in an infinitesimal shrug.

'CORA.'

'Quite something, our Cassandra, isn't she?' piped up CORA. 'Look at all those firm, flowing curves. Those angel eyes. Isn't she to die for?'

'Wouldn't know,' Dredd gruffed.

'That's your problem, sir.'

'You're really starting to drokk me off, disc-head!' Dredd snapped. 'Just fill me in on the Nameless and the Judges and keep your opinions to yourself. And no fancy talk.'

'As a matter of fact, I've restricted myself to the most elementary lexicon since I first spoke to you. Primate-friendly, so to speak. So, before you burst a blood vessel, here is the pithiest of summaries of Dreadcity. The eight hundred million Nameless endure lives of abject misery, ruled by terror. Mega-City One, at its worst, has nothing to equal it. The Nameless have a sole purpose, to serve the Judges. They are controlled by ultraterror, which is transmitted from a most unpleasant computer known as the Conglomeration.'

'What the drokk *is* ultraterror?'

'Psionic waves of amplified terror that cow the entire population into total submission. A trace of those waves has leaked into Mega-City One through the Cafe Cesare fistula, creating the Zone Pacifica. The displaced ultraterror effect on our home continuum is, however, negligible compared to the overpowering force it exerts in the dominion of Chief Judge Dread. The Nameless, controlled by fear, slave eighteen hours a day for the Judges in an economy directed solely towards interplanetary conquest. In little more than a decade, the technology of this society has leaped centuries, especially in the area of psionic weaponry. Chief Judge Dread himself is crammed with the latest in psionic implants, constantly updated, to make up for his originally low level of psychic aptitude.'

'If this guy's me, he shouldn't have *any* psychic ability,' Dredd cut in.

'Everybody has *some* psychic potential, sir. Yours happens to be extremely low, as of course was Judge Dread's in the early days. But he cultivated what he had, and boosted it with UltraTek psionics. Clear enough? Now let's get back to the issue at hand. The Nameless are controlled by ultraterror, and creep about in fear and dread, but this state of affairs is sometimes lifted when the Chief Judge declares a Carnal Carnival. During one of these carnivals, psionic waves of lust and rage replace ultraterror. The entire population goes berserk. Those of the Nameless who display exceptional viciousness and outstanding sadism during carnival time are later taken to a Judgement training camp where, if successful in the tests – which include killing all the members of their family – the trainee is promoted to Judge once he's leaped over the ritual bonfire. Male Judges must neither marry nor live with a partner, but are encouraged to take any Nameless woman by force whenever they choose. Female Judges – a mere two per cent of Judges are females – must remain celibate, unless they achieve membership of the Hammerfist, this world's equivalent of the Council of Five, composed of the five Judge Governors. Present Judge Governors: Caligula, McGruder, Hershey, Memnon and Mean Machine Angel – '

191

'Mean Machine!' Dredd exclaimed. '*Judge* Mean Machine? How come one of the biggest perps in Mega-City One ends up as a high-ranking Judge?'

'This is Chief Judge Dread's dominion, sir. Psychopathic violence is a plus in the Judgement force. The Chief Judge openly avows Fascism, and encourages savage treatment of the cities' various populations. Judge Mean Machine, Governor of Antarctic City, is one of the staunchest supporters of the regime.'

Dredd took a deep breath. 'Something doesn't add up. How the drokk did shooting Rico back in '79 make the Chief Judge so different from me?'

'He's not *all* that different, sir,' CORA remarked.

Dredd ignored the remark. 'Okay, so he killed Rico twenty years before I did. Two warnings had been given – he was justified in firing. Doesn't explain why he became a worse tyrant than Judge Cal.'

'Indeed it doesn't, sir. As a matter of fact, Anderson believes some crucial event occurred after the killing to warp Judge Dread's mind, but said event has not been identified. Anderson, however, suspects that it might be connected with the Chief Judge's morbid fascination with Resyk. And there may be a tie-in with his apparent fear of clones.'

'That fear of clones again. Any ideas on the subject?'

'None at the moment, sir, but soft – the yellow-haired angel approaches . . .'

Cassandra Anderson strode up, a retinue of elite Bleeding Heart soldiers at her back. 'Get ready, Joe Dredd. The rebellion's starting.'

'Not sure I want to be part of a rebel army, Anderson. Now if you Bleeding Hearts still called yourselves Judges, upholders of the *Justice* force, it'd be different.'

She shot him a heated glance. '*Justice?* The word has been censored from Dreadcity. All we have here is *Judgement*. And don't try to tell me that justice is the top of your agenda. The Law comes first for you. Law, not justice.'

He thrust out his jaw. 'Same thing.'

'Like hell.' A surge of anger was visibly building up in her taut body, threatening to erupt in fury 'Who authorised the Judges to take power in the first place? Nobody. They just took power because they had the strength to do it, and the people were too weak to resist. You rule by force, *Judge* Joe Dredd. Keep it up, and one day your world will be like ours, invasion or no invasion. Stick that in your helmet and chew on it.'

He folded his arms, and stared.

Anderson stared right back.

At length, he gave the tiniest of nods. 'Maybe I'll think about it. Just *maybe*.'

Some of the heat went out of her anger, but it still simmered. 'Want to see thirty-seven years back, Joe Dredd? Want to see the first act that made your name a byword for fear?'

He twisted his lip. 'I'll watch whatever you've got to show.'

'Then have a look at this psionic hologram,' she said, light streaming from her fingertips to form images in the air, images from a long-ago Mega-City One. 'Take a look at yourself a couple of days after the confrontation in the Cafe Cesare.'

The psionic hologram had a substance and sense of reality absent from the electronic holos of his own world. Slipway 77 in Sector 40 virtually came alive before his eyes . . . .

A small crowd was cheering on the pedway verge as Judge Dredd roared down Slipway 77 on his Lawmaster, fresh from his latest arrest.

One short, tubby citizen, cheering more wildly than the rest, jumped off the pedway and on to the slipway surface, arms waving in greeting:

'Well done, Judge Dredd! That's the stuff! Show the

193

perps what the Law means. Three cheers for Judge Dredd! Hip-hip – '

'HOORAY!' shouted the crowd.

Dredd screeched his Lawmaster to a halt, dismounted, and walked up to the excited citizen on the slipway.

'Hip-hip – '

No 'hooray'.

Dredd had pulled a gun. 'Jaywalking,' he growled, indicating the man's trespass on the slipway.

Sweat broke out on the man's moon face. 'But – I'm one hundred per cent behind the Law. Always cheered when the perps got what they deserved. Judges are the best thing that ever happened to us. Without Judges, this city would be in a right drokking mess.'

The Lawgiver pistol lowered. 'So you're right behind the Justice force?'

'Oh yes, mister Judge, sir. All the way.'

'Then maybe I'll give you a chance.'

'Uh. Oh thank you, thank – '

Dredd fired the lowered pistol – lowered to the level of the man's knees. A slug in each kneecap.

The victim crumpled with a yelp.

Dredd stood over the writhing figure, gun trained on the citizen's head. 'Here's your chance – it's five metres to the pedway. You've got ten seconds to reach it. Start crawling. One second, and counting . . .'

Despite his agony, his shattered legs, the man heaved himself by his elbows towards the slipway's verge.

'Ungh . . . Aaah . . .'

One metre covered.

'Three seconds.' Dredd intoned.

'Uh . . . Ach . . . Nngh . . .'

He forced himself two more metres, arms scrabbling frantically.

'Six seconds.'

The tortured man tore his fingernails in his desperation to reach the safety of the pedway.

Two metres to go.

'Eight seconds.'

In a superhuman effort, the man clawed over the last two metres.

'Nine seconds.'

With a cry of triumph, the kneecapped citizen launched himself on to the pedway.

'Ten seconds.'

Face streaming from pain and exertion, the man looked up at Dredd. 'Made – made it – Judge Dredd, sir.'

Dredd pointed at the man's left foot. It trailed over the pedway, its toecap touching the slipway surface.

'Jaywalking,' Judge Dredd said.

He aimed the Lawgiver between the man's eyes and pulled the trigger.

The man's head exploded into disunity, each skull fragment going its own way.

Dredd holstered his Lawgiver and mounted the Justice motorbike.

He rode away from a dead silence.

The psionic hologram dissolved into the perpetual night of the Undercity. A hush from the assembled rebel host, all witnesses to the grim spectacle, lingered after the hologram vanished.

Anderson laid a withering stare on Joe Dredd. 'That was the act that brought you to the public's attention. Made you notorious.'

'That was your Chief Judge Dread's past, not mine,' he retorted.

She was unmoved. 'There's a lot of overlap between the continua. You could just as easily have done that yourself.' Her smile was mirthless. 'Maybe you did.'

Dredd balled his fist. 'You think I'd do a thing like that, lady – you need your own mind reading. I just carry out the Law, and what you showed me there had nothing to do with the Law.'

Anderson tilted her head. 'You'd never do anything like that?'

'You heard me. And that's it. Now if you want to get a war started with the Chief Judge, then start it. I'll let you know whose side I'm on – when I'm ready.'

Giant loomed up behind Anderson. 'After all you've heard, you still don't know whose side you're on? Cassandra, we can't use this jerk. Let's waste him.'

She kept her maybe-grey maybe-blue eyes on Dredd. They probed deep. 'No. He's not sure we're giving him a true picture. Suspects we might be fooling around with his brain. He's thinking Judges Hershey or McGruder could be turned against the Chief Judge. That right, Joe? Your mind's on the wrong lines. They're not the same as their Mega-City counterparts. Hershey – well, she's a long shot, I'll grant you that. McGruder – forget it. Prize bitch. In the ranks of the Hammerfist, the only one who might turn renegade is Caligula.'

'Judge Cal!' he snorted. 'The day I join forces with Judge Cal, you can have my badge!'

'Caligula,' she corrected. 'He hasn't been called Judge Cal for a decade.'

'Whatever – I won't have anything to do with that drokkhead Caligula. The creep's a raving lunatic.'

'He's mellowed with age, although rejuvenations have made him look younger than way back when he was Chief Judge. Lunatic he may be, but his governorship is the least oppressive of any in the Hammerfist. There aren't any Nameless in his jurisdiction of Nova Roma. He rules a population of plebs, the old Roman model.'

Dredd displayed frank disbelief. 'You trying to tell me Caligula's less oppressive than Hershey? Judge Dread couldn't have corrupted her that much.'

'She's scared of him. Grud, we're *all* scared of him. Except for Caligula, and even he's scared on the occasions that he's sane – which aren't often. Besides, Caligula's got an ally of ours at his side. Name of Patchwork. Patchwork's a very special – '

'Anderson,' Dredd interrupted.

'I don't know. But it's something to do with Resyk.'

'Drokk, I haven't asked you yet! Gruddam Psi precog!'

'I've saved you the trouble. Like I said, I've no real idea what twisted Judge Dread into what he is, but Resyk's involved somewhere. Anyway, if we get into Dreadhead, you can ask the Chief Judge face to face. Or rather visor to visor. He doesn't take his helmet off either, not ever.'

'Grud – you think I wear this helmet in the bed or the shower?'

A quirky smile twitched her lips. 'Wouldn't surprise me.'

He swatted away the remark as though it were a fly. 'You mentioned something about Dreadhead. What the drokk's that? Come to that, what's this Conglomeration I keep hearing about?'

Anderson arched an eyebrow. 'I've got some news for you, Joe Dredd.'

'Uh-huh.'

'The world doesn't revolve around you.'

'You've got something in common with the Anderson back home,' he grunted. 'Always trying to be funny.'

She shook her head. 'I wasn't trying to be funny. By the way, I haven't cried since I was eighteen.'

His lip tightened. 'I'm getting tired of you poking into my mind. Sure, Judge Anderson cried when she experienced other people's pain. She was the best empath on the force. Felt things deep.'

Anderson's eyes clouded. 'She's not the only one. But I didn't have the luxury of letting my feelings show. Different world, different rules.'

He studied her pensive expression, downcast gaze. 'Maybe not so different,' he said.

She half-smiled. 'Maybe I'll meet my other self one day. Compare notes.' The smile, what there was of it, vanished into the stern expression of a seasoned veteran of the rebel underground. She flicked her head at Corey. 'I sense Patchwork's ready.'

Corey nodded. 'I sense it too.'

Anderson straightened her spine. Squared her shoulders. 'Then let's go.'

She marched to the front of the stage, surveyed her army of ex-Judges, Dreadcity refugees and mutants.

Then she raised a clenched fist high. 'Love hurts!' she proclaimed.

Hundreds of clenched fists rose in response:

'LOVE HURTS!'

The reverberation of the response had hardly died away when another reverberation took its place.

A rumbling.

A rumbling from above.

Every gaze was raised to the plascrete roof of Old New York, which seemed to rest on the World Trade Center's twin towers.

Anderson couldn't keep the tremble from her tone. 'Corey, can you feel it too?'

Corey's face was a mask of dismay. 'Yes. I never thought he'd do it before you were safely locked up in Dreadhead.'

Anderson's heart sank. 'Seems he's given up on taking me alive. Decided not to tolerate us creatures in Dreadcity's cellar. Too much at stake.'

Dredd glared up at the roof, listened to the mounting rumble. 'What's going on?' he asked Anderson.

'The roof has several old vents. We're about to be flooded,' she replied, eyes fixed on the Undercity's plascrete lid.

He snorted dismissively. 'What's the problem? Can't you people swim?'

The rumble intensified to a continuous roll of thunder.

'It's not going to rain water,' Anderson said.

A deluge of yellow-brown fluid burst from a corner of

198

the roof. In swift succession, other sickly downpours flooded in continuous streams from vents in the plascrete and splash-landed on the streets of Manhattan.

Joe Dredd gave a shrug. 'Looks like sewage. I've swum in worse.'

Anderson swerved a sharp stare on Dredd. 'It's not sewage, Joe. That gunge up there is from the Conglomeration. It's the Secretion. The Stew.'

'The MetaSecretion,' Corey supplemented, glancing at the Judge. 'Extract of brains stewed with bio-fluid and bombarded with ultraterror waves to form a psionic morphing agent.'

'Uh-huh. So what's that mean to us?'

'It means that if the Stew floods over you, even *splashes* you, you metamorphose into the thing you most loathe and fear,' Anderson said. 'If you're scared of spiders, you'll turn into a spider, fully conscious as a human being and in horror of the body you inhabit. And you stay that way, unless someone has the mercy to kill you.'

Corey nodded, the fear raw in her eyes. 'Total and irreversible metamorphosis.'

The wails of rebels went up like the chorus of the damned. Terrified witless, they raced for the escape route of the World Trade Center's towers.

A turbulent, stinking flood rushed in their wake, streaking in from West Side Highway and Broadway. It slammed into the makeshift stage and swept it along, Dredd, Anderson and their few companions struggling to keep their footing on the lurching surface of the impromptu raft. Close up, it no longer resembled sewage. And it smelt a lot worse.

'Cassandra,' Corey warned. 'Twin Tower Two . . .'

'I know,' Anderson responded, arms windmilling to preserve her balance. 'There's a disused vent at the top of it.'

Dredd glanced up. A roiling, urine-coloured spillage

was gushing down inside the second tower, already flooding fifteen floors in its downward rush.

Judge Dredd immediately took command. He bellowed above the thunderous fluid. 'EVERYONE INTO TOWER ONE – NOW!'

'You loud-mouthed stommhead!' Anderson cried out, seeing a large number following Dredd's order. 'Tower One's foundations were blown to Grud years ago. The pressure of the flood will tear them loose and bring the whole damn thing down!'

Dredd curled his lip. 'You can't know that. And what other way is there?'

She tapped her head. 'I sense it. And what I sense, happens. As for the other way . . . Give Joe Dredd some cling-pads, Corey.'

The stage, spinning in the maelstrom where two Secretion floods collided, had careened close to Tower Two. Anderson sprang off the stage and clung on to a sheet of glass, knees and hands pressed tight to the sheer surface.

As Corey slapped two pairs of cling-pads on to Dredd, he frowned at Anderson. 'She's not wearing these.'

'We have our own kind,' Corey said. 'They come with the uniform.'

'This way!' Anderson shouted to those few still clear of the rising, muck-yellow stew. 'Climb the outside of Tower Two!' She glanced back to the people on the foundering stage. 'Come on!'

Dredd leaped, cling-padded hands and knees thrust forwards. They made contact with the glass and stuck.

Giant landed securely to one side of him, Corey to the other. A few others made it. The rest didn't.

Anderson was a metre above him. 'Don't look down,' she urged. 'The Secretion has metamorphosed everyone down there. You won't like what you see, believe me.'

'How do I move these Gruddam cling-pads?' Dredd bawled out. 'I'm stuck here like a fly in a web.'

'They're retroactive,' she called down. 'Press *hard* and

200

they come loose. Keep pressing hard as you slide upwards. And don't press hard on all the pads at once, or you'll drop off.'

Dredd attempted the exercise. It worked. His Justice training, geared to instant adaptability to all situations, did the rest. He succeeded in keeping abreast of Corey and Giant as they scaled the first floor of the tallest building in New York. It was going to be one long drokk of a climb.

Glancing around, he spotted only twenty climbers. Anderson's army, tiny as it was, had shrunk to the size of a commando unit.

The roof was still gushing rivers of the Secretion's bile.

'How much of that stuff's likely to pour in?' he shouted at Corey.

'As much as it takes,' she yelled back. 'Until the Undercity's flooded – right up to the roof.'

'But we can't get inside the tower! How are we going to get out?'

'With considerable difficulty.'

He climbed with renewed determination. Intent on the ascent, he failed to notice the sudden clouding of the glass immediately. Then he peered into the interior. The dark yellow Secretion swirled inside, licking the windows. The tower was a glass container, brimming with nightmare fluid. A few cracks in the glass would spread fast.

He felt someone probing his mind. His stare darted up. Anderson was glancing down at him, a humourless smile on her lips. 'Don't worry, Joe, twentieth-century reinforced glass is all it's cracked up to be.'

'Big joke,' he muttered, concentrating on the climb.

He hadn't ascended two floors when he felt the tower shake. Despite the cling-pads, it was difficult to maintain a grip.

A Grud-Almighty roar made havoc of the air.

'Oh, *man*,' groaned Giant, staring past Dredd. 'Look at *that*.'

He followed the direction of Giant's gaze.

Tower One was reeling. As he watched, it buckled near the base.

The twin edifice hovered in mid-air for a stretched moment. Then the tower toppled. Its summit tumbled down, heading straight for Tower Two.

The deafening impact of tower on tower threw Dredd clean off the wall.

As he dropped, his eyesight skimmed the boiling yellow sea below. A sea swimming with monstrosities that had once been humans.

Dredd was on his way to join them.

Weller flexed the throbbing fingers of his psionics-crammed hand. The digits pulsed rhythmically.

'I've got rhythm – let's make music.'

The suicide squad of ten Bleeding Hearts, grouped along the plascrete tunnel, glanced questioningly at their leader.

'We carry on,' he stated quietly, answering the unspoken question. 'It's passing through the disused vents. The tunnels are safe.'

The roar of cascading fluid was all about them, shaking the tunnel walls. The smell of the Secretion seeped down the plascrete passage.

'What's the point in going on?' someone asked. 'They'll all be drowned – metamorphosed. We're finished.'

'We carry on,' Weller insisted. 'And *we're* not finished. There are hundreds of tunnels to go. Remember Jericho, and keep going.'

He placed his throbbing hands on the wall. 'We've all got rhythm. Let's all make music.'

Reluctantly, they complied.

Twenty-two hands pressed against the walls.

Their hands transmitted rhythm to the walls.

They gave the walls their music.

* * *

Helmeted head resting on fist, elbow propped on the black obsidian fist of the DreadThrone, Judge Dread smiled as he heard the news.

«Undercity flooded, sire,» the transmitted slish-slosh voice of the Conglomeration slurped in the Chief Judge's helmet. «The level of the MetaSecretion will soon reach the Undercity's roof, but it can be presumed that all Undercity dwellers have already been metamorphosed.»

'Excellent. Now it's done, I realise it should have been done long ago. No resistance to my rule is to be tolerated, even Anderson's token resistance. As for Joe Dredd, best that he's quickly dispensed with. After all, he's a clone, like me. Just like me. Dangerous.'

«Your judgement is sound, my Lord. Best dispose of all clones, especially Joe Dredd. Your way is now clear.»

Chief Judge Dread scanned the vaulted arches and shifting, living shadows of DreadCourt. 'Yes, the time's come,' he said. 'In a day I'll enter Mega-City One – in the flesh.'

«Did your previous visits not give you satisfaction?»

Judge Dread waved a dismissive hand. 'They were no more than projections of myself. Psionic holo-probes to lure Joe Dredd into my dominion. They did lure him, and whatever feeble threat he might have presented is cancelled. So much for Joe Dredd. Now: Mega-City One and the universe it inhabits. I want to absorb Mega-City One's continuum – in person.'

«Shall I start the first phase of invasion, Lord?»

Dread nodded. 'Yes – why wait? Some five or six hours' subjection to ultraterror and every last creep in Mega-City One will be dead of fright. A city of the dead. That'll teach the rest of the mega-cities to bow the knee before they get the same treatment.'

«There will be four survivors, sire. Judge Death and his Dark Judges. You cannot kill what does not live.»

Dread sneered contemptuously. 'I'll keep them as pets.'

«Very well, sir. I'll start to pour ultraterror through the Cafe Cesare fistula, Lord Dread.»

Dread's smile widened. 'Yes, flood Mega-City One with ultraterror. They won't know what's hit them.'

Part Four

Circle of Dread

'Weave a circle round him thrice
And close your eyes with holy dread . . .'

Samuel Taylor Coleridge
Kublai Khan

TWENTY-ONE

He dug the bullet out of Hershey's back with a crude, curved knife.

Naked to the waist, Hershey checked the Pits doctor's expression and movements in a mirror, her gun pointed over her shoulder, trained between his eyes.

A dangerous flicker showed in those eyes. The knife shifted to the gap between her fourth and fifth vertebrae.

'Don't try it, doc,' she warned. 'Or you'll be wearing a third eye – made of lead.'

He thought better of sliding the knife between her vertebrae. 'All finished.' The dislodged slug plinked into a metal bowl marked DOG.

She swung her legs off the ancient, grimy sofa and stood up, flexing her back and leg muscles. The oil-fired lamplight cast her shadow over a small, grubby room plastered with pornozine clippings.

Even for the Pits, she reflected, this underworld surgery was – the pits. She'd be lucky not to die of infection.

She scratched. 'You sure you got rid of all those bugs? Doesn't feel like it.'

He picked at a scab on his nose. 'Normal skin reaction. The bugs are well and truly fumigated to death.'

'Uh-huh.' Hershey shrugged on the ragged overcoat. 'And I'd have ended up just as dead without a gun in my hand. There's a thriving trade in body parts, right?'

The doctor held out his hand. 'I do a job, I expect a reward.'

She rammed the Lawgiver into his groin. 'Here's your

reward.' She watched the sweat pop in beads on his forehead. 'You get to keep your balls.'

She withdrew the pistol. The doc heaved a sigh of relief.

Sliding the gun into an inside pocket, she kicked open the door and plunged into the night.

'Bitch,' she heard the doc snarl at her departing back.

'Ultrabitch,' she corrected.

Eyes sharp on the lookout, she threaded a path through narrow, down-sloping alleyways.

Luck had been kind to her.

Some four hours had elapsed since she'd hit the Pits. No sign of pursuit from the Helmets. Sure, Justice Central was all screwed up with double trouble, but it didn't make sense that no one had tracked her down yet. Jeez, they had Spies-in-the-sky everywhere, and she was labelled as the worst kind of perp: a renegade Judge.

How come they hadn't pinned her down and drilled her full of holes?

'Ah, shut it, Barbara,' she berated herself. 'When you're handed a heap of luck, just say thanks.'

Staying clear of Pits dangers was trouble enough. She'd run foul of three gangs since the tattooed eye-suckers.

Or rather, three gangs had run foul of her. Their bodies were busy decomposing somewhere back there in the ribbon-development of shanty towns.

She checked her ammo counter. Not good. All the fancy bullets used up on the gangs. Just three standard slugs left.

Her next underworld encounter might be her last.

'Got to hold out till Dredd gets back.' She'd repeated that line more than fifty times. It didn't get any more convincing with the repetition.

If only there was somewhere *safe*.

She halted abruptly. For the first time in the Big Meg's history, there was somewhere safe in the bulging citi-blocks between the West Wall and the Atlantic Wall.

The Zone Pacifica.

Not one crime in an entire month.

Somewhere safe.

Matthew Meldrew handed over his last charity package to the Winstons of Shack 11/235, Shanty Town 497/21/396.

'You're a treasure, that's what you are, Mr Meldrew,' Mrs Winston beamed as she opened the door for him to leave.

'Not at all, Mrs Winston,' Meldrew smiled benevolently. 'We who are more fortunate must do what we can for those less blessed. The Inner Light of Grud Confraternity is only too happy to aid the poor misfortunates of this troubled city.'

Her hand clasped her roomy bosom. 'Oh, what can I say, Mr Meldrew?'

'Say nothing, Mrs Winston. Just spread the Word of Grud among your neighbours, and I will be more than recompensed.'

'Goodnight, Mr Meldrew.'

'Goodnight, Mrs Winston.'

Meldrew headed for his hover-pod with warmth in his heart and the love of Grud in his eyes.

He voice-activated the pod's plastiplex cover to swing wide open.

'Another good night's work for Grud the Firm but Fair,' he sighed, stepping into the pod and sinking into the front seat.

The vehicle tilted fractionally as he heard someone jump into the back seat.

Meldrew felt a cold circle of metal pushed into the nape of his neck. Staring into the rear-view mirror, he saw a young, black-haired woman in a ragged black overcoat.

She held a gun in her hand – a *Judge's* gun. A Lawgiver.

Her mouth smiled. Her hard grey eyes didn't.

'Take me away from all this,' she said.

* * *

Hershey's pistol sank to her side as she watched Meldrew's hover-pod glide into the night. She had knocked out his communications and preset his course to take him on a long, circular tour of Mega-City One. He wouldn't be squealing her whereabouts to Justice Central until the night was well over.

'Appreciate the ride.'

Lawgiver still in hand, she surveyed the length of Degradability Avenue that ran down the centre of the Muttering. Not a soul about. A few weeks ago, you'd have been guaranteed at least a couple of prowling gangs and several bands of muggers.

Something had emptied the Muttering's streets. Hershey could taste that something in the air. Anxiety? Fear?

'Dread,' she said.

The street *dared* you to walk down it. She took up the challenge, hearing the echo of her footfalls in the eerily deserted avenue.

Her palms sweated. She ignored them. Her heart thudded a rapid pulse. She told it to slow down. It didn't listen.

Passing an unshuttered window, she peered inside.

There were five people within: three seemed to be curled up in terror, two were evidently stone dead.

After a hesitation, she pushed open the door and strode in. The three – a woman and two men – remained in their foetal position, oblivious of her presence. Lost to the world, locked in a private nightmare.

She knelt down by one of the corpses. A small girl. The conventional wisdom of forensics insisted that you couldn't diagnose a victim of death by fright simply by looking at them. Hershey studied the stark, bulging eyes, the mouth agape in a frozen rictus, its scream unvented. And she knew.

Dead of fright.

Gently, Hershey closed the girl's eyes. She glanced at the embroidered name on the small, pink jersey: Lynn.

210

'It's all over now, Lynn,' she whispered. 'They can't hurt you any more.'

Bowing her head, she remained still and quiet for several breaths. When she finally spoke, her voice was a hoarse murmur. 'It's getting harder to be hard.'

She rose slowly, then moved to the other corpse, a man in early middle age. Lynn's father? She gave the other corpse a cursory examination. The same as the girl. Killed by fear.

Hershey let herself out of the house with slow, hushed movements. Her pace barely quickened once she was back on the street. Gaze lowered to the ground in front of her, she'd covered fifty metres before realising the Lawgiver was still in her grip.

Slipping the gun inside the overcoat, she pressed on, glancing neither to left nor right.

She was safe, sure enough. Oh yeah, she was safe. Protected by terror.

Something had imposed a ring of fear around the Muttering.

A circle of dread.

Right now, she didn't give a flying drokk about the waves of dread that beat on her. She was still thinking about Lynn.

Finally, she glanced to one side.

Her eyes narrowed. Robinson Street, a little way off down the avenue. Epicentre of the Zone Pacifica. Location of the Cafe Cesare.

Arriving at the corner of Robinson Street, she debated for a moment, then headed down its long, straight length.

Two minutes later she stood outside the cafe's open door. Someone must have removed the giant heart that Maximin reported. All that remained was a wide-brimmed hat and an extensive brown stain.

Hershey walked straight into the cafe. Easier than hanging around, letting fear build up.

A few steps inside, and she drew to a halt. Some of the

lights at the back of the cafe were on, spilling pools of illumination over purple tables and yellow-tiled floor, but leaving the rest of the area in semi-murk.

Stealthily, she moved through the cafe. And pulled to a stop after a few paces.

There was a black box on one of the round tables. She leaned over it, and a smile crossed her lips.

It was a signature-box, marked HERSHEY.

No prizes for guessing who'd left that for her to find.

Hershey allowed the box to read her palm-print and DNA, then opened it and examined the contents. A microcorder. She pressed play and listened to Joe Dredd's grim tones:

'Hershey, if you hear this, consider me dead. A while back I wondered if I'd have to take on Rico's ghost. I was wrong. The man I'm going after is – myself.'

'Toughest enemy of all,' she muttered, and followed the rest of the message up to the final lines:

'. . . If I don't make it, I know you'll put up a hell of a fight. You've got my posthumous vote for Chief Judge, if you want it. See you on the streets, Hershey.'

'See you on the streets, Joe.'

Hershey pocketed the microcorder and wove a path to the kitchen door. An instinct told her to have her gun at the ready as she pushed open the door.

A flood of yellow light streamed out of the door. The disused kitchen was ablaze with Hi-Glo wall-lights. The thick coating of dust showed that the kitchen hadn't served up food for years.

Until now.

A man squatted on the floor, dining on a giant heart. He wasn't even using a knife and fork.

Judging by his torn overcoat and battered hat, the munching diner, squatting with his back to her, was one of the city's millions of vagrants.

Hershey pocketed her gun.

The vagrant stiffened, apparently sensing her presence.

He turned round, his hand pulling something metallic from inside the overcoat.

Hershey's mind flashbacked:

She let loose a volley at the shambling shape, its hand pulling a glittering object from an inside jacket pocket . . . She saw what the lumpy-headed mutant had drawn from his jacket. Not a weapon – a plastiplex card with an embossed message:

MY NAME IS JOHN MERRECAR. I AM OF GRADE ZERO-TWO INTELLECT AND CAN ONLY UNDER-STAND VERY SIMPLE INSTRUCTIONS. PLEASE DO NOT FIRE IF I FAIL TO RESPOND TO JUSTICE OFFICERS' COMMANDS . . .

Hershey's Lawgiver was back in her hand but her finger hesitated on the trigger, the flashback stark behind her eyes.

The vagrant spun round, a Lawgiver in his grip. She registered the face the instant the muzzle fired.

Mathers. Judge Mathers, mouth dripping with blood and clogged with heart tissue.

The slug bit into her shoulder, way off target. Wild shot.

Mathers's vacant expression explained everything. The SJS Judge had lost most of his marbles.

He dropped his pistol. 'Sorry, lady,' he giggled. 'Been waiting for ya here. Eliphas told me to. Said you . . .' He gripped his head, pain creasing his forehead. 'Said you might come here. Yeah – that's it. I left the little black box where you could see it, lure you in.'

A gleam of intellectual light was dawning in Mathers's eyes. 'Found the signature-box hidden under a table. Who put it there – Dredd?' The gleam of understanding faded. He put a hand to his bloodied mouth, 'Oh, shouldn't say that name. Fear and Dread.'

Hershey thought she was catching on. Eliphas had left Mathers here in civilian disguise to catch her unawares.

But the scheme had backfired. 'How long have you waited here, Mathers? A couple of hours?'

Mathers's suddenly nervy glance darted about the kitchen. 'Hours and hours. Days and days. Years and years.'

She was certain now. The inimical aura of the Cafe Cesare, cold heart of the Zone Pacifica, had unseated his wits. He'd probably lain in wait here for an hour, at most. More than enough for the atmosphere to get to him, *into* him.

That was Mathers's problem. She wouldn't cry any tears for him.

Hershey nodded at the massive heart with a mouth-sized chunk missing. '*Bon appétit.*'

Then she backed out of the kitchen and made her way through the comparative gloom of the dining area. If Eliphas had ordered Mathers to stay on watch for her here, then Eliphas wouldn't be far away. The SJS had been one jump ahead of her, Gruddammit. They'd reasoned that a Judge on the run might head for the safety of the Zone Pacifica. And they'd been right.

With SJS hunters around, the Zone Pacifica wouldn't be so pacific. Time to run again.

On the threshold of the doorway, she heard the kitchen door creak open. She spun round fast, the Lawgiver aimed before she completed the turn.

But Mathers was unarmed as he stumbled across the room. He mumbled something.

She kept her Lawgiver trained on his heart, alert to any sudden tricks.

'They're coming,' he said.

'Who's coming?'

He cupped chunky hands around his head. '*They're coming!*'

Psychic creepy-crawlies made a steeplechase race-track of her spine. Something *was* coming.

Something wicked.

Mathers's blood-stained mouth stretched to a gaping oval, the eroded teeth on full show.

'*THEY'RE COMING!*'

A metre from where the SJS Judge swayed in fear and agony, the air shimmered.

'*THEY'RE HERE!*'

A rosy glow emanated from the murk. It spread in a pool between floor and ceiling, deepening to an angry crimson.

Then an invisible pebble was dropped into the crimson pool. Ripples in the pool.

Concentric waves of red rippled across the cafe.

Mathers caught the first wave. It lifted him off his feet and threw him to the floor. He threshed on the tiles, arms lashing, legs thumping.

The Judge was being pumped full of dread. Raw dread. His body swelled with it, belly bulging through the civvy clothes. Like a blocked bladder filling up with water, he kept on expanding.

Fit to burst.

Hershey retreated in shock. She'd witnessed more than her fair share of grisly sights in her time, but not until now had she been faced with the living essence of terror.

If it touches me, I'll die of fear.

Mathers was now unrecognisable as a human being. He had ballooned out into a round, stretched expanse of skin, the pout of his mouth emitting the piercing whistle of a cooked lobster.

The skin split at the seams. Burst apart from the inner pressure.

Pale flesh blasted in chunks from the red heart of a visceral explosion.

The red ripples accelerated their flow across the cafe.

A crimson wave sped towards Hershey's face.

She took to her heels.

Her feet devoured the metres as she sprinted down Robinson Street.

215

A backward look flipped her heart over. The red waves were rippling down the street, matching her panicked pace.

Spurring herself to greater efforts, she sprinted with all the fear of red hell in her veins.

Almost losing her footing, she skidded round the corner into Degradability Avenue.

Eyes trained on the ground in front of her, she maintained a gruelling pace with grim determination.

run-run-run-run-run-run

'HERSHEY!'

The familiar, hated voice wrenched her gaze from the ground.

She was running straight into the mouth of an SJS hover-wagon. Its wide hatch was open, revealing Eliphas and a dozen black-visored SJS executioners, each with a Widow-maker in their hands, muzzles aimed in her direction.

'Surrender, Hershey,' Eliphas ordered. 'Or – well, you know the rest.'

She darted a glance over her shoulder. The glowing, crimson waves were surging down the avenue.

'Put up your hands, Hershey!'

Her head sank in defeat.

She was between the SJS and a red tide of terror.

She'd sooner be between the Devil and the deep blue sea.

TWENTY-TWO

Dredd plunged down the glass face of the shaking tower to a boiling sea of dark yellow muck, ready and willing to suck him in.

His mind speeded faster than his fall.

The cling-pads on his hands and knees adhered on contact. If only he could reach –

He thrust a palm at the windows that blurred past. Just short.

Doubling up, he shifted his equilibrium forwards, stretched out a hand.

It made contact.

Don't press too hard, pad won't stick.

He slid down the glass, his descent slowing.

A jolt ran up his arm at the abrupt deceleration, threatening to pop his shoulder from its socket.

He slapped the other hand on to the glass. Pressed the cling-padded knees to the surface.

The slide eased to a halt. He glanced down.

'Drokk!'

The Secretion was a mere few metres under his feet. A tentacular green arm writhed out of the yellow slush and stroked the sole of his boot. More tentacles lashed out of the stinking guck. A distorted, cephalopod head emerged in the wake of the threshing limbs. The eyes in the head had a human quality, awash with self-loathing, self-horror.

It was one of the rebels, metamorphosed into the thing he most feared, locked inside his personal nightmare made flesh. The sloppy slit of a mouth parted and gave vent to a scream that chilled Dredd's normally chill-free blood.

Just one splash from that seething stew, and he'd join the hideous company below, changed into his worst fear.

The flood was rising fast. Even as he looked, it mounted almost half a metre.

'Joe!' Anderson yelled from twenty metres up. '*Move!*'

'Don't need you to tell me that,' he growled, crawling up the glass surface. A few centimetres of glass was all that separated him from the nightmare fluid inside Twin Tower Two, brimful from top to bottom, like a bottle of poison.

A violent shudder of the skyscraper almost threw him. Tower One had crashed against its twin, punching a Titan-sized hole in its side and straining the building frame beyond its limits.

It wouldn't be long before Tower One brought Tower Two tumbling down. He'd better not be on it when the crash came.

Dredd glanced up at the tower's summit, tight against the Undercity's flat, plascrete roof. Once at the top, then what? They couldn't go inside – the floors were flooded with the Secretion. As for crawling across the roof, no way were his cling-pads up to that.

'You sure you know what you're doing, Anderson?' he bellowed.

'Always,' she shouted back. 'Now *move!*'

With a grunt, he moved.

Hand by hand, knee by knee, Dredd crawled up the remaining tower of the World Trade Center.

From time to time, he threw a downward glance. He was ascending quicker than the roiling stew that deluged Manhattan. But the yellow broth rose steadily, metre by metre.

Teeth gritted, he fought to catch up with Giant, the lowest of the climbers. Far from catching up, he couldn't match Giant's speed.

It fitted in with everything Dredd had seen of this world's fighters. They were tougher, stronger and faster than their Mega-City One equivalents. It seemed like psionics enhanced performance way beyond anything imagined by Tek labs in his own world.

All the same, he kept on trying to catch up.

Dredd was halfway up the skyscraper when one of the windows above burst, unleashing a crud-yellow jet. Two of the climbers took the jet full in the face and hurtled backwards off the glass face of the tower.

They screamed and threshed a long time before they hit the turbulent surface.

A stream of Secretion gushed down the building's exterior. A couple more men fell foul of the cascade, kicking and yelling as they dropped.

Dredd had scrambled sideways the instant the window shattered. The tumbling fluid missed him by a fraction before he side-crawled clear. A quick upward glance revealed the rest had done the same.

Dredd kept on climbing with renewed resolve.

The yellow sea continued to rise, drowning Manhattan's smaller skyscrapers. Tower Two strained its joints as its crashed twin threatened to push it over. And the windows were groaning under the pressure of the Towering Flood.

He concentrated on ascending, hand by hand, knee by knee, fixing his eyes on the next move.

Don't think about what might happen. Keep going.

He was Dredd, and he never gave up.

Hand by hand. Keep going.

'Joe!' he heard Anderson shout.

He glanced up. Anderson and a few of her companions were perched at the summit of the tower. Just twenty metres above. Giant was a few metres ahead of him, still scaling the glassy face. Dredd had almost caught up with him.

'You don't do too badly when you put your mind to it,'

Anderson called down. 'That's what it's all about, Joe — the *mind*.'

'Yeah,' he grunted.

By the time he reached the roof, he was almost level with Giant.

'Now what?' Dredd demanded of Anderson. 'What do we do? Fly?'

'Turn into a fly,' she said. 'A fly on the ceiling. See those tiny X signs in the plascrete? X marks the spot. Each spot contains an embedded bio-attraction plate. Place your hands and knees on each X, and you'll crawl like a fly across the ceiling. Keep to the path, and you won't fall. Mind you, it's murder on the shoulder muscles.'

He squinted through the visor. 'A magnetic path?'

'Of sorts.'

'How far does it go?'

'That's the bad news: about seven hundred metres to the nearest melt-hole plug.'

He threw a look at the ever-rising fluid. 'Then we'd better get going.'

'Yes,' she responded, thrusting a hand on to the first X. 'We'd better. It's a race between us and the tide. Come on, Joe, you follow me.'

An ominous groan reverberated from the tower's steel bones. 'Hurry!' she yelled. 'Damn thing's going to topple any second.'

Dredd was right on Cassandra Anderson's heels. Corey followed him, muttering, 'Get a move on.'

The last of the survivors had barely got his boot off the tower when it finally gave way with a thunderous roar. Mercifully, it fell away from the human flies on the roof.

But the almighty splash it made threw up murky spumes that drenched the rearguard.

Howling as if burned by acid, seven of the band tumbled, fluid-soaked, into the waves.

Of those that had started the climb, only half remained.

The rest were alive, down in the fluid, but would have been better off dead.

After three hundred metres, every muscle in Dredd's body was screaming blue and red murder. He ignored them and kept on going.

He could hear Giant's huffs and puffs over the booming of the mounting sea.

Corey, following in his wake, winced with pain.

Even Anderson was showing signs of strain. She glanced over her shoulder. 'We've got to speed up,' she urged. 'Damn Secretion's rising too fast. It'll swallow us at the pace we're going.'

Setting an example, Anderson set to with an iron will, covering ten metres in under half a minute.

Dredd, through sheer bloody-mindedness, kept pace with her.

'A hundred metres to go,' Anderson called back. 'Don't flag now. Drokking Secretion's a couple of waves away.'

Dredd glanced down for a split second. Too right. The stinking yellow fluid couldn't be more than ten metres from the ceiling.

A disinterested onlooker wouldn't have given a hundred to one for their chances.

That didn't bother Dredd. As far as he was concerned, you made your own chances.

'Get a move on, Anderson,' he barked. 'You're slowing me down.'

'Stop showing off,' she riposted.

At that moment something big and grey and sluggy reared out of the yellow muck, an agonized human face locked in its slugskin folds.

It sank back with a loud slurp.

'Oh Grud,' Anderson groaned. 'Jonathon. That's – that *was* Jonathon. The one thing he was afraid of was slugs. Never understood why – oh *Grud*.'

'Good friend of yours?' Dredd asked.

'More than a friend. One of my lovers.'

The sight hadn't put Anderson off her stride. If anything, she pushed herself along at a more frantic rate.

'About thirty metres to go,' she yelled out. 'Move, move, move!'

Dredd gave the swelling flood a couple of minutes, tops, before it lapped their backs. Thirty metres in under two minutes was one hell of a gruelling prospect.

An insectile limb, sprouting black barbs of hair, extruded its articulated length from the Secretion. The clawed extremity skimmed Anderson's yellow mop of hair.

'Their shapes are starting to affect their minds,' Corey cried out. 'They're turning hostile.'

'I know,' Anderson said. 'I can feel it.'

Dredd barely caught her following remark:

'I can feel their torment.'

He cast a glance at the yellow swill beneath. Less than five metres from the roof.

The heaving surface of the Secretion wouldn't have to rise the full five metres to reach them – *change* them; less than four metres would do the dire trick.

'How much further?' he roared.

'Twelve metres or so.'

'For Grud's sake, Anderson, shift it! Break records!'

'I'm breaking them,' she snarled. 'It's you that's slowing Corey and the rest down. So move your butt, lawman!'

True enough, she was drawing away from him.

He squeezed every last drop of energy from his powerful physique, and made up some of the distance.

'Here!' Anderson exclaimed, halting under a small circle inscribed in the plascrete. She shut her eyes, furrowed her brow in concentration.

Searing light flashed from her palms, and the plascrete flowed away from her hand, receding into a round hole.

Dredd expected her to climb up into the hole, but she moved to the other side. 'Quick, Joe. Get in.'

'No, you go first.'

She rolled her eyes and groaned. 'You're the weakest.

222

The rest of us might have a chance of affecting the mind of a hostile creature from down there. You wouldn't. Now get in!'

Scowling furiously, he clambered into the hole and emerged in a tunnel.

Peering down, he saw that the turbulent fluid was within licking distance of the roof.

Then Corey's head blocked out the view as she hauled herself out of the hole.

'Where's Anderson?' he asked.

'She'll wait till last, of course,' Corey replied, eyeing him curiously. 'What do you expect a leader to do?'

Giant emerged, barely squeezing his burly shoulders through the gap.

After Giant –

Nothing.

'What's going on down there?' Dredd muttered.

Still nothing.

Just a noxious swirl of puke-yellow.

Then Anderson's head appeared. She swung herself up with athletic grace.

Her expression was bleak.

'They've gone,' Corey said. 'I felt it.'

Anderson nodded. 'A sudden surge in the fluid. Gulped them down in one go. Tierney called out to me as he fell.'

Corey glanced at Dredd. 'One of Cassandra's lovers.'

He opened his mouth to say something, then slammed it shut.

In the blink of an eye, Anderson's features hardened. 'Come on, it's four of us against the world. Let's die with style.'

Giant moved over to Dredd as Cassandra Anderson strode up the tunnel, fists clenched at her sides.

'You see that, man? Maybe you begin to understand what's so special about that woman.'

Dredd followed in Anderson's tracks. 'I always did.'

Lengthening his stride, the Mega-City Judge drew alongside the rebel leader.

'Anderson?'

She stopped, swung round. 'Yeah?' The anger in her sparked from her gaze.

'Now that I've seen what the Chief Judge is capable of – what he did to the people down there – I've made up my mind whose side I'm on.'

Cassandra Anderson glared at Judge Dredd. 'You with me or against me?'

Dredd stared Anderson right in her blue-grey eyes.

'With you. I'll kill every Judge I see, then rip out the Chief Judge's heart.'

TWENTY-THREE

A helmeted head the size of a mountain ascended from the summit of Judgement Central.

Dreadhead, seat of Judge Dread's power on Earth and in the heavens, made a turmoil of the frosty cloud that canopied the City of Dread.

It glided over the graniteen spires and gulfs of the buildings psych-moulded from the Chief Judge's own consciousness. The colossal head, its mouth stretched wide, seemed to glare down on the mad fushion of Gothic and Cubist architecture that was Dreadcity.

'CREEPS!' blared a titanic voice from Dreadhead's biosteel mouth. 'START CREEPING.'

Out they crept, from the stalagmite warrens, on hands and knees. The multitudes of the Nameless, identically dressed in grey uniforms, only differing in the Judgement number branded on their foreheads at birth. They were nameless, but not numberless.

'CRAWL!' bellowed the cavernous mouth.

In unison, eight hundred million people dropped on to their bellies and crawled, shivering in the biting cold.

For long minutes, they slithered over the icy ground.

'LOOK UP!' the voice of Dread commanded.

As one, they looked up at the shroud of mist.

'SECTOR 59 IS FIVE PER CENT BELOW PRODUCTION TARGET. FIVE PER CENT OF THE CREEPS OF SECTOR 59 WILL BE PUNISHED. WATCH AND LEARN, NAMELESS CREEPS.'

A bolt of blue-white lightning forked out from Dreadhead's mouth, cracking the sky as it swooped over the horizon to let fall its wrath on Sector 59.

A psionic holo-screen appeared on the underbelly of the cloud canopy. It depicted an area of Sector 59 in close-up.

On the screen in the clouds, blue streaks of radiance swept through the ranks of the sector's Nameless. Most were unaffected. One in twenty fell victim to the cold fire from above.

Five per cent of the sector's grey-uniformed masses tumbled to the ground, limbs threshing as their torsos expanded.

The swelling bodies burst through the thin uniforms, the reddening flesh pulsing with mounting beats.

Arms and legs retracted into the burgeoning hearts.

Soon, a million boulder-sized hearts pumped on the ground. They bled richly.

'Seen enough?' Cassandra Anderson muttered through tight lips, gazing at the gruesome holo-show in the sky.

Dredd stood motionless, visored gaze fixed on the clouds. 'I get the picture.'

In the cover of a sculpted cave near the summit of a stalagmite block, Dredd, Anderson and their two comrades in arms viewed Chief Judge Dread's grisly lesson.

'Is this usual?' Dredd asked.

Anderson shook her head. 'It's usually worse.' Abruptly, she turned to Corey. 'Can you sense an ultraterror leakage?'

'Yes,' Corey replied. 'I'm not sure of the location.'

'I think I can sense it. The Cafe Cesare fistula. If I'm right, Judge Dread's pouring ultraterror into Mega-City One.'

'He's messing with my city?' Dredd burst out. 'What will ultraterror do to the Big Meg?'

Anderson stared him right in the visor. 'Kill everyone in the city. Kill them with waves of concentrated fear.'

He stuck out his jaw. 'The citizens might crumble, but the Judges don't scare easy. They'll handle it.'

Expelling a sharp breath that steamed in the gelid air, Anderson folded her arms. 'When are you going to grow up? There are some things that kill, no matter how you try to tough them out. Anyone that's capable of experiencing fear will be struck stone-dead by ultraterror. You've experienced fear plenty of times – I can feel its echo in you. Ergo, ultraterror can kill you, and any other Judge.'

He remained impassive. 'Maybe.'

Anderson grimaced. '"Maybe," the man says. *Maybe*. Listen – a slight ultraterror overspill has been affecting your world for weeks now. It's a sure bet at least ten per cent of the people will be dead of fright in its area of influence. And that wasn't much more than a sniff of the stuff. Now the stuff itself is flooding through.'

Dredd shook his head. 'I'm still not convinced. If ultraterror's so lethal, how come the Nameless aren't dead of fright?'

'Can't you work that out yourself? The terror waves can be modulated, of course. Here in Dreadcity, the Conglomeration sends out signals on a low frequency, about three per cent of maximum. In Mega-City One, the dose will be well over ninety per cent. That's thirty percent above anyone's level of endurance.'

Judge Dredd glanced over the frosty city, his mouth a grim scowl. 'Okay, I'll take it on trust. I figure Anderson's double won't put me far wrong.'

His stare returned to the giant head in the sky. A pale object emerged from the gaping mouth. 'What the drokk's that?'

'You wanted to know what a Fist is,' Giant said. 'Now you know.'

As the object swooped closer, Dredd discerned that the Fist was exactly what its name implied. A fist. A huge chunk of white stone in the shape of a tightly clenched fist.

'It's an attack craft,' Anderson said. 'Fifty metres' span

of reinforced marbleen, bristling with psionic panic-inducers and body-morphers. Sometimes, just for show, it punches buildings or enemy aircraft – not that there are any enemy aircraft left.'

Dredd curled his lip. 'A warship shaped like a fist, and it punches things?'

She shrugged. 'Different world, different rules. Anyway, they're what *you* would have created if you'd taken Judge Dread's path.'

'The guy's a psycho,' he snorted. His scowl was never more pronounced. 'What twisted him? Come to that – why's he so afraid of clones? There's got to be a reason . . .'

'Joe?' Anderson was studying him closely.

'Uh-huh.'

'I can't go into Judge Dread's psychology now, but there's a more urgent matter. At a rough guess, I'd say ultraterror waves will wipe out ten thousand Mega-City One citizens in the next hour. Twenty thousand the hour after that. Then forty thousand. Eighty thousand. Before five hours are up, the body count will be on the way to two million. And that'll be just phase *one* of his invasion. Are you willing to take any risk to save your continuum?'

'You name it, I'll do it.'

'Okay, then go into the open. Attract the Fist's attention. And get yourself captured.'

Dredd squared his shoulders. 'Right.' And marched out into the open air, bellowing at the Fist.

'I'm in love. I am. This time it's the real thing. From now on, it's owls all the way.'

Caligula gazed longingly at his new altar, a holo-image of Judge Hershey, draped in a white himation, adorned with a helmet of gold and flanked by candles and the owls of Athena, Goddess of Wisdom.

'Here we go again,' sighed Drusilla, propped disconsolately on a couch in the Hollywood-Roman interior of Caligula's quarters.

Agrippinilla glowered at Hershey's august holo-image, three times life-size. 'Just because you saw her in skimpy black leathereen,' she grumbled. 'A flash of backside and you're anybody's.'

He swirled round, arms wrapped around his breast-plated chest, head flung back in a theatrical pose. 'Speak not thus of the woman I love. Nay, more than woman. A goddess. How blind I've been! Barbara Hershey is Athena. The warrior virgin, spear in hand. Did you see her battle with the hag-goddess Hecate, disguised as McGruder? What martial skill, what grace divine!'

'Whatever happened to Aphrodite-Helena Bonham-Carter?' grumped Lesbia.

He twirled a hand in the air. 'Oh, that was no more than an idle fancy of my young and foolish youth, when I was a callow and gadding thing.'

'It was only a few hours ago,' mumbled Lesbia.

'What was that?' he snapped.

Lesbia was suddenly all sweetness and light. 'Nothing, darling Little Boots. I also see how high and awesome is Athena-Hershey. How – how blind I've been not to spot it before.'

'Hmm . . . well, I only just spotted it myself,' he conceded. 'And I'm a god. No wonder you missed it.'

His entranced gaze returned to the deified holo-figure of Hershey. 'Leave me now, exalted sister-wives. Go and disport yourselves in the Anti-Gravitorium pool or something. I must commune alone with Athena.'

Left to the solitude of his temporary temple, Caligula ran shy fingers through the auburn shock of his hair which always gave the impression that he'd just seen a ghost.

'Athena – or may I call you Hershey? I can? I'm so pleased. Well you'll be delighted to hear that I've chosen you as my wife. What did you say? Oh *no* – perish the thought. Not one of my *ordinary* wives. My Top Wife.'

He adopted a winsome smile. 'Hershey – may I call you Barbara? Oh, thank you. Thank you, *Barbara*. I've always believed that husband and wife should be on first-name terms. So, er, Barbara, I think you put up a spiffing show against that old bag McGruder. And I really think it was very bad of Chief Judge Dread to subject you to the pain of the asphyxion collar and the indignity of the skimpy black leathereen. Mind you, I expect to see a lot of you in that gear, just between the two of us, or with a few suitable friends, if you catch my drift. Now, as I'm a god and you're a goddess, we can't tolerate the present state of affairs with an inferior like the Chief Judge at the top. What I'd suggest we do is – '

Caligula.

He jumped at the sharp psi-call in his head. The shock of it sobered him to the dangers of voicing anti-Dread sentiments in the heart of Dreadhead.

'Patchwork,' he hissed softly. 'I told you never to call me here.'

Answer me in psi-speech.

Caligula pouted his lips, sulked. 'Can't. Not in the mood.'

Then listen. I have received intelligence that a last-ditch attack is about to be launched on the Chief Judge.

Caligula's eyes darted about nervously. 'It's not safe. Dreadhead's psi-sensors can pick you up – '

Now don't utter another word unless it's yes or no, understand? This psi-call is scrambled. Virtually impossible to intercept and decode. I've received a similarly scrambled call less than a minute ago from Cassandra Anderson. She has a man with her – that man is Joe Dredd, the Chief Judge's better self, and the man whom he fears, deep in his warped soul. When the time comes, I'll give you the signal. If you wish to be the Chief Judge, you must side with Anderson and Dredd, and respond promptly to my signal. Understood?

'Can't be bothered,' Caligula said, forgetting the simple

yes-no injunction. 'Not in the mood. Some other time. Don't feel quite up to snuff at the moment.'

There won't be another moment, Caligula. It's now or never. Remember, the only safe man in this world is the Chief Judge. While Dread rules, you live at his whim. A bold strike now and you can make yourself the Lord of the Seven Suns. Fail to act, and sooner or later Dread will have you killed.

'I can't be killed,' muttered Caligula. 'I'm a god.'

Well . . . You can be killed in your human form. That happened to you over two thousand years ago, in your first incarnation, remember? Hacked to death by the Palatine Guard. Not a pleasant experience.

Caligula's blue eyes bugged. 'That's a thought.'

I – I sense that you're worshipping a goddess, and a woman. Athena, is it? And – Hershey. That right?

'Yes, that's right, clever boots.'

Hershey's one of Dread's bedmates, against her will, I suspect. While the Chief Judge lives, you will never have your Hershey-goddess by your side. Think on that.

Caligula rubbed his chin, eyes fixed on Athena-Hershey. 'All right, I'm thinking on it. Now go away, you're bringing on one of my headaches.'

Then when the signal to arms comes, you'll answer?

The Nova Roman emperor folded his arms and grimaced. 'I'll think about it.'

A last thought, then I'm gone. If for no one else, do it for your new goddess, Athena-Hershey.

Caligula continued to stroke his smooth chin. 'Hmm,' he murmured, eyeing Hershey's image with a speculative air.

TWENTY-FOUR

'Out of my way,' she snapped, bumping into two young Judges as she left Chief Judge Dread's quarters.

Hershey, reinstated Judge Governor of SinoDread, was back in uniform and bristling with anger. Anger at the man-bitch McGruder, anger at Grud-Almighty Chief Judge Dread, anger at the whole damned world.

Her skin still crawled from Dread's touch. Almost an hour she'd endured on Dread's bed, she and Judge Perrier playing yes-sir-no-sir, one on each side of the Chief Judge on top of the sentient mattress. Dread's playthings. It was all right for Perrier; she *liked* that sort of thing.

Strange woman, Perrier. Used to be a good Judge before Dread got to her. Since then, she played the role of bimbo to the hilt. No one had seen her without bright red lipstick on her lips for at least five years.

Stuff Perrier. Hershey wanted to indulge her anger against Chief Judge Dread. But she had to be careful what she thought, despite her – protection.

Anger directed against the Chief Judge was suicidal in Dreadcity, let alone inside Dreadhead. Suicidal for anyone except Hershey, and the hyperpsychic Judge Karyn.

Karyn had been shielding Hershey's mind for months. Hiding all of Hershey's rage and resentment against the Chief Judge's absolutist rule under a mask of submission. As SinoDread Governor, out of Dread's immediate range of awareness, she'd exercised a little justice when she could, as much as she thought she might get away with. She'd reckoned without his spies. And McGruder.

If it wasn't for Karyn's mind-shield, Hershey would have been fed to the Conglomeration or inducted into the Orchestra by now. Nothing so merciful as execution.

She rubbed her neck, free of the asphyxion collar and rapi-healed of its effects, but with the strangulation memory embedded in the flesh. She could still feel that tightening collar.

She had a rage in her, and ached to let it loose. Slaughterhouse Six was the place for it, just two corridors away.

Heading for Slaughterhouse Six, Hershey approached one of the doors to Resyk Entertainment. The corridor was crowded with Judges on their way to the savage amusement of Resyk. Ghouls. Sick ghouls.

'Coming to Resyk, Judge Governor?' asked Judge Merriman, tapping her elbow as he drew alongside. 'Should be a good show tonight. Family groups.'

Hershey adopted a convincing smile. 'Love to. But a Judge Governor's got a lot of duties. Some other time.'

'Last chance you'll get for quite a while. The population of Mega-City One will be dead in a few hours. Then the invasion starts in earnest. Not much time for Resyk fun after that.'

She hoped the smile wasn't slipping. 'Like I said – some other time.'

'Congratulations on your reinstatement!' he called out as she walked away. 'Heard about your victory in the trial by combat. It's the talk of Dreadhead.'

Glancing over her shoulder, she shrugged. 'It was nothing.'

The corridors soon emptied as she neared Slaughterhouse Six, one of ten psionic firing-ranges in the vast labyrinth of Dreadhead.

The door of living shadow parted at her approach, whispered shut as a she entered the slaughterhouse. Pulling the Exterminans psionic rifle from her boot holster, she warily scanned the murky, multi-pillared spaces. There was a lot of blood on the floor. Judges' blood.

Slaughterhouses had superseded the old holo-firing-ranges. In the original holo-shoots, no Judge could be killed. The holo-targets with their holo-bullets were simply that: holograms; tricks of the light. Slaughterhouses changed all that. Psi-generated attackers, solid as biosteel while the system was activated, replaced holo-targets. Their weapons were psi-generated too. If they hit, it was death by ultraterror, pain induction or organ dysfunction – such as heart enlargement, Dread's favourite form of organic disruption.

You had to keep your wits about you in a slaughterhouse, or you ended up dead. No better way to hone the reflexes.

A movement from behind one of the gargoyle-sculpted pillars.

Hershey crouched and aimed her Exterminans in a single, eye-blink motion, mind pre-attuned to the rifle's psionic amplifier. The figure emerged from thick shadow.

A helmeted Judge.

One of the few female Judges.

Hershey swung her Exterminans to one side. 'Dekker,' she nodded, hiding the hostility she felt.

Dekker, a few years Hershey's junior, was the only female Judge to copy Dread's habit of never removing her helmet, at least in public. The Chief Judge was Dekker's supreme role model. Dread's girl. And she was McGruder's sidekick and bedmate. Dekker was ambitious, and it paid to be close to McGruder even if it churned your stomach.

'Hershey,' Dekker acknowledged, tone as cold as the twist of her mouth.

'Still hiding behind your helmet, Dekker? Extra protection from psi-fire, huh? Why not take it off and run the extra risks, show what you're made of?

Dekker's icy expression was as fixed as her helmet visor.

'You're playing an old tune, Hershey. Let's play with fire and see who wins. First to fifty?' She lowered into a crouch, visored gaze roving the dark spaces, Exterminans at the ready. 'Your call, *Barbara*.'

Hershey's nervous system went on red alert as she delivered the activation code:

'Carnal Carnival.'

Slaughterhouse Six erupted into the noise, colour and mayhem of a Carnal Carnival. The slaughterhouse's figures and settings were one step away from reality. A short step.

The Nameless, bombarded with lust and rage, went berserk at Carnival time, inflamed from the Nameless to the Reckless, numbers exchanged for bizarre personae. The lid clamped on their unconscious was yanked off, and all hell burst forth. A regular Pandora's Box.

Dressed in grotesque clothes psych-woven from graniteen, their anatomies freed to extrude prolific flesh weapons, the Reckless were a tricky handful even for a Judge.

The terror twins Blockhead and Clockhead stormed at Dekker, their transformed physiologies drinking in the Exterminans' ultraterror bursts like milk sweetened with honey.

A clownish figure cavorted in the twins' wake, wearing a totem pole of stacked human heads as novel headgear for his shaven scalp.

But Hershey was concerned with the Reckless that charged her from the left. As a Nameless, she was a grandmother, number 23/57/649746. As a Reckless, she was one of the most formidable killers in Dread's megalopolis: Bizzie-Lizzie.

Bizzie-Lizzie was the most busy woman in the Carnal Carnival. Busy committing every crime known to history, and a few more she'd invented herself. She was always in a frantic hurry to get through her murderous chores.

'So much to do, so little time,' fussed grey-haired Bizzie-

Lizzie, her stocky body clanking with a small armoury. Her mouth opened wide and a brain-seeker dart whizzed out, homing on Hershey's helmetless head.

Wrong weapon, despite her lack of energy-shielded helmet. At the precise nanosecond, Hershey raised her gauntleted hand in front of her head. The uniform's force shield atomised the dart on contact.

In the ensuing second, Hershey wiped out four Carnival grotesques that rushed in on both sides.

'So much to do, so little time.' Bizzie-Lizzie's purple-and-yellow-striped tongue protruded in an elongating streak, sizzling with psychic menace. Streaks of purple and yellow lightning flashed from the prehensile tongue.

A burst of blue-white light from the Exterminans met Bizzie-Lizzie's striped lightning halfway. The Exterminans' psi-charge drove the striped lightning back to its source.

Blinding radiance spilled through cracks in the manic grannie.

'So much to die, so little – '

Bizzie-Lizzie blew apart.

A figure streaking from the right . . .

She spun, squeezing the trigger. And released her finger at the last instant.

A Judge.

Lose five points if you shoot a psi-generated Judge.

Lose your *life* if you shoot a real Judge sharing the slaughterhouse.

The psionic Judge jumped out of sight.

A gang stormed into the vacated space.

Hershey made short work of the gang of many-headed monopeds before the next real threat showed itself in the shape of a small, thin boy in a suit of razor-blades.

Whipper-Snapper.

Whipper-Snapper hurtled at Hershey as if a speed-of-light monster was biting his backside.

236

'Don't want to!' he screeched. 'Shan't! Gimme gimme gimme!'

She fired a psi-blast. The animated little brat, quick as you like, dodged the blast.

A flock of razors flew from Whipper-Snapper's suit, Hershey-bound.

'*Now* you'll be sorry!' he shrieked. 'Gimme gimme gimme!'

She somersaulted over the lethal flight of razors, simultaneously firing a psionic burst at Whipper-Snapper's zigzagging, hip-hopping figure.

'Gimme – '

He detonated and was heard no more.

Hershey landed on her feet, and blinked blood from her eyes. A few of the razors had sliced her face. Luckily, her eyes had been spared.

Demondwell and his Fallen Angels dropped from the arched roof. By the time they reached the floor, they were already vaporising in a continuous spray from the Exterminans.

Hershey's body count soon mounted up: forty five, forty six . . .

'You're dead, you *slag*,' snarled Yob, leaping on her back, his knife-fingers flickering.

She rammed the Exterminans muzzle in his mouth, and he was wiped out of existence.

'Forty-seven.'

'Fifty!' Dekker shouted out. 'Terminate Carnal Carnival.'

The hosts of the Reckless disappeared.

Slaughterhouse Six became its shadowy, silent self.

The scores appeared, glowing in mid-air:

Hershey	Dekker
47 Reckless	49 Reckless
0 Judges	1 Judge
Score: 47	Score: 44

'Tough luck,' Hershey said, permitting herself a smile. 'Some of those Judges come and go so fast you don't know who you've hit until the scores come up.'

She holstered the Exterminans and strode out of Slaughterhouse Six.

'Better luck next time, Dekker.'

The living shadow parted to permit her exit.

Dekker stared through her reflective visor at Hershey's departing figure, and didn't speak a word.

Minutes after Hershey's departure, Dekker still lingered in the slaughterhouse.

You think you're clever, Hershey, she thought. You're not so clever. Not clever at all.

I aimed to take out one Judge, *Barbara*. Preset the Memory before you arrived. The Judge I killed was you. This time, a holo-image. Next time –

'For real.'

McGruder wanted Hershey to meet with an accident. If Dekker obliged, McGruder would nominate her as Deputy Judge Governor of EastDread.

In all the activity preluding the continuum invasion, an accident would be easy to arrange. The Conglomeration, which normally scanned the minds of every Dreadhead Judge, was directing most of its energies towards Mega-City One and the world it inhabited. No time to keep track of each individual psyche, not unless you were on the List.

Hershey was on Dread's list of potential traitors; Dekker wasn't. Hershey had to guard her thoughts. Dekker could think what she liked.

You're a dead woman, Hershey.

'Civil War!' she voice-activated Slaughterhouse Six, initiating a holo-show of renegade Judges battling it out with loyal Judgement troops.

The pillared hall boiled with psionic Judges, the renegades distinguished by a small black raven motif on the red of the helmet nose-guard.

Each rebellious Judge wore a different face, bore a different name on the golden badge.

But Dekker saw only one face, only one name:
HERSHEY
Dekker fired a quick psionic burst.
Killed Hershey.
Fired again.
Killed Hershey again.
And again.
And again . . .

An appreciative roar issued from inside Resyk Entertainment. The show had begun.

Hershey halted momentarily in the corridor, flicked a sour glance at the door to Resyk, then moved on to the black door at the end of the passage. The door led to a speed-chute. The chute would take her to the Conglomeration Domain near the base of Dreadhead. In Chamber 265 of the Domain, Judge Karyn was awaiting her arrival.

There had been a time, not that long ago, when Hershey would have turned Karyn in on a charge of treason.

But times – and Hershey – had changed.

Strange, Hershey reflected. Strange how a single encounter can change you. But then, encounters with yourself didn't happen every day.

Her experiences as Governor of SinoDread had inspired the first stirrings of rebellion. A few weeks in the job and she started to see a hundred ways that she could improve on Dread's regime. That was when Karyn had come calling, on DreadCourt business. It had been a fortuitous meeting. Karyn had perceived Hershey's growing misgivings, and confided her own opposition to the Chief Judge and all he stood for. Hershey wanted to know if there were other malcontents, aside from Anderson's crew.

Just two others, Karyn informed her. One was Caligula.

The self-styled emperor of Nova Roma was the only man insane enough to believe he could oust Judge Dread as Chief Judge, and Dread, so taken with Caligula's entertaining madness, failed to note the Roman emperor's native cunning. Frequently, there was method in Caligula's madness, and madness in Dread's method.

The other was the mysterious Patchwork, Caligula's secret adviser. Karyn had been unable to read his mind, but his utter hatred of Chief Judge Dread radiated from him like solar flares.

After the disclosures Karyn had psi-shielded Hershey's mind, hiding the subversive intent from the prying attentions of the Conglomeration. Such intent was death, if discovered.

In the end, Hershey had decided on escape. How could anyone take on Judge Dread and survive? He was the most invulnerable man in history. Best get out while the going was good.

There were areas in the Conglomeration Domain, close to the loathsome computer, where power could be drawn from the Conglomeration to continuum-hop to the precise location of your double. She'd leaped the dimensions and landed directly behind the Mega-City One Hershey. But for her plan to succeed she needed to push the Mega-City Hershey into Dread's continuum, then take her place in Mega-City One.

Without that transference, she wouldn't last a minute in the Mega-City before she was dragged back to her home continuum. Each Hershey had to be in one continuum. It all boiled down to balancing the equation.

Equation balanced, she'd have been up and running. Taken flight for the furthest habitable planet on the celestial map. It would have taken Judge Dread many years to conquer all the known planets of the alternative universe. She'd have been free and safe all that time. Who knows, she might have had the opportunity to form an effective resistance movement.

Yeah – the plan was all worked out.

But it hadn't worked: defeated on the first move. Her double was weak, by Dreadhead standards, but she'd fought like a panther. Hershey was propelled back to Dreadhead and a heap of trouble.

But, in retrospect, she'd gained something from the encounter. The Hershey of Mega-City One might be a tough cookie in her own world, but she was a mild, kindly *saint* compared to her counterpart.

As governor of SinoDread, Hershey's notion of mercy was not randomly killing too many people in one day, or occasionally cutting short a torture interrogation with a slit throat.

The Hershey of Mega-City One cared about Justice. She cared about individual people, even the nonentities. That sense of care had haunted Judge Governor Hershey since that briefest of encounters. The sheer force of her double's concern had knocked the Judge Governor's psi-enhanced senses for six.

She had simply never imagined that Judges could be like that. Or perhaps Dread's influence had made her forget.

Chief Judge Dread had done things his way for years. He was the Law Incarnate.

Now there was another game in town: another Law. Judge Dredd.

Judge Dredd versus Judge Dread.

Sure, the word was that the Secretion had drowned him, along with Anderson's army.

But Karyn, next to Judge Omar, was the most powerful empath in Dreadhead, and she sensed that both Dredd and Anderson were alive.

The Chief Judge wasn't having it his own way for once. It was time to strike. Now or never.

A brief conference with Karyn, and Hershey would make the first move.

It was a hell of a long shot, but if it worked she would achieve her ambition.

Hershey would become Chief Judge.

She'd be a good Chief Judge.

She wouldn't execute *nearly* as many people as Judge Dread.

Karyn tried not to give in to fear as she waited in Chamber 265 of the Conglomeration Domain.

But fear was in the very molecules of the air and an empath had little choice but to inhale the fear.

Was it possible that the Conglomeration had pierced her defences, and in piercing hers, probed Hershey's inner thoughts also?

But she'd taken such trouble to protect herself from the Conglomeration's attention: thrown all her resources into the effort.

One thing was sure. McGruder and Dekker were plotting Hershey's death: McGruder the will, Dekker the instrument. While keeping track of Hershey, Karyn had felt Dekker's mind way up in Slaughterhouse Six. The slaughterhouse's concentrated psionics had revealed Dekker's mind in sharp relief:

Kill Hershey.

Kill Hershey again.

And again.

And again.

Hurry up, she urged Hershey. Get here fast. Got to warn you.

She's near. Be here any second.

Footsteps outside the door.

The door *whished* open.

Someone walked into the Chamber.

It wasn't Hershey.

And Karyn realised she was right to be afraid.

Part Five

Dead Men's Boots

'Be bloody, bold, and resolute;
Laugh to scorn
The power of man, for none of woman born
Shall harm Macbeth.'

William Shakespeare
Macbeth: Act 4, Scene 1

TWENTY-FIVE

Resyk Entertainment had begun, and the show was on the rollers.

The fifty-metre-wide rubbereen belt carried its cargo of Nameless creeps to the psych-morphed Mouth. Paralysed, and fully conscious, the creeps screamed their terror of the approaching meat-grinder of a mouth, framed with fifty-metre lips.

Laughter and jeers rang from the graniteen of Resyk's nightmare-sculpted walls and vast, vaulted roof. The Judges of Dreadhead, crowding Resyk's seven galleries, were relishing the creeps' anguish to the full.

Terror was the name of the show.

The Conglomeration gave out terror in abundance.

In turn, the Conglomeration needed to be fed. It required the nourishment of stark fear and agony in the flesh of those consigned to the Resyk belt.

As the Nameless were swallowed by the Mouth and chopped, sawn and crushed in the bioplast Stomach, psionics sucked out the secretions of pain and fear and pumped them through ducts into the pulsing mass of the Conglomeration.

Fear and pain were bread and wine to the Conglomeration.

And the torment of the souls on the moving belt was a savoury experience for the Judges on the seven-storeyed balconies.

But this was just a taster. The main item was soon to follow.

A cheer went up as another creep materialised from nowhere, slipping through the interdimensional net. Another Waker from Mega-City One Resyk, propelled from the Mega-City recycling plant and drawn to its Dreadcity equivalent by sheer terror and the remorseless pull of the Conglomeration.

The Waker, a middle-aged woman, clambered to her knees, too weak from narcolepsy to rise further.

'Help me!' Her cry was thin and plaintive.

Gales of laughter greeted her plea.

Twenty metres to the Mouth.

She struggled to crawl away from the whirling blades and buzzing saws, but her enfeebled muscles couldn't match the belt's steady four kilometres an hour. Her bewildered gaze alternating between the maw of steel and her paralysed companions in woe, she was carried remorselessly towards the mouth of sharp, churning blades, awash with foaming blood.

'That's it, creep!' a Judge shouted down from the first gallery. 'Keep crawling!'

The shouter acknowledged the loud guffaws of approval with a wave of the hand.

'I'm alive!' she called out desperately, eyes streaming with tears.

Ten metres to the Mouth, and she still couldn't manage more than a slow crawl despite the fear adrenalin that pumped energy through her narcoleptic veins.

'*I'm alive!*'

The laughter and jeers rose in intensity.

Five metres to the spinning blades.

She lifted a hand, pleading.

'HELP ME! I'M ALIVE!'

The plea only increased the Judges' mirth.

'I'M – '

Her words were swallowed in a tortured scream as the Mouth's sharp teeth munched her body.

The vaulted roof echoed to thunderous applause.

When it finally died down, an expectant hush descended as the last of the paralysed creeps were crunched up.

So much for the starter. The main course was to follow, once the Chief Judge arrived.

Judge Dread never missed Resyk's main course.

'Rico . . .'

Chief Judge Dread sat bolt upright on the obsidian DreadThrone, fists clenched tight, eyes shut behind his reflective visor.

Inside the helmeted head, an old scene was replayed again and again, a nightmare vid-loop.

Thirty-seven years ago, when he was a young Judge by the name of Joe Dredd and the megalopolis was still called Mega-City One.

Two days after he shot his clone-twin in the Cafe Cesare.

He had stood in Resyk 3 and watched his brother's body, sprawled among the pale corpses on the rubbereen belt. Watched Rico slide towards the Mouth. He noticed the Med-work on his brother's chest, the bio-sealed wound, leaving barely a scar, but thought nothing of it. Med often experimented on cadavers before passing them on for recycling.

Some ten metres from the Mouth, he thought he saw a twitch in Rico's hand.

Instantly, he checked that the sensors' red lights were on. They were, every last one. Normal functioning.

He glanced back at Rico as he slipped into the Mouth.

Rico lifted his head and stared straight at his brother.

'*Joe* . . .'

Then he disappeared in a whirl of razor-sharp blades and a spray of red.

'Rico . . .'

Chief Judge Dread leaned forwards on the Dread-Throne, and clutched the name-badge inscribed DREAD.

It was Rico's badge, an A inserted in place of the bullet

247

hole. He'd had the alteration done within an hour of leaving Resyk. From that day, it became his own badge.

One man doing the work of two.

Rico had wanted to milk the system. Okay, Judge Dread would milk it too, his own way. Rico had bedded women, flouting the Justice celibacy law. Judge Dread would have any woman he wished.

Rico's way led to Resyk or Titan.

Judge Dread knew a better way.

He planned to sit in the Chief Judge's chair. Once you were Chief Judge, you could do as you wished, so long as your plans were well laid and your co-conspirators well placed.

And Chief Judge Dread had done exactly as he wished. It was going to stay that way.

When the last clone was purged from the Judgement force, he would be safe. The purging had been gradual and discreet. He had waited two years before closing down all clone banks, on a suitable pretext. He had gone to great pains to hide the real reason for the systematic abolition of clones:

The prophecy.

The prophecy that must never be allowed to reach fruition. Now that Joe Dredd was destroyed, metamorphosed in the Secretion, the prophecy *couldn't* reach fruition.

Could it?

'Conglomeration,' he summoned.

From the bowels of Dreadhead, the living computer reached out its manifold thoughts, and echoed in Dread's helmet.

«Here, my Lord.»

'Does the prophecy still hold?'

The Conglomeration slurped and slopped its reply:

«Be bloody, bold, and resolute;
Laugh to scorn
The power of man, for none of woman born

248

Shall harm Judge Dread.»

'But how many are left that are not born of woman? How many clone Judges survive to offer me a threat of harm?'

«Less than a hundred, and none poses a threat.»

'Then the prophecy no longer holds.'

«I have not yet confirmed Joe Dredd's destruction in the Undercity. Until that is confirmed, the prophecy still holds. Dredd, cloned from the DNA of the same father as yourself, is the one clone that might do you harm.»

Dread leaned back in the black obsidian throne. 'Can you probe the Undercity and maintain the ultraterror flood of Mega-City One?'

«It would mean withdrawing yet more surveillance from Dreadhead, sire. Internal surveillance is already at minimum level. As it is, I would prefer a closer watch on Hershey and Caligula.»

Dread snorted dismissively. 'Hershey's been taught a lesson she won't forget. I know about women, and she's a woman who's learned her place: under my heel. As for Caligula – the man's a joke. An exceptionally funny joke. That's why I've let him live. He's no danger.'

«As you say, Lord Dread.»

'That's right. As I say.'

«Lord Dread, the main course is about to be served. Do you wish to attend?»

The Chief Judge smiled grimly. 'I wouldn't miss Resyk Entertainment's main show for anything. How's the food and drink? To your taste?'

«The pain and fear of the Nameless is most palatable, my Lord. I have ingested much nourishment from the body-souls devoured by the Mouth.»

'Rico . . .' Judge Dread whispered, fingers brushing the name-badge.

«My Lord?»

'Nothing.' He lifted an arm. 'DreadThrone. Resyk.'

Responding to his command, the Dread-effigy throne

rose and glided across the gloomy spaces of DreadCourt, parting the living shadows before it.

Dread inhaled the scent of the shifting shadows. The scent was fear: the psychic residue of those fed to the Conglomeration. A clotted memory of Resyk terror, clumped into inchoate masses and wrapped in darkness. They weren't worthy to bear the name of ghosts. The living shadows were the aftermath of terror. The Conglomeration's psychic excrement, left free to roam Dreadhead but attracted more often than not to the throne room of DreadCourt.

As the DreadThrone descended the winding, semi-organic tubes to Resyk, the living shadows followed, Fear following in the wake of Dread.

The Chief Judge entered Resyk to a deafening shout of acclaim:

'DREAD! DREAD! DREAD!'

He silenced them with an upturned hand, and the DreadThrone flew through a vast hush to hover above the Mouth's upper lip.

'Tonight is more than an entertainment,' he proclaimed. 'It's a celebration of the invasion. So let's celebrate. Tomorrow we enter a dead city. After that, we'll lay claim to new worlds. So enjoy the spectacle in honour of your Chief Judge. Let the show's highlight begin.'

At his word, a section of wall dematerialised at the far end of Resyk, and scores of naked Nameless were dumped on to the rubbereen belt.

By the time the wall resumed solidity, two hundred people milled about the far end of the hall, ten-metre walls rising sheer above the belt, trapping the unfortunates in the moving path to the Mouth.

These two hundred were special. They had the full use of their limbs. They could run. And run.

The unlucky batch was also a group of families. Fifty families of four apiece, carefully selected. A mother, a father, a son, a daughter: ranging in age from ten to forty. Nice and neat. Judge Dread liked neatness.

He surveyed the quaking families at the other end of the belt, then raised a high fist.

'Listen, you creeps,' he addressed the family groupings. 'You're going to run. Run for your lives. Tonight all but one of you will be devoured by the Mouth. The one that runs the hardest and fastest and stays the course will live. Only *one* can survive.' He looked up at the ranks of his troops, gallery above gallery. 'Tonight's a special diversion . . . Family entertainment.'

Roars of laughter boomed about the vaulted hall.

When the noise died down, he slammed down his fist. 'Nine kilometres.'

The belt, which had maintained a constant four kilometres per hour, sped up to nine kilometres an hour.

The victims had to stop back-pedalling. They were forced to turn around and walk at a brisk pace. Some mothers and fathers lifted their children and carried them in shivering arms.

'Only *one* can survive,' Dread reminded in a bellow. 'Which will you sacrifice? Yourself? Your son? Your daughter?'

After two minutes, Dread again slammed his fist on the armrest. 'Twelve kays.'

The belt accelerated to twelve kilometres an hour. For the wretched families, the walk changed to a trot. The two hundred were still at the far end of the belt.

The Chief Judge relaxed in his throne, and let five minutes pass.

Some of the runners were starting to gasp.

'Survival of the fittest,' Dread murmured. 'First Law.' His fist came down.

'Fifteen kays.'

The trot became a run. A boy stumbled and shrieked before he scrambled back to his feet.

Dread smiled.

251

Keep it at fifteen kays for a while. Wear them down. Especially those who'd volunteered to carry their children. They'd weary the quickest. Serve them right. A salutary lesson to the rest.

Survival of the fittest.

They ran at fifteen kays for more than ten minutes, each family assisting the other to keep going.

Time to rid them of their self-deception, the illusion that anybody could care for anyone but themselves.

'Twenty kays.'

The run was now at a seasoned marathon pace. The children and those foolish enough to carry them would be the first to go.

Slowly, inexorably, the weak began to slip and slide down the belt. Their neighbours no longer held out a hand of assistance. The bond between the families was broken, each family concentrating on its own survival.

Every back was sweat-slicked. The stink of fear wafted up to the galleries.

'Twenty-three kays.'

A dark-haired man side-stepped and landed a bone-crunching blow on his male neighbour's skull. The stricken man toppled, senseless, and sped down to the Mouth, his wife and children too intent on staying alive to try and help.

A roar of applause went up from the Judges.

'It's starting,' grinned Dread.

Another man had followed the dark-haired runner's example. Then another. And another.

Dread chuckled. Family against family.

They'd taken the first step. The next step wouldn't be long in coming.

He let the runners' torture drag out.

Mothers let drop their children when they came within blood-spray of the Mouth. The children didn't keep pace with the belt for more than a minute. The blades took them, one by one.

Dread's gaze moved to the foremost creep on the belt. A red-haired man with sinewy muscles. He hadn't turned on anyone yet, *and* he carried his daughter on his back.

At first sight, he wouldn't have identified the red-haired creep as a sturdy runner. But he was showing his mettle, despite the burden of the girl.

But he'd learn. He'd learn.

Sooner or later he'd have to face the demands of survival and drop his daughter.

From his vantage point on the Mouth's upper lip, Dread glanced down. The mouthful of spinning blades was doing brisk business.

It had chewed up a third of the creeps, and was hungry for more.

So, for that matter, was the Conglomeration, ingesting the juice of individual terrors, restoring its depleted reservoirs of psionic liquids.

'Feed well, my pet,' he addressed the Conglomeration.

«The food is much to my taste, Lord Dread,» the Conglomeration slurped inside his psi-conductive helmet. «A tasty feast. Family fare.»

Dread leaned back and enjoyed the show.

Twenty-three kays was just about right. No satisfaction in hurrying the entertainment to its conclusion.

Let it drag on.

The red-haired man was still ahead of the pack. And his daughter was still on his back.

How long would the creep keep deluding himself? Sooner or later, he'd have to drop the brat if he wanted to last the course. In the end, everybody looks after Number One.

If he wished to live, he'd have to give up his daughter's life.

Very simple.

Even for a Nameless creep.

His gaze moved to the rest of the herd.

Ah! A youth had just tripped up his mother, kicked her

in the face. The example was soon taken up, mutual suspicion and raw terror driving family members against one another. The old principle, old as life: hit them before they hit you.

Everything he witnessed proved his philosophy true: no one can be trusted. Everyone's guilty.

The more the creeps fought each other, the faster the Mouth fed, and the quicker the Conglomeration was nourished.

After fifteen torturous minutes, there were only twelve runners on the belt: three women and nine men.

Twelve runners, but thirteen survivors, scattered around the middle section of the belt. The red-haired man still bore the girl on his back.

'You're taking a long time to learn your lesson,' Dread muttered. 'But learn it you will. Everyone does. When it comes down to blood and steel, everyone's a killer.'

Two minutes later there were ten runners left.

Those ten lasted five minutes, then two met the blades and saws in a matter of seconds.

A couple of minutes later another was swallowed by the metal mouth.

The remaining seven were the pick of the bunch. As the odds against them decreased, their efforts increased. Too widely spaced to attack one another, it became a basic contest of endurance.

The red-haired man had lost his lead, but he was still hanging on to his daughter.

'You're a slow learner,' Judge Dread growled.

But the man who thought he prized his daughter so highly was a good thirty metres from the Mouth. He'd change his mind when he felt the wet, sticky spray on his back.

The minutes stretched out.

Under the gruelling pace, they collapsed one by one, and went their bloody and bone-cracking way.

Finally, two runners remained on the deadly racetrack.

A blond and a redhead. Two runners. Three survivors. The red-haired man was taking his time learning the lesson of Judge Dread.

If he had the stamina to endure with the burden on his shoulders, he would have won the contest without great exertion if he had run alone and for himself.

He *would* drop the girl, of course. At the last moment, they always did.

The last moment would be too late. The blond man had a determined set to his physique. He was a winner. He was going for it, and to hell with anyone else.

The Chief Judge marked him down for a post in the Judgement force. He had what it took to be a Judge.

The two contestants were almost level, fifteen metres from the Mouth.

For the next five minutes, they stayed level, only losing a couple of metres.

'Redhead can't keep it up,' Dread murmured, brushing fingers over his name-badge. 'It's impossible.'

The cheers and jeers from the galleries had long since subsided. An expectant silence hung over Resyk; thousands of eyes were riveted on the gruelling race. Dread's troops didn't like Redhead any more than he did. He wasn't behaving like a creep. He was throwing a challenge in the face of Judgement.

A snarl twisted the Chief Judge's lips.

When it comes down to it, you'll have to sacrifice the girl or the Mouth will swallow you both. That's how the game works. Can't you see that, creep?

The blond man's legs suddenly buckled.

By the time he regained his balance, he was in the Mouth.

Ten metres from the meat grinder, Redhead glanced over his shoulder and saw his opponent's fate.

He lifted the girl above his head.

Dread laughed. *Now* Redhead had got the message. Get rid of the girl.

Be a survivor.

Redhead gave a superhuman heave, and hurled the girl a good four metres *away* from the Mouth.

Almost simultaneously, he threw himself backwards into the whirl of blades and saws.

The belt pulled to an abrupt halt.

The silence was only broken by the sound of chopped meat as Redhead was carried down the internal conveyors to the Stomach.

The girl's momentum tumbled her within a hand's breadth of a swishing blade. She pulled back and crouched on the rubbereen, eyes running with tears as she stared at the meat grinder.

The silence in the hall was so thick you could eat chunks of it. The girl's father had made a nonsense of Dread's Law, and everyone in the hall knew it.

The girl's voice was small.

'Dad . . .'

Judge Dread rose in rage from the DreadThrone.

The brat's father had proved him wrong.

The Chief Judge was *never* wrong. He was the Law, and the Law was always right, therefore he was always right.

But her father had proved him wrong.

'What are you, brat?' he roared. Close up, the girl looked younger. Ten years old. No more.

She crouched lower, her gaze sank. Her mop of red hair fell over her face. 'My – my name's Cassie.'

'I want your *number*!' he bellowed. 'Who gave you a name? Who *dared* give you a name?'

'My – ' She threw a tearful glance at the vast mouth of grinding, slashing teeth. 'My – father.'

'You have a name,' he hissed softly. 'Where there's one, there's many.' His fist tightened. 'Cassie, short for Cassandra. What do we have here? Cassandra Anderson admirers? I've news for you, *Cassie* – Anderson has been metamorphosed into her worst nightmare. If you saw her, you'd scream. What do you say to – '

'CHIEF JUDGE DREAD! URGENT!'

The broadcasted voice boomed around the hall. 'FIST 24 REPORTING, CHIEF JUDGE. JOE DREDD'S ALIVE. HE'S SURRENDERED. WE'RE BRINGING HIM IN.'

'Alive!' Dread exclaimed. 'How – never mind. Bring him in, but watch him carefully. You've paralysed him, I presume?'

'YES, SIRE.'

'Then take him straight to Dungeon Unbreachable.'

'OBEDIENCE, SIRE.'

Dread sank back in the throne, resting in the obsidian lap of his own image.

His glare descended to the girl. 'You survived, but you didn't run. The rules were broken. You have to run to survive.'

She bent lower, arms wrapped round her waist.

'You'd better start running, brat. The belt's about to move again. If you last an hour, I'll allow you to live. Now *run*!'

She sprang up and sprinted away from the Mouth.

'Fourteen kays!' he roared. 'Keep it constant.'

His second command was pitched too low for the girl to hear. 'And keep it *perpetual*. Hour after hour after hour. As long as it takes for the Mouth to swallow her.'

His troops knew the score. They were grinning, anticipating hours of amusement at the brat's expense. It was the kind of practical joke that appealed to them.

He lifted a fist. 'Rise.' The DreadThrone lifted into the air and soared over Resyk.

The sight of the girl running below did little to allay his misgivings.

Joe Dredd was alive.

An ominous whisper came from the back of his skull:

'. . . *none of woman born,*
Shall harm Judge Dread.'

He cast a final glance at the Mouth.

A memory flickered into life . . .
Rico lifted his head and stared straight at him.
He shut his eyes tight, struggling to exorcise a ghost.
'Rico . . .'

TWENTY-SIX

Between Judge Eliphas and the red surge of terror sweeping down the avenue.

Between the Devil and the deep blue sea.

Hershey chose the Devil.

'I surrender,' she said, dropping her gun as she ran towards the hover-wagon's open hatch. 'I *surrender*, okay? Now let's get the drokk out of here. Those crimson waves back there are lethal, and they're coming *fast*.'

Whatever he was, Eliphas wasn't stupid. He took one look at her, another at the advancing red tide.

'Must be lethal to make you surrender so easily,' he said. 'Get in.' He turned to the pilot. 'Emergency take-off!'

Hershey slumped into a seat, and watched the avenue drop away. The sight of a dozen Widow-makers pointed in her direction didn't worry her too much after the rippling crimson menace below.

'What was that down there?' Eliphas asked. 'Some sort of deadly laser?'

She shook her head. 'Nothing so familiar. I think it's psionic. Just an intuition. It killed Mathers – with terror.'

'Mathers is dead?'

'Yeah.' Hershey grinned. 'Breaks my heart.'

Eliphas shrugged. 'Plenty where he came from. As for you, say your prayers, Hershey.'

She gave a tired lift of her shoulders. 'I led you a merry dance, but it's over. You've won. Take me back to SJS Interrogation and throw away the key, but for drokk's sake warn somebody at Justice Central about those crimson ripples down there. Look, see how fast they're spreading.'

'You're not going to Interrogation, Hershey. You're not going anywhere near Justice Central.'

'Where the hell am I going?'

'To the nearest hell we can find. Somewhere out of the way. To the Cursed Earth, where we've a special little camp with a very small cell. Nobody will know you're there. And you'll be there a long, long time. After a year, you'll be too crazy to scream.'

She raised an eyebrow, determined to face the SJS dirtbag out. 'You're good at playing the gloating villain, Eliphas. Do you practise in front of a mirror?'

Eliphas turned away, unimpressed by her defiance. 'Willoughby – head for the Cursed Earth, Area 17.'

'Sir,' the pilot acknowledged.

'Eliphas,' Hershey called out. 'You've got to warn Justice Central about that psionic terror back there.'

He kept his back to her. 'It'll blow itself out. I don't want any contact with Control for a while.'

'Call in, you piece of stomm!'

'When I'm ready. Maybe.'

She expelled a sharp breath and studied the black-visored Specials surrounding her.

'A dozen Widow-makers to keep one lady in her place. Yeah, you'd need the most powerful rifles in the force's armoury to watch over me. Tough guys, you SJS.'

'Shut your mouth, woman,' snapped one of the Specials. Like his comrades, he had no name-badge. No names, no pack-drill.

'You talk to me, you use my name,' she said. 'Hershey. What's your name, soldier?'

'My own business, woman.'

'Oh, I see. It's something embarrassing. Let me guess – Jerk-off.'

He rammed the hefty assault weapon into her stomach, whooshing the air from her lungs.

The dork had fallen for it.

As she doubled up, she gripped the barrel in both hands, wrenching it to the right as she twisted her body to the left, landing a knee in the Special's midriff for good measure.

The gun was in her hands and pointed at the pilot within half a second of the muzzle ramming her stomach.

The second still wasn't up when she sprayed Pilot Willoughby and the flight console with a shower of explosive slugs.

The h-wagon tilted crazily.

Everybody went flying.

Hershey slammed into the console and heard her shoulder crack. Wits dazed, she saw half a dozen Specials hurtle through the bullet-shattered windscreen.

The angle steepened from 45 degrees to near-vertical.

There was a block roof below.

It was rushing up fast.

Goodbye, cruel world.

There wasn't a lot of point to it, but she held on to a corner of the console for dear life.

A slug thwacked into the wall a few centimetres from her head. She nosedived behind the pilot's seat before the explosive bullet blew her to Grud.

The explosion damn near snapped her neck, but she managed to loop her legs around the chair runners.

Willoughby was still in his seat, strapped in tight, but he wasn't wearing a head.

And there was a Widow-maker lying within reach, caught under the seat.

She grabbed it with the arm that still worked, and let loose a series of rounds shooting blind, using the seat and pilot for cover.

She heard three separate screams. With luck, one of them belonged to Eliphas. Hershey wanted to waste that creep herself before the craft crashed and flung them all to oblivion. A bullet – from me to you. The personal touch.

'Hershey!'

Eliphas's distinctive tone. Drokk.

'You're still outnumbered, you bitch! Three to one.'

Unbidden, wild laughter rang from her mouth. 'Outnumbered? That must really cheer you up no end, considering we're all heading for a block faster than the speed of sound.'

'I'm taking you out before we hit, Hershey. Matter of honour.'

'The feeling's mutual, slime-features.'

'Hey!' another voice cut in. 'Manual panel's still lit!'

Glancing up to the console, she saw that the observation was right. The manual might still be functional.

Eliphas changed his tune.

'Listen, we've got a trainee pilot back here. Hershey, I swear, I *swear* I'll set you free if you let him take the controls.'

'Fat chance,' she snarled. 'Whatever happens, I'm dead. McGruder's got me down as a renegade Judge. And I wouldn't trust your word in a month of Fargo Days.'

'McGruder's out, Kelleher's in,' Eliphas shouted desperately. 'You were reinstated hours ago. You're free as a bird.'

'Unfortunate simile, seeing as we're in a nosedive,' she retorted but wondering: *what if*? It would explain why no one but Eliphas had tracked her down.

She glanced at the uprushing block.

Jeez.

Ten seconds to impact, max.

'I've got my gun stuck to the manual,' she announced. 'You shoot me, the manual goes, and we all go.'

She sat in the dead pilot's lap, Widow-maker muzzle pressed to the pilot controls.

'Anyone want to blow my head off, do it now,' she

262

called out, the gale storming through the broken wind-screen whipping the words from her lips.

Her head stayed intact. Seemed they loved living more than they hated her.

Yanking back the control lever, she braced her legs and heaved with all her strength.

For a heart-stopping moment there was no response.

The craft was so close to the block that its bulk filled the entire view.

Two seconds left, tops.

Not a chance of lifting the nose and changing a near-vertical drop to vertical ascent.

Then go down, you idiot!

Loop the drokking loop.

She thrust the lever forward. The steep fall became a straight drop.

She pushed the lever for all she was worth.

Still a straight drop.

Great – now they were heading for a crash at Ground Level.

The craft turned upside-down with a suddenness that startled even Hershey, almost dislodging her leglock on the seat.

She heard the SJS slam into the roof with a howl and a snap of bones. Best thing she'd heard in days.

Keeping the pressure on the control, she gradually righted the craft into a 45-degree ascent.

Behind her, the SJS thudded to the floor without so much as a grunt. Must be out cold.

Squinting through the gale, she spied the flat summit of a tower block up above. A flat roof. It was a chance, the only chance she'd get. Most block roofs were rounded.

She nosed the craft up to the summit. Watched the brink loom perilously close. . . .

'Just a few metres,' she growled. 'Give me a few drokking metres. That's a prayer, by the way.'

Someone up there heard her. The hover-wagon literally

scraped over the rim, almost throwing the craft off balance.

Its belly thumped down on the roof and skidded across the smooth surface.

Hershey eased back on the lever. And discovered it was dangling in her hand.

Her eyes bugged. Damn thing had torn loose. Might well have torn free *before* she crested the roof rim.

Talk about close calls.

She was about to breathe a sigh of relief when she realised that without the lever she couldn't stop the airship. And the emergency brakes were shot.

Well, the drag on the underside would slow the vehicle down.

Peering ahead, her mouth fell open. The craft had skidded clean across the block roof. The far edge couldn't be more than two hundred metres away. And she was still doing a good 400 kph.

The only option was to jump. Drokk, they'd still be scraping her off the roof in a week's time.

But jump was all she could do, unless she fancied suicide.

She leaned forwards through the shattered windscreen.

And spun round as an explosive bullet took her in the side, sending a chunk of flesh hurtling through the windscreen.

Eliphas was crouched behind a plasteen chair, Widow-maker in hand.

Hershey dropped before the next slug hit, and fired her Widow-maker at the SJS Judge's cover. The plasteen chair was blasted asunder.

But Eliphas wasn't there. Gruddam creep must have slipped behind another chair.

She darted a look through the windscreen.

The roof rim was gone. They'd gone right over the edge, in a ship that was as flightworthy as a brick.

'Damn you, Eliphas!' she roared, rearing up and spitting flame and death from the Widow-maker. 'Burn in hell!'

'Let's burn together!' he screamed, rising up and blasting a spate of bullets at the woman top of his hate list.

The craft tilted and they plunged through empty air in an exchange of fire and fury.

TWENTY-SEVEN

Joe Dredd had bellowed at several Fists for the best part of two hours. Not one of the fist-shaped marbleen airships took any notice. They glided sedately on.

During a lull, he stomped up to Cassandra Anderson, mouth scowling, fists firmly on hips. 'What the drokk's going on? They jump me the moment I step into your world, then they don't drokking well want to know.'

She heaved a wry sigh. 'The Judges are creatures of routine. Always following orders. They've probably been told that you've been gulped by the Secretion, so, in their minds, you're history. On top of that they wouldn't expect you to do the ridiculous and try to get yourself arrested. So I suppose they look at you, see a Judge on foot, and reckon he's one of theirs who's lost his airship, and deserves to leg it home. Here, the Judges fly; they never walk, except out of necessity. And the Nameless always walk – they're not allowed even a wheeled vehicle.'

Dredd jabbed a finger towards a group of Nameless. 'Wondered why they kept staring at me. Couldn't work out what kind of Judge I was.'

'Another Fist coming,' Giant announced. 'Go get yourself arrested, Mega-City man.'

'Fair warning,' he said. 'If this drokker doesn't pick me up, I'm doing things my way.'

Anderson arched an eyebrow. 'And what way would that be, lawman? A knuckle fight? Go on – and shout louder this time.'

'Last time,' he warned, marching off.

Corey glanced at Anderson. 'Shouldn't we have filled him in, at least about Patchwork? The way it is, he's working blind.'

Anderson gave a thin smile. 'If I read him right, he works best when he works blind.'

'What if a Fist doesn't stop within the next hour?'

Anderson threw up her hands. 'We're drokked.'

The Fist pilot glanced at the figure below, then turned to his copilot. 'Look at that stupid drokker. He's standing down there like a Nameless creep.'

The other gave a shrug. 'Maybe we should go down and take a look-see.'

'Nah, drokk him. Serves him right for losing his flier. Automatic dismissal from the force. He'll have a number on his forehead and be creeping with the creeps this time tomorrow.'

'Hey,' the copilot chuckled, 'let's go down and jeer at him.'

'*Now* you're talking. Yeah, let's rub his face in it. Stupid drokker.'

The pilot brought the Fist in low, hovered over the solitary figure, and opened a marbleen pore in the hull to confront the Judge visor to visor.

'You're drokked, drokker!'

'I surrender!' the Judge bellowed.

The copilot grabbed his companion's arm. 'Grud! Who does he remind you of?'

'What?' The pilot increased the visor magnification. 'Stomm! He's like a drokked-up version of the Chief Judge!'

'And check that uniform, that titsy-bitsy boot holster – that's not standard.'

The two exchanged glances. 'Couldn't be, could it?' the pilot whispered. 'I mean, he got drowned in the Stew. News was all over Dreadhead.'

'Take a look at that name-badge. DREDD.'

'Okay, run psi check,' the pilot ordered the psi-conductive material of the Fist.

A few seconds later, the Fist walls replied:

'DNA IS IDENTICAL TO THAT OF CHIEF JUDGE, BUT PSI-PROFILE AND PHYSICAL CONDITION DIFFER. THIS MAN IS JUDGE JOE DREDD. YOU MUST ARREST IMMEDIATELY.'

'Freeze him,' the pilot ordered. The sentient Fist instantly paralysed Dredd's nervous system, leaving him standing rigid like a spire of rock.

'We'll have to tell the Chief Judge,' the copilot said.

'You serious? He's probably in Resyk. He'll drokking murder me if I interrupt the fun.'

'He'll feed you to the Conglomeration or stick you in the Orchestra if you don't.'

'Hmm . . . yeah.' The pilot instantly relayed a message to Judge Dread while his sidekick opened the marbleen pore to maximum. He hefted an Exterminans as he stepped through the round aperture.

'Just to be on the safe side,' he called over his shoulder.

The pilot, his urgent message concluded, curled his lip. 'What you afraid of – drokking creeps?'

The copilot turned round, gave him the finger.

And exploded.

The helmet and uniform sank to the ground, filled with mush.

'What the drokk?'

Something hit the pilot. Inside his skull.

The cells of his body parted company. He felt his veins pop.

By the time he exploded, his mind was long gone.

Dredd, mobility and circulation restored by Anderson's psi-healing, chucked the mush-filled uniform out of the Fist.

'Pretty strong stuff, psionics, blowing guys to crud with

268

a thought,' he admitted. 'Hope Psi Division never get hooked on it.'

'The way things are going, there won't be a Psi Division if you ever get back to your city,' Anderson said. 'There won't be a *city*.'

'Where to now?' Dredd demanded.

'We fly this Fist somewhere quiet and hide,' Corey answered.

'Hide!' he snarled.

'Yeah, hide,' Anderson stated firmly. 'Hide and wait.'

'What the drokk for?'

Anderson leaned up close, parted her lips. 'A mysterious stranger.'

Caligula knocked on Hershey's door, a bouquet of flowers held behind his back.

'I hope you don't find me forward, but your spellbinding beauty has captured my heart,' he rehearsed, tapping his foot.

The door swung open, revealed a grim-faced Hershey. 'What the drokk do you want?' she glowered.

'Er – I hope you won't find me forward, but your spellbinding beauty has – '

'Drokk off.' The door slammed shut.

Caligula rubbed his smooth chin. 'Hmm . . . Playing hard to get.'

The door opened again. 'Have you fallen in love with me?' she asked severely.

'Oh yes, madly, hopelessly. I know you now for the goddess Ath – '

She grabbed him by the breastplate and dragged him in.

I knew she was playing hard to get, he triumphed inwardly.

He handed her the flowers. She threw them aside and pushed him into a chair.

It was then he saw Judge Karyn, her pallor grey, her posture slack where she slumped in a chair opposite.

'Is she dead?' he asked.

'As near as. She's been drained of her psyche. She's a shell. I went to meet her – found her this way.' Her stern grey eyes studied him closely. 'You think you're in love with me, right?'

'I don't think, therefore I am,' he asserted stoutly. 'You're the goddess Athena – or Minerva, if you want me to be pedantically Roman about it.'

She wasn't listening. 'You're the only one crazy enough to . . .'

'To what?' he demanded. 'I hate pregnant pauses.'

'You led three rebellions against Judge Dread. That's pretty crazy.'

He looked at the back of his hands, abashed. 'They weren't very successful. His Dreadness thought they were funny.'

'But deep down you think you're far superior to him, don't you? You're a god.'

'And you're a goddess,' he burst out. 'And I come as a god to unite with my adored goddess.'

Her keen stare lanced straight through him. 'If you're a god, you must prove it. Then I'll – unite – with you. But what sort of god bows down to a mortal like Judge Dread?'

'Oh, not that again,' he complained. 'Everybody's always picking on me about that. Honestly, Athena, I could take Dread any time I wanted to. It's just not convenient at the moment.'

'Athena . . .' she murmured. 'Remember the Statue of Liberty?'

'Yes. What about it? Dread blew it up years ago.'

'Did it remind you of anyone?'

His brow creased, lost in thought. 'Remind me of anyone . . .'

'Like a goddess,' she prompted.

He shot up a finger. 'Athena!'

'Yes,' she nodded.

His hand flew to his mouth. 'And Dread blew her up.'

'And you saw what he put me through with that bitch McGruder.'

'Yes,' he muttered angrily. Then, in a doubtful tone, 'But if you're Athena, how come he has control over you?'

'Well – I'm trapped in my mortal guise.'

He threw up a hand. 'Oh, tell me about it. So am I. Know the feeling.'

She grasped his hand. 'Together, we can rule the universe.'

'You said it, Athena!'

'But first you must assert your divinity. Perform a task which only a god could accomplish.'

'You name it, I'll do it.'

'Fine.' She put her lips close to his ear. The lobe wiggled in anticipation. 'Take the *Head Imperial* and blow up every Judge Dread statue in Dreadcity in retaliation for his destruction of the Statue of Lib – of the Statue of Athena.' She pressed his hand to her breast. 'When I'm avenged on Dread's statues, I'm yours to command.' She pushed his groping hand away. 'Until then, we must stay apart.'

A gulp travelled down his throat.

Hershey held a fist aloft. 'Caesar or nothing.'

'Yeah,' he mumbled, backing away. 'Caesar – and all that.'

With Caligula finally gone, Hershey slumped into a seat and sagged into a sigh.

Quick thinking could save your life. But sometimes it could lose it.

Caligula was a poor substitute for Karyn, but he was all that was left. Old-fashioned insanity was rare in Dread's new world. The Nova Roman emperor's belief in his divinity gave him the courage of his delusions. He might well attack Dread's sacred images, distracting the Chief Judge from – other threats. Or he might fold before the

271

enterprise was under way – toss of the Roman coin where Caligula was concerned.

Not until she saw Caligula at her door, proclaiming undying love, flowers in hand, did she think of inveigling him into openly defying the Chief Judge. As for the method, she'd worked that out as she talked, picking up on the Roman emperor's obsessions.

Needless to say, Caligula was doomed. Dread would crush him for blasting the Judge Dread statues. A court jester can go only so far.

Hershey raised her gaze to the corpse-like figure of Karyn, propped in her chair. She looked no better or worse than when Hershey had first stumbled across her down in the Conglomeration Domain. At first sight she appeared dead, but a quick check had disclosed that her heart beat a faint pulse. But there was not the slightest resonance of psych presence in her body. What was once called the soul had left its fleshly home.

And Karyn's left hand formed a prearranged sign: the thumb hooked between the index finger and second finger.

Hershey went morgue-cold when she saw that sign.

It meant that Karyn's soul had gone to hell.

And she thought she knew who'd sent it there.

Hershey crossed the room, gathered the scatter of discarded flowers, and placed them tenderly in Karyn's lap.

The black DreadThrone circled about the vast spaces of DreadCourt, the Chief Judge rigid with fury as he sat on his seat of power.

Fist 24 had reported Joe Dredd's capture. Then the Fist had disappeared. And the Fist's crew had been turned to slush in their uniforms and dumped on the ground. There was only one psi-talent outside Dreadhead capable of such a feat: Anderson.

So if Joe Dredd was alive . . .

'Cassandra Anderson's alive.'

272

None of woman born shall harm Judge Dread.

'Conglomeration,' he summoned.

«Yes, my Lord?» surged a multiple voice in his helmet.

'How close are you to locating Anderson's and Joe Dredd's whereabouts?'

«Not yet pinned down, sire. But the search goes on.»

'What's taking so much time?' Judge Dread snapped. 'They can't be in the Undercity. I would have thought you could locate anyone on the surface in a matter of seconds.'

«Not while simultaneously maintaining maximum ultra-terror levels in both Dreadcity and Mega-City One.»

'Then cease the terror-flood of Mega-City One until Anderson and Dredd are found!'

«Obedience, sire.»

As the voice of the Conglomeration rippled away, Judge Dread guided his obsidian throne back to the summit of its hill-mount in the Circle of Dread.

Once ensconced on the mount, he raised his hand. Clenched it into a fist. 'First Blood Symphony in Red Major,' he ordered.

The graniteen walls heaved, pores swelling and dripping blood. The entombed human instruments of the Orchestra gurgled their anguish, a multitudinous death-rattle that never reached its conclusion.

The living shadows, psychic excreta from the Conglomeration's digestion, moved with the throbbing rhythm, swaying black silhouettes.

The Blood Symphony failed to divert him. Too much on his mind.

'Judge Omar,' he summoned, the psi-conductive helmet transmitting the summons down to the chief of hyper-psychics in the Conglomeration Domain.

Omar's mellifluous tones vibrated in the helmet. 'Yes, Lord?'

'What's the latest on Judge Karyn?'

'Same as before, sire. The moment I walked in on her

she fell to the floor, psych-shelled. An empty vessel. When I returned with assistance, she'd gone.'

'This is old news, Omar,' Dread scowled between clenched teeth. 'Did she get up and walk or did someone take her?'

'I'm sorry, Lord Dread, old news is all there is. She hasn't been located.'

'Then extrapolate.'

'I'll do my best. She must have sensed that I'd intercepted a scrambled psi-emission from her to someone inside Dreadhead. The wave pattern of the emission suggested that it was continuous. Psi-shielding of another's mind portrays such a pattern. As such shielding is forbidden, I can only surmise she ejected her psyche when I entered her chamber, realising that I was about to psi-freeze her and probe her mind. Karyn had readied herself for the psyche ejection before she saw me; most likely she sensed my approach as an unspecified fear.'

Dread tightened his lips. 'That doesn't tell me how or why she disappeared.'

'She couldn't have got up and walked. Not possible. Someone spirited her body away in the short minute of my absence, most likely the same person Karyn was shielding. The one who took her had to be someone with the skill and means to circumvent standard surveillance. That means someone above the middle ranks. The one thing I'm sure of is that the perpetrator – and Karyn – are still aboard Dreadhead.'

'Then ask the Conglomeration to trace Karyn, you fool!' Dread thundered. 'If she's inside Dreadhead, she can be located in a nanosecond.'

'I – I have asked the Conglomeration, sire,' Omar said hesitantly. 'An hour ago. It cannot locate Karyn inside Dreadhead. The puzzle is – sensors and Memory show that she hasn't left.'

'If the Conglomeration can't locate her, she *must* have left!' Dread rumbled.

'Forgive me, sire, but anyone who leaves, living or dead, is instantly registered in Memory. The system cannot be circumvented.'

Dread slammed a hand down on the armrest of his own obsidian fist. '*Anderson*. The Saint of the Bleeding Heart. It's Anderson. She's found a way into the system.'

'That's – not possible, my Lord.'

'How dare you question a Judge Dread judgement!' Dread bellowed, drowning out the Blood Symphony. 'I am the Law, and the Law is always right!'

'Forgive me – my Lord. I spoke out of turn. You are the Law.'

'Now don't trouble me again until you've found Karyn and the one who's hidden her,' Dread growled. 'Get to it.'

'Immediately, Chief Judge,' Omar signed off.

Dread was left to the shifting shadows, the undulating, blood-dripping walls and the exquisite torment of the Blood Symphony in Red Major.

'It's Anderson,' he murmured.

Anderson.

And behind her, a more shadowy figure, familiar in outline.

Joe Dredd.

His other self. It reminded him of Rico.

Rico's ghost.

They knew she was going to die and so did she but she kept on running.

Cassie maintained a steady pace on the rubbereen belt, ignoring the Judges' laughter and jeers. She had seen her father eaten alive in that meat-grinder mouth at the end of the belt, and Cassie was sure what her father would expect of her.

Keep running. Don't give up.

Against all the odds, you might survive if you don't give up. There was always the unforeseen.

275

And there was always Cassandra Anderson, after whom she'd been named.

She wanted to cry for her father, for herself, for everyone devoured by the Mouth.

But she followed Cassandra's example. She gritted her teeth and carried on, dry-eyed.

Keep running.

Never give up.

TWENTY-EIGHT

A marbleen head flew out of a biosteel mouth.

Caligula's *Head Imperial* whizzed out of Dreadhead's cavernous mouth and sailed under the glittering ice-crystal shroud that canopied Dreadcity.

Eyes bulging, hair standing on end, Caligula yelled his defiance.

'I was born in the morning of the world, and when the last star falls I shall still be! I am Lord above lords. God above gods. *CALIGULA THE ULTIMATE!*'

'Yes, dear,' Drusilla smiled uneasily, glancing at her apprehensive clone-sisters huddled at the rear of the flight deck. 'Whatever you say.'

'Huh,' he snorted. 'Order *me* around, will he? Make *me* worship *him*! Not any more, Helmet-head! Smash Athena's effigy and think you can get away with it, do you? Well, I'll give you what for!'

A statue of Chief Judge Dread, three kilometres high, loomed over the pinnacled horizon.

'There's the first of them!' the emperor cackled.

A press of a button launched a Diabolus missile, aimed at Judge Dread's groin. 'Take that, you swine!'

The missile hit. The statue detonated. Hovered in various huge pieces for a split second. Then fell to the ground in thunder and ruin. Twenty stalagmite blocks were flattened.

'Hee-hee-hee-hee-hee,' Caligula chortled. 'One down, thirty-six to go. Hee-hee-hee-hee-hee . . .'

'But you've only got nine more Diabolus missiles,'

Drusilla reasoned, stroking a cool hand over his fevered brow. 'Arithmetic doesn't work out, Little Boots.'

'I don't need missiles!' he shrieked. 'I'm the Supreme God of the Universe and I only have to *sneeze* to blow the earth from its orbit!'

'We've really had it now,' moaned Agrippinilla, head in hands.

'Fear not, sister-wives!' declared Caligula, spotting the head of another Judge Dread statue in the distance and making for it with all haste. 'Fear not, you who shall be in the company of Athena-Hershey hereafter. The time of Dread is done, and Zeus-Jupiter-Ammon-Caligula is his undoing!'

A jab at the ignition button. A Diabolus streaked to the sky-high Dread statue. 'Take that!' He jabbed again. 'And that! And that!'

'Easy, Little Boots,' Drusilla cautioned, shaking in her sandals. 'We're running out of macro-missiles fast. One for each statue, eh? *Please* . . .'

He stuck out his lower lip, wiggled his head. 'Oh – well . . . All right then. Just for you. And because you asked me nicely.'

He peered around. 'Right, where's the next Dread-shaped giant phallus?'

Caligula.

'Oh no! Get out of my brain, Patchwork. Bad time to call. Got a hundred and one things to do.'

Caligula, you must listen . . .

'No, you listen! I've decided to stop pretending I'm mortal. I'm taking over the universe. Then I'll blow it up. And – and I'll create another one in five days. Go Jehovah one better. Are you taking all this down? It's a seminal chapter in my great autobiography, *I, Caligula*.'

I can't quite sense what you're doing.

'Blowing up Judge Dread's giant statues. Good, eh?'

Patchwork was silent in Caligula's head for a brief space. *Yes, that's good . . . Carry on the good work.*

Caligula touched his temples. 'He's gone. Whew! I hate psi-calls, don't you?'

He squinted through the *Head Imperial*'s blue glasseen eye. 'Ah, there's another one. Five kilometres tall, or I'm not Zeus-Jupiter-Ammon.'

Caligula smiled a wicked smile. 'I think I'll attack from the rear. You're not going to like the spot I've chosen for the next missile, Your Dreadness.'

Seated on the DreadThrone, the Chief Judge raised both fists in rage. 'He's doing *what*?'

«Judge Governor Caligula is blowing up your thirty-seven Statues of Dominion,» the Conglomeration slushed inside Dread's helmet. «He has declared war on you again.»

Very slowly, Dread's fists lowered. 'For the last time. Fancy-dress rebellions in Nova Roma are one thing. Destruction of Dread colossi here in Dreadcity is another matter entirely. Concentrate waves of ultraterror on the *Head Imperial*, maximum strength.

«The Head's marbleen is saturated with psionic reflectors. Caligula's craft is fully psi-shielded, sire.»

'Then send out a squadron of ten Fists!' he bellowed. 'And order *Dialhead* to lead the squadron. I want Judge Mean Machine to head the attack!'

Reclining in one of Fist 24's bio-attraction seats, Cassandra Anderson's eyes sprang open.

'He's doing *what*?'

Dredd frowned. 'Who's doing what?'

Anderson waved an irritated hand. 'Be quiet. I'm getting a scrambled psi-call.'

Dredd folded his arms. Simmered.

At length, Anderson glanced at the Mega-City Judge. 'The plan's fallen through. Caligula was supposed to attack Judge Dread in DreadCourt, create a diversion for Karyn.'

Corey darted a look between Dredd and Anderson. 'Cassandra, is it wise to mention – you know . . .'

Anderson shrugged. 'The plan's been blown to bits by Caligula, so he might as well know. And if the plan had worked, we'd have to tell him soon.'

The Judge stuck out his chin. 'Tell me now, drokk it!'

'Watch your lip, lawman,' Giant warned, hefting a meaty fist.

'It's okay,' Anderson said. 'He's entitled. Patchwork is Caligula's mentor and right-hand man. And he's been working with the Bleeding Hearts for years. He's a mystery man, supposed to have come back from the dead twice. That fascinated Caligula – he's terrified of death. Patchwork primed Caligula to attack the Chief Judge at just the right moment, the moment our one and only saboteur in Dreadhead – Judge Karyn – attempted to disable the Conglomeration. Two simultaneous diversions: our signal to enter Dreadhead in a Fist and launch a full-scale assault on the Conglomeration and the Chief Judge.'

'Why wait till now?'

'We needed a larger diversion to set the scene: Judge Dredd's invasion of Mega-City One. And we had to wait until the final hour to steal a Fist. No point in attracting attention too early.'

'But now you've lost what army you had,' Dredd said. 'It's just the four of us.'

Anderson flashed him a quirky half-smile. 'Like I said, let's die with style.' She gave a flick of the wrists, a flicker of the fingers, and the marbleen Fist rose from its block-cover. 'Anyway, Caligula *has* handed us a diversion, although not the one we expected. But Karyn – ' Her face became sombre. 'She hasn't responded to Patchwork's psi-calls. Seems like the line's dead at her end. She's either given up the ghost or been desouled.'

Corey nodded sadly. 'Can't feel her psyche inside Dreadhead or outside.'

'What the hell,' Anderson responded, blue-grey eyes radiating an undaunted will. 'Let's go to hell.'

The Fist sped into the sky, part of the marbleen becoming transparent and serving as a window.

Within minutes, the massive bulk of Dreadhead came in sight.

Ten Fists erupted from the mouth of the colossal head.

In the vanguard was a metallic head, four times the span of a Fist. The Head bore the pugnacious features of Mean Machine: Antarctica Judge Governor in Judge Dread's world, imprisoned perp in Mega-City One. A circular biosteel plate covered the upper forehead of the craft, a five-point dial fixed to the plate, marked by an arrow.

'*Dialhead*,' Corey groaned, eyeing the Head airship with trepidation. 'Judge Mean Machine's flier.'

'The dial markers look different from the Mean Machine I know. He only had four, unless you count the four and a half when he went apestomm,' Dredd observed. 'Can you get me magnification?'

'You've got it.'

Dialhead ballooned in the oval of translucent marbleen. Dredd made out the signs on the dial's markers, counting from one to five:

SURLY – MEAN – REAL MEAN – DROKKED OFF – NO MORE MR NICE GUY

The arrow was on MEAN. By Mean Machine's standards, fairly mild. By anyone else's standards, homicidal rage.

Ignoring the rebel craft, *Dialhead* and the ten Fists swept to the south.

Anderson glanced at Dreadhead's kilometre-wide mouth. Touched fingers to her brow and frowned.

'Get a move on, Anderson!' Dredd barked. 'Way's wide open. What you waiting for?'

She reeled, only held in place by the bio-attraction seat.

'What the drokk's wrong with you, Anderson?' Dredd roared.

'Take that, you Fascist scum!' Caligula cried, blasting another cloud-scraping statue of Judge Dread.

'But *you're* a Fascist, dear,' Lesbia said sweetly.

He straightened up in his seat. 'Am I? Well, we can't have that. I'll not lower myself to Judge Dread's dreary politics. From now on I'm a – a Totalitarian Liberal Democrat.'

'Yes, dear.'

'*Excuse me, Gaius Caesar Augustus Germanicus Caligula,*' the Head ship's psionic walls broke in, '*but Dialhead and ten Fists are on our tail.*'

Caligula waved an airy hand. 'Don't worry. Helena Bonham-Carter will blast them out of the sky.'

'*With all due respect, Caesar, that is extremely unlikely.*'

'What d'you mean? She's Athena, isn't she? Or is it Aphrodite?' He glanced around, puzzled. 'What am I doing here?'

'I don't think he's a god at the moment,' Agrippinilla stage-whispered.

'What's happening?' he asked in utter confusion.

'You're blowing up Judge Dread's Statues of Might,' Lesbia hesitantly informed him.

His hand shot to the horrified oval of his mouth. 'Uh-uh-uh-'

'So much for Athena-Hershey,' Drusilla wryly remarked. 'Another undying love that lasted an hour.'

'Athena-*Hershey*?' he scowled. 'Don't be absurd. I mean – I wouldn't kick her out of bed – nice rear, firm but fair – but *Athena*? That's downright silly. I mean, she's no Helena Bonham-Carter of Troy or anything.'

'Yes, dear.'

'*Caesar, the situation is thoroughly dire,*' the walls warned. '*Judge Mean Machine and ten Fists are about to launch a full-scale attack.*'

He threw up his hands. 'All right, tell His Dreadness I'm sorry and all that. Won't do it again.'

'*Too late for apologies, Caesar. You are about to be terminated.*'

'Well I like that!' the emperor snorted, totally disgusted. 'After all I've done for him! He *used* me, you know, ages ago. Sneaked me into the Chief Judge's chair, then booted me out and sat in it himself. Me, what did I get – years in a cell, that's what, pronounced dead by Zeus-Almighty Judge Dread.' He stood up and stamped his foot. 'That's it! I've had enough!'

One hand on breastplate, the other stretched aloft and balled into a fist, he declaimed in ringing tones:

'By the phallus of Priapus, Caligula shall suffer wrongs no more. To war! To war!'

Flinging himself into the pilot seat, he swung the *Head Imperial* around and confronted *Dialhead*, face to marbleen face.

'Come and get me, Butthead!' he yelled, his voice amplified to a boom by the *Head Imperial*'s mouth.

'Butthead!' laughed a young Judge standing behind Mean Machine. 'That's a good 'un!'

The rest of the *Dialhead* crew shrank back. 'He's for it.'

Judge Mean Machine, a daunting mesomorph with a brain-attuned dial on his Neanderthal head and a robotic arm that could bend biosteel, froze at the young Judge's derision.

He turned, very slowly, a mountain of rock-hard muscle. Then he shifted the dial on his head-plate. 'I'm going up to *three*,' he growled, moving the arrow from MEAN to REAL MEAN, incidentally switching the arrow on *Dialhead* to the same position.

Judge Mean Machine stomped up to his victim, who suddenly wasn't laughing any more. 'Just kidding, Judge Governor sir – only kidding . . .'

Mean Machine bent backwards . . . and bent backwards

283

. . . He arced back until the top of his head touched the floor.

He stayed there a moment, like a taut bow, quivering to lash back.

Lash back he did, releasing all the power in his massive physique in a forward swing. His head-plate impacted on the young Judge's forehead.

BOK!

The young Judge's head cracked like an egg and ended up somewhere inside his neck.

'Anyone else laughing?' bellowed Mean Machine, the volume deafening. His crew wore earplugs to keep their eardrums from bursting. Mean Machine *always* hit the high decibels.

'Think I'm THICK, huh?' he roared. 'I used to be SENSITIVE! Used to like PRETTY FLOWERS and NICE PICTURES! Then Dad stuck this drokking dial in my head and DROKKED ME UP! Anyone want to laugh at that? No! RIGHT! BATTLE STATIONS!'

'War!' Caligula shrilled, launching a Diabolus at *Dialhead*. The Head ship's psionic intelligence predicted the launch and shot sideways.

The missile swept on and hit a Fist.

The explosion vaporised the Fist and destroyed four of its companions. Three tumbled earthwards, disabled.

Dialhead shot a Diabolus from its own snarling mouth.

The precognitive *Head Imperial* had already moved out of the missile's lightning-fast path.

The *Head Imperial* replied with another Diabolus. *Dialhead* evaded it with ease. The last two Fists were blown to oblivion.

Caligula jumped up and down excitedly. 'Look at that! Boom! Whoom!' He reached for the launch ignition.

Drusilla caught his wrist. 'Easy on the macro-missiles, Little Boots. *Dialhead*'s bound to have a bigger stock than us. Duck and dodge for a while. Let Mean Machine use up his last Diabolus, then strike.'

Caligula slapped his thigh. 'Well said, Mrs Caligula.'

Dialhead kept on firing.

The *Head Imperial* ducked and dodged.

Finlly, *Dialhead*'s major fire-power was spent.

The Nova Roman emperor readied himself to unleash two Diabolus missiles. 'Dodge this, *Dialhead*,' he chuckled, finger poised over the button.

That's when a fleet of Fists arrived.

A hundred of them.

He flapped his arms wildly. 'What do I do – what do I do?'

Drusilla gulped. 'Launch all macro-missiles at the Fists. No other choice.'

He stopped flapping, slammed away at the button. 'Take that – and that – and that – '

The sleek missiles homed in on the charging Fists.

Impacted.

When the dust cleared, a loud cheer went up from the *Head Imperial*'s flight-deck.

'The gods have smiled on us!' rejoiced Drusilla, scanning the empty skies and the Fists plunging in flames far below.

'Did we get all of them?' Caligula marvelled. 'Wow!'

'A lot of them must have crashed into each other with the force of the explosions,' mused Agrippinilla.

'Don't go all technical on me,' Caligula grimaced. 'It's so – unaesthetic.'

Dialhead floated back into view, an exact replica of Mean Machine above the neck.

'Look,' Lesbia said, pointing at the dial. 'He's gone up to number four. "DROKKED OFF".'

'Well, tough luck on him. His arsenal's spent. Let's flit off back to Nova Roma.'

Drusilla clapped a hand to her mouth. 'Oh no . . .'

Even as she groaned, they all saw what was coming.

More Fists.

Hundreds and hundreds and hundreds of them, each faster on a straight run than a Head ship.

Caligula leaned over to Drusilla. 'I think we're in a spot of bother, Mrs Caligula.'

TWENTY-NINE

The semi-organic walls of Dreadhead were shrieking their alarms like a million banshees.

Leaving Karyn propped in her chair, Hershey slipped out of her quarters and mingled with the manic throng.

Dread's command boomed through the banshee wail:

'ALL FIST CREWS TO STATIONS! BLOW THE *HEAD IMPERIAL* OUT OF THE SKY! DESTROY CALIGULA!'

Hershey tried not to smile. *All* Fist crews? The entire drokking fleet? That amounted to half the middle ranks of Dreadhead. The most able fighters. Caligula must be putting up one hell of a battle. Who would have thought it? The emperor of Nova Roma was full of surprises.

She had hoped for some confusion when and if Caligula blasted a few Judge Dread statues. But she'd been handed chaos.

Weaving unnoticed through the hither-and-thither rush of Judges, Hershey entered a speed-chute and sped down into the bowels of Dreadhead.

After several minutes, the descent slowed. And a rank smell wafted up the flexing duct of the chute.

She stepped out of the chute into an unusually deserted Conglomeration Domain.

The floor pulsed beneath her booted feet as she ran through winding passages, the pulse of the floor mounting as the noxious stink intensified.

She was nearing the heart of the Domain – the soft core. The Conglomeration. Running to her death.

'For you, Karyn,' she whispered under her breath. 'For you.'

'We've got rhythm,' Weller said, planting his psi-charged palms on to the wall of the melt-hole that snaked through the Undercity's plascrete roof. 'Let's make music.'

Expelling a weary sigh, one of the suicide team slumped to the tunnel floor. 'What's the point?' she asked, face drained with exhaustion. 'The Bleeding Hearts army – what there was of it – is wiped out. Drowned in the Secretion. We haven't got a hope. Why go on?'

'Because I sense Cassandra Anderson is still alive, and while she lives, there's always hope,' Weller responded, stepping back from the plascrete wall. 'Come on, Julie, keep going. We've covered almost all the tunnels. Struck up a rhythm in the plascrete.'

'Julie's right,' another chimed in. 'A suicide mission for a purpose – I can see that through. But when there's no purpose . . .' He shook his head. 'I doubt that Cassandra's survived the Stew. She's not invulnerable.'

'I never said she was, Martin,' Weller conceded. 'You're all forgetting something. She's saved our lives, many times, every one of us. And at great risk to her own. We owe her. Besides, we all gave her a promise when we volunteered. A promise to see this thing through to the end, no matter what it took. I wouldn't break a promise to Cassandra, would you – *really*?'

Julie stood up. 'Okay, I hear you. Let's finish the job. But not out of hope. Just – for Cassandra.'

Weller glanced at Martin.

Martin gave a dour smile. 'For Cassandra.'

Weller planted the rhythmic throb of his hands back on the wall. 'Remember Joshua and Jericho,' he exhorted. 'When Joshua fought the battle of Jericho, the walls came tumbling down.'

Julie thrust her palms on the plascrete and forced a smile on her lips. 'We've got rhythm,' she announced.

'Let's make music,' responded Martin.

Weller gave a nod. 'Groovy.'

Her lungs were bursting.

Her heart was banging like a drum.

But Cassie kept on running.

Never give up.

The rubbereen belt kept up its steady, remorseless pace, wearing her down, wearing her down . . .

Most of the Judges in the galleries had gone away now. Alarms were ringing. She hardly registered the changes.

She only had one task. Stay alive as long as she could.

Metre by metre, she was losing ground to the Mouth.

That didn't matter.

Just keep running, and never give up.

The last of the Fists shot out of Dreadhead's mouth, trailing the vast fleet.

After three minutes and ninety kilometres, another Fist slid in behind the tail-ender.

In the frantic activity, no one noticed that the new tail-ender was Fist 24.

Cassandra Anderson glared through Fist 24's oval of transparent marbleen. 'So we've lost one plan,' she said grimly. 'Let's make up another. I can take out a few of the tail-enders as we go. The rest are too busy looking ahead to notice – I hope.'

She twisted her hand. Lightning flashed into the walls. The walls absorbed it, then released the energy in blue-white bolts. Four Fists melted like hot wax.

She repeated the procedure, again and again.

By the time the embattled *Head Imperial* came in sight, she'd accounted for seventy Fists.

Seventy out of nearly two thousand.

Corey had been increasingly withdrawn as the flight progressed. 'I'm not sure,' she kept muttering. 'Not sure.'

'Not sure of what?' Dredd finally snapped.

Corey glanced at Anderson. 'Cassandra, can you open up? I think I feel something.'

'I've got my hands a bit too full at the moment to open up,' Anderson muttered.

Corey turned to Dredd. 'I may be wrong, but I think I can sense Karyn's psyche. But if I'm right, it's lost in a crowd.'

'*Drokk*,' Anderson swore. 'They've spotted us.'

Dredd took it in at a glance.

Fifty Fists were wheeling round to hit Fist 24 with everything they'd got.

Anderson's voice resonated in the cockpit. 'He's here.'

'Who's here?' Dredd snapped, surveying the night skies beyond the Fist fleet.

'The mysterious stranger.' She pointed upwards.

A monstrous Head airship plunged through the frosty clouds, churning the vapours in its descent.

The Head's face was lopsided, the eyes mismatched and askew. The biosteel face was a mish-mash of crudely slotted bits and pieces, a jigsaw that didn't fit.

'Patchwork,' announced Anderson, with a fond look. 'Patchwork face, patchwork body, patchwork clothes. His insides are patchwork too.'

The Patchwork Head spat out missiles like a salvo of bullets.

The fifty Fists that had swung round to confront Anderson's craft were blown to Grud. She had to force the Fist into a deep ascent to avoid the hurtling debris.

She maintained the ascent until the Fist grazed the cloud canopy's underside, then slowed the ship to an easy glide.

'Don't tell me,' grunted Dredd. 'We're gonna wait again.'

'Only for a minute or two. After that, it's hell all the way, you'll be pleased to hear.'

'Patchwork!' Caligula exulted, peering up at the grotesque Head dropping from the clouds on to the Fist fleet. 'Give 'em hell, Patchwork.'

Diabolus missiles stormed down on the marbleen fleet. Caligula had barely blinked ten times when half the Fists were blown to smithereens.

Then the Patchwork Head paused in its attack.

'Keep it up,' Caligula prompted. 'Smash the oafs to atoms.'

Lesbia shook her head. 'He deluged them with his Diabolus arsenal. I don't think he has any real fire-power left.'

'Would Patchwork make such a mistake?' He frowned. 'Hard to believe.'

'Look at that!' Drusilla thrust a finger at Patchwork's Head.

The air was rippling underneath the bizarre Head ship, spreading out in prodigious shock waves.

When the first wave hit the *Head Imperial*, they tumbled and rolled across the flight-deck with the abrupt lurch.

'You're not supposed to hit *me*, you buffoon!' Caligula screeched, struggling to his feet.

He squinted through the blue glasseen eye-window. 'Oh . . . he's hit *everybody* – I think.'

His clone-wives peered over his shoulder.

'Yes,' Agrippinilla observed. 'The fleet seems to be – drifting.'

'Inert lumps,' said Lesbia.

Caligula clicked his fingers. 'Of course. Patchwork developed some kind of polarising psi-field thingamajig that drains psionic energy. We're all operating on low power. Cancels out missile launches for starters. As for flying – anyone want to get out and push?'

Drusilla glanced at a readout in the holo-shape of an unrolled vellum scroll. 'We have some motive power. Up to forty kays an hour.'

'*Caligula* . . .'

All four glanced about the flight-deck.

'This can't be another psi-call,' the emperor muttered. 'Doesn't sound right.'

'It's audio-psionic,' Drusilla said, rolling her eyes upwards. 'You know – standard communication.'

'Ah, that's all right then.'

'*Watch out for* Dialhead! *I've almost depleted the reserves in that last surge. All I have is motive power, but I can't reach you in time.*'

Dialhead was floating up close to the *Head Imperial*. The two Heads stared at each other in a head-to-head.

'So?' The emperor shrugged. 'I can't fire on him, but he can't fire on me. What can *Dialhead* do?'

Judge Mean Machine pushed the dial on his head-plate up to five.

'No more Mr Nice Guy!' he roared.

Some drokker had drokked up *Dialhead*'s psionics, but Mean Machine had a special relationship with his craft, verging on symbiosis.

If he thought *hard*, until his head hurt, Mean Machine could make *Dialhead* do what Mean Machine did best.

He furrowed his brow. Thought hard. His head started to hurt.

'RIGHT!'

He leaned back . . . and back . . .

Dialhead tilted back . . . and back . . .

Mean Machine bent back until his head touched the floor.

Dialhead turned in the sky until it was upside down.

Mean Machine whiplashed upwards, snapping his head forward in the king of all head-butts.

Dialhead spun round and forward, and nutted the *Head Imperial* hard on its noble brow.

BOK!

The *Head Imperial* went flying, whirling like a top.

Caligula's laurel-crowned marbleen Head plunged towards a graniteen block, out of control and out of luck.

* * *

Dredd watched the *Head Imperial*'s downfall with a stony expression. 'Gives me an idea,' he said. He rounded on Anderson. 'How d'you feel about a fist-fight?'

Their craft, thanks to Anderson's prescience, had stayed well clear of the Patchwork Head's polarising surge. Fist 24's armaments had been used up in earlier attacks, but the motive power was intact.

The rebel leader winked. 'Way ahead of you, but first we've got to save Caligula.'

'Save Caligula!'

'He may come in useful. Watch this.' She was already accelerating the Fist up to a thousands kays, dropping in pursuit of the *Head Imperial*. 'Fists have an energy shield when fully functional,' she said. 'Seems like we're the only ship of the fleet that's functional. If we weren't, my next trick would be my last.'

Swooping under the *Head Imperial*, with a kilometre to go before it bashed into a block, she aimed the Fist at the huge head of marbleen.

And landed an uppercut on the marbleen jaw, punching the Head back into the sky.

The recoil was barely registered in the shielded Fist.

Anderson raised an eyebrow at Dredd. 'See? Now let's give *Dialhead* a smack in the face.'

The Fist zoomed up to Mean Machine's Head ship and socked it on the side of the jaw.

Dialhead rolled with the punch, and went on rolling over Dreadcity.

Then it was Anderson's Fist against Judge Dread's Fists. She was energy-shielded. The rest had their knuckles.

Darting to and fro, she punched them out of commission, sending dozens spinning to explode in the moulded graniteen valleys and steeps.

'Groovy,' she murmured.

Corey put a hand on Anderson's arm, just below the Bleeding Hearts badge. 'That's enough, Cassandra. That's enough.'

Anderson eased back. 'You're right. Too groovy.' She peered up at the *Head Imperial*, which had righted itself in the air. 'Seems like we're playing in Caligula's world. Some freaky game.' Her expression hardened. 'It's no game. Let's fly to Dreadhead.'

She shut her eyes, reaching for Patchwork.

You hear me? It's time. As far as we know, Karyn's out of it. But Caligula's diverted Judge Dread's attention. Let's make the best of it. Let's go.

Patchwork's Head descended. Anderson threw a glance at her companions. 'He wants us inside the Patchwork Head. Last-second change of plan. We'll fly into Dreadhead's mouth together. He's recharged the *Head Imperial*'s psionics so that Caligula can keep up some kind of diversion.'

'We're gonna ditch the Fist and go inside that thing?' Dredd scowled. 'Not sure I trust this Patchwork. Who the drokk is he, anyway?'

She guided the Fist up to the mutilated features of Patchwork's Head. 'You're about to find out.'

As they soared towards the Patchwork Head, Corey gave a sharp gasp, hands covering her eyes. 'I know where Karyn is. No wonder she was hard to locate.'

Anderson snapped a look at her. 'Where is she?'

Corey lifted bleak eyes. 'She's inside the Conglomeration.'

Whatever Anderson felt, she didn't show it. 'Bad place to be,' she said in a flat tone.

THIRTY

Hershey crept to the thumping heart of the Conglomeration Domain, nose wrinkling at the smell.

Whatever Caligula was doing out there over Dreadcity, he was doing a great job of it. Dreadhead was in turmoil. Normally, the Conglomeration was surrounded by hyperpsychics, under Judge Omar's watchful eye.

Apart from the occasional sound of footsteps in the winding labyrinth of tubular passages, Hershey might as well have been alone in the Domain.

'For you, Karyn,' she said under her breath. 'For you.'

The hand sign that Karyn had left told Hershey all she needed to know about the young hyperpsychic's whereabouts. If Karyn's psi-shielding of Hershey was discovered, she'd attempt to eject her psyche into the Conglomeration. That way she would be hard to trace, and although Judge Dread would know of the psi-shielding, it would take him some time to uncover *who* was being shielded.

The odds were that Karyn wouldn't make it into the Conglomeration. Failure meant that she'd float about Dreadhead's interior, at the whim and beck of the living shadows. But if she succeeded, she faced the likelihood of a worse fate: total absorption in the Conglomeration. Complete loss of self.

The passage widened; the pounding in floor and air intensified.

Hershey slowed her paces as she entered the great dome that housed the most powerful computer in history.

The dome was two hundred metres in height and width.

The Conglomeration filled most of it.

Hershey tried not to retch.

The heaving mass was not one brain, but more than ten thousand, drawn from a decade of psychic talents. It was a vast clump of barely recognisable human bodies. Each head was enlarged through Resyk feeding, but not sufficient to contain the fear-secretion-enriched brain that bulged through the split skull.

The heads were the largest parts of the bodies. Torso, arms, legs – they'd atrophied into dangling pink scraps. Vestigial rags of bodies hanging from inflated heads.

The clumped mass of ten thousand heads was interconnected and nourished by a tangle of transparent, vibrating tubes that pumped an amber guck into the brain lobes. The guck oozed and dripped on to the floor, spreading in a wide pool.

It was a conglomeration of brains, and it beat as one.

If Karyn had projected her soul into one of those heads, and been ingested by the hive-mind of the pulsing mass, Hershey had promised herself she'd blow the Conglomeration to Grud.

It was impossible to attack the Conglomeration. Everyone said so. The bio-computer's collective mind would absorb your psyche the instant you entertained a hostile thought towards it.

Well, she'd indulged in a range of hostile thoughts, and the Conglomeration hadn't sucked out her soul yet.

She started to pull the Exterminans rifle from her boot holster.

Aimed it at the centre of the flexing clump of brain-oozing heads that seemed to vibrate with a sudden alarm.

Hershey squeezed the trigger.

For you, Karyn.

Karyn's corpse-like figure sat immobile in a chair in Hershey's apartment, a bunch of flowers in her lap.

Her left hand rested on a blue hyacinth.

The finger of the left hand twitched, just a fraction.

Hershey never got off a single shot.

An invisible force lifted Hershey off her feet and propelled her away from the Conglomeration and down the passage.

Rifle still clutched in her hand, she flew through the Domain maze like a bird.

In her befuddled wits, she believed at first that the pulsing mass of brains had proved how invulnerable it was. Then she heard a voice in her head as she hurtled down the corridors.

I'm inside the Conglomeration, Hershey, the one place it can't look for me. And I'm still myself. I'm blocking the bio-computer, tangling it in paradoxes. It's going slowly insane. It's feeding Judge Dread lies and half-truths. Leave me here. YOU MUST!

Hershey landed with a thump beside the speed-chute.

Okay, Karyn. You're calling the shots.

She staggered to her feet, shaking her head.

'HERSHEY!'

Whirling round, she saw the helmeted figure of Dekker aiming an Exterminans. Behind her was a grinning McGruder.

'Tracked you down here,' cackled McGruder, stroking her bearded jut of a chin. 'Shouldn't be down here, should she, Dekker? We'd be in our rights to punish you.'

Dekker's mouth curved into a mirthless smile. 'The punishment's death.'

Caligula rubbed his forehead. 'I think I'm suffering from blood on the brain.'

After *Dialhead*'s head-butt, he and his sister-wives had tumbled round and round the *Head Imperial*'s interior as the craft spun downwards. Then another *thwack* and the

Head ship was launched skywards. And they tumbled round and round again until the craft finally righted itself.

'Ooo . . . I ache all over,' complained Lesbia.

The others grunted in accord.

Groggily, Caligula lurched up to the left glasseen eye. *Dialhead* floated nearby. 'Look! There he is! Judge Butt-head of Antarctica!'

'Stay clear of him,' Drusilla warned. 'He'll nut you out of the sky.'

'I'm a god, and I can outnut anybody!' exclaimed the Nova Roman emperor. 'Hey . . . what's that?'

The low thrum and heightened illumination of restored power was enlivening the *Head Imperial*.

'*Full motive power has returned, Caesar,*' the psionic walls announced. '*Power regeneration transmitted from Patchwork's Head.*'

Lesbia clapped her hands. 'We can fly back to Nova Roma. On second thoughts – let's head for the furthest planet we can find.'

'Fiddle-faddle!' Caligula snorted. 'I'm going to teach Judge Head-butt a lesson. Beat him at his own game.'

'Oh *no*,' the three clone-wives groaned as one.

'Oh yes. Nobody nuts the divine Caligula and gets away with it.' He raised an arm, fingers outspread. 'Let battle commence. Ramming speed!'

From the flight-deck of the Patchwork Head, Dredd and Anderson watched Fist 24 speed away, pre-programmed to keep up the knuckle fight with the remnants of the fleet.

A door sighed open, and Patchwork entered.

The face was instantly recognisable: the Head ship's features were an exact replica of the man within. The patchwork suit was a cross between a clown and tramp's outfit.

He nodded at Dredd. 'Glad to meet you, Joe Dredd,'

he husked harshly, as though his lungs laboured to keep on pumping.

He rested his gaze on Dredd for several seconds, then turned to Anderson. 'Maybe it's as well the original plan didn't work out. Caligula's made more impact by drawing out the fleet than he'd ever have done by launching an attack on Judge Dread himself. Besides, the first plan meant the emperor's certain death. Better this way – I rather like the guy.'

'Patchwork,' Corey said, stepping forwards. 'Karyn's merged with the Conglomeration. I'm sure of it.'

He twitched his maze of a face. 'Has she retained her own mind?'

'I think so. Shall I try to psi-call her?'

'No. That would alert the whole of Dreadhead. Leave it up to her. If she can hold on, she can do more good inside the Conglomeration than outside. Anderson, would you fly the craft to Dreadhead? I want to talk to Joe Dredd.'

She flicked a look at Dredd, at Pachwork. 'Uh-huh. I get it – finally.'

Patchwork waved Dredd into a room decorated in mismatched mosaic tesserae. Mosaics on walls, floor and ceiling.

Stopping in the middle of the floor, Patchwork swung round and faced Dredd.

'Don't you recognise me, Joe?'

Dredd shook his head. 'Can't say I do.'

Patchwork thrust his head forwards. 'Look at me, Joe. *Look at me*!'

Dredd tensed in every muscle. 'Face different. Voice different. No way I could recognise you. But I reckon I do.'

Patchwork nodded. 'I'm your brother – Rico.'

'You're Chief Judge Dread's brother – but yeah, it amounts to the same thing.'

'What did you do to me in the Cafe Cesare?' Patchwork asked.

'I waited you out. You surrendered, and ended up serving twenty years as a cyborg on Titan.'

'Huh, I'd sooner have been *shot*. I was waiting for you to shoot me, you know.'

'I often wondered about that. Tell me, what twisted the Chief Judge into the maniac he is? It couldn't have come from firing a bullet into you.'

'I can guess. I woke up in Resyk and looked straight at him before the Mouth swallowed me. I think that drove him over the edge.'

'Grud!' Dredd exclaimed. 'You survived the shooting *and* Resyk?'

'Yeah.' What might have been a smile trembled the near-rigid mouth. 'I'm the man who came back from the dead twice. Impressed Caligula no end. I've been his closest adviser since I told him about how I cheated death twice.'

'How did you survive?'

'When I was taken out of the Cafe Cesare I was as near dead as you can get. Heart was in a mess. On a Med-slab, a faint trace of brain activity was picked up. Trouble was, the guy who picked it up was Judge Rutter. A day in rapi-heal and I was brought round. Rutter was crazy keen on a woman I was seeing. Ranted on about me making her pregnant. That was true enough. I had a daughter – called her Vienna.'

'Same thing happened in my world,' Dredd said.

'Uh-huh? Well, Rutter had his vengeance on me. He paralysed my motor functions and fed me to the Resyk belt, fully conscious, unable to lift a finger. Until I was a few metres from the Mouth, that is. I got control of my limbs back and ducked, dodged and dived my way through Resyk's Stomach. It cut my flesh to ribbons and my bones to snapped sticks, but my heart was still beating when I came out the other side. Next thing I knew I was in some unofficial surgery, bits and pieces put back together into the Patchwork you see now. Reckon the Resyk operatives must have worried about their jobs when a live one came out the other end; I suppose they shunted me off to the nearest underworld doc.'

'*Grud*,' Dredd murmured softly, lowering his helmeted head. 'I never heard of any Waker making it alive through Resyk.'

Patchwork stared Dredd straight in the face. 'I'm a Dredd,' he stated simply. 'And by the set of your jaw, you're more of a brother of mine than the Chief Judge Dread of my own world.'

Joe Dredd's mouth worked in tiny spasms. 'I did have to shoot you – twenty years later when you came back from Titan. I think you wanted to die.' A tiny hesitation. 'Rico – Patchwork . . . Were you some sort of Christian?'

Patchwork gave a throaty laugh. 'Me, a Christian? No way.'

'The last thing you – I mean your continuum double – said was, "Mother of God – is this the end of Rico?"'

'That's what *I* said in the Cafe Cesare when the slug plugged my heart. Different continua, same death-gasp words, huh? No, it wasn't anything to do with religion. If you'd watched some old movies, you'd know that. It was a quote from a death scene in *Little Caesar*, a 1931 gangster movie, starring Edward G. Robinson as a hoodlum, name of Rico. Edward Gee was the owner of the Cafe Cesare on Robinson Street, and Cesare's Italian for Caesar, right? I croaked with a pun on my lips.'

'Yeah – come to think of it, that'd be your style. Does Anderson know who you are?'

'Only from a minute ago. I opened my mind to her a little. Come to think of it, the time's come to bring everything out into the open. We're about a minute from Dreadhead. I've got several thousand scores to settle with the Chief Judge, starting with the murders of Vienna and her mother.'

301

'He killed them? Jovus Drokk . . . How come he turned out so bad and you turned out okay in the end?'

'People change. He got worse. I got better.'

'PATCHWORK!' Anderson's voice shouted through the audio. 'Someone's declared a Carnal Carnival!'

The two men rushed on to the flight-deck and studied the magnified holo-vista of a sector of Dreadcity.

Mayhem, frolic, havoc and saturnalia reigned in the spires and gulfs below. The Nameless were transformed into the frenzied celebrants of a carnival of delights and horrors that outmatched Mega-City One at its most bizarre.

'The Nameless have become the Reckless in this dark hour before the dawn,' Anderson grinned. 'And Judge Dread had nothing to do with it. Last thing he wants in the first phase of invasion is a Carnal Carnival.'

'Karyn?' Patchwork queried.

'Got to be. She must have drokked up the Conglomeration from within and redirected its aims. Corey and I both sense that ultraterror's been withdrawn from both continua. And sure as sin she's sent a Carnival command into the people's minds. Just as well our first plan was shot to pieces. This way we've got a better chance.'

'Seems like some luck's on our side,' Giant rumbled.

'We're going to need it,' Patchwork commented. 'Anyone who's crazy enough to challenge Chief Judge Dread needs all the luck they can get.'

The colossal helmet of Dreadhead loomed into sight. In seconds, it filled the screen.

The kilometre-wide mouth, stretched as though to roar or swallow, gaped to engulf the craft.

Patchwork's Head flew straight into the mouth of Dread.

THIRTY-ONE

Dekker's finger was on the trigger of the Exterminans. Hershey's Exterminans was in her grip but the finger wasn't on the trigger. The difference between life and death.

That's if you bothered to fire, which Dekker was expecting Hershey to do.

Hershey did the unexpected. She leaped backwards into the speed-chute.

Hurtling up the chute, Hershey took aim directly below. Dekker, always a gung-ho character, flew up in Hershey's wake, blasting streaks of blue-white psionic lightning up the narrow channel that gradually wore down the energy field of Hershey's uniform. As for her unprotected head, the lightning played havoc with the inside of her skull.

Hershey met fire with fire, pouring down deadly psionic jets that spilled harmlessly off her pursuer's psi-shielded helmet.

It was the helmet that made the difference. On a level battleground, Hershey would back herself against Dekker any day.

Have to get underneath.

Firing a fierce burst for cover, she slowed and jumped out on Level 732.

Dekker didn't slow in time to emerge on to the same level. She kept on rising.

Hershey jumped back into the chute, inverting her body in mid-jump, her boot soles pointing upwards. No way

303

was she going to offer Dekker a bare-headed target to blast to Grud.

But the shoot-out was still loaded in favour of the helmeted Dekker. Some of the psionic spillage seeped over Hershey's unprotected head. As things stood, Dekker was going to wear her down, sooner or later.

Soaring up through Dreadhead, the two women exchanged bursts of lethal lightning.

Time was on Dekker's side. Hershey knew it. Dekker knew it.

The ascent accelerated as they neared the crown of Dreadhead. Floors whizzed by.

Soon be journey's end, Hershey grimly reflected.

'Run, little girl,' Chief Judge Dread growled as he sat in the hovering DreadThrone above the yawning Mouth of Resyk.

The Nameless girl who had the *nerve* to call herself Cassie kept up her hopeless running-to-stand-still battle against the rubbereen belt.

Resyk's galleries were emptied of Judges, called out to man or observe the fleets. Judge Dread had the graniteen hall of Resyk all to himself. He glanced up at its high, pointed arches, its leering gargoyles.

Resyk was Dread's cathedral, the Mouth the gate to his altar, the Conglomeration his tabernacle.

If he had a religion, this was its ritual.

The Mouth's devouring of Rico had been Dread's baptism of blood.

'RUN, LITTLE GIRL!' he bellowed.

He leaned back in the obsidian throne and enjoyed the spectacle. A while ago, he had been plagued by doubts, but the Conglomeration had allayed them.

The Conglomeration had assured him that Joe Dredd, Cassandra Anderson – the whole crew – were dead. So was Caligula, blasted from the skies by *Dialhead* on first contact. Not that the Nova Roman clown was of any consequence except as a salutary lesson that no one was exempt from Dread's Judgement.

The entire fleet was intact, and on its way back to base. In fact – they should have arrived by now . . .

'Conglomeration,' he summoned.

«Yes, sire,» slurped a multi-tongued voice in his head.

'Status of the fleet.'

«On its way back.»

'It should have arrived. You – you sound subtly different, as if you've gained an extra tongue.'

«The feeding was good, my Lord. It gave new vigour to thought and tongue.»

'Very well. Report the moment *Dialhead* returns.'

«I was about to inform you, Lord – Judge Mean Machine has scooped Caligula from the *Head Imperial*'s debris. Caligula survived the blast. Mean Machine wishes to bring the presumptuous jester directly to you through the private duct. You might care to observe Caligula race against the speed of the belt.»

A smile split Dread's features. 'Excellent, arrange for *Dialhead* to come through Duct Prima to Gate 1 of Resyk. Caligula can join the brat on the belt.'

The exhausted girl, thirty metres from the Mouth, stumbled and crawled on her knees, gasping for breath.

'No,' Dread grinned. 'Looks like Caligula will be alone on the belt. Can't let him run the futile race without suitable musical accompaniment.'

He raised a fist to the vaulted spaces.

'Slaughter Symphony in Shriek Major!'

From the Orchestra far above, in the crown of Dreadhead, the music was transmitted through the conductive walls.

A savage symphony tinged the air red within the grey walls of Resyk.

Cassie fought to regain her footing.

But her limbs failed to respond.

She felt the wind of a spinning blade on her skin.

'Never give up,' she whimpered.

The words sounded hollow in her ears.

The Patchwork Head sped through a voluminous duct that reminded Cassandra Anderson of an intestine.

Dredd scowled. 'Lost control?'

'Yes and no,' Anderson replied. 'The Conglomeration's in control, but Karyn's in control of the Conglomeration. We're being taken where we need to be taken.'

The craft decelerated rapidly, halting in front of an expanse of glittering metal marked RESYK GATE 1.

Momentarily, Anderson shut her eyes. 'Me and Corey will have to travel a little further. The rest of you – out. And Dredd, don't forget what I told you about the Jericho plan.'

'I won't.'

Dredd was the first to spring out of Patchwork's Head, Patchwork and Giant close on his heels.

The gate slid open.

Dredd stormed inside, with only his fists for weapons in this psi-dominated world.

He found himself on the lowest of five galleries in a nightmare version of Resyk.

And he saw a nightmare version of himself, seated on a huge throne shaped in the likeness of –

'Judge Dread,' Dredd growled.

Then he saw the girl sprawled on the belt, speeding towards the Mouth.

'GIRL!' he bellowed, leaping the ten metres on to the belt. 'RUN! RUN!'

She looked up, five metres from the meat-grinder Mouth, shrank back for the briefest instant at the sight of Dredd, then flung herself away from the spinning blades and buzzing saws.

He could see she'd put all the grit and guts she'd got into the desperate run.

He pounded down the belt towards her.

'You're not Judge Dread!' she gasped out.

'Not in this world,' he growled.

He darted a glance at the man seated in a throne fashioned in his own likeness, his posture rigid as if frozen.

Then he concentrated on the girl who was battling for every meagre metre she put between herself and the Mouth. Barely ten metres.

Aided by the belt's speed, he pounded down the rubbereen surface and grabbed her in his arms.

'Never give up,' she panted, arms encircling his neck, eyes aglow.

'You said it, girl.'

He sprinted away from the Mouth, then heard a weighty thump on the rubbereen. A quick look showed Giant charging towards him.

'Give me the girl!' Giant boomed. 'You haven't got the strength to jump out of here!'

Dredd studied the sheer, ten-metre walls. 'And you have?' But he passed the girl over.

'I'm Cassie,' the girl said, clinging to Giant's back as he charged the wall.

'Good to meet you, Cassie,' he said, then blasted his huge, muscular frame at the towering wall.

Patchwork appeared above him, and slipped through the railings, dangling by his hands from the lowest railing.

Giant leaped.

The prodigious leap took him three-quarters of the way up the sheer expanse.

He shot up a hand. Just managed to grasp Patchwork's ankle.

Hand over hand, he clambered over Patchwork and swung himself on to the gallery.

Patchwork let go and dropped on to the moving rubbereen.

'Judges are coming!' Giant yelled down before placing Cassie in a niche. He hefted the Exterminans he'd let go to save the girl. 'Time to kill Judges. I'll leave their Chief to you guys!'

Sure enough, a stream of Judges flooded the far end of the gallery.

Giant let fly a storm of lightning bolts. 'Die, you drokkers!'

Dredd and Patchwork left Giant to it and raced back down the belt, glares fixed on the enthroned Judge Dread.

'You gonna come down and fight with your fists like a man, drokkhead?' Dredd bawled.

Chief Judge Dread reared up in his throne, balling his fists.

'Although you are born of no woman, and rebellion has come to Dreadhead, do your worst, and damned be the man who cries mercy!' Judge Dread thundered, leaping down from his throne.

He thumped up the belt, mighty fists raised, each thump underscoring the Slaughter Symphony in Shriek Major and the thunder-crack of battle on the gallery overhead.

'My skin is bioplast!' he roared. 'My skeleton is adamantinium! I am invulnerable!'

'Oh yeah?' snarled Dredd. 'Try this on for size!'

He slammed a fist into the Chief Judge's jaw.

And broke every bone in his knuckles.

Chief Judge Dread didn't even flinch.

He swatted Joe Dredd with the back of his hand. Dredd's jaw cracked and his body spun as he flew metres through the air to land with a thud.

Teeth gritted, he was back on his feet.

Patchwork was hanging back, making some obscure signal to Dredd. Dredd ignored it.

Chief Judge Dread was a *man*, and a man could be beaten, if you had the guts to keep at him.

He launched a flying kick at the Chief Judge. It was like hitting a steel wall. His spine jarred as he fell to the floor.

Judge Dread gave him a kick.

It cracked his ribs and sent him soaring.

He crash-landed with a pained grunt, vision swimming. When it cleared, he saw that the belt had carried them within fifteen metres of the Mouth.

Shaking his head clear of supernova stars, he forced himself upwards to see Patchwork still hanging back, but pointing at the Mouth.

Then he realised what Patchwork was trying to tell him.

The significance of it would have turned any normal man's blood to red ice.

If Chief Judge Dread was to be defeated, Dredd and Patchwork would have to die.

Cassandra Anderson and Corey raced through the maze of the Conglomeration Domain, summoned by Karyn's psi-call.

At every twist of the semi-organic tunnels, hyperpsychic Judges appeared, ready to unleash a flood of psionics on the two women.

Anderson and Corey lightning-flashed the Judges to psychic smithereens.

'*Love hurts,*' snarled Anderson as another one bit the biosteel.

'*Love hurts,*' responded Corey.

Heaps of blasted flesh lay in their wake as they raced into the dome of the Conglomeration.

They skidded to a halt.

The clumped heads, split-skulled with burgeoning brains, and dangling flaccid drapes of vestigial bodies, pulsed fiercely with the amber fluid pumping through a tangle of tubes.

'Hello ladies,' smiled Judge Omar, emerging from the other side of the Conglomeration, an Exterminans in his hand. 'I'm afraid you've met your match in me.'

Anderson gave a slight flicker of the fingers and the Exterminans melted in Omar's hands. His hands melted too. So did the rest of him.

So much for Omar.

The women closed their eyes . . . reached into the hive-mind of the Conglomeration.

Sought an individuality.

An individual.

Karyn.

Karyn. Anderson-Corey psi-whispered. *I sense the Conglomeration can't be destroyed from the outside. Retroactive shield against hostility. Psi-attack is turned back on the attacker.*

Think no hostile thoughts, Karyn psi-murmured. *The Conglomeration can only be destroyed from the inside. I'm not strong enough. Feed me your loving thoughts . . .*

Anderson-Corey transmitted what love they had to Karyn's trapped psyche.

A flood of love.

Bleeding Hearts love.

Killing love.

Karyn was brimming with love.

She let it out in hate.

It burst out from the centre of the pulsing brain-hive.

THIRTY-TWO

Hershey's resistance was wearing down fast under the constant barrage from Dekker's Exterminans.

Ascending the speed-chute upside down, she returned Dekker's fire, burst for burst.

The floors blurred by at a dizzying pace.

The psionic onslaught tormented Hershey's unhelmeted head, despite the fact that her boot soles faced her adversary.

She was losing it, but she threw her last drop of will-power into maintaining the ever-accelerating speed.

600 kays and rising.

Floor 900 flashed by.

901.

902.

They were ten floors from the crown of Dreadhead.

Hershey, from her inverted position, looked up the speed-chute.

Dekker, her visored gaze glaring down at Hershey, didn't think to look up.

Two more floors to Dreadhead's crown and the ceiling of the speed-chute.

The biosteel ceiling of the speed-chute.

Hershey activated her psionic uniform to operate emergency braking.

Dekker spotted her opponent's abrupt deceleration and looked upwards.

The instant Dekker looked, her helmeted head rammed into the biosteel roof with a crack of metal and bone.

There was no sign of Dekker's helmet. She was buried to the neck in biosteel.

The Exterminans dropped from her dead hand.

Hershey caught it as it fell.

'So long, Dekker, and thanks for the ride.'

The Conglomeration erupted, drenching Anderson and Corey in a mess of brains and oily liquid.

Karyn had done her work. She'd blown the bio-computer from within, and blown herself with it.

Anderson spat out a glob of brain tissue. 'Let's get going. The Conglomeration's destruction will send Dreadhead haywire for a while.'

They sprinted out of the dome, jumping over the threshing bodies of hyperpsychics crazed by the psychic backlash of the brain-hive's death throes.

The two rebel women felt the aftershocks too, but they endured them, not batting an eyelid.

'She did it,' panted Corey. 'Sacrificed herself. Blew the stinking mass to hell. We owe her.'

'You may be able to thank her personally,' Anderson said, racing down a passage that led to a speed-chute.

'Huh?'

'Just a feeling.'

The woman in the chair looked like a corpse, her chalky face in stark contrast to her red-gold hair.

A bunch of flowers lay in her quiet lap.

A white hand rested on a blue hyacinth.

A flush of pink invigorated the hand.

It twitched.

Stirred.

Grasped the hyacinth's stem.

Lifted it up.

The scent was inhaled.

* * *

312

'She's alive.'

Corey nodded in agreement with Anderson. 'I know, Cassandra. I can feel it.'

She glanced up the speed-chute they were ascending. 'She's close by. A few floors up. Do you sense that?'

'Yes.' She raised her hand. 'It's this floor.'

Following Karyn's spiritual echo, they exited the chute and ranged down a series of corridors.

'Here,' Anderson stated, stopping in front of a purple door, marked JUDGE GOVERNOR HERSHEY.

Corey arched an eyebrow. 'Hershey?'

Anderson shrugged as she opened the door. 'Why not?'

They walked in to witness a smiling Karyn, flowers in hand. And the muzzle of an Exterminans, held in Hershey's hand.

'You won't need the gun, Hershey,' Corey said calmly. 'If I read you right, we've ended up on the same side.'

Hershey lowered the rifle. 'If the rebels have taken over, then I declare myself Chief Judge.'

'Who needs a Chief Judge?' Anderson scowled, then turned to Karyn and broke into a broad smile. 'You did well, Karyn. You okay?'

'Fine. I escaped from the Conglomeration the instant I blew it. But you're wrong about not needing a Chief Judge. We'll have to reform the force into a Justice system, then gradually restore political power to the people. Anything else would end in chaos.'

Anderson thumped her brow. 'Give me chaos any day! Besides, all this talk is premature. Chief Judge Dread is still alive, and the odds are still against us. It's all down to Patchwork and Dredd – and Weller's Jericho team. Long odds, ladies. Long odds.'

Dredd responded to Patchwork's hand signal by throwing himself at Judge Dread's feet.

Anticipating the move, Patchwork flung his full weight at the Chief Judge's upper chest, throwing him off balance.

313

Judge Dread was strong, but he couldn't defy gravity.

He hit the deck. And the deck was moving – at 14 kph.

It was less than ten metres to the Mouth.

A few seconds to keep Judge Dread pinned down, keep him occupied before he realised the nearness of the Mouth of whirling blades.

'You're *stomm*, drokkhead!' Dredd snarled, jarring his fist on a punch at Judge Dread's throat.

'Look into *my* head, brother,' Patchwork hissed. 'What do you see there? *Who* do you see?'

The Chief Judge suddenly lapsed into immobility. His lips barely moved.

'Rico . . .'

Patchwork leaned close to Joe Dredd. 'Get away *now*! Operation Jericho!'

'Rico and Dredd!' bellowed the Chief Judge, clamping spine-breaking arms around the two men. 'My brother and my brother! I'll break you in two!'

Dredd, tensing his back muscles against the inhuman pressure, saw a rotary blade *whish* past his face.

Then the three men were inside the Mouth.

'NO!' bellowed Judge Dread, releasing his hold as the reality struck home.

'No good howling to me,' Patchwork snarled as a saw ripped into his back. 'I'm a dead man.'

They were on the inner conveyors leading down to the Stomach. There was no way back. And even the Chief Judge's adamantinium-skeletoned, bioplast-coated body couldn't pass unscathed through the bowels of Resyk.

'Duck and dodge!' Patchwork yelled at Dredd. 'I made it once. So can you!'

Dredd gritted his teeth, turbo-boosted his nerves to lightning-reflex, and ducked, dodged, twisted, leaped and squirmed as blades, saws, hammers and roving rollers sought to slice and grind.

It didn't do much good.

His body was cut, crushed and punctured.

He heard Patchwork's agonised scream close by.

It was succeeded by Judge Dread's bellow above the roar of the abattoir machinery. 'I AM THE LAW!' A tortured *skreak* of ruptured metal accompanied the roar.

'Follow the Judge!' Patchwork yelled from inside a windmill of razor-sharp blades. Blood geysered.

Follow the –

Dredd caught on.

The Chief Judge. Body of adamantinium and bioplast. Can smash his way through. SO FOLLOW!

He followed in Judge Dread's path, still ducking and side-stepping whirring blades, darting saws. But the Chief Judge was clearing a tortuous path through Resyk's Stomach. And Dredd kept close behind.

'*Acids! Shelter!*' Patchwork gasped somewhere at his back.

Dredd grasped Patchwork's meaning, and used Judge Dread's bulk as a shield against the sprays of searing acids, leaping from left to right as the deadly jets changed direction.

When the acid stopped spouting, a bass rumble sounded up ahead.

Rollers.

Giant rollers.

Wall-to-wall, floor-to-ceiling rollers.

No way round. You could only go through the middle. And come out the other side as paper-thin tissue.

Patchwork couldn't have faced *this* back when he was Rico. Must be an addition by Chief Judge Dread.

Bellowing, the Chief Judge battled with the rollers.

Punched, kicked, ripped metal asunder. The rollers shuddered and squealed in protest.

Judge Dread's bioplast skin was tough.

But it wasn't that tough.

It started to split at the seams even as he began to win his titanic struggle with the grinding barrels.

Howling, he forced his rupturing body through a ragged

gap. Just after he squeezed through, the rollers ground to a halt, defeated.

Dredd pushed through moments later, and entered a down-sloping duct. By the looks of it, he'd passed through the Stomach.

He glanced back through the gap in the rollers.

Patchwork was in bits and pieces, sliding along.

'Thanks – Rico. Couldn't have made it without you.'

He drew a deep breath. 'Operation Jericho.'

He slid down the duct, tensed for any sign of Judge Dread. But he emerged into a small, domed area, awash with amber-coloured guck. Tunnels radiated in all directions.

'Now where the drokk do I go?'

'Forgotten me, sir?' CORA asked inside Dredd's helmet.

'Truth is, in all this excitement, I had.'

'I'll show you the way out, sir,' the disc computer said.

'But Operation Jericho –'

'I'm fully primed on that, sir. Shall we go?'

'JOE DREDD!'

Dredd spun round. The damaged figure of the Chief Judge stood ten paces away, seething with rage and ready to rip.

'Time to run, sir. You know why.'

Dredd ran.

Dread pursued.

'We've given it the rhythm,' Weller said. 'We've given it the music. Now all we need is Anderson to blow the horn.'

The suicide team of Operation Jericho sank in sheer weariness to the floor of the last tunnel on their list. They'd transmitted the rhythm and music to every tunnel in the plascrete lid on the Undercity.

The walls were ready. The task was done. And the Secretion was just a bonus.

Now it was up to others.

* * *

316

'In here, sir.'

Joe Dredd looked at the small hover-pod in Dock 5 of Dreadhead's landing area, then glanced over his shoulder. No sign of the Chief Judge. Hadn't been for the last twenty minutes.

'You sure he's following?'

'He's pursuing in the DreadThrone. Anderson's psi-tracking him. He's psi-tracking you.'

He leaped into the pod. 'Sector 17,' CORA instructed.

The pod zoomed through a duct at a remarkable speed, and under a minute later was out in the open air.

'Ground Level's pretty close,' Dredd observed.

'Dreadhead's gradually sinking, sir. Psionic backlash from the Conglomeration's destruction. Ah, don't look now, but we're being followed.'

Dredd glanced back. The black shape of the Dread-Throne flew in his wake.

'You've really riled him, sir. Anderson was banking on that. He'd hound you all the way to hell. Good gracious me! He's carrying a couple of Lawgivers.'

'I figure I know why. A side of him wants to take me on equal terms.'

'Hardly equal, sir. The rips in his bioplast skin are already healed, and his organs are self-regenerating. Keep to the plan, sir. *Please.*'

Dredd grunted something.

'Land here,' CORA ordered the pod.

It settled in a flat, frosty arena, tinged orange by the early dawn, and encircled by stalagmite blocks alive with the bedlam of Carnal Carnival.

Dredd stepped out and stood on the icy ground.

The DreadThrone landed within spitting distance.

The Chief Judge descended from his throne, tossed a Lawgiver to Dredd. 'Okay, lawman – draw.'

Dredd snorted. 'Even armour-piercing wouldn't dent bioplast. Some shoot-out.'

'It amuses me. That's good enough. I won't kill you –

317

just disable you. Then you'll learn what it's like to play in the Orchestra.'

Judge Dread's mouth twisted into a snarl. 'Draw, I said.'

Anderson, Corey and Karyn knelt with eyes closed inside the high walls of DreadCourt.

The living shadows had gone. The Orchestra was quiet. Each human instrument had been put out of its misery by Anderson's mercy-killing thoughts.

The silence thickened.

'NOW!' the three women said in unison.

'NOW!' CORA shouted in Dredd's ear.

The command was barely uttered before he'd jumped into the pod and streaked skywards, leaving Judge Dread standing on the ground, peering warily up at him.

'NOW!'

The psi-order rang in Weller's head.

'Now!' he shouted at the suicide squad.

They sprang and planted their psi-charged hands on to the plascrete, and transmitted the signal for the plascrete to crack.

Tunnel by tunnel, wall by wall, they'd riddled the Undercity's plascrete lid with rhythmic music.

A disruptive rhythm, pressuring existing fault lines, creating others where none had existed.

Spreading a web of cracks.

Just a single beat and the cracks would widen. The plascrete lid would shatter.

As when Joshua fought the battle of Jericho, and the walls came tumbling down.

The suicide squad issued that single, catastrophic beat.

'Love hurts,' Weller said.

'Love hurts,' they replied.

And the walls came tumbling down.

* * *

The ground Judge Dread stood on trembled.

He glanced down.

The earth opened under his booted feet.

The earth in question being the Undercity's plascrete lid. It collapsed into a million pieces, ruinous in its downfall.

He fell straight through, his flailing hand missing the hovering DreadThrone by centimetres.

On the long drop, jostled by huge, plascrete chunks, Judge Dread had time to remember . . .

Remember that he'd flooded the Undercity with the Secretion. The Stew that transformed anyone into their worst nightmare.

Anyone – including the Chief Judge.

Howling, he plunged into the Secretion.

THIRTY-FOUR

'Where to now, sir?'

Dredd stared down at the wild festivities of Carnal Carnival. 'Ought to be arrested,' he rumbled.

'Where to, sir?'

'Home, CORA.'

'Through the Cafe Cesare fistula? I doubt that's possible. The Chief Judge created the fistula. With him gone, I'd say the way back was closed.'

'Go there anyway, drokk it!'

'Whatever you say. Incidentally, you took quite a slicing and mangling in Resyk. You're leaking all over the place. Shouldn't you seek medical attention?'

'It's nothing but a few broken bones and missing flesh and a small bucket of blood.'

'Oh, I give up. Cafe Cesare it is. It's not far. ETA three minutes.'

As the pod sped over the grim spires of Dreadcity, Dredd cast a last look at Dreadhead. It had descended to ground on the edge of the crater which now led to the Undercity.

He turned his back on it, and kept his eyes fixed ahead.

Soon the hover-pod was arcing down to the lower flanks of a block, and an aperture came in sight. The tunnel entrance to the cafe.

He alighted from the vehicle and entered the tunnel, the frost crunching under his feet as he walked into the derelict Cafe Cesare.

'Now what?' asked CORA.

Dredd rubbed his chin.

'Good question.'

Cassandra Anderson and Hershey faced one another across the former Circle of Dread in DreadCourt.

Anderson grimaced. 'This is stupid.'

'Take it or leave it. If I win, I become Chief Judge. If you win, I'll step aside for Karyn.'

'I don't want it this way,' Karyn sighed. 'If anyone has to fight Hershey, it's me.'

Anderson shook her head firmly. 'You wouldn't stand a chance against her.'

'And you don't stand a chance against me, *Cassandra*,' Hershey sneered.

'In your dreams, *Barbara*,' Anderson rejoined.

Hershey leaped without warning.

Anderson had already foreseen the attack and jumped clean over Hershey's head, kicking her teeth in the process. She landed lightly and spun round in a low crouch.

Tigerish, Anderson and Hershey circled each other.

Corey, Giant and Cassie watched the contest with mixed feelings. The Judges had fled Dreadhead after the psychic upheavals following the Conglomeration's destruction.

This was no time for battling it out over the Chief Judge's seat.

The two women charged each other.

A flurry of foot and fist blows ensued, too fleet for all but the quickest eye to follow.

When the fighters finally drew apart, breathing heavily, both were bloody but unbowed.

Giant studied the two women. 'Anderson's standing up the best.'

Corey gave a so-so shake of the hand. 'Hard to say.'

Snarling, Hershey flew at Anderson.

Anderson booted her in the stomach while executing a miraculous backward somersault.

Everybody was so intent on the struggle that no one

noticed McGruder creeping through an arched gateway, her crazed eyes fixed on her most hated enemy, an Exterminans pointed at that enemy's head.

What had once been Judge Dread climbed out of the Secretion and scaled the jagged walls of the newly formed crater with seething Stew for bubbling lava.

Judge Dread had metamorphosed into the thing he feared most. His worst nightmare.

The shape of his worst nightmare clambered within sight of the hovering DreadThrone. He called it. It came.

He sank back in the lap of Judge Dread's obsidian image, and issued a command.

'Cafe Cesare – now.'

McGruder pointed the Exterminans at the woman she loathed, heart and soul.

Cassandra Anderson.

McGruder hated Hershey, but at least Hershey was on the side of Judgement. The Law. She was a Judge.

Anderson was the queen of the rebels.

McGruder trained the muzzle on Anderson's head. And squeezed the trigger.

Karyn sensed the threat simultaneously with Corey, but Karyn moved first.

She flung herself in front of Anderson, yelling, 'Watch out!'

The Exterminans' psi-lightning blew Karyn's head from her shoulders.

Anderson and Hershey stopped, aghast.

The momentary silence was broken by a roar and a rush from the gate at McGruder's back.

A herd of Reckless charged into Dreadcourt, headed by a grey-haired matriarch, chock-a-block with weaponry.

'Poor Bizzie-Lizzie,' complained the grey-haired lady. 'So much to do, so little time.'

Anderson and Corey instinctively raised a psi-wall in front of the Reckless hordes. It just so happened McGruder was on the wrong side of it.

Spotting a Judge, the Reckless descended on McGruder and dragged her out of the hall, kicking her heels and screaming.

Bizzie-Lizzie's voice echoed from the gateway. 'So much to do, so little time. Look – first you pluck out the eyes – so.' McGruder's screams rose in pitch. 'Then you peel off the skin – so.'

McGruder's howls of agony were hardly human.

Anderson walked up to Karyn's body. She stroked the red-gold hair. 'Love hurts,' she murmured.

Hershey stood alongside, hands on her hips. 'Now what? What do we do about deciding on a Chief Judge?'

Anderson turned on her heel and walked away. 'I don't know and I don't damn well care.'

Before she strode out of earshot, Anderson glanced up at the soaring arches of DreadCourt. 'Sometimes I wish I could cry.'

'Hide, sir, hide!' CORA urged.

'What the drokk for?' Dredd growled.

'If you want to return to Mega-City One, *hide*!'

Dredd took the advice, running to the kitchen door and pulling it near-shut, a thin crack showing.

'He's coming,' CORA said. 'Judge Dread. He's been metamorphosed into his worst nightmare.'

Dredd squared his shoulders. 'Fill me in.'

'He's full of terror, panic, rage. He's driven by a death-wish. He wants to destroy himself.'

'What's he become?'

'He's become you.'

'Me!'

'His worst nightmare – you. He's flesh, blood and bone. The image of yourself, but not with your mind. He still

323

has Chief Judge Dread's mind, in every particular. If he can't be the best, the supreme, he wants oblivion.'

The soft thunk of boots on graniteen issued from the tunnel. Judge Dread strode into the cafe. Joe Dredd stared at his living image, right down to the lines in the chin and the cut of the Justice Lawgiver.

Then he noticed one difference. The name-badge said DREAD.

Judge Dread halted at the spot where he'd shot Rico, thirty-seven years before, and, in a low voice, quoted the lines of a poem:

> *'Like one that on a lonesome road,*
> *Doth walk in fear and dread.*
> *And having once turned round walks on,*
> *And turns no more his head;*
> *Because he knows, a frightful fiend,*
> *Doth close behind him tread.'*

The air rippled, shimmered . . .

'SIR!' CORA cried in alarm. 'He's not simply out to destroy himself. He's still attuned to the fistula he created. He's going back in time to destroy his past, and that means the destruction of *two* continua: his and yours. Follow him. Stop him!'

Dredd charged out of the kitchen, Lawgiver levelled.

But Judge Dread was already disappearing into a stormy vortex.

Dredd leaped into the vortex, looking for a target . . .

His wits spun.

He was spinning up-down-sideways.

Then he felt himself falling backwards through a tunnel of years.

The bewildering fall slowed . . .

And he dropped to his knees on shiny yellow tiles. He looked up. He was in a brand new Cafe Cesare. Just like it had been a month after it opened – thirty-seven years ago.

He saw himself as an eighteen-year-old Judge, fresh from the Academy, a Lawgiver levelled. He saw Rico crouched above the corpse of Edward Gee, Lawgiver in hand.

The apparently motionless figures resembled a tableau, but he got the feeling they were moving in the slowest of slow motion.

He darted a glance to one side. Judge Dread stood a few paces from the young Joe Dredd and Rico. Judge Dread's gun was aimed at the young Dredd's chest, finger squeezing on the trigger.

If Joe Dredd was killed at the age of eighteen, history would be changed for both continua, just like CORA said. Two universes would be wiped out, Dreadcity's and Mega-City One's.

Total oblivion.

Judge Dread fired at young Joe Dredd.

THIRTY-FIVE

Hershey lifted her head from the pillow and glanced through the window of Justice Central's med-centre and her gaze roved the bulbous blocks of Mega-City One.

She'd come to an hour ago, and was amazed to discover she wasn't dead after hurtling off a block roof in a drokked-up hover-wagon exchanging bullet for bullet with Eliphas. She should be full of gratitude (even though Gruddam Eliphas had survived as well), but she was troubled with a bone-deep fear.

Be satisfied, she told herself. The airship shot off the block roof so fast it only dropped a hundred metres in a gentle arc before crash-landing on the roof of a smaller block.

And Med had arrived in thirty seconds.

Lucky, lucky, lucky.

But the fear wouldn't go away.

Dredd was in trouble, big trouble.

Everything was in trouble, teetering on the brink of – nothing.

'Joe,' Hershey muttered, restless in the Med Unit bed. '*Watch out . . .*'

Joe Dredd fired a fraction before Judge Dread.

Judge Dread's shot went awry, zinging harmlessly out of the open door.

Joe Dredd's slug hit home. Slam in the name-badge. Boring a hole and obliterating the A of DREAD. Bang in the heart.